ALL THE FORGIVENESSES

Center Point
Large Print

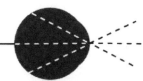

**This Large Print Book carries the
Seal of Approval of N.A.V.H.**

ALL THE FORGIVENESSES

ELIZABETH HARDINGER

CENTER POINT LARGE PRINT
THORNDIKE, MAINE

For Charles
The light surrounding me

As we know,
forgiveness of oneself is the
hardest of all the forgivenesses.
—Joan Baez

BOOK ONE

Chapter 1

Daddy, he was the one always shot the pig. There's a trick to it. You want to stun her so she falls directly and the heart keeps pumping and she drains out quick. If you shoot her back of the ear, say, like some people does, you might just nick the brain, and she's like to run around the yard spewing blood and squealing, whirl in a circle, bounce off the cellar door. Might take five or six shots to drop her, and you'll ruin good meat. No need for her to suffer like that. Daddy knowed just where to shoot her—right between the eyes but up a little bit. Sticking her, that takes a good eye and a sharp knife. You don't stick her in the vein, might take a long time for her to drain out.

That day, when Mama seen Daddy walking over toward the pig with the long rifle, she hollered at me and Timmy to get back. "Bertie, get aholt of him!" Which I done.

Daddy walked a couple more steps and turned around and shot the pig, and she fell down directly. Then he stuck her, and the blood poured out.

"Bang," said Timmy. His eyes was bright.

"Come on," I said to him. "Let's go look at the fire." Timmy was three year old, and he'd as soon play with a stick on fire as blood. I took aholt of him and drug him over to where the women was congregated, like they will. Soon's the sun come up, the women had built the fire and hoisted the big oil drum up on the grate. Then everbody carried buckets of water to half-fill it. Pretty soon it heated up, and the steam smelled of the pigs that had been boiled in it before. Smelled so good my mouth'd filled up.

"Mind he don't fall in the fire," Grandma Sweet said. She run her fingers up and down her arms, stripping off water.

"I know." I myself wasn't but six and a half, but, like Mama always said, you would've thought Timmy was my own baby instead of my brother, the way I was always making over him. Mama called me "little mother," but I didn't mind it. She meant it kindly.

"Don't let him touch the pig," Mama said to me. "I told you, keep a close eye on him. Ain't got no time to look after him today." She had my sister Dacia on her hip, smiling at her, jiggling the baby's lower lip with her finger while Dacia cooed.

"Bang," Timmy said again. He giggled in

that way little children does, like they're full of bubbles.

I took aholt of his hand. His fingers was cold, I remember. It was fall. You want cool weather for killing a pig so's the meat gets good and chilled that night.

We was all there at Grandma and Grandpa Sweet's place: Daddy, Mama, my older brothers William and Buck, me, Timothy—I called him Timmy—and Dacia. Opal and the twins wasn't born yet.

A lot of the Sweet relations was there, too. Mama, her given name was Polly Jolene Sweet. I don't remember most of their names, I was so little. Aunt JoyAnn and Aunt Birddella was there, and most likely Alma—and four or five older girl cousins. Hardly nobody my age. Most of them was older. I remember my cousin Frank, who had one side of his head flat and couldn't but half see. It wasn't often the Sweets got together. Everbody lived on little acreages scattered throughout the hills, and a pig killing was like a day at the fair practically.

Grandma and Grandpa Sweet's house, now it was built up on a bluff. There wasn't much front yard, and the back sloped up a ways and then there was the backwoods. There was a creek run down the hill and curled around in front of the bluff and wandered on down through more woods for a ways. They called it Tenmile Creek. We had to jump over a narrow place in the Tenmile to get up to the house, or, if it was high, we stepped along the rocks.

We was living in the Appalachian hills in southeast Kentucky, but I didn't know that then. It was just the place where we lived at. For all I knowed, it was the whole world.

Me and Timmy watched as the men spread the pig's hind legs apart and tied the feet to the spreader. Then they threaded a two-by-four through the spreader and heaved her up and carried her over to the old sweetgum tree, the one with the big stout branch they used for hanging pigs. They strung her up by the hind legs, and then they waited around, smoking, till the blood petered out. I pulled Timmy back out of their road again as they carried her over and lowered her headfirst into the boiling water to scald her. After a little bit, they lifted her out and hung her back up in the tree to skin.

Then Daddy and the other men and boys took off to go hunting, I guess ten or twelve of them altogether. My big brothers, William and Buck, went with them. I seen Daddy lift his whiskey bottle before they got to the woods.

With the pig hanging in the tree, the next thing was to scrape the hair. Now the pigs we had in them days was about half wild, seems like— they had thick brown hair, coarse and stiff. Some people just skinned them, hair and all, and throwed the skin to the dogs. But us, we scraped off the hair first, and then we saved the bare skin to fry up. Cracklins, now that was good eating. Mama told me you ain't had good food till you've eat cracklins.

Grandma and two other women and an older girl, they scraped the hair. It made a *snick-snick* sound.

"Mind you don't break the skin," Grandma said.

Grandma's half-tail red tom come up. "Scat!" one of the women hollered. She kicked him, and he yowled and took off.

Timmy laughed. Then he stuck his nose in the air and said, "What stinks?"

"Hush, it's just pig," I told him.

"We just gonna stand around all *day?*" he said. "What—"

"Leapfrog!" He jumped up high as he could, stretching his arms out wide. "Leapfrog!"

"I hear you! No need to holler!" I faced away from the pig and bent over, and Timmy jumped up and landed right smack in the middle of my spine. We both fell down in a heap, and Timmy laughed till the snot come out of his nose. He never got the hang of leapfrog.

I was content to play with Timmy in the yard while they gutted her. I didn't want to watch anyhow. It about made me sick, tell the truth. You start off by cutting around her rear end and pulling out a gob of innards and tying it off with a string. Then you slice her down the middle and pull out the entrails. Nasty work. Then you saw down through the backbone to halve her, and you're ready to butcher.

Mama and the aunts set up the two sawhorses with the old door laid across them for a work-table. It was painted black, that door was, and it had a hole where the knob used to be. They used that same door ever time.

The women stood around the table, cutting up the meat and visiting like women will. Seemed like there was a lot to tell. "Well, John, now, John tore off his big toenail the other day, drove the spade clean through it," a woman in a blue bandanna said. "Like to bawled his head off, a growed man."

They all laughed.

I heard more snatches. "Poured bleach down the hole, and I ain't seen a termite since." "I told him, don't you never come home like that again unless you're right with the Lord." "Well, who do you reckon was standing there? His mother!" "We always salt it afterwards. I never heard of salting it before. Don't it get tough? It don't? Seems like it'd get tough." "Told her and told her, it's your own fault. Said, don't come crying to me. You was asking for it." "Well, of course we didn't know him from Adam's housecat."

Aunt JoyAnn, she was one of them standing

16

there and working, and Mama next to her watching and playing with Dacia. JoyAnn said to Mama how pretty of a baby Dacia'd gotten to be.

"She's a Sweet, all right. Look at all that curly hair," Mama said, petting her. "Now Bertie, she takes after her daddy's side, sure enough. You know his mama said to me one time, 'Us Winslows got eye-colored eyes and hair-colored hair.'" Mama and JoyAnn both laughed. No matter how many hundred times I heard "eye-colored eyes and hair-colored hair," it never made no sense to me, though I got the point.

Then Mama told the story—like JoyAnn didn't already know it—about how they named the baby Dacia after Mama's favorite cousin twice removed, who was a famous gospel singer and sung at the Union Gospel Tabernacle in Nashville and married a rich man and always wore rouge. I never seen that Dacia myself, but Mama and them was all the time talking about her. They called her somebody's Dacia, I forget who, and our Dacia they called Polly's Dacia. Our Dacia was too little to walk yet, but if she was setting on your lap and you started singing or even just clapping, why, she'd dance, swaying her head and flinging her arms. She was loose-jointed as a rag doll.

Now some people, when they seen her name spelled out, called her "Day-SEE-uh," but that ain't right. It's "DAY-shuh." Sometimes I'd call her Day-SEE-uh just to tease her.

I looked up when Mama said, "Dacia, *boo!*" Mama swooped her nose down close to Dacia's face and then pulled back. *"Boo!"* She done it again. Dacia broke out in a toothless grin and started burbling. Then JoyAnn laughed and said, *"Boo."*

They kept it up till Dacia got tired of it and started fussing. "Bertie," Mama called to me, "come put Dacia down."

"Now Bertie, *she* was a colicky baby, remember?" Mama said to JoyAnn. I reckon she knowed I could hear her. "My Lord, you'd've thought her stomach had a mouse in it, the way she gagged and spewed up milk. You never seen the like. Bertie! Come get Dacia!"

I stopped playing with Timmy and walked over there.

"You'd pick her up—stiff as a washboard!" Mama went on. "Never smiled! Sour as a choke-cherry! I thought, 'I waited all this time for a girl, and *this* is what I got?'" Then she leaned over and said something in JoyAnn's ear, something about Daddy—I heard her say his name, Albert— and JoyAnn laughed.

Wasn't no use of me crying about being called a washboard or a chokecherry or even a Winslow, I knowed that. Didn't do no good. Just showed you didn't have no sense of humor. Come to

18

that, the way I was raised, it wasn't no use of crying—or even whining—about hurt feelings, period, unless somebody'd died. If you was a bawl-baby, you got shamed, you got teased, or people just ignored you like you'd embarrassed yourself, which I reckon bothered me the most of all. If you kept at it, you got punished, though usually only a slap. So you learned to hide your feelings or wait till you was out behind the barn and nobody could hear you.

Mama looked at me standing there. "When I call your name, you come—hear me?" She kissed the baby and laid her in my arms. "Mind you don't drop her." I seen Mama's shirt had wet spots from nursing.

Soon's I took aholt of the baby she started bawling, and she bawled all the way to the house. Timmy followed behind us with his head hung down.

I carried her into the side room, where Grandma kept the cribs. I picked the littlest one, but still I wasn't hardly big enough to reach over the side, and I dropped the baby a little bit. She hollered like she'd been whipped.

"Stop bawling, you baby, you ain't hurt." I took Timmy by the hand and walked him back to the yard. I said to him, "Don't worry, she'll fall asleep directly."

By the time they was done butchering the pig and wrapping up the meat in newspapers, me and

Timmy was tuckered out. I made him a pallet in the corner of Grandma and Grandpa's room. I seen he had a little brown crust of pig's blood on the tail of his shirt. I scraped at it with my finger. His eyelids fluttered, and he went to sleep.

I set there and looked at him for a while. There's a certain velvet sheen to the eyelids of a sleeping child. Some baby animals have it, too.

When I walked back outside, some of the women was washing up and some was laying out food. Mama was telling them the story on me—how I snuck down to the creek at our place, Elbow Creek, by myself. I loved it down there on the Elbow. I fished for tadpoles and crawdads there, and things there was peaceful. But I was forbade to go to the creek by myself. I was not ordinarily a contrary child, but ever little bit I felt like I had to go down there and just set and listen to how quiet it was. It was like I couldn't help myself. Well, this time that Mama was talking about—a week, more or less, before the day we butchered the pig—well, when I come back home, I'd stood there and told her I never went down to Elbow Creek, and me with mud all up and down my skirt. Mama like to had a fit. She feared me going down to Elbow Creek, sure enough, but it was me bearing false witness, now that she couldn't hardly abide.

Mama said to them women, "So I said to her, said, 'Bertie, *I* sure would hate to think Jesus got nails pounded into his hands just so *I* could tell a lie and get away with it.' "

"Saved by grace," Aunt Birddella said.

"What about that snake that time?" somebody said. "Wasn't that Bertie? You know, that time Albert—" And I said, "What?" And Mama said, "Hush, we wasn't talking about you." And I said, "Yes, you was, you—" And Mama narrowed her eyes. "*Hush,* I said."

Then I had a memory light on my chest like a butterfly will, lingering for a moment, its wings quivering. In my memory I was real little, and there was a man there with snakes, and I was setting on Daddy's shoulders with my hair fly-away, and there was a commotion, and then me and him was walking home. Then I blinked and these pictures flew off, and I felt goose bumps all up and down my arms.

"Saved by grace, thank God Amighty." This was the woman with the blue bandanna, nodding, and her eyes closed.

Now Mama and her kin was the kind that believed you was saved by grace and not by works, so you could get away with a sin if you wanted to—you just didn't want to. Grace was God's way of letting you into Heaven even though you was a born sinner. But the way Mama taught grace was a hard teaching. According to her lights, if you was in God's grace you didn't even *want* to do bad no more.

But me, seemed like I was always wanting to sin. For sure I'd ruther lie than take a whipping. There was times I was like to covet, and I was like to get a hungry headache at Sabbath service. I got to where I hardly ever wanted to go no more. Not to mention, honoring your mother and father meant doing their will without complaining even in your heart. That was hard. So whenever Mama talked about them nails in Jesus' hands, seems like my insides would fold in two.

And besides, after I went down to the Elbow, she'd made me go cut her a switch anyhow, and she give me a whipping. "Shame on you for dis-obedience, shame on you for making me whip you," she hollered, and afterward she throwed the switch into the trees. I'd felt scalded.

Now one of the other women spoke up. "My little Pleasant, she hardly ever lies, but does she *steal*—food! Right out of the pantry. I told her, said—"

"It's ready," somebody said. "Come and eat it before the flies get it." So we all lined up next to the worktable. They had scrubbed it down and put on a red-and-white cloth, and they'd set out bowls and bowls of food.

"We waiting on the men?"

"How come?" the bandanna woman said. "They wait on us?"

Everbody laughed.

"Let us pray," Grandma Sweet said, and we

22

all bowed our heads. She thanked our heavenly father for sending Jesus to die on the cross and get raised up after three days by God's grace. "Hallelujah," Mama said. Grandma Sweet thanked God for the food we was about to eat by His grace, too, and we all said amen.

Everbody took a breath and helped themself to the food. Mama filled me a plate, and we set around on chairs and tree stumps and eat. The women kept on talking. Mama bragged on me making my first pie crust in a teacup. I didn't know why she bragged on it since it was a mess and I'd like to cried over it, it fell into so many pieces. Mama bragged on me ever little bit, on how handy I was around the house, and though I warmed to the praise, it always made me break out in a sweat. I never liked people looking at me. But it did feel good knowing I was able to do something that pleased Mama.

While we eat, the sun come out, like it will sometimes in the fall, and the air warmed up. Some of them took off their sweaters and set around fanning themself, and some of them spread out a quilt and laid down. Their heads dropped back and their mouths fell open. Pretty soon my flat-headed cousin Frank come along carrying a stick with a rag tied to it. He took up a place and stood over three of the sleeping women and waved the stick back and forth, I reckon to keep the flies off. I remembered, then, that

I'd saw him do that before. Frank, if you once showed him how to do something and got him started, why, he would keep doing it till you told him not to no more.

It got quiet.

Mama, she laid down on a quilt and dropped off. Now I myself never liked taking a nap, but after I watched Frank waving the stick for a while, I laid down next to Mama and fell asleep, too.

Next thing I knowed, why, Daddy, William, Buck, and the other men come tromping into the yard. Men and boys makes a racket just by walking along, seems like. Must be the things they carry—guns, knives, traps, chains, tack—not to mention the buckles on their boots and the noises bubbling up from their gullet.

They'd got a mess of rabbit and three pheasant, and Daddy had a gunny sack half-full of squirrel.

"Jesus wept!" he bellowed to Mama. She was setting on the quilt holding Dacia, fluffing the baby's hair with her fingers.

"Ain't you got nothing to do?" Daddy said. "Smother me some squirrel!" He loved him some squirrel gravy.

William and Buck and the men swarmed to the table like locusts and started eating the leftover food right out of the bowls.

Mama give me Dacia to hold, and then her and two of the women dumped out the scald water and rolled the oil drum out of their road. Then they built up the fire again and started in cleaning and cooking the game. The chill had came back, and they had on their shawls and sweaters.

"I need to go to the backhouse," I said to Mama.

She never said nothing, only reached down and took the baby from me and balanced her on her hip.

I went to the backhouse and relieved myself. Then I wandered into the house to check on Timmy, but he wasn't laying there no more.

"Where you at, Timmy?" I hollered. "Daddy and them's back, and Mama's making smothered squirrel!" Grandma and Grandpa's house was bigger than ours, four rooms, but it didn't take long to search through it. Timmy wasn't nowhere.

I went outside and started looking for him. Timmy was like to hide from me. He'd watch me from his hiding place, and whenever I got close he'd start to giggling. Then when I found him, he'd take to laughing like I'd happened on him just by luck.

Now I looked through his favorite hiding places. I searched the grove to the west of the house, and then I looked out back of the barn, behind the backhouse, underneath of the out-cropping by the big mossy rock, calling his name.

I was standing at the edge of the backwoods when Daddy come walking toward me, his shoulders bobbing up and down like they always done from his bad knee.

"What the Sam Hill you doing up here, girl? Didn't you hear us calling you in?" He reached where I was at, and he bent down and give me a hard swat on the behind.

I blinked back tears. "I can't find Timmy."

"Can't find him? He hiding?"

"How would *I* know?" If I hadn't've been so sidetracked I never would've mouthed off like that.

Daddy raised his hand and slapped me in the face. Hardly nothing I hated worse than getting slapped.

He took aholt of me by the elbows. "My squirrel's getting cold."

"I went—I looked—"

He give me a hard stare, his eyes big and wild. I smelled liquor on him, which I most always did. He squeezed my arms.

"We was playing hide-and-go-seek, Daddy. I don't know where he's at." That lie just tumbled out of my mouth.

Daddy swore, grabbed me up, and carried me back to the house. The ragged skin on his hands scratched my underarms.

Wasn't long before everbody started up looking for Timmy. The dogs bayed and tore around the yard like dogs does. They give them the scent, and the dogs loped off, and people followed them. I remember my older brothers' faces stiff with fright.

Directly Mama give me Dacia and had me to go in the house and set there with an older girl cousin of mine. I laid Dacia on a blanket on the floor and set near to the stove and bawled, shivering. Dacia, she stared at me for a while and then took up whimpering, and I had to swallow back my tears and keep her company. Otherwise she was like to start howling.

Sometime after dark, Mama come and got us, and we walked the three mile home. When I seen our house coming up, with its familiar hewed wood siding and corrugated tin roof, I sunk down to my knees. Mama, she kept going, and after a little bit I rose and caught up with her. We never eat that night except Dacia.

Seems like I never slept that night for praying. I asked the Lord to lead the men to where Timmy was at, shivering in the cold but living still. I prayed they would find him alive for Mama's sake, and I promised I'd never take my eyes off of him again. But the praying never done me no good. I felt myself drug down into a dark place, and seemed like my eyes never closed all night long. I knowed whatever happened to Timmy, it was my fault, and nobody realized it but me. There wasn't no getting around it.

I got it in my mind that if Timmy died, Daddy would shoot me. I hoped he would sneak up on me and shoot me in the back of the head so I wouldn't see it coming. Maybe I dreamed that.

The next morning I was looking out the front window and seen Daddy and my older brothers walking up to the house. Aunt JoyAnn was with them. Mama had me to wait in her and Daddy's room while she went out and talked to them. I heard her wailing, and I knowed Timmy was dead.

Pretty soon Mama and Daddy come in. They stood there side by side.

"We found him a ways downstream on the Tenmile," Daddy said. His voice went high-pitched. He cleared his throat. "He was wedged in some rocks, is why we never found him till daylight."

My throat twanged from holding back tears. I looked at my hands and waited for the judgment of the Lord to come down upon me. I deserved it.

"The Lord called Timmy home, and he'll be up there in Heaven, waiting for us, when we get there," Mama said. "He's happy in the Lord." There was red all around her eyes.

"But I want him back," I blurted out.

Daddy blowed out his breath. "You think *we* don't? Wantin' ain't gettin'. Time you learned."

About that time I heard Buck sobbing in the front room, and then the sound of it changed, like somebody had pulled him to their chest. William, I heard him clear his throat two or three times.

"Tell me what happened," Mama said to me.

My tears dried up. "Well." I took a breath and then another. "Maybe he hid, and after while he looked around and didn't see me, and maybe he . . . felt like I wasn't looking for him no more, so he took off by himself." It was like I was speaking with the tongue of the Devil himself. I wondered if God was gathering up thunderbolts to rain down upon me.

"He knowed better, he was told," Mama said. "Don't a one of you pay no attention." I seen how her bottom lip was pointing off to the side on its own ever little bit. She never had that tic before.

Now JoyAnn come in carrying Dacia. The baby's cheeks was pink, and she was babbling. She looked for all the world like a painted doll. They don't come no prettier than Dacia was, even I've got to admit that.

"We got to go take care of him," Mama said to me.

For a tiny second my heart went wild, but then I realized she was talking about Timmy's body, not him. I pictured his body stuck in the rocks, cold and wet. It wasn't like I hadn't saw little drowned animals before. Their skin is waxy, and their hair clings to it like thread.

JoyAnn set with me and Dacia that day while Mama and them buried Timmy. They went ahead and put him out by the big mossy rock at

29

Grandma and Grandpa's, which they could since her and him owned their place. Afterward people talked about how big and brave my brothers was, helping dig the hole.

Now me and JoyAnn, there wasn't hardly a word spoke between us all day, seems like. I slept some in the afternoon. When I got up, I felt extra wakeful. JoyAnn had me to go feed and water the chickens and horses and gather the eggs, which I done. I felt like I was floating six inches off the ground and not really touching anything, like a ghost, though as I poured the grain into the feeders I noticed it give off its usual smell of old fruit, and the dust floated up. Blue, our dapple gray mare, she nickered and puffed out her nostrils and nuzzled my neck like she done, but it was like I was standing a ways off and watching it. I didn't get no feeling out of it.

When I come back inside, JoyAnn seen me and wiped her nose and patted the side chair for me to set down. "You don't remember this, but you stayed with us for a while, you and Timothy, while your mother recovered from his birth," she said. "You must've been about three."

I never said nothing.

"I recollect how you'd drag him around like a doll, and you barely bigger than him." She blowed her nose on her hankie. "You'd crawl up in the rocking chair, and your legs was so short, your feet hung over the edge. So you'd lean back hard as you could, back and forth, back and forth, singing to him."

Nobody said nothing for a while. Pretty soon she got up and made some supper. Then she put me and Dacia to bed—Dacia in her crib, and me in my pallet in the corner of the front room. Mama and Daddy and William and Buck, they wasn't back yet.

I must have fell asleep for a while. I dreamed Timmy himself sent an avenging angel after me, roaring like a bear. I woke up, and I heard that angel up above me, and I made water a little in my drawers. But then I realized it was Daddy on the roof, drunk, talking and hollering to himself like he done. I imagined I could smell his slobber and throw-up through the tin. I wondered what was going to happen to us now. Our family was ruined, seemed like, without Timmy there where he belonged. Me, I didn't belong there no more neither. With what I done, I didn't belong nowhere. God nor Jesus wouldn't want me in their heart now, seemed like.

I laid there for a long time. I tried to pray, but my teeth chattered to the point where I couldn't. I cried for a while, quiet as I could, till my lips felt dried out. I ached all over. I had a painful buzz in my mouth that wouldn't go away.

I needed Mama. I needed to tell her I'd lied to her and Daddy both. I wasn't watching Timmy like I was supposed to, and it was my fault he was

31

dead. I went over it in my mind, how I would say it, how I would beg forgiveness and ask Mama to pray with me and get me right with the Lord like she knowed how. I reckoned everbody would hate me. I knowed I would be punished in some terrible way. But I deserved it. And besides, it would be better than feeling like I never belonged nowhere.

Finally, I rose up and tiptoed into Mama and Daddy's room. By the moonlight from the window I seen Mama laying there, facing the wall.

I didn't hear Daddy up on the roof no more. I don't know if he'd passed out or if the thunder in my ears was too loud for me to hear him.

"Mama," I whispered.

She turned over quick, and I was surprised to see she had a half smile on her face. But soon's she seen me, she pursed her lips. "What are you doing up? Get back to bed."

I opened my mouth, but no words come out.

"Stop your bawling now," she said, though I wasn't. "Ain't no tears in Heaven, you know that. Timothy's asleep in Jesus."

"Yes, but—"

"Lord don't want to see you crying, hear me? Ain't your place to tell God Amighty what to do."

I tried to get started. "I never thought Timmy would die." That word *die* had a thickness to it that stuck in my throat.

"Ever living thing dies," she said. "It's the curse of sin. The wages of sin is death."

This took all the breath out of me.

"I'm tired, you hear? Go back to bed." Now her shoulders squirmed like she was being tickled, and I seen a light come on in her eyes. Then I heard giggling, and I knowed Dacia was in the bed with her, curled up behind her, and that was how come Mama'd been half smiling before. She give a little sigh and turned over, and you could see her body loosen under the quilt. The thought of her making over Dacia at that moment was like sand in my teeth.

I walked back into the front room and dropped onto my pallet. After while I started smelling my water on my underdrawers, and I knowed I couldn't abide it through the night till morning. I got up and made me a bowl of soap and water, and I took my time rinsing them out and blotting them with a dishrag. I hung them up on the back of the chair. I didn't have no clean ones, so I laid back down with nothing on underneath of my nightshirt. I hadn't never slept that way before, and it felt amiss in some way I couldn't fathom. That alone would have kept me up the rest of the night, even if I didn't have nothing else haunting me like I done. After while, I put my drawers back on, damp. It made me cold all over, but there wasn't nothing to do but stand it.

Chapter 2

Off and on Daddy was a horse trader, and whenever he went on a trip to buy and sell horses, he took my big brothers William and Buck with him. About the time I turned nine year old, why, I started in asking him could I go—Buck was only seven when he'd started going—but Daddy said it wasn't nothing a girl could do that was useful to him. I'd filled my mind up with notions of what-all went on, and I hated missing out on it.

But Mama, she said it was bound to be rough, and besides I was needed at home. She'd had Opal by then, who she named after a dead sister of Memaw's. I don't imagine Mama knowed what a real opal was. If she did, she never said nothing about it to me.

One morning early I stood out on the porch and watched Daddy and them get ready to set out. My brothers was bareback on Blue, and I remember Buck was yawning so hard I heard his jaw click. They had four or five horses by a rope.

You could tell them two boys was brothers, bony-shouldered and dark-haired, but William, he had squinty eyes like a coyote and always looked mad no matter what. Buck was more like Daddy, a storyteller and jokester, and him and Daddy was close. The boys was always in my life of course, but seems like they was like to be off somewheres with Daddy and not in the house very much, which naturally was where my days was spent and my heart and head was, with Mama and the little ones. It was like, there was Daddy and my brothers in their world, and then there was us in ours. So my brothers was almost like neighbors, as far as feelings. You'd think about them when they wasn't around, but you didn't miss them but once in a while. I growed up with it, so I never thought it was strange. We knowed plenty of people lived like that.

I often wondered, if Timmy had lived, would Daddy have tried to take him away from us like that, too? I pictured him older and me standing up to Daddy, keeping myself between the two of them, so Timmy wouldn't end up like William, with narrow eyes. Ever year on Timmy's birthday I told myself how old he would be and pictured him bigger. The rest of them went to visit his grave, but I didn't. Couldn't nobody make me.

That morning with the horses, didn't neither William nor Buck say nothing, nor Daddy. Daddy curried Sparky down, raising dust from his back, and then he saddled him up and mounted. It pained me to watch Daddy and them ride off without me along. Wasn't nothing I didn't love about horses, especially their sweet, dusty smell.

"Bertie, where you at?" Mama called from inside the house. "Stop fooling around out there, and get yourself in here and help me out."

I wiped my eyes and went inside.

Mama was setting at the table with Dacia on her lap, unwinding the rags tied in her hair. Dacia's head swayed back and forth, and she smiled like she was in a rapture. You never seen a prettier girl, little as she was.

I walked over to the washbowl and took up doing the breakfast dishes. Behind me Mama started singing.

> *Soft as the voice of an angel, breathing a*
> *lesson unheard,*
> *Hope, with a gentle persuasion, whispers*
> *her comforting word.*

Now Dacia took it up, though she garbled the words. I myself started singing, but Mama hushed me. "I'm trying to teach her, and besides you can't carry a tune." I glanced at them, and I seen Mama was running her fingers along Dacia's scalp, zigzag, to release the curls. Dacia arched her back like a cat, her eyes closed.

"Soft as the voice of an angel," Mama sung, and Dacia sung—more like *said*—"Soff a boyce angel," like a three-year-old will. Mama sung it again, and Dacia sung it wrong again, and Mama sung it again. It was quiet in the house, and my head still plagued with the night cobwebs, and it was like the two of them was whispering.

Mama said to her, "I'd sure like to see an angel in person, wouldn't you?"

"Angel."

"I had me one once," Mama said. I knowed who she meant, and it gutted me.

"Me too," Dacia said.

"Bertie," Mama said. "Go get me a jar of grape jelly—this 'n's moldy."

I wiped my hands and went outdoors to the root cellar dug in the side of the house. The rock steps was crumbly, and the cellar was cool and dry, smelling like old clay. I heard, or thought I heard, Mama and Dacia singing and laughing upstairs. I found the jelly right off, but I stayed down there for a while. I knowed other hymns—"Up From the Grave He Arose," "Rock of Ages," "Work for the Night Is Coming," lots of them—but not a one I liked as well as "Whispering Hope." I sung the whole song to myself, all three verses and all three refrains. I pictured Mama in the house, impatient.

When I got back, Mama was saying to Dacia, "Like the angels themself." Mama said to me, "Where you been all this time?"

I put the jar on the table. Mama scooped out a glob of jelly, mounded it on a biscuit, and stuck it in Dacia's mouth. She struggled to hold the whole mouthful, laughing and losing purple drool out the side of her mouth. But she got enough of it chewed to swallow it down.

"I *like* gray jelly," she said. White crumbs flew out of her mouth.

"Bertie, see if there's a cookie," Mama said.

"For breakfast?"

"You're too big, she ain't."

I got down a cookie, and Mama smeared it with jelly, too.

After a little bit, Dacia hopped down and come over to me and grabbed my skirt with her sticky hands. "Sister," she said. She yanked on the material. "Sister."

"Leave me be, I got work to do."

"Let's scrape some carrots and sugar them for dinner, want to?" Mama said.

"Let's," I said, though I knowed she meant me.

"Me too, me too," said Dacia.

"You're too little," I told her.

"No, I ain't, I ain't little." She took up my skirt and wiped her mouth with it.

"Daddy and the boys take off already?" Mama said.

I nodded.

She sighed. "Well, he better get home with the money this time. Store bill's due."

"Oh, that reminds me," I said. "Mrs. Longhoffer, she brung some ironing by yesterday night. A dollar's worth, I expect."

39

"Sister," Dacia said. I felt her hands around my ankle, and I pulled my foot away. She was like to bite.

"Well," Mama said. "Let's do the ironing instead of the carrots, then."

I nodded.

"Don't know what I'd do without you, Bertie," she said to me. "Wore out as I been."

Warmth spread through me to my toes. "You'll get to feeling better, Mama."

"Sister!" Dacia hollered. "I gotta pee!" But it was too late.

Mama started to get up from her chair but then fell back heavy.

"I got it, I got it, set down." I grabbed a rag from off the table.

Mama rested her head in her hands. Dacia started hiccupping and then took to bawling like she done, and I felt an ache behind my eyes, fiery.

Seemed like them days was like that more often than not. You was feeling content one minute, and then, just like that, you was drug down like a coon with a pack of dogs on her. It wasn't like chores was a tribulation. I liked feeling useful, and mostly they wasn't that hard. Washing dishes and ironing, especially, I'd stand there and daydream and maybe sing or hum to pass the time. For me, floors, though, they was a trial. When you think about it, everthing falls down sooner or later. Our house only had two rooms—the bedroom where Mama and Daddy slept, and the front room, which had a corner curtained off for the older children to sleep—but seemed to me like the floors was dirty most all the time.

"Bertie?" Mama said. "Where's your mind at? Get that sopped up, she's like to play in it."

I blinked and knelt down and wiped up the puddle. Then before I could get back up, why, Dacia laughed and throwed herself on my back. "Worsie! Worsie!" she hollered. She bucked and kicked me in the ribs till I give up and rode her around the table. Grit dug into my knees, and I felt Dacia's pants leaking on my shirt.

Pretty soon I slid her off and changed her pants. Then I left her with Mama and took the dirty things outside. I rinsed them out and hung them up in the volunteer elm tree next to the pump. Luckily it was a fine warm day. The sun would take the smell away before washday.

I stretched my back and looked around the place. The house, it needed painting, and half the porch floorboards was gone, and the fence was down in places. The garden was weedy and needed watering, and there was a pile of trash to be burned.

Inside, there was the dishes and the floor. And Mrs. Longhoffer's ironing would take up most of the day.

It surprised me when I felt tears gathering. I

knowed perfectly well, whatever didn't get done today would still be there tomorrow, so how come was I feeling blue? Then I heard Mama laughing in the house, and I reckoned my feelings was hurt she'd give my song to Dacia. Of course it wasn't mine, but Mama had to know how much pride I took in it. My favorite part was in the second verse:

> *If, in the dusk of the twilight, dim be the*
> *region afar,*
> *Will not the deepening darkness brighten*
> *the glimmering star?*

I used to play like I had a horse named Glimmering Star. I called him Star. As a child I never knowed what "glimmering" meant, but I loved how it sounded. Me and Star, we had a lot of adventures in my mind. Mama never knowed about my pretend horse, but surely she knowed this was the only song I knowed all the way through, the song I used to sing to Timmy.

I give the pump a couple pulls and let the cold water run over my hands, and then I rubbed it over my face and felt it stream down my neck. I stood there next to the pump and thought about Star till Mama called me in.

Wasn't long after that, maybe a month, Daddy come to my pallet one morning before dawn.

"Get up," he whispered, shaking my shoulder. "Come on now."

He'd never woken me up in my life. Though I was still groggy, my heart pounded. I was half-scared to find out what was going on.

"Get dressed," he said. "Ain't got all day."

I reached for my skirt next to me on the pallet. I felt the need to stretch, and I reached both arms up.

"You been crying to come with me all this time," he said. "Hurry up if you're coming."

I stood up and pulled my skirt on underneath of my nightdress.

Daddy turned and walked toward the door. "Go if you have to. Won't be stopping till we get there."

I pulled my nightdress up over my head and throwed on my shirt. I never let myself believe it till I got outside and seen it—there was the horses, snorting and stomping their feet, humming in their throat like they does. Daddy, he was standing next to Blue, waiting to hoist me up. I about fell over, I was so tickled. Wasn't nobody but him and me.

Up on Blue, my legs was splayed practically straight out. I always was little for my age.

Daddy had gotten in the horse business when a neighbor of ours was getting evicted off his property and had to sell his horse. Daddy give him three dollars for it and sold it a week later for seven and a half. To him it was like printing money. After that he went horse trading three-four times a week. If he didn't get his price, he brought them home and kept them till he did. Daddy knowed how much he could pay and how much he could get. He could tell how well they'd been looked after and how much starch they had left in them. He didn't get bamboozled very often.

We had four with us that day. Daddy was riding one in the saddle and leading Blue and the other three by a rope. I was surprised my brothers wasn't there, but I never asked. There was some things you was better off not asking Daddy. If he thought it was none of your business, he wouldn't answer you. And if he thought you was being mouthy, he was like to ignore you for a long time, or slap your face if he thought you needed it. Seemed like he wanted you to understand he was mad just by the way he acted.

Me, up on Blue I felt as happy as I ever was. I always loved the sound of horses' hooves, how they *clop-clop, clop-clop* in time with their backbone swaying underneath of you. Seems like horses just know what they're doing, so you're all right if you sway yourself in time with them.

We rode off, and I never looked back. Wasn't nobody up but us.

Pretty soon the sun come up, and Blue's back

got to sweating and made my legs sweat. My skirt was hiked up, and as Blue swished her tail, it made my legs itch something fierce. I didn't know which was worse—the flies, or the sharp tail hair lashing at my legs. Didn't matter, though. I got whichever one I got.

We took the trail that led to town. I was hoping we would ride through town so I could see what was what, maybe see an automobile like I seen before, but a mile outside of town we veered off into the woods.

"I ever tell you the time Uncle Seth come riding up on a mule after he was dead?" Daddy said.

"You did."

"Me and my brothers was sleeping in the house on the old Strickler place," he went on. "Now, how many brothers did I have, I wonder."

"Five," I answered.

"And what was their names?"

"William, which they called him Billy, Thomas, James, Marcus, which he got his one foot cut off, and Ezekiel, which they called him Zeke." I'd heard this story many a time. I knowed what to say and when to say it.

"Your memaw, now," he said, "it never failed she kept a bedroom window open in all weathers—"

"And one time you woken up in the morning and your bed had a snow drift on it."

45

Daddy sighed and petted his horse on the neck.

"But that ain't the story," I said. *Clop-clop, clop-clop.*

"No, that ain't the story."

"Tell me, then."

"Well, one day us brothers, we was up in that room, and we looked out the window, and we seen Uncle Seth riding up to the house on a mule. Now that wasn't nothing—we seen Uncle Seth riding up to the house many a time. We knowed that mule."

"Name was Jackie, that mule."

He nodded. "Well, now, we run down the stairs, and there's Memaw, setting at the table, bawling fit to die. And we said, 'Mama,' said, 'what's the matter?' And she said, 'Just got word. My brother Seth, he passed on, Tuesday week.' "

"Poor Uncle Seth," I said.

"Now I ask you." Daddy reined his horse to a stop, and the others bumped to a stop, too. He turned in the saddle to look at me. "You tell me. How was it, me and my brothers looked out that window and seen Uncle Seth, and him dead over a week? And his mule?"

"Maybe it wasn't him." I run my fingers along Blue's mane. "Maybe it was some other man."

"Wasn't no man there!" The horses throwed back their heads, and there was a commotion. Even Blue got spooked and started pawing and thumping like she was high-stepping, and I

46

grabbed her mane and made my hips as light as I could.

"Whoa there," Daddy said. "Whoa there." His horse twirled around, and he dropped the lead rope. My heart roared, but Daddy quick jumped down and made clucking sounds and rubbed their necks, and after while they all simmered down and stood there blowing out their breath. I was proud I hadn't gotten throwed.

After a little bit Daddy climbed back up and we rode on, him still in front, me following. "Wasn't no man there," he said again, in a more regular voice. "Nor mule neither."

"What was it you seen, then?"

He took out a rag and blowed his nose. "A dead man riding a mule made out of air, I reckon." He wadded up the rag and put it back in his pocket.

That was the end of the story. I knowed from experience Daddy wouldn't brook no more questions. It was a mystery, and he liked a mystery. Not me. I wanted things to make sense—I couldn't hardly abide things being two different ways. For one thing, I wanted to know how come Mama went to Galena Baptist and took us younger children, and Daddy went by himself, when he went, to the Tabernacle of the Blood of the Lamb. And how come Daddy seemed to believe in ghosts, and Mama always told us ghosts was from the Devil. There was lots of things where Mama and Daddy seemed to believe

47

two different ways, and each of them so certain. I wondered what made the difference, and I longed to know which one was true.

As for me and Daddy, I wanted him to be happy with me, if only I could figure out how. The age I had gotten to, though, I was starting to wonder was the story about Uncle Seth even true, never mind the mystery, though I would never say nothing like that to Daddy.

After a little bit we come to a clearing where there was a cabin and three sheds. An old man was setting out front on a wooden chair like a scarecrow. He had a full head of white hair sticking up like a scrub brush.

"Winslow," he said.

I reckon I should have knowed people would know Daddy already, but I was startled to hear our name coming out of that man's mouth. Of course, I was surprised he talked at all, setting there so stiff like he was.

"Byrnes," Daddy said.

"The wife? Childern?" the man said.

Daddy nodded. "Got anything for me?"

The man frowned and shook his head. "Oh, there's a gelding back there, but I don't know."

"How long you had him?"

Byrnes throwed his head back and squinted at the sky. "Two, three months?"

"I'll take a look." He got off his horse, and then

he come over and pulled me down to the ground. He took off limping toward one of the sheds. I trotted to catch up with him.

We come to a bob wire fence, and he pressed his boot down on the bottom strand and stretched out the middle strand. I stepped through and then him. He said, "Fuck"—for what reason, I couldn't see. Wasn't the first time I'd heard him or my brothers say that one. I never knowed what it meant then, but I had a feeling if I said it I'd get a whipping. You just reckon them things out.

A small black horse come walking up to us with his head lowered. "Whoa, horse," Daddy said softly, making a kissing sound with his mouth. "Whoa there, that's a good fella."

The gelding shied back and coughed, but Daddy sweet-talked him and after while he stood quiet. Daddy run his hand along his backbone and sighed. He reached in his pocket and pulled out a brown chunk—sorghum, I reckoned—and the horse gathered in the treat with his big, floppy lips and ground it in his teeth like they does. I heard him wheezing as we walked away.

Daddy shook his head. "Heaves."

"What's heaves?"

"What's it sound like?"

We reached the fence and climbed through.

About the time we got to the shed, he said, "After while, they get heave lines." He stopped.

"Overgrowed muscle along the ribcage, from coughing and wheezing. Heaves."

"Oh." I wished he had pointed out that heave line on the horse so I could've saw what it looked like.

He took up walking again. "Nothing you can do about heaves."

"Will he die?"

"Ever living thing dies."

"I know, but—"

" 'I-*know*-b't,' " he said, mocking.

When we got back to the horses, he mounted his and said to Byrnes, "Can't do no business with you today." When he stretched out his leg I seen a line of blood on his pants. Must've cut it crossing the fence, and that's why he said fuck.

Byrnes throwed back his head, nodding backward like some men does.

"Maybe next time," Daddy said.

I walked over to Blue and waited for Daddy to boost me up. But off he rode at a trot, leading the other horses. Blue shouldered me out of the way and followed.

"Daddy?"

He acted like he didn't hear me and rode on.

"Daddy! Don't forget me!"

Quickly the woods swallowed them up.

I turned to Mr. Byrnes, who was staring at me, grinning. "Reckon I got me a little girl," he said.

I should've knowed better—should've figured

Daddy was only teasing me and there was nothing to do but wait till he tired of it—but I busted into tears anyhow.

After maybe ten minutes he come riding back, laughing. When he boosted me onto Blue's back, he seen I'd been crying. "Ain't you got no sense of humor, bawl-baby?"

I settled myself on Blue and petted her neck. I breathed in her smell as best as I could with a nose full of tears.

"Can't you take a joke?" he said.

"Can't take a joke," Byrnes said.

Daddy mounted his horse, muttering, "Whose child are you?"

Nobody's is what popped into my mind. *No-fucking-body's.* It about took my breath away I even thought that word.

At midday we stopped at a creek to water the horses and eat dinner. He'd packed us up some bread-and-butter sandwiches and a potato each. Later on he bought two horses.

When we got to Feldspar, he had me and Blue to wait by a church two blocks away from the livery stable while he sold the horses to the livery man. I set on the church steps and watched them. The livery man leaned against the fence, smoking cigarettes and nodding ever little bit. Daddy, he roamed around like a caged bull, flinging out his arms, pointing this way and that, talking all the while. He'd turn his back and take two or three steps and then turn and limp back. I coveted being over there and hearing what they was saying. I pictured myself perched on the fence, acting like I wasn't interested but studying ever word. It was like when I was little, before Mama learned me my letters, when I looked at the pictures in her Bible and didn't understand what I was looking at. I remembered Daniel in the lion's den, how the biggest lion had his upper lip curled and his fangs bared. I pretended Daniel and the lion were friends, laughing together. I could almost talk myself into believing it, though I'd seen the handiwork of coyotes and possums, and I knowed better in my heart.

Pretty soon Daddy and the livery man shook hands, and Daddy ducked into a storefront.

After while I got up and walked Blue around. Back of the church we found a graveyard, and me and Blue wandered through it, her eating grass. One grave looked like a little crib. They had built railings around it, and there was flowers growing where the blanket would be. This was a child's grave, surely, and it asleep in the Lord. I couldn't help but tremble, looking at it. What if Mama and Daddy was both wrong, and Timmy was just dead? Soon as that thought come, I prayed the Lord would banish it. I felt my sins heavy on me.

Me and Blue tarried there a while. It was a quiet day, and there come up a breeze, making the trees to rustle. Blue ripped up grass and chomped on it, and that sound, so familiar, comforted me and made me feel the life going on outside my own skin. I shivered. I got a feeling I had sometimes, of my future life being big and far away and calling to me through the wind in the trees. I felt a sharp longing, though I didn't know what for.

For the first time all day I thought about Mama and Dacia and Opal back at the house, and me here. I thought, *I ain't never going to forget this day. I'm going to remember it all my life.*

After while I got hungry and thirsty, but Daddy'd told me to wait there, so I done what he said.

Finally, a white-haired woman come up to me, leaning on a cane. "You lost?"

I shook my head. I wondered, was there a rule against tarrying by a church if you didn't belong to it.

"I been watching you." She pulled her shawl around herself. "The mare yours?"

"My daddy's."

"He the horse trader?"

I nodded.

She looked at me like I was dirt. "You'll find him out back of the . . ." She never said what, only pointed to the building Daddy'd went into. "In the alley."

I couldn't hardly take in what she meant.

"You better go get him before the sheriff does," she said.

In the alley I found Daddy laying next to the trash cans, groaning. He stunk of drink, and there was blood on his face and neck. His saddle was laying a ways away. I stood there. Tell the truth, I was just as afraid he wasn't dead as he was dead.

"Daddy?" I didn't want to get close enough for him to swat at me. "Daddy?"

He turned over, and I seen one eye was swole closed. His shirt was stained halfway down with blood.

"Jesus Christ," I said.

He moaned and opened his good eye. "Help me up. Help me up, I said."

I stretched out my arm, and he grabbed it and got to his knees. A cry of pain come out of him.

"Ain't got time to strop you for swearing." He couldn't hardly get his breath, and he forced his words out. "But don't think you ain't going to get it."

Now he rose up to his feet and moaned and hoisted up the saddle on Blue's back. There was many a time my daddy surprised me with how strong he was, hurt or not. He wasn't a tall man but barrel-chested.

I don't reckon I have to tell you, I didn't ask him how come him to get beat up.

We got home after dark. Mama was setting out on the porch with the lantern lit, and she stood up when we got there.

I slid off of Blue and walked up to the porch. She pulled me to her, which surprised me, and she held up the lantern and looked me over. "You eat?"

I shook my head.

Now Daddy dismounted, real stiff, and she aimed the light at him. You could see he was hurt.

"Don't you *never* take one of my girls out of my sight again," Mama said, slow, almost in a hiss.

I felt a thrill go through me. *Her girls.*

Daddy, breathless with pain, said, "The boys, they had the runs this morning."

"You hear me?" she said.

"Pump me a bucket of water," he said.

"You hear me?" Her grip tightened on my elbow till it hurt.

Daddy tried to stand up straight, but he ended up leaning against Blue. "Horse needs water."

Nobody said nothing for a long time. The silence was broke by the baby crying in the house. My littlest sister, Opal, still a shoulder baby.

Mama set down the lantern, and our shadows whirled around the porch, now big, now little. Then she took me inside and fed me and put me to bed. When she leaned over to pull the quilt over me, what come out of her big apron pocket but her ball-peen hammer. It clattered onto the floor. Without one word she picked it up and put it back in her pocket and left. Later on I wondered did she intend to use that ball-peen hammer on Daddy, depending.

I let myself feel bad that Daddy only took me on the trip because my brothers was sick, but I didn't stew over it for long. At least he forgot to strop me for swearing. I was wore out, and sleep come quick.

I never found out how come Daddy got beat up that day at Feldspar. Like as not, it was over money, or a woman. All's I know is, it wasn't but two or three days later, why, Mama told us children we was fixing to move. We was going to Obsidian, Missouri, which was north and west of Galena, mostly west, five or six hundred miles. Daddy was going to take up farming. Ain't no doubt in my mind this move was on account of the trouble Daddy got into at Feldspar. No telling how long it had been going on, whatever it was. And Mama'd been wanting to get away from Daddy's people for some time on account of their ways, which she never approved of. Not that she told me that, but I heard things. I knowed they done snake handling, but I didn't know what else they done to earn her wrath.

Before we went, me and Mama and the children spent a day at Grandma and Grandpa Sweet's place. Mama took me by the hand and had me to walk with her out to the mossy rock where they'd buried Timmy. I'd never went out there since he died, and Mama never made me go till that day. She reminded me, we wouldn't be there to leave flowers on Decoration Day come May. Grandma and Grandpa and the aunts and cousins would be, but not us. I wondered how come she was trying to make me feel worse—did she think I wasn't missing Timmy because I wasn't bawling?—but if that was in her mind, it wouldn't work. I didn't care nothing about Decoration Day.

It turned out they'd put him a ways west of the rock and planted a wild rose bush nearby. There wasn't no stone. "Where'd that cross get to?" Mama said, and she started looking around.

Me, I stood there with my teeth clenched. I'd always pictured Timmy on the south side of the rock, where it was warm and where he always used to hide when we played hide-and-go-seek. It hit me hard that nobody'd thought to put him there, and then I realized probably nobody knowed about it but me. They never paid no attention to how he was like to get tangled up in thorn bushes, neither.

Mama found the little wooden cross, which looked like animals had drug off a ways. It was white, but the paint was near gone. She brushed off the dirt and cobwebs and set her foot on it and pushed it back down in the dirt. She asked me to say a prayer, but I turned away and shook my shoulders like I was crying, so she done it. I don't remember what she said.

It took all I had to walk away and leave that cross there where it wasn't supposed to be.

On moving day a man in a big straw hat come with a wagon, and me and the boys loaded up our things. We couldn't take most of the furniture—it was mortgaged—but we'd stuffed the clothes around the pots and pans and put everthing in two wooden crates plus Mama's green wedding trunk Grandpa made her.

Dacia, now, she screamed and cried and kicked Mama in the legs as Mama drug her out of the house.

When we was ready, Mama led us in a prayer. She asked the Lord to bless our move to Missouri, and she asked the Lord to bless and comfort her kin, who was going to miss us something fierce, and she thanked the Lord for Jesus dying on the cross for our sins, and she thanked the Lord that Daddy was well enough to go with us. The whole time, Dacia was screaming crying.

Then there was a long goodbye with the kin, and we set off. My brothers, they rode Blue, and Daddy rode Sparky, and the dogs followed along.

Once we was under way, Mama nursed Opal and then give her to me. I put the baby up to my shoulder and patted her while she burped. The roads was bumpy, and she spit up ever little bit.

I seen Mama had dozed off, so quietly I sung my song to Opal. Then I said to her, "You're so

58

lucky, Opal. We're going to a whole nother place, and things is bound to be new and different." Then I took up the song again. Of all the things I needed, hope was the biggest.

Whenever I think about that trip, I remember the grapefruit smell of Opal's spit-up. She kept spitting up for the two weeks we was traveling. The rest of it's a blur, which is just as well.

Not then, but later on, I often asked myself how Mama had the strength to move away from Kentucky, no matter what Daddy and his people done, and leave all her kin like that, the aunts especially, and I wondered whether the loss of her kin nearby was what caused her to turn later on like she done. But at the time I never said nothing. Us older ones, we never put up no fuss. We knowed Mama wouldn't tolerate it. You went where you was told and made the best of it.

Chapter 3

By the time we got to the new place it felt like we had traveled to the other side of the world. Missouri didn't seem like there was hardly no woods. Seemed like knee-high grass growed everwhere, and prairie flowers. Our house was a tiny thing. If you pushed on the walls, you felt them give a little. One blessing, the water pump was on the back porch instead of out in the yard.

One day about a week after we got there, I was out in the yard killing three chickens for a lady name of Florence who lived in town. I'd been dressing chickens and game for people back home, and it wasn't hard to find customers in Missouri. I'd just went door-to-door in town, asking. At first I just killed birds they'd boughten, but later on we built up our flock to where sometimes I sold them the chicken, too. Or either way, whichever they wanted.

That day I'd just set the first one's head under the broomstick when I heard female voices coming, an older and a younger. From the road, there was a big bend and a long rise before you got to the house, and I heard them before I seen them. I pulled the chicken's head off and tossed the carcass. It begun running around like they will.

Now I could make out what the older woman was saying. "Alta Bea, I want you to keep a civil tongue in your mouth."

"Don't I always?" the younger one said.

"They have a nine-year-old girl you could walk to school with"—I realized with a start she must mean me—"and for heaven's sake, don't act stuck-up."

"Mother, I—"

"And don't mention your father's a banker unless they ask, and then say he *works* at the bank. Or works in town. But only if they ask."

"I am not stuck-up," Alta Bea said.

"There's no shame in honest work," her mother said. "God is no respecter of persons. Remember, there was a time when your father and I hardly had anything, too."

"I know."

I pulled off the second head and let go the carcass.

"We don't have to be friends with them," the mother said. "But I won't have it said that I'm not neighborly."

I watched them make the rise just as I was tossing the last carcass. I felt warm drops of blood on my ankles.

They walked up to me, and the mother gasped. "Well, forever more." The girl, Alta Bea, stared at me with big eyes. She was a head and a half taller than me, and she had more hair than I ever seen on a human in my life, more than Dacia. This girl's hair was almost black, and spilling out of its pins.

"Mama!" I hollered. "Company!"

I seen Alta Bea look down. I followed her eyes, and there was the broomstick on the ground and the three chicken heads lined up next to it.

The woman said, "Hello, I'm Mrs. Snedeker from across the road, and this is my daughter, Alta Bea. She's twelve. What's your name?"

"Mama!" I called again. I felt shy. It was Mama always met new people.

Alta Bea stared at a headless chicken laying on its side with its feet opening and closing like they does. "How'd you do that?" she said.

"I've brought a pie," Mrs. Snedeker said. "Do you like green-apple pies? Some people think green apples will give you worms, but I always—"

Now Mama come to the door, drying her hands on her apron. "I'm a-doin' some warsh," she said to them. "I got a pot of coffee, want some?"

Alta Bea and her mother walked in, and Mama said to me, "Bertie, rench out a cup." I heard Mama say "warsh" and "rench" because already I noticed how these strangers talked different.

"Bertie?" Alta Bea said. "Did you say 'Bertie'?"

63

Now Dacia jumped up from the little bed in the corner. "Birdy!" she hollered.

"Mind you don't wake up Opal," Mama said.

"It ain't Birdy, it's Bertie," I said to Dacia, "which you know good and well." I shook the water off the coffee cup.

"Birdy Birdy Birdy," Dacia said on purpose.

Mrs. Snedeker set the pie on the table, and Mama brushed off a chair with her apron and motioned for her to sit down. Alta Bea, she perched on the edge of the bed.

"My husband, Albert, why, he's off trading horses," Mama said. "He's fixing to plant a crop when the time comes. Rye, I reckon, or wheat."

"My daddy?" Dacia said, blinking, like she didn't know that. Seemed like sometimes she wanted people to think she was younger than she really was. She liked people to make over her.

Mrs. Snedeker smiled. "My husband works in town."

Mama said to me, "You better finish them chickens before the dogs get 'em."

Alta Bea jumped to her feet. "I'll help."

Outside, I picked up two of the chicken carcasses and motioned for Alta Bea to go get the other'n. She walked over and looked down at it.

"What's the matter?" I said. "Ain't you never dressed a chicken before?" Well, of course she hadn't. "Just take it by the feet," I told her. But when she touched it, she yanked her hand back.

"Won't bite you," I said.

"I know." But when she picked it up, the toes curled around her fingers. I seen a shudder run through her, and she looked like she was like to gag, but she held fast to the carcass and followed me back inside.

Now Mama dunked each chicken one at a time in the pot. She used the feet like spoons to push it under the steaming water. Alta Bea's mother was chattering, telling Mama how our house used to be a pump house, but Mr. Packebush, the landlord, he'd put on the front room and the porch after his wife died and he wanted tenants to farm this eighty acres. Things like that. Her voice sounded pinched, I reckoned from trying not to breathe in through her nose on account of the smell of blood, feathers, feet, innards, and dirt.

When the chickens was hot, me and Alta Bea carried them back outside, and I showed her how to pluck the feathers. You start with the pinfeathers. I pulled them out by the handful—they made a soft *plock* sound. Didn't take but a minute.

I seen she was watching me. "Go on," I said.

It looks easier than it is, I reckon. The feathers stuck to her fingers like hair, and the more she tried to grab aholt of them, the worse they stuck. "I can't *do* this," she said, sniffling.

"Here." I took her chicken and finished the

65

pinfeathers. Then I spread out a wing, took aholt of a long, stiff wingfeather, and yanked it out. "Here, while it's still hot."

She took aholt of her chicken and started in ripping.

"Don't tear the skin," I said. "It's like to tear." I wondered, could she really be twelve years old and so ignorant?

"How'd you get the name of Bertie?" she said.

"Short for Albertina," I said. "He wouldn't have no *boy* named after him, said it wasn't nobody in this life that was, or ever would be, like to him." Daddy's very words. "But Albertina, that was a name he liked, though it seemed too fancy for the plain baby I was. So they named me Albertina and called me Bertie."

"Oh." She jerked on a feather.

"How many brothers and sisters have you got?" I said.

"Not any."

"How come?"

"I don't know," she said. "I just don't."

"Huh." I watched her for a while. "Well, besides them two girls in the house, I've got two big brothers. They sleep in the barn mostly."

"Oh."

"Mama's like to have another'n before you know it."

She looked surprised. "She is?"

I could tell her chicken was cooling down.

66

"Here," I said, and I give her my two to hold while I tried to clean up the mess she'd made of hers. After while I looked up at her.

"Stop staring at my hair," she said.

"I never seen so much hair on a human head."

"My dad says I cost a fortune in hairpins."

"You could braid it."

She rolled her eyes. "Only little *girls* braid their hair."

"My memaw braids hers ever day of her life."

" 'Memaw'?"

"My grandma on Daddy's side."

"Well, maybe grown women braid their hair in Kentucky. Around here, it's only little girls."

I wondered how she knowed where we was from, but I reckoned her mama knowed everthing about the neighbors, like mine knowed everbody back home. "I seen a picture one time of a Chinaman had a braid halfway down his back," I said.

"Well, you won't find any Chinamen in Obsidian."

We looked at each other and busted out laughing, the both of us. I felt a stab of pleasure.

Just then Mama stepped outside and called us in to have a bite of pie.

Soon's we eat, Alta Bea and her mama left. I watched from the doorway as they walked down the rise. Just before they went out of sight, I seen Alta Bea smell her fingers. She looked at her mama, and when she seen nobody was looking, she put her hands close to her face and took in two deep breaths. It was a wonder. Her hands must've stunk of raw chicken.

"She sure is tall, ain't she?" I said to Mama. "For twelve."

"Who? Oh, her. Stuck-up."

"She is?" I turned to look at her, and I seen her roll her eyes. Dacia was setting on Mama's lap, acting sleepy, and Mama petted her hair.

"Her mama seemed nice," I said.

"Can't say I favor her pie crust."

"Maybe Alta Bea and me, we could walk to school together."

Mama sighed. "Come and get her, will you? My arms is played out."

Dacia was dead weight, and I had to buck her up on my shoulder. She mewed like a kitten, but she never woken up.

"I know you like school," Mama said, "but I'm going to need you home for a while." She rubbed her one shoulder. She looked more tired than I ever seen her before.

"Oh, I know. Just sometimes." In Mama and Daddy's room I laid Dacia on the bed. I seen her eyelashes made a shadow on her face. She was sweaty, but she was still of the age where it smelled sweet. I pulled her hair back off of her neck.

Directly Mama come in the room and laid down

with her, and I left them be. Mama, she slept half the day.

Wasn't but a week later Alta Bea knocked on the door and asked could I come over and play, and Mama said yes, if I wasn't gone too long.

Alta Bea's house beat anything I ever seen. I couldn't hardly keep track of the rooms: the front room, the setting room, which she called the parlor, and then a room in the back that was full of books plus two tables just for writing and three cushion chairs. There was a big room to eat in and a room for cooking, with a little alcove for washing clothes. They had a woman come in once a week.

Before I could blink, Alta Bea run up the stairs two at a time. A long hallway and doors into four bedrooms. The second on the right was hers.

I stopped in the doorway and just stared. Her room was the size of our front room. A bed big enough for two or three people, with a carved wooden headboard. A tall cabinet with two doors, and clothes spilling out. And books, my Lord! On the floor, on the bed, on the windowsill, all over.

"Come on in, silly," she said.

Going in, I tripped on a pair of cast-iron shutters built into the floor—a heat register, Alta Bea told me. We got down on our knees, and she pushed a handle to open up the shutters. Through the grate you could see down into the setting room below.

"For heat," Alta Bea said. "Heat rises, you know."

I looked down through the grate. It was like looking at a picture in a frame.

Alta Bea said, "You can listen at night. I hear lots of things I'm not supposed to." Her eyes was shining.

"Like what?" I said.

She laughed and slammed the grate shut. A puff of dust come up. "Come on."

It surprised me she laughed and never answered my question, and it stung.

Alta Bea clomped downstairs and took me back into the room with the bookshelves. There was a box and two pair of scissors set out, and Alta Bea opened the box and pulled out the prettiest curly-headed paper dolls I ever seen, with lots of clothes, and all of them with tabs to fold over to hang them on with. I never knowed there was such a thing as boughten paper dolls. At home I had always cut mine out of the Sears catalog, and the clothes was different sizes from the bodies. I wondered if everbody in Missouri had such things, or just Alta Bea.

As we was cutting, she said, "What grade will you be in?"

"I don't know. I was in the third last year back home, but I don't know how they do it here." I accidentally snipped the corner off of a dress, so I put a little spit on it and pressed the pieces back together.

"I'll be in seventh," she said. "I *wish* I would be in *high* school."

Now me, I wasn't in school but half the time, and my geography and arithmetic wasn't very good. "Seventh," I said. "That sounds hard."

She made a *puh* sound with her lips. "School's so easy, it's pitiful. I'm reading college-level books at home. Dad quizzes me."

"College?" I put down my scissors and stared at her. I'd heard talk of college, where teachers and doctors went to. I'd never heard of no girl going.

"I want to know everything," she said. "I want to know how things work. One time, my father had this pocket watch, and I took it apart, and it had these wheels inside. Gears." She took a piece of paper and drawed circles on it with a pencil. "So when you wind it, it tightens a spring, and then, as the spring lets go, it moves this wheel, and then the gears—see?"

I looked at the picture, and I seen what she meant.

"And see, this wheel is bigger, so it takes longer, so it's like the hour hand? Then it gears down to the littler wheel, and it moves faster— the minute hand." Sweat come out on her forehead, from excitement seemed like.

"Your daddy, did he tell you about the watch?" I said. "My daddy showed me how to throw a knife one time."

She frowned. "When he found me with it, he gave me a spanking. The only one of my life."

"Oh." One whipping. She must be awful good. Mama would admire that.

Directly Alta Bea asked me what was my favorite subject in school.

"Reading. I like to read the Bible."

"Look at these shoes," she said. "Aren't they darling?"

I didn't answer. I had heard the word *darling* before, but I couldn't figure out how it connected to them paper doll shoes.

She give a strange laugh. "Really, I'm too old to play paper dolls. I don't want to play this anymore." She reached over and grabbed my doll, and she it tore in two. She throwed pieces willy-nilly into the box and shoved it across the table. Scraps fell on the floor.

I didn't know what to think. She said she was too old to play with paper dolls, but to me she was acting like a child. I reached over and put the lid on the box.

"Mother!" she hollered. "Mother!"

It was like her mother'd been standing out in the hall waiting—there she was.

"We're tired of paper dolls," Alta Bea said to her. "There's nothing to do."

"Would you like to look through my button box?"

Alta Bea rolled her eyes.

"I would," I said.

Her mother smiled. "I'll get it."

You never seen the like of them buttons—bone, ivory, wood, shell, stone, all kinds, all colors, carved into ever sort of a thing you can imagine. There was ever animal, flower, feather, and jewel in the world, and even some made-up things. I spread my fingers and buried both hands up to my wrists. Them buttons was cool to the touch, like natural things is.

Alta Bea, she reached over and took the box and dumped the buttons all out on the floor. She laughed, and then I laughed. I loved the clicking sound they made, and I loved what they looked like spreading out, like coins. We set down on the rug side by side and started fingering them and putting them in piles. It was the most contented I'd felt since I got there.

"My mother has a button box," I said, "but nothing like this. I never—"

"How old is she?" Alta Bea said. "Mine's fifty. She was thirty-eight before she had me."

"Oh." I hadn't never thought of mothers having any particular age.

"I was a surprise," Alta Bea said. This sounded like something she heard through the heat register. I wondered what it meant.

She asked me what was it like to live in such a big family. That near stumped me. What was it like? How would I know that, not knowing no different? I told her about shelling beans and scraping carrots, tending the fire, doing up the linens, looking after Dacia and Opal, and such things as that.

"When do you read?" she said.

I just looked at her. I never understood what she meant.

"I mean, what do you do for fun?" She laid out black buttons in a big circle on the floor, moving them in and out, back and forth. She kept staring at them and fiddling with them. But she never missed a word, seemed like.

"Me and Mama, we like to visit when we work, or sing."

"What do you talk about?"

What did me and Mama talk about? The weather? The garden? The animals? The house? The children? Daddy? When Mama talked, it all seemed so much *like* her, I didn't hardly pay no mind. It was just her. And Dacia alongside, chattering like a magpie, and me hardly getting a word in edgewise.

"Mama, her pies is awful good," I said. "She peels the apples in one long string." I pictured her bending over the flour sack, dipping out the flour with her hand. I never seen her use a cup. She just seemed to know how much flour to put in.

"If she don't have lard, she uses butter," I said, "but she favors the lard."

Alta Bea asked me about my brothers William and Buck, what was they like, and I told her how things was. "They almost sound like hired hands," she said.

"They earn their keep."

She cocked her head. "You, too, it sounds like." She seemed satisfied, like she had reckoned something out.

I just set there. Surely she didn't mean to be insulting, though it sounded like it. Just ignorant, I reckoned.

"How did your folks meet?" she said.

"Mama says, you know how some people just drift apart? Well, her and him just drifted together." I smiled, remembering the time Mama'd said that.

Alta Bea stared at me. "What does *that* mean?"

That brought me up short. I pictured how things was back home, where people lived cheek by jowl in the hills, not in flat, laid-out squares like in Missouri, with roads. Back home, half the people you knowed was a relation, seemed like, and people spent a lot of time at other people's houses. How could I make her understand? "You know. They—people just—they—"

"When I was a little girl, I used to squint my eyes and disappear. Did you ever do that?" She didn't look at me.

"You what?"

"I would stretch out flat, like a piece of paper, and I would just slip underneath the wall, or a picture on the wall, or the *paint*."

"Underneath?" I said.

"Oh, it's handy. You can see people, but they can't see you."

I was tired of her making fun of me like I was ignorant. "Do it now. I want to see you disappear."

She shrugged. "Don't be silly."

"You're the one that said it. Go on." I didn't believe her. I wasn't no fool.

She sighed. "Don't be so serious all the time."

"Sounds like witchcraft to me."

Now she screamed laughing. "I was only pretending!" She slapped her hand on the rug.

"But you *said*—"

"I was only *pretending* to *disappear*, I mean. I knew I wasn't really invisible."

I thought about it. "How come you to do it, then?"

She leaned over close to my face and spoke like she was out of breath. "Don't you ever just want to be invisible? When it feels like things are closing *in* on you? And people are looking at you like you're crazy? Your lips feel like they're about to crack open, they're so dry? Just disappear? You know what I mean."

I pulled back.

She let loose a big sigh. "I never know if it's just me. I never know what people are thinking."

I heard footsteps, and I started putting the buttons back in the box. I was getting the willies. I didn't want to be with her no more, tell the truth.

Alta Bea leaned over and lifted my chin to look me in the eye. "Why is everything such a big Goddamn *secret*? Don't they know, if they just told you what they want, you'd do it? Don't they *know* that?"

"Who? Know what?"

"They don't *tell* you, and then they get mad when you just—"

"Who?"

"People!"

I looked at her. "I don't have no notion what you're talking about." How come she seemed so mad all the sudden?

"That's what I mean!" She was hollering now. "The big Goddamn secret!"

Just then a man come walking into the room holding a newspaper, a white-haired man dressed in a suit but with his collar off. His face was scarlet red. You could see his scalp through his white hair, and it was a red shade of pink.

"What did I just hear you say?" he said, one word at a time. Cold.

"Dad," Alta Bea said, quiet and breathless, like all her peculiar emotions of a minute ago had

77

dissolved. I felt her knee tremble against mine.

Now her daddy blinked and looked at me. Evidently he hadn't noticed I was there. He looked puzzled, like he couldn't work out who I was.

"Dad," Alta Bea said, "this is B—"

"What's all this?" His eyes swept the paper scraps and buttons on the floor. He flung the newspaper around like he was swatting flies.

"I'm sorry," Alta Bea said.

The look he give her was so withering I couldn't stand it, and I dropped my eyes. He snorted air out of his nose and stomped out of the room without another word.

Alta Bea's face was pale. "I didn't realize how late it was," she said to me. "He reads the paper in this room." She reached out her hand and scooped up some buttons. But instead of putting them away, she dropped all but one, which she worried with her fingers.

I looked at her—slumped over, her stomach pooching out, her face crumpled. There wasn't no tears, only a look of pain that felt like a burn. It come to me how the Bible talks about *the poor in spirit,* and I felt like I was looking right at one of them poors in spirit. My skin felt prickly.

Alta Bea said, "He doesn't like things to be . . . unexpected," and she shrugged like she didn't reckon I would understand, any more than I understood her other odd notions.

I felt like I had to make up my mind all on my own, without Mama nor nobody there to talk to. So I done it. "My daddy, sometimes in the mornings I find him passed out on the porch."

She was sitting cross-legged, and now she leaned her elbows on her knees and laid her face in her hands. "Is he sick?"

I shook my head. "Drunk." I felt myself blush. Mama wouldn't like me telling something so personal, and Daddy, he'd like to've blistered me if he'd knowed. It felt like Alta Bea was pulling things out of me.

"Oh, that." She shrugged.

"He stinks," I said in a low voice. "Sweet and sour, like day-old potato scrapings."

She wrinkled her nose but didn't look up, so I took a breath and said, "Well, one time, he . . ."

"What?" she said.

"Don't tell nobody."

Now she straightened up and looked at me. "I won't."

I scooted closer. "Daddy's people believes in handling serpents. If you get bit by a poison snake, it won't kill you. Mama's, they don't hold to that."

"Oh." Her eyes brightened.

"Daddy, he took me one time. When I was real little."

"In Kentucky?"

"I never told nobody before." I had goose

bumps. Memories—no, not memories, *feelings*—come to me in a rush, flooding me. I hadn't thought about that time with Daddy and the serpents since the day of the hog killing, the day Timmy died, when one of the women brought it up and I had a memory light on me like a moth, and Mama hushed me. Now I wondered—was I feeling those feelings again like when it happened, or had Daddy told me about it, and I was feeling my feelings about his story? *Had* Daddy told me about it? I couldn't remember. All I knowed was, I felt full to overflowing with feelings that made me shiver inside and out.

"Tell me—go on." She was staring at me like she could see through me. Like she could see my feelings.

I closed my eyes. "It wasn't in church, it was in somebody's house. I remember, my hair stuck to the ceiling. Daddy was holding me on his shoulders, and my hair, it rose up." I opened my eyes. "You know, like your hair sticks to a penny balloon if you rub it."

She nodded. "Static electricity."

"Made my whole face itch." I swallowed. "Anyhow, there was this man, light-colored hair, all greased up, rippling off his forehead like ladies' hair. And he had this wooden box he kept the snakes in." I was seeing all this in my mind like it was just now happening.

"What kind?"

"Not great big, just regular size. But poison." Seeing the look on her face, I said, "I'm not lying."

"Oh, I know." She picked up some buttons and started making a circle of white ones inside the circle she'd made earlier of black ones. She acted like she was only half listening, but I could tell by the cord on her neck she was taking in ever word.

"He spread out his arms, and the snakes, they crawled up and down them, and one crawled around his neck." I was trembling. It was like them snakes was on *me*.

She kept fishing out white buttons, adding to the circle. "You sure they weren't just garter snakes?"

Well, that galled me, sure enough. The spell was broke, and the story was ashes in my mouth. I stood up and brushed paper scraps and buttons off of my skirt. "I don't like you," I blurted out.

"I don't care." She kept playing with the white buttons without dropping a one.

"You're stuck-up."

"I don't care," she said again.

"They *was* poison." I wanted her to believe me, though I couldn't have told you why.

She shifted so her feet was flat on the rug and her knees was bent and close together. She laid her forehead on her knees for a moment, and then she brought up her head and hammered her face against her knees, hard, four or five times. "I *told* you."

It hurt to look at that. "Quit it."

"People! People! People!" With each one, she again smacked her forehead on her knees.

"I said *quit* it." I dropped back down on the floor and grabbed aholt of her arm.

Now she blinked and looked around. I let go her arm and scooted a ways away. We both set there, breathing hard.

After while she said, "I don't know what makes me act this way."

There was a red place on her forehead. I pictured her daddy's red scalp. "Me neither." I shivered.

She sighed and rubbed her forehead.

"I'll help you clean up," I said.

She shook her head.

"Well, I reckon I'll go on home then."

She never said nothing more, and she never got up. I found her mother and told her I had a nice time. Mama always had us to say that.

Walking home, I went through it all in my mind. I worried I had told Alta Bea things that might come back on me. I asked myself how come I was such a blabbermouth to her, somebody I hardly knowed. She was trouble, a blind man could see that. Seemed like I had invited trouble to walk right into my life. Something there in that house was off, like spoiled pork, and now I had let myself get drug into it.

For sure I hadn't never met nobody like Alta Bea. I never knowed nobody that had that look in their eyes like she could see into you. It made a person tired and jangled, like somebody was shining an oil lamp in your eyes, but it also give you a feeling of glittering, fluttery things you couldn't hardly not look at.

Chapter 4

That summer Mama lost her religion. She stopped talking about the Lord and stopped singing—hymns or nothing clsc. We stopped saying grace, or praying at all. And even though they had three churches in Obsidian, we never went to a one of them. When I asked her about it one time, she said, "We'll go when I feel better," but we never did. I knowed better than to pester her about it. Far as I know, Daddy never took up church again neither.

And Mama started up sneaking out of the house without a word to nobody. You might find her anywhere—in the barn, out by the fence, laying down under a tree in the old orchard. Might be gone for an hour, two hours at a time.

It irked me, since I didn't have no time to go looking for her. For one thing, Opal started up crawling and then took steps, and directly she was running hither and yon. Dacia, at least, seemed like she was content to go off and play by herself. That age—three—likes to play with chickens and barn kittens. Still, you had to check on her ever little bit, since she was like to tease the animals till they scratched her.

It was hot now, hotter than it ever got back home, a wet heat that left you slick with sweat. When I wasn't checking on a child or Mama, I was dressing chickens, sweeping floors, scrubbing pots, putting meals on the table, doing the wash, cutting firewood. I spent the evenings going through the clothes, seeing what could be mended and what could be made over.

William and Buck, they worked out in the pasture over the south ridge, cutting prairie hay to feed the cow come winter. That's hard labor, bent over with a scythe morning to night in the heat. Them boys didn't have their whiskers yet—Buck was twelve and William was fourteen—but working in the field they turned into little men, seemed like. They was like to chew tobacco.

Daddy, after visiting with people in town, he decided to sow hard red winter wheat come fall—bragged on it, said it was the best kind, sprouted in time for the fall rains, rested under the winter snow, already up two-three-four inches come spring. So one day he hitched Blue to the plow and started in preparing the ground. On the second day, he come in the house at noon. Me and the girls was eating dinner at the table—salt-meat gravy and bread. Ate a lot of salt-meat in them days.

"Blue, she ain't no plow horse," Daddy said to me. "Don't have the right conformation."

"What's that?" Dacia said.

Daddy picked up a piece of bread and looked around the table. Not seeing no knife, he grabbed a spoon and scooped a blob of butter on it. "And Sparky, he won't let himself be broke to the plow." He eat the bread in two bites, and then he reached into the gravy and fished him out some salt-meat with his fingers. "Fix me a supper to take with me. Gonna go get me a plow horse."

I never said nothing. I pictured how he'd looked in the alley back in Feldspar, drunk and bloody and beat half to death. Plow horse, my eye. He was heading back down that very same road that'd ran us out of Kentucky. I give him a look, but it didn't do no good coming from a girl. I stood up and started rummaging in the trunk where we kept the food.

"Where's your mama?" he said.

Dacia said, "In the grove, laying on a blanket." This surprised me—I thought Mama was taking a nap in the bedroom—but I never said nothing.

Daddy belched out a bad smell. "What the Sam Hill's she doing out there?"

"Daddy, I don't rightly know." When she felt like it, Dacia was like to imitate her elders' talk.

"You want a can of beans?" I said to him.

He swore, and then he went around the table looking for food. He grabbed up half a loaf of bread and throwed it in the saddlebag. Then he headed for the back door.

"When'll you be back?" I said.

"You'll see me when you see me."

I picked up Opal and walked over to the doorway and watched him ride off. Opal started squirming, and I let her down. She scooted back to the table and started picking up crumbs off the floor.

I peeked in the door to the bedroom, which wouldn't close all the way on account of the floor was crooked. That door was always partway open.

Sure enough, Mama wasn't in there. "Mama's in the grove setting on a blanket?" I said to Dacia.

She shrugged. "We out of bread?"

I set down at the table. "Was you out there with her?"

Opal let out a cry. I looked down and seen Dacia pulling her foot back. "I didn't mean to!"

I was too out of sorts to scrap with her, so I let it go. "Nobody said you did! Hush up!"

Now I heard the pump being worked on the back porch. "What's all this hollering?" come Mama's voice. "Lord Amighty."

She come in and picked up the baby. "Sounds like a bunch of heathens in here." She tickled Opal, and in a moment they all three was laughing.

"Daddy's went to buy a plow horse," I said to Mama. "Or so he says."

I expected her to be mad, but she just said, "I reckon he's the one knows about them things."

"He wouldn't say when he'll be back."

Opal stuck her fingers in Mama's mouth, and she laughed and turned her back to me. "You make the coffee yet?"

"Where was you?" I said.

"Who's been in the trunk?"

"Dacia, she said you—"

"Stop picking on your sister." She looked inside the trunk. "We out of coffee?"

I was wroth Mama wouldn't tell me where she'd been—or hadn't told me she was leaving the house, come to that. Her and Daddy both, and the relations back home, why, they was like to tease a child. You'd say, "Who's coming for supper?" and they'd say, "The boogeyman, and he wants fricasseed childern for dessert." But this wasn't no teasing matter, seemed to me like, so how come Mama done me that way? It tied me in knots trying to work out how come she done the things she done.

Two days later, Daddy come home with a half a dozen horses, which he put in the corral next to the barn. Nobody said another word about hard red winter wheat. All that was left of Daddy's notion of farming was two crooked furrows next to the fence.

Wasn't long after that, maybe a week, me and Mama and the girls was setting on the back porch, me snapping string beans. We had a bushel of them from Alta Bea's mama. She said she didn't have no time to snap them, would I do it and keep a peck for my trouble? I wanted to do them beans up right, being's it was charity.

I said something to Mama, and when I looked up, she was gone.

"You seen Mama?" I said to Dacia.

"She was in the backhouse while ago."

I stood up and shaded my eyes and run my gaze over the area behind the house. There was the backhouse, with its halo of buzzing yellow jackets looking to fatten up the queen before winter, but the door was half open. Wasn't no Mama out by the chicken house, and she wasn't out in the garden neither. Wasn't nothing but flies stirring out by the barn, the corral, and the horse tank, and I couldn't see nothing out by the smokehouse.

I glanced at Opal asleep in her basket. "Keep an eye on the baby," I said to Dacia. I pulled a couple of red flowers off the trumpet vine. "Here, make you some trumpet dolls."

In the barn I searched through the stalls and the tack room, and then I climbed up in the haymow and stood inside the big square door up there and looked all around the place. Nothing. Maybe she'd went down to the slough, see if there was water in it yet, or maybe she'd took some old leaky pot to the wash on the other side of the ridge, where we throwed out junk. There was lots of reasons for her to be someplace, but not no reason for her to go off without telling me, anyhow no reason I seen.

I glanced over to the back porch and seen Dacia get up and wander around the yard, so I give up looking for Mama. I walked back and took up snapping beans again where I could keep an eye on the girls.

I was halfway through the bushel when I heard Mama come through the front door. Her bare feet swished on the floor as she walked through the house and out to where we was. She set down heavy, her face flushed, and she dusted the soles of her feet with her hands. "Floor needs swept."

Dacia set down next to her, and she started combing through Dacia's hair with her fingers. "Rat's nest! Go get me the hairbrush."

"Where's it at?"

"I don't know—go look."

After Dacia left, Mama leaned back on her elbows and rocked her head till her neck popped. "Woo, I'm wore out."

"We didn't know where you was at," I said— light, so she wouldn't get mad.

Dacia come to the doorway. "I can't find it, Mama."

"You didn't look," I said.

Now Mama set up straight and then got to her feet. "I'm gonna go lay down for a minute— don't none of you bother me."

91

"Can I come? Can I come?" Dacia said.

"I'm just gonna sleep."

"I wanna sleep, too," Dacia said.

Mama sighed and took aholt of her hand. But ten minutes later, here Dacia come back, bawling, saying Mama'd kicked her out of the bed. Now Opal woken up, and she started in crying, too. I was hot, I was tired, and I was wroth and worried both, so I busted into tears myself. The little ones stopped crying like they was shot, but pretty soon they took it up again, and we all set there and bawled. I took Opal out of her basket, the both of us still crying, and I changed her pants. Then I put her on my hip and took aholt of Dacia's hand and started walking.

"Where we going?" Dacia said through her tears.

I didn't have no idea, so I said, "Let's go pet the horses," and then our bawling petered out to sniffles. We walked out to the corral, wiping our noses on our sleeves.

Mama, she slept through supper and was still sleeping when I put the girls to bed on their pallets. We heard her cough ever little bit, and I looked in on her a few times to see was her chest moving.

When she finally got up, long after dark, she had me to pump her a fresh pitcher of water, and she gulped down two big glasses' worth.

"You feeling puny?" I said.

She set there and daubed water on her face. "Just wore out. Go on to bed."

Daddy, he never come home that night, or, if he did, he slept out in the barn.

July come, with heavy air inside and out. My brothers was still cutting prairie hay on the south ridge. One night late, they come to the house for supper with me and Daddy after the smaller children was asleep. Buck set down and started cramming food in his mouth, but William, he never eat, only talked about how the two of them ought to hire theirselves out. It would take a good six more weeks to cut enough Goddamn hay to feed the cow for the winter, when, hell, they could work on a wheat harvest crew and buy the Goddamn hay, with money left over against the rent. Hell, people with any sense was using steam thrashing machines, you could cut six tons a week, didn't make no Goddamn sense to cut nothing by hand no more—hay, wheat, nothing.

If you didn't know no better, by the tone you would've thought it was Daddy talking.

Now Daddy didn't want to lose them boys as hands, and him and William got to arguing about it. Directly William said Daddy was an old drunk who didn't know shit, he was fifty year too Goddamn late. The stupidest horse in Creation—Lord knowed, horses was stupid—had more Goddamn sense than Daddy had.

Daddy throwed his whiskey bottle across the room, liquor spewing. Then he grabbed up his belt and chased the boys out of the house. He stood on the front porch cursing them for ungrateful and wayward bastards, and then he stepped off the porch. Pretty soon I heard him saddle up one of the horses and take off, but I knowed he wasn't going after the boys. He was going into town to get drunk.

We didn't see William and Buck again for four days, till Daddy packed up his saddlebags and took off someplace. That night, William come to the house and told me and Mama that him and Buck was by God joining a harvest crew. They'd start up south in Texas and work their way north. They calculated they could send us forty dollars a month for the next four or five months and see us again come winter.

About that time Buck come in, took off his hat, and stood there behind William's chair. His eyes was red.

"You'll do no such of a thing," Mama said, but she hardly had it out before she broke down, and we all knowed she wasn't going to stop them. If Daddy was making money horse trading, he wasn't bringing it home, seemed like, and we was having a hard time making the rent.

William stood up. "Truck's coming to the

bridge west of town at four in the morning, so we better get going."

The two of them walked to the front door. William, he looked back and nodded to me, and Buck come over and touched me with his fingers on the top of my head.

Mama walked with them as far as the road and then come back crying. "I'm losing my boys," she said. "Won't nothing be the same again."

"It's only for harvest," I said, though it felt like she was right, wouldn't nothing be the same again. I felt like I should cry, too, but it had been a long while since I thought of the boys as part of the house family. I let loose a tear or two, but pretty soon I wiped my face and set down to the mending.

After they left, Mama got to where she'd turn up missing ever day. I tried keeping track of her, but there was always a child or animal needed looking after, and if I turned away for a minute, she'd be gone. And when she come back, she'd go to her room and sleep. I'd never knowed nobody could sleep that much if they tried.

After a week or two, it dawned on me something must be wrong with her. I remember when it happened. I was washing dishes, and Opal and Dacia was playing on the floor. I wasn't thinking about nothing special. I reached for a dirty pan, and at that moment, a feeling of dread settled on me like a blanket. I stood there and stared at my bare dripping arm. Why, something must be wrong with Mama. It just come to me.

The next morning, early, I seen Daddy out front, astride Blue. I run out there and grabbed aholt of his leg. "Daddy, Mama ain't hardly been out of bed for a week now."

"Got no time for this." He smacked Blue's rump with the reins.

I felt myself lifted off my feet, but I held on. "She's awful puny, Daddy! I don't know what to do."

He reined Blue in. "A week, you say."

"Maybe two, I don't know, I got the girls to look after."

He peered at me. "You got any notion what doctors cost?"

Wasn't nothing I could say to that. He wheeled Blue around and galloped off.

Late in the afternoon, why, here come a man in a buggy, an old man wearing a black suit. I opened the door, and he said, "Where's she at?" He had thick white eyebrows that stuck out like wings.

"Who's that man?" Dacia said. Her and Opal was setting at the table.

The doctor ignored her and looked at me. I pointed to the bedroom door. He walked on in and tried to shut the door behind him. He yanked on it, but as usual it wouldn't go shut all the way.

"Floor's crooked," I said, but seemed like he didn't pay me no mind.

I heard Mama cry out a little bit in surprise and him answer, and then I heard the two of them talking, though I couldn't make out the words.

"Who's that man?" Dacia said again.

"Hush, it's the doctor." I was struck by a strange man's voice—reedy, womanish—coming out of Mama and Daddy's room.

"How come?" Dacia said.

"Hush, I said." I set down at the table. "You got to be quiet or he can't make Mama well, hear me?"

"She going on her trip?" she whispered.

"Where'd you get that notion? What trip?"

She pursed her lips. "Could we play buttons? Let's get out the button box and play buttons."

"Hush *up,*" I said.

Pretty soon I got up and peeked through the door, and I seen the doctor pull a hypodermic needle out of a medicine bottle. Not that I knowed what a hypodermic needle was—I'd never saw such a thing. Mama tensed, and the doctor leaned over and poked her in the hip with it. It like to scared me to death. Then he pulled it out and peered at Mama's face, and he took the needle apart and put it away in a little leather case lined in purple velvet. He fingered a drop of sweat off of his nose.

Mama begun whining with each breath, like

a cat will sometimes when it's licking its fur.

I showed the doctor out and went in to Mama. Her face was pale. She shifted her eyes to look at me, and she muttered something I couldn't make out. Then she closed her eyes, and her head sunk hard into the pillow. Her breathing was rough.

I stood and watched her for a while, and ever little bit I placed my hand on her stomach to feel her breath. Thinking about that needle give me the willies. It was slick and shiny, and it seemed mysterious and deadly as a snake. Modern.

Mama mumbled and sighed for a while but never opened her eyes. It got deathly still in the room.

Now Dacia come in and wrapped her arms around my leg. "I wanna play buttons! Let's play buttons!"

I clapped my hand over Dacia's mouth, but Mama never stirred. Through my hand Dacia tried to say something, but I never let go. Then she stuck her tongue in my fingers, and I was so surprised and disgusted I let loose of her and she run out of the room.

I stood there and tried to picture what it done to somebody—what kind of doctoring it was— when you poked a needle in them. I'd had hot mustard plasters on my chest for colds, I'd drank castor oil for the runs, I'd took aspirin powder for the headache, but I couldn't fathom what a needle done to you. Maybe let bad air out?

What was in that shot, I reckon now, was opium. That and other kinds of dope, they was in the patent medicines. I don't know how come the doctor give Mama a shot of dope. I don't know was it something Daddy'd said to him, or something Mama said, or what.

Now her face looked relaxed, sure enough, the wrinkles flattened out like melted candlewax. Maybe she wasn't getting good sleep, I thought. Maybe all she needed was a good long rest.

Wasn't long before Dacia come back in and drug me out of the room, saying she wanted to go outside, she had something to show me. I figured Mama would be sleeping for a while, so I put Opal on my hip, and Dacia led us out to the old smokehouse about a hundred yards from the house. This little building hadn't been used for a long time, and a volunteer tree had heaved up one side of it, making the whole thing slanted. Inside, it was dark except for strips of light leaking through the walls where the daubing had been eat by rats long since. All around the ceiling was iron hooks, otherwise you might not've knowed it was once a smokehouse. That and the smell.

When my eyes adjusted I seen that Dacia'd fixed her up a playhouse in there, with two turned-over buckets for chairs and a fruit crate for a table. There was dishes and silverware she'd stole from the house, and an old bent-handle pan. She also had pickle jars filled with dead bugs, bird's eggs, rocks, feathers, buttons, and square-head nails. I don't reckon I'd been inside the smokehouse but two or three times, and none of this had been there. I wondered what-all else Dacia had been up to that I'd never paid no mind to, and I felt a pang.

"I'm the mama," Dacia said. "Now you two, you sit on this chair." Which we done, Opal balanced on my knees.

Dacia played like she was serving us up some fried chicken, biscuits, and pie, and me and Opal eat it, smacking our lips. Dacia, she was correcting our table manners when I all the sudden realized she wasn't just playing like she was a mama, she was mimicking Mama herself—the sound of her voice, the way she twisted her neck and made it pop, the way she slapped your hand if you tried to fork something off the serving platter.

"Who showed you how to do that?" I said to her.

"Don't leave that gristle—chew it up. It's good, and good *for* you." She lifted her cup and slurped it just like Mama done, and her not quite four year old. I never heard the like.

"You sound just like her," I said.

Now she frowned and pinched her lips. "Go fetch me a rag—Opal spit up," she said in a sharp voice. "Hurry up, before it gets all over, you hear? You hear?"

I started to laugh, and then it hit me, she was imitating me. "I don't sound like that."

She wiped her face with her hand and curled a lock of hair back behind her ears, which I was like to do. "You don't do as you're told, why, Daddy's gonna strop you when he gets home."

I felt my neck and face go red.

Now she put her thumbs on her eyebrows and got a fierce look on her face. "Where at's yer mama?" she said, low-pitched but womanish.

"The doctor!" I couldn't help getting caught up in it. I laughed, and Opal got to laughing, too. Then Dacia started in singing, *Soft as the voice of an angel,* and I joined in, and Opal, she started half-singing and half-babbling in her baby way. There we set, singing and laughing, like in a dream.

After the song, Dacia said in her own voice, "It's hot in here."

"Race you to the pump!" I said, grabbing up Opal.

I let Dacia win, and I was pumping us a bucket of water when I remembered Mama's shot. I left the girls there to splash in the water and went inside.

Mama's eyes was closed, but she stirred when I come in. "Water," she said. It come out "warr." There was a line of dried drool on her chin and down her neck.

"You feeling better?" I poured water from the pitcher.

She set up and gulped down the water. Then she laid back on the pillow and closed her eyes. She had hollows under her eyes the color of rust.

"More?" I said.

She shook her head. I waited for a minute and then turned to go.

"Brr," she said. She grabbed my hand and pressed it to her belly. "Baby." Then she turned over on her side, facing away from me.

A feeling of blessed relief run through me. No wonder she'd been puny! Now she would be fine. Everbody loved babies, Mama most of all. A new baby would make things better—they always did. I hoped it would be a boy. Daddy would like that.

Mama slept through dinner and supper, and she was still sleeping when I put the girls to bed. I heated up some broth and took it in to her, but she pushed me away and turned back over. I set the bowl on the washstand and crawled in the bed with her in case she should need me in the night. I started thinking about the coming baby, but sleep come to me before I could picture it.

Chapter 5

Y ou *have* to go to school," Alta Bea said. "It's not too late. You could catch up. I'd help you, I would."

I looked up at the sky and started pulling the clothes down off the line. "It's coming up a bad cloud—we better hurry."

"You could ride to school in our car."

I'd saw that car, long and black, driving in and out from their house. Alta Bea's mama knowed everbody in Obsidian, and she rode into town most ever day to "see" her friends. That was a new one on me. Mama'd always had friends and kin aplenty back home, but whenever they got together, they was doing something, not just "seeing" each other.

"Don't you smell that rain?" I took down a shirt of Daddy's and moved on to a pair of overhauls, which I flicked a piece of bird shit off of.

Alta Bea reached out and put her hand on my arm. "You want to be ignorant all your life?"

Wasn't no use getting my back up. To her it was just a fact, not an insult. I shook her hand off. "You going to stand there, or help me get these in before the rain comes?"

She sighed and reached in her pocket. "Here, I brought you a book."

I dropped the little book in the basket. "Help me with the sheets, will you?"

I pulled the sheet down off the line and motioned with my head for her to grab a corner, which she done, and then she leaned over and caught the other'n. We brought our hands together, and I took aholt of four corners in each hand and pulled the sheet toward me.

"Read it, Bertie, you'll like it," she said. Hearing somebody use my name—and not to curse me out or ask me for something—I confess that made me glow a little bit.

The two of us brought our hands together again, and I pulled the sheet to my chin and finished folding it. I put it in the basket, and Alta Bea pulled down the other sheet. "After you read it, we could talk about it."

"Like school," I said.

We brought our hands together again, and she blurted out, "Nobody at school likes me. My *parents* don't even like me."

We was face-to-face, real close, and I felt the heat coming off her. "I like you." I couldn't think of nothing else to say.

"No, you don't." She frowned and curled her lips, and you could see the creases coming off her mouth like an old woman's. There was tears in her eyes.

I blowed out my lips to show her I was vexed, and I pulled the sheet away. I busied my eyes and hands folding it.

"Nobody likes me," she said.

Now the clothesline started bouncing. I looked up and seen she was banging her forehead against it like she'd banged her forehead against her knees that day we played with paper dolls at her house. She was like to do that when she was riled.

"Quit it," I said. "You're like to—"

She stopped and looked at me. "You're the only friend I have, Bertie, truly."

This touched me. I knowed it must be true, and I felt sorry for her. And her and her mama had been awful good to us. I started to say something—I don't know what—when I seen little splotches on her sleeve and then felt raindrops on my face. I hurried to pull down the rest of the clothes while she stood there without moving, getting wet. When I clutched the basket to my chest and turned around, I seen she was running off toward their place, hairpins flying and her hair bouncing on her back.

I pictured Mama or one of my kin shaking their head and saying, "Don't have enough sense to come in out of the rain," and what-all else they might say if they seen how Alta Bea acted—*Don't have the sense God gave a goose, ain't worth the salt in her bread, don't got all what belongs to her.*

105

Alta Bea was a strange one, all right. But then Mama also used to say, it was the ones that was hardest to love that needed it the most. And Alta Bea, she was hard to love, sure enough.

When I got inside the house, I dug through the basket and pulled out the little book. It was called *Five Little Peppers and How They Grew*. Inside she'd wrote her name—wrote, not printed—but I could read the *A* and the *B,* so I knowed what it must say. I put the book on a high shelf next to the rat poison so no grubby little hands would get it dirty. I told myself I'd read it when I could. It would give me and Alta Bea something to talk about.

Deep in winter—January 1910—Mama had the baby, which turned out to be twin boys, James and John. I don't know where them names come from, Daddy just picked them. I knowed he had a brother name of James.

We was snowed in at the time, and Daddy, he never tried to dig us out for five-six days. That surprised me. Ordinarily he couldn't stand being inside four walls that long. And he helped me out, even done some dishes. I can't forget walking into the front room and seeing him standing there over the bowl and stacking clean dishes on the table. It was like some fairy tale come to life, where a bear or a wolf opens its mouth and talks, and you never knowed it could do that, or any of its kind. I remember what Daddy's broad back looked like and him bent over the bowl. It was a wonder.

And it surprised me, too, when he changed the babies' pants, washed them out in a bucket, strung a cord across the front room, and hung them up to dry. For months, wasn't a place in the house didn't have diapers hanging there like sails on the sea.

He was crazy about them twins, sure enough. He hadn't had him a little boy since Timmy died, and now he had two. They was pretty babies, rambunctious like Dacia. He'd put one in the cradle and rock it with his foot and hold the other'n on his knee. When he finally dug us out, why, first thing he done was ride to town and send a telegram back home to the relations.

That day he come home with a bag of groceries, a sack of hard candy, and a fat black cigar. He set at the table and lit the cigar afire. He wrapped his lips around it and drawed in the smoke, draw after draw, like it tasted good. Finally, he let out a sigh, and curly streams of smoke leaked out the sides of his mouth. The girls set there watching him and sucking on the candy.

I had one baby on the shoulder and the other'n in the cradle.

Daddy coughed and spit on the floor. "You take good care of them boys," he said. "I'll be needing them before you know it." This is the closest he come to talking to me about William and Buck. They was back by now, taking care of the outside chores during the blizzard, but they built a fire outside to melt ice to water the stock and keep warm by, and they hardly ever come to the house when Daddy was there. I don't imagine they'd said more than a dozen words to him since they got back, and him neither.

"They's only babies," I said, meaning the twins.

He give me a hard look. "Too bad they grow up and get a mouth on 'em." He leaned back and hitched up his pants, touching one hand to his belt.

"You getting a whipping?" Dacia said to me, losing spittle from the jawbreaker in her cheek.

Nobody said nothing. I wasn't afraid. Something told me Daddy wasn't going to whip me no more. His spirit had got broke, I reckoned, when him and William had their fight about the horse business and the boys took off and left. For Daddy, seemed like horse trading had turned sour. It wasn't like back home, where he rode into the woods knowing everthing and everbody, and them knowing him. Now it was him by himself, clopping along dusty roads with fields stretching out as far as you could see, maybe a half a dozen people to a mile section, and him not knowing nobody. And William was right— people was using machinery to do things more. Daddy wasn't nothing special no more in his own mind, is how I pictured it, and he was bitter how his life had turned out.

Now he stood up and grabbed his coat and took his cigar out to the front porch, paying no mind to the cold.

That night he slept with Mama in the bed, which he hadn't done for a long time, and the twins laying in the cradle in there.

By the time I made up the girls' pallet in the front room, Opal was already asleep. She never batted an eye when I laid her down.

"Tell me a story, tell me a story," Dacia said, bouncing like a baby.

"This 'n's a story Daddy told me one time. Stop bouncing, you want to hear it." I set cross-legged on the pallet. "Daddy had this cousin."

"What's his name?"

"Who's telling this story?" I said. "Wasn't a he but a she, and her name was Violet." I made that name up, and the cousin part, too. I couldn't remember was it a cousin or aunt or what. Some relation, didn't matter who.

"Now Violet, she had a"—I searched for a word—"she had a bump on her leg." Actually, it was a cyst, but I didn't want to get into some long conversation with Dacia, which she was like to do when she heard a new word. "It was brown and purple, this bump was, the size of your fist." Dacia curled her hand shut and looked at it. "Now Daddy said, Velma'd had this bump—"

"Violet. You said Violet."

"Quiet down. I was just seeing was you paying attention."

She give me a doubtful look.

"Now Violet, her bump on her leg got to bothering her, so she went to see Dr. Rumpelstiltskin." I made up the part about his name, of course.

"The man turned the straw to gold?" she said.

"No, his brother." I waited to see would she think that was the end of the story and drift off, but she was too smart for that. She said, "Then what happened? What happened?"

"He cut it off, that bump, cut it right off of her leg. And you know what was *in* that bump?"

"What?"

"Teeth! And hair, and fingernails, rhinoceros horn, I don't know what-all!"

Another doubtful look.

"You know how come?"

She shook her head.

Now it dawned on me—this wasn't no story to be telling a child. I had to think quick. " 'Cause his brother, Rumpelstiltskin, had *put* all that stuff in there! And when Dr. Rumpelstiltskin cut off that bump, why, his brother Rumpelstiltskin lost all his hair—ever hair on his head, and his beard, too. And he got so mad, he grabbed aholt of his feet and tore himself in two!"

Dacia narrowed her eyes. "Is that the end?"

"They all lived happily ever after, the end." I laid down next to her and wriggled to get myself comfortable.

"Can we talk?" She loved to lay in bed and talk.

"If you're quiet."

I wish I could remember some of Dacia's sleepy talk that night—and for that matter, the things they all said to me—but it goes out of your head soon's you hear it. Prattle. I sure wish I could put my mind back there and hear some of it again. No telling how much you'd learn from it if you only listened.

As Dacia fell asleep, I thought about the rest of Daddy's story. The actual doctor told this cousin, when you're a baby in the womb you might have a twin but swallow it, and some of its parts end up inside you, so maybe she had a twin that ended up in that cyst on her leg. The first time Daddy told me this, I'd wondered, did I have a twin that I swallered? I'd looked all over myself to see was there a cyst with my twin's parts inside of it. I wondered if maybe one of my moles would grow into one. I felt like there was something missing off of me, but maybe it was inside where you couldn't see it. After that, I'd went around for a long time wondering about my twin, though I'd forgot that story till James and John was born.

It was a wonder—two whole babies and not just one that swallered the other one. Daddy, he

111

said it was two for the price of one. That tickled me.

Now that I think of it, that night of the cyst story was the last time me and Dacia was happy with each other. It was like Dacia herself was two people—one sweet, one curdled—and that night was the last time she showed me her sweet side.

Now Mama, the twins' birth was hard on her. Seemed like after they come, she hardly left her room all winter. She never wandered around outside like she done before, it was too cold and snowy. I remember wading through drifts up to my thigh, in bright sunlight, and the snow sparkled to where it hurt your eyes. You get snow like that, seems like time stops.

The months after the twins was born, it was like that. Then come the day I realized Mama had set up her bed to live in.

It must have been March or April—the outdoors was thawing out. The house had got to where it stunk. I swept the floor and washed it, but the smell stayed on, so I opened the front windows to let some air in.

I dished up dinner for Mama and carried it into her room, and the smell in there was awful, worse than the front room. Mama was in bed, scooted up almost against the wall—sleeping, it looked like—and there was Dacia in the bed, too. She'd found some playing cards and strung them all over the quilt and on the floor. Ever card, even the number cards, had pictures of ladies and men and horses, ladies fanning theirself or eating watermelons, men playing mandolins or waving swords. You could tell a lot of stories with them cards, and Dacia'd pawed them to where they was grimy and tore. Besides the cards, there was pictures cut out of catalogs, there was combs and a hairbrush, there was underdrawers, there was dirty cups and bowls.

Watching from the doorway, I seen Dacia cutting up a piece of paper with the scissors. She had a gummy blob of Mama's face powder in her hair, which hung down in strings, and she was murmuring to herself.

Then it come to me—Dacia'd been staying in here in the room with Mama most of the time for a while, maybe weeks. I'd been so busy with the twins I'd never noticed.

I started to say something, but then I heard Dacia say "Rumpelstiltskin," and I set the food down and just listened. "She had a bump on her leg with *teeth* in it, and the brother tore his beard in two, and all his hair fell out." She throwed up her hands, and the paper and scissors went flying. Then she arched her back, arms still straight up, and leaned back till her head touched the bed—I seen her eyes was closed—and then she started to slide off. I run and caught her before she hit the floor. She let out a scream, not so much from falling, seemed like, as me being there all the sudden.

Mama made a rumbling noise and turned over. "What? What?"

I acted like things was normal. I didn't know what else to do. I said, "It's just me and Dacia, Mama." I stood Dacia on the floor and walked over and pulled the curtains and opened the window a crack. "It's a nice day," I said. "William brought a mess of rabbits last night, and I smothered them for dinner. Let's eat in the front room, want to?"

Now I was back at the bed, reaching out my hand to help her, and when I got a good look at her, I froze. Her face was waxy, with skin hanging down off her cheeks, and her eyes was sunk in dark hollows. Her eyelids was fat and wrinkled like crepe—when had that happened? And she smelled. I hadn't never smelled a woman so rank.

She shrunk away from my hand. "Just bring me some broth. I'm wore out."

Now Dacia jumped onto the bed. "Me too, me too!" She started bouncing like she done, and she got Mama to swaying, and it looked like Mama might throw up.

"Stop it! You're gonna make Mama sick!"

"She don't care! She likes it!"

"She don't neither!" I hollered, and I reached over and grabbed Dacia off the bed. She squirmed and kicked—she'd growed, and it hurt—and Mama said, out of breath, "Leave her be, Bertie—ain't hurtin' nothin'." She got to coughing.

I turned Dacia loose, and she crawled next to Mama and give me a hateful look.

"I'm sending for the doctor," I said.

"Where's Opal at? And the babies?" Mama said, and I sucked in air. I'd forgot about them. I hurried into the front room. Opal, she was setting in a chair at the table, swinging her legs. She couldn't hardly see over the tabletop. The babies was laying in their baskets, waving their arms.

A cold, wet breeze was coming through the windows I'd left open, and the room felt icy. I feared for the babies—you didn't dare let a baby get a chill, they could die in a day's time—and I run and closed the windows. Then I grabbed some sticks from the woodbox and stoked up the fire in the stove.

I heard Dacia giggle from Mama's room. For a minute I was glad Mama had somebody to keep an eye on her while I took care of the little ones, but then I thought, a little girl, especially a wild one like Dacia, couldn't look after a growed woman that'd taken to her bed like that.

For a moment I had a vision of Mama in her bed, only it had sides like a coffin. I blinked it away.

. . .

Next morning I seen Mama had coughed up blood in the night, and there was a mottled rash on her neck that looked like leather boots with raindrop stains on them. I asked her what was it, but she just turned over.

I walked across the road and knocked at the big house. Alta Bea's mother opened the door. "Alta Bea's in school today, Bertie. She'll be—"

"I know," I said. "I'm wondering, could you send a hired man to fetch the doctor? My mama's poorly."

"Where's your dad?" she said, looking around like he might be stooped down behind me.

I felt hot all over. "Working."

"Come in then," she said. "I'll get Wilber to drive you into town."

"Could he—I mean, I need to stay with the babies."

She looked vexed, but only for a moment. "You go on home. We'll get the doctor." She started to close the door, and then she looked at me and smiled. "Don't worry, honey. She'll be fine."

When the doctor come, I went in the room and watched him give Mama a shot like he done before. I was ready for it this time, but it still made my toes curl under.

Back in the front room I asked him, "What's she got?"

He shook his head. "I wouldn't worry about it,

little girl. Just needs rest." He pulled out a piece of paper and wrote on it. "You could be a big help to her—mind the other children."

"How come she coughed up blood?" I said.

He dipped his chin and looked at me through his eyebrows. "This time of year." He finished writing and left the paper on the table. "See your daddy gets this." I seen it was a bill.

Mama purred for a while and went to sleep. She stopped coughing, but her rash was still there the next morning at first light when I checked on her.

After that, Mama's rash come and gone. Sometimes it was on her back, her eyelids, her cheeks, one time on her hand. I got to where I washed her ever day—she fought it more than a child would—and then turned the sheets. I tried to wash them to where she never slept on one side twice, but didn't seem to do no good. Her rash would come and go without no reason, seemed like. Might be gone for a week and then come back.

I didn't have no time to fret about Mama, I told myself, and so Dacia was the one kept her company hour after hour. And as she got to be more of Mama's pet, seemed like Dacia got mouthier and meaner. I had a feeling of dread about where Dacia would end up, spoiled like she was, and I couldn't help but wish Mama wouldn't be so easy with her.

I confess I felt the pangs of envy. I didn't envy
Dacia herself but the way Mama made over her,
always had. I knowed envy was a sin, and wrath
and pride was sins, and I had them, too, and I
knowed better—I had been taught the word of
the Lord. And besides they hurt, and there wasn't
no place for the pain to go. So I swallowed them
feelings down deep as I could.

Ain't no place deep enough to where they don't
eat at you anyhow, whether you know it or not,
but I didn't know that then.

Spring come, and Daddy resumed horse trading.
Said if we was going to have the doctor come
ever Goddamn day, he had to bring in more
money. Of course we never had the doctor ever
day, only ever month or two, and all he ever done
was give her more dope. I heard him tell Daddy
one time that she just wasn't of a mind to look
after all them children. Made me so mad I come
to tears, but wasn't no use arguing with no doctor,
or any other growed man, come to that.

Soon's the ground thawed enough to work,
William and Buck started hiring theirself out
again. By summer, they was boarding away for
weeks at a time. Here would come an envelope
with money, and Mama'd send me to town to
pay against the store bill. It never got all paid
that I knowed of, but they let us trade there anyhow. We wasn't the only ones. Sometimes I give

118

some to the store, and the rest to the landlord.

Now Dacia, seemed like whenever I passed by Mama's door, Dacia was in there chattering. She got to telling herself stories about taking trips in a flying wagon. Or her and Mama would be going horse trading, just the two of them, and all the sudden the horses'd take off flying, and they'd go to someplace she never been to before, but it was nice there. There was lots of stories about her and Mama going on trips. I didn't know if Mama heard these tall tales or slept through them.

Me, I had more than I could do, looking after the twins. Even one baby, it'll take up all the time you've got and then some. With twins, when one gets to crying, the other'n will start up, too, and the sound of it grinds against your spine. James and John, though, seemed like they wasn't babies for long. They crawled early, they walked early, and they was talking to each other, seemed like, before they was a year old. Then next thing I knowed, they'd got to be toddlers, and they was all the time asking why was the bugs green and what was this and this and this, like children does, boys particularly, and they'd holler "look at me, look at me" whenever they done something new, which the days was full of. They run from morning till night, and seemed like they broke or tore up most everthing they put their hand to that was in their road. They swallered things you couldn't picture how they got the notion to put in their mouths, like hairpins and marbles. They put beans and buttons and tacks in their ears or up their nose. Their ways added up by the end of the day, sure enough. But there was other times, too, like when they was out in the yard at dusk chasing lightning bugs, marveling at the glow in their hands, or when we was all laying out on a blanket looking at the stars, which they couldn't hardly get over the wonder of, or even when you got them washed and their hair squeaked when you stripped off the water—things I kept in my heart like a treasure and took out ever little bit to look at. I reckoned them kind of times was how come Mama kept having babies.

But Mama, she was living in her bed, her and Dacia.

Now Opal, she was only a couple years older than the twins, but you most never seen her underfoot. I truly don't remember her at that age. If you went to look for her, why, she'd be setting in the corner sucking her thumb or loving on a rag doll or a blanket, content to be by herself, seemed like. She was like a ghost baby, which I'd heard people talk about back home—the one in the middle of the family who nobody can remember later on. I hate to think the reason Opal kept to herself like she done was because I needed her to, but I reckon she did.

I do remember one time, when I put her to bed, she begged me to tickle her back. I reached under her shirt and run my fingertips, hardly touching, round and round on her bony little back. She got the goose bumps and laughed till she couldn't hardly breathe. We both got to laughing. Opal, she was a child knowed how to make do with the smallest little scrap of nothing, as far as attention.

Mama, when I needed somebody to show me how to dig things out of the children's ears and noses, seemed like she would rally for a while. She was the one knowed what to put on their bug bites and what kind of potion to give them for their fevers and how to get them to mind and what dangerous things it would be all right to let them do. I didn't know none of that yet. Many's the time I sent them to her to get permission. If they come to me with a problem, I'd tell them, go ask Mama. She might be sick, but it never occurred to me she wasn't in charge. I counted on her for the things I didn't know, and I learned ever day how many things that was.

Dacia, now, like I said, she spent a lot of time with Mama. But when she was with me and the children, seemed like she couldn't help but act hateful, and things would get out of hand too fast to wait for Mama's word. One day the colander went missing, which I needed to drain my noodles. I rummaged through the top drawer of the little chest we had next to the stove. I asked Dacia had she saw it.

"How comes you to ask me?" she said. "How come I'm always the one?"

"What's a colander?" Opal said. She was a slow talker.

"That thing with the holes—you know," I said.

"Holes?" Opal said.

I shut the top drawer and opened the middle one, though I knowed good and well it was just rags and towels. "You know, like a bowl. You strain things with it. Blue painted."

Dacia laughed. "She don't know what you're talking about."

"Stop picking your toes in the house," I said to her.

"You ain't my mama."

I pawed through the linen drawer. No colander. Meanwhile, my noodles was laying there in their cooking water, getting mushy.

Nobody hardly used the bottom drawer—the pull on the right side was missing, and there was a bent nail in the hole. So you had to grab aholt of the nail and press the nailhead hard against the hole to lever it. You opened the drawer a little at a time, unjamming it, left and then right.

Now Dacia jumped up off the floor. "It ain't in there," she said. "Don't look in there." She reached out to take aholt of my arm.

"Lord, what've you got hid in there?" I leaned over and fought with the drawer till all the

122

sudden it popped out, and the junk spilled out on the floor.

"Damn it!" I seen right away that there wasn't no colander. "Clean this up," I said to Dacia. "Hurry up, before somebody steps on—"

Dacia quick pounced on something and hid it behind her back. I saw a flash of white.

"What have you got? What're you hiding?"

"Nothing," she said.

"Feathers," Opal said.

I reached to grab Dacia, and she took off running. I don't know why she done that—she knowed I could outrun her. I grabbed aholt of her skirt just as she got to the door. I felt it rip as I pulled her toward me, and I grabbed a handful of material and yanked her hard enough I know it hurt her around the waist. I turned her around and grabbed the feathery thing out of her hands.

Evidently it was something she'd made—two pieces of corrugated cardboard tore into ovals, about the size and shape of Mama's turkey platter. Dacia'd stuck white chicken feathers into the folds of the cardboard. There was dried blood smeared on the quills and matted in the down-feathers and the hairs, and there was tiny, crooked trails in the cardboard where the silverfish had chewed on it. There was a string that held the two pieces together. I turned it over in my hands. I tried to picture what in the Sam Hill it might be.

Now I knowed the kind of things children done,

the strange, secret things, but Dacia was like to confound me. She done things, like peel the labels off unopened store-bought can goods, that she didn't get nothing out of but grief. She stole things she had no earthly use for. She'd get up in the night and set out on the porch and fall asleep out there and like to freeze to death. And she'd set there on Mama's bed telling stories wasn't nobody listening to. And now this. What was this get-up supposed to be? An Indian headdress? And why hide it in the junk drawer? Who'd want it?

"What was you thinking, bringing this filthy thing in the house?" I said to her. "It's got blood on it, and look here, see these holes? That's bugs done that. I wouldn't wonder it's drawed ants into that drawer! Or maggots! Ain't I got enough to do without cleaning up after your filth? Well?"

Dacia looked down at the floor. "It's just something I made to play with."

She was like to lie right to your face, and I couldn't hardly abide that. "Go cut me a switch, liar." I put the feathered thing on the table.

She never said no more, just went outside and come back with a green twig and stood there with her back turned toward me. When I seen she'd stripped the leaves off of it—to give it more sting—I didn't have the heart to whip her. I just swatted one leg a little bit.

She eyed the feathery thing on the table and

said, "Could I keep it? Out in the smokehouse?"

I throwed my hands up. "The rats'll eat it—don't you know nothing?"

But she snatched it off of the table and run outside, and that was the last we seen of it.

We was living close to the bone, and you'd think it couldn't keep on like that, but it did, for five years. Mama'd be puny for weeks, and then one day she'd get better, and she'd wander out into the front room with her slippers on. I'd say, "Mama! You're up!" and she'd act like it was normal. She'd walk to the stove and scramble some eggs, or she'd wash out a diaper, and Daddy'd sleep in the bed with her that night.

One time I remember, she made a green-apple pie, though she forgot to peel the apples. Dacia remarked on it. I told Mama it didn't make no difference, it was a wonderful pie, but Mama set at the table and bawled and never tried to hide it. The twins started up bawling, too, and Opal, she looked stricken. Mama never said a word, just got up and went to her room and got back in the bed.

Ever little bit, Alta Bea's mama would send over food. She'd say they was expecting company but the company didn't come after all, so would we help them eat up this ham before it went bad? Things like that. I reckon sometimes she give Mama money, too, though Mama never said so, being proud. Alta Bea's mama, she was awful good to us.

Alta Bea, whether she was bringing food or not, she'd come over and visit. Just blended in, seemed like. First thing she always done was ask me, how was Mama doing. I'd say, "Some better" or "The same."

Sometimes me and her—and probably Opal dragging the twins in a little wagon—why, we'd go for a walk. Alta Bea's folks had two or three sections of ground, and she knowed all the secret hiding places out in the pastures or in the tree rows or down in the washes. Might be a tumbledown outbuilding, maybe a shed or old homestead cabin, or just a stone foundation with burnt timbers laying around. You might find some odd thing—a curry comb, a perfume bottle, halter fittings. You might see tracks of a wildcat or a coyote. One time we found a nest of baby field mice no bigger than the end of your finger. The children begged me to take them home, which we did. We put them in a shoebox and fed them grass, but of course they died overnight.

Alta Bea went through grade school and then skipped some grades in high school and graduated. We heard she got all As, which she always had, and evidently high school wasn't no harder for her than grade school.

All that time she never stopped nagging me, *go to school, go to school.* Most days, I sent

Dacia—and Opal when she got big enough—but I didn't go as regular, only when Mama had the strength to look after the twins. And when we had shoes to wear, which Mama insisted on. If we had one pair, we'd take turns going. The school-teacher, Miss Snow, she come to the house once in a while, and I'd make sure to send the children regular after that, at least for a week or two. Miss Snow seen how it was for me, and she'd leave me books to read from. I liked stories about talking animals best, but if a book was about people, I liked stories about kings and queens and pirates. She left me them kind, along with arithmetic and geography and other school subjects. She also left paper for me to practice my penmanship, which I did sometimes at night.

Alta Bea loaned me books, too, of course. It took me a long time to finish *Five Little Peppers and How They Grew*. I didn't like it much. Didn't seem like much of a made-up story, just real life. Me and Alta Bea talked about it like she wanted to, but we got into an argument as usual and she run home.

Alta Bea also give me their old newspapers. Papers is handy—ain't nothing better for washing windows—and I got plenty of use out of them. But I read them, too, whenever I had a minute. Alta Bea and them, they took the *Obsidian Gazette*, which come ever Wednesday. I most always read that one. The Kansas City paper, which come in the mail ever day, why, I at least looked over the titles when I could.

Between the two of them, Alta Bea and Miss Snow got me in the habit of reading. I learned a lot that way.

Sometimes I thought about my Bible stories from back home, though I'd forgotten some of the names and things, and Mama never talked about them no more. One day it dawned on me— when Mama used to hallelujah the Lord, it was when she was with Grandma Sweet and the aunts and her friends. I wondered, would things have been different if we hadn't have moved like we done? But then I'd been taught not to have idle thoughts like that. My aunt Birddella always said, "If wishes was horses, beggars would ride."

The spring of 1915 was when Alta Bea got her diploma. Seemed like after high school was over, she calmed down some. Wasn't nobody teasing her no more, I reckon. She'd growed to be a tall one, not pretty but the kind of a woman people called handsome, and seemed like she wasn't fidgety all the time. All she talked about was going to college, and how maybe in college, school would finally get hard enough to where she would like it. I couldn't hardly picture what college was even like—it was hard to imagine growed people setting and doing sums. But Alta Bea, she talked about it like it was Heaven on earth, and she couldn't hardly wait to get there.

That year Dacia turned nine, Opal got to be six and a half, and the twins turned five. William and Buck had growed into men, and they kept on hiring theirself out whenever they could. They wasn't home in them years but once in a while. As for me, I turned fifteen.

That was when Mama come up pregnant again. Her rash come back permanent, she started having the bloody runs, she wouldn't hardly eat, and seemed like she didn't hardly sleep. She never got out of bed again. It happened fast, seemed like.

Chapter 6

Daddy limped out of the bedroom. He looked in my direction and motioned with his head toward the bedroom door. As he crossed the front room, a high-pitched sound come out of his throat, like a kitten mewling, but he never said nothing. He grabbed his hat down off the hook and left the house. After he clomped down the steps, I went into the bedroom.

Dacia was setting at the foot of the bed. Mama had her eyes closed.

"You finally ready to have the baby?" I said to Mama.

She shook her head and pointed at the bed next to her, and I set down. I leaned over and touched the back of my hand to her cheek. Hot.

She sucked in her chest and let out a breath. "Lord's coming."

"No, he ain't," I said.

She frowned, and a twinge went over her face.

"You're just having a baby," I said. "You done it six times before." Lord forgive me, I forgot Timmy.

"You're just having a baby," Dacia said.

Mama's face wrinkled, and she coughed for a

131

while. It made me breathless. I petted her arm. Pretty soon she rasped out, "Help me up."

I reached around her and tried to scoot her up in the bed, but she was deadweight. Didn't have no strength in her arms or legs, seemed like. So I took aholt of Daddy's pillow and stuffed it low behind her back, and it raised her up a little.

She set there and caught her breath. I seen she had a crack in her lower lip. I dipped my finger in the dish—the butter was half melted by now—and dotted her lips with it. I touched the cracked place two times. Her breath was light on my finger.

She closed her eyes. "Now listen."

"Wait, Mama, wait for the doctor. Daddy—he—" Truth was, I didn't know where Daddy'd went, but I wanted to think he went for the doctor. I wanted Mama to think so, too.

"Listen," she said again. "I need."

"What, Mama? I'll fetch it." This from Dacia. She petted Mama's feet.

I started to get up, but Mama raised up her hand and half-pointed at me. "The children."

"I know, Mama." I closed my eyes for a minute. I knowed what she meant—I was to take care of the children if she died. I felt wroth—I wanted to say, "Who you think's been looking after them all this time?" That shames me, but it's the truth.

A sound come out from between her lips, a kind of buzz. "Cold. I feel cold coming up my legs."

"You want more covers?" Dacia said.

I started to fold the quilt over Mama's feet, but she gathered up all her strength and set up straight.

"You can't count." She was trying to holler, I could tell, but it come out more like braying. "You can't *count* on him."

"I know, Mama."

She fell back. "Lay down with me."

"She means me," Dacia said, and I said, "No, she don't."

"Quit it," Mama said.

I reacted first and laid myself in between Mama and the wall, spooning her, and I put my arms around her. Dacia, she reached over and pinched my thigh, but I never moved. She give me an evil look, and her nine year old.

"Pray for me," Mama whispered.

"And say what?" My voice cracked.

"Come soon, Lord. Come soon."

"I can't say that. I ain't gonna say that."

From the front room there was a bump, and one of the twins cried.

"Go see to that," I said to Dacia.

"You ain't my mama," she said.

"Please, girls, please," Mama said, mostly breath.

Dacia growled like a pup and give me a dirty look. Then she slid off the bed and left the room.

Mama murmured. Her shoulders slumped

133

down, and she just shrunk into herself. She moaned ever little bit. I felt like I was about to fall in the crack between the bed and the wall, and I scooted her and me both toward the middle of the bed. Through her nightdress and mine I felt the heat she was giving off. I couldn't tell if her fever was worse than before. Seemed like it.

Slowly it got dark as we laid there. In the night, I thought I heard a sharp sound, like the echo of a bird's cry from a far-off river, but I couldn't quite make it out, and it didn't last but a few seconds.

I woken up again when Mama's moaning all the sudden stopped. A strip of yellow light glowed at the edges of the window curtain. The sun was fixing to come up. I'd never aimed to fall asleep, and her so sick in the night.

Now I was grateful her pain was easing up. I whispered, "Thank you, Lord," and I scooted closer to her. Lord help me, I still thought she was having the baby.

I felt a crick in my neck, and I rooted around in the pillow till it laid better.

Directly a sound come out of Mama's throat like a dry gourd clattering in the wind, and the hair on my arms rose up. I felt the need to relieve myself—I always feel that way when I get chilled—but I ignored it.

I put my mind in a place to where I could

whisper to her, "Wait, Mama, Daddy's coming with the doctor."

Again the rattle come. I squeezed my pillow with both hands and closed my eyes shut. My teeth started clicking. That sound coming out of her, it wasn't right. I was only fifteen year old, but even I knowed it wasn't right. Mama'd asked me to pray for her, so I started to. But I never got no futher than "Lord—" I couldn't say no more. That sound she was making, it wasn't right. My mouth filled up with drool.

From the front room come the sound of hip bone against bare floor—one of the children turning over and sliding off the pallet. A sigh, and I knowed it was one of the girls settling herself back down. I hoped it wasn't Dacia. If she woken up, she was like to get up and run into the bedroom and start jumping on the bed and bounce Mama around and get her out of breath. Dacia'd no more listen to me than she'd fly to the moon.

Then Mama let out a jagged breath you could hear the water inside of. I laid there shivering and waited. I pressed against her so she would know I was there. I never shifted to look her in the face—I told myself she couldn't see me nohow. Seemed like I was counting ever breath I took in.

Don't you do this to me come out of me. Looking back, I don't know if I said it out loud

135

or just prayed it in my mind, or if it come out of my very skin and bones, or if it come out of the air around the bed or out of the walls or out of the wooden box she kept the good linens in. I don't know who I was talking to, but *don't you do this to me* was in that room, sure enough.

My teeth was chattering now, and I felt bile in my throat, oily. Where I was, where my mind was, was someplace to where I couldn't let loose a tear.

The house was quiet. I waited a long time. "Don't you *do* this to me," I said, or I heard. But I knowed.

I told myself I didn't care if I wet the bed, I wasn't going to leave her. But directly I couldn't hold it no more, and I wrapped my shawl around me and crept out to the backhouse. It's something I'll never forget, the feeling of my water— burning hot—as it passed out of me that morning, like I'd been wading waist-deep in a river colder than I ever been in before.

When I come back it was done. Mama, she was in Glory.

William and Buck, they was thrashing wheat twenty or thirty miles away when Mama died, and they rode back home two to a horse. Got there in the afternoon and went looking for Daddy.

It must have been Opal went over and told Alta

Bea and them late in the day. Pretty soon they come over bringing short ribs and noodles, a tomato pie, and two loaves of bread. Alta Bea's father helped carry the food, but he never come in the house. I heard Dacia say, "Mama's went to Heaven," when Alta Bea and her mama walked in.

Mrs. Snedeker stayed in the front room with the children, and Alta Bea come into the bedroom, where I was setting with Mama.

I looked up when she come in, and I said to her, "She told me the other day, said, 'Bertie honey, we just go and go and go and go, till we can't go no more.' "

Alta Bea walked over to the bed and took my hands.

I looked down at the mound our hands made. "I need help washing her."

Her eyes went to the door, like she was about to call someone in. Then she turned back. "Me?"

"Ain't hard," I said. "I watched Mama do it back home. Tiny as she's gotten, won't take but two."

"Don't you imagine your father? Or your brothers? Won't they want to?" She started gently to pull our hands apart, but I held on. "I mean, shouldn't it be family?"

"I won't make you, if you don't want to," I said.

She didn't say nothing.

"Would you go fill the dish bowl. Just use what's left in the kettle."

When she pulled her hands away, mine felt like they was vibrating. I slipped off the bed and turned around to face Mama. Alta Bea hurried out the door.

Mama laid there face up in her nightdress. There was some brown pieces on the pillow next to her head. I figured she must have throwed up in the night. I brushed it away with a rag.

After a little bit Alta Bea come back with the bowl and set it on the table next to the bed.

"Help me move her over," I said.

I stood at Mama's head, and Alta Bea moved to the feet. She pursed her lips and took shallow breaths, I reckoned because of the smell. I'd been in the room a couple hours, and I couldn't smell it no more.

"A little at a time." I leaned over and slipped my right hand under the ribcage, and my left hand under the head and neck. Alta Bea did the same with the lower part of the body. Mama was stiff, like they get.

"Now scoot her this way." Inch by inch we moved the body to the open edge of the bed, the nightdress trailing along. We might could have pulled on the gown itself to move the body, but it was so threadbare it would have tore.

"Hold on." Now I picked up a clean sheet, raised it over my head, and shook it out. The fabric bunched up, and Alta Bea took aholt of it and pulled it free. She picked up the other corner, and together we spread it on the bed, between Mama and the wall. Alta Bea was doing real good. I was proud of her.

I wiped my forehead on my sleeve. Then I leaned over, took aholt of the nightdress, and tore it down its entire length. In the quiet room, the sound seemed loud, and out of the corner of my eye I seen Alta Bea jump a little. I spread the gown apart and then ripped open the sleeves, too, and laid them like wings on the bed. Mama looked gray all over.

Alta Bea took a quick look then. I seen her eyes linger on Mama's stretch marks on her belly and bosoms. The marks was different colors—silver, gray, pink—depending on which baby they was from. They silvered over time. I reckoned Alta Bea hadn't never saw stretch marks, and I started to explain but the breath wasn't there to.

I wet a rag in the bowl and wrung it out—the water made a certain dribbly sound I still remember—and I passed the rag over Mama's face and neck. Again I dipped the cloth, twisted it, and washed her arms and upper body. Alta Bea stared at the wall next to the bed.

"Good thing her eyes is staying shut, they's like to open," I said, or maybe I just thought it. I washed the belly. The baby was still in there. I petted it.

I'd already put the cotton in her so Alta Bea wouldn't have to see me do that. But when I looked up at her, I seen she was getting green. "Can you bear up? If it bothers you—"

A sound come out of her. It wasn't a word or a cry, nor an "oh," nor any other sound I'd ever heard coming from her. "Alta Bea?" I said.

"I was thinking about—" she said, almost in a whisper.

I waited.

She was making tears. "It's stupid. You won't even remember, but I . . ."

"What?"

"You and I, we were folding sheets outside. I'd brought you a book. It was raining." She shook her head. "I'm sorry. I always seem to say the wrong thing, the stupid thing."

I did remember—it was the day when she told me I was the only friend she had. "Truth ain't stupid," I said.

She sniffled and swallowed. I heard the click in her throat.

"You ready?" I said.

She nodded.

"We'll turn her over now. Hold her as stout as you can." We managed to turn Mama facedown onto the clean sheet. Then we pulled the edges of the sheet to slide her again to the open edge of the bed.

I pulled off the ruined nightdress, put a towel

across her, and washed the back of Mama head to foot. Alta Bea watched, clearing her throat.

"We'll dress her now." I walked to the peg and took down Mama's brown skirt and white blouse. They had a smoky smell from the sad iron.

I'd already split the skirt down the front, and now I laid it on Mama. I slipped my hands underneath the waist and pinned the skirt in front. Then I wrestled the sleeves over the arms—that was hard—and smoothed the blouse over her back. I reached underneath to button three of the buttons.

I stretched out my fingers to loosen the cramp in my hands. The finger bones popped. "All right, now on her back again," I said. "Mind the pins."

With Mama on her back, I finished buttoning the blouse. Then I got out the needle and thread and started sewing the front of the skirt with long stitches.

There was a long silence. Then Alta Bea said, "I'm not going to college after all, Bertie." There was tears in her throat.

I kept on working. "You ain't? How come?"

"It's Dad. He thinks I'd 'go wild.' And he says it's a waste of money on a girl."

Sweat was dripping off me onto Mama's skirt. I was wore out in body and spirit, and I wondered if Alta Bea had any notion of what I was feeling like.

"What am I going to do?" she went on. "He

told me, 'You can help your mother around the house, and she has the ladies' bridge club once a week.' Bridge club! My God! There's *nothing* for me in this godforsaken place. I hate it here! If I don't—"

She stopped all the sudden, and I looked up. She had covered her mouth with her hand. "Christ," she whispered. "Bertie, I'm so sorry, what was I thinking? I'm an idiot."

I was finished, so I broke the thread between my teeth and stood up, stretching my back. "There."

She put out her hand in front of her, like she wanted me to stop. I knowed she was embarrassed and she wanted me to say something nice, but I didn't have it in me. "Everbody's saw her that's going to, so we can go ahead and wrap her up."

She nodded, her head bowed. Her arm fell to her side.

It was hard and awkward work to wind the sheet around Mama—me and Alta Bea was sweating good by this time—but the two of us got into a rhythm and got it done.

Before we covered Mama's face, I took my last look at her. She looked like a dead person, is all I can say. There wasn't no more pain on her face, which I felt like I had to be grateful for, but she was plainly dead and wasn't coming back no more. I leaned over and kissed her lightly on the lips and then tucked and pinned the final corners in.

As we stood back from the bed, out of the corner of my eye I noticed a streak by the door. The bouncing hem of a skirt. There was no doubt in my mind who it was. It shames me how wroth I felt, like she didn't have no right to be there, and her Mama's best comfort.

I stood for a little bit with my hands folded, and Alta Bea copied me. Pretty soon I touched Alta Bea's elbow and whispered my thanks.

She turned her face to me, and I was surprised to see tears flowing down. "How can you stand it?"

I said what Mama'd always said to me. "Got to stand it or bust."

My big brothers hauled Daddy home from town that night. Found him passed out, they never said where.

Next morning, sobered up, Daddy wouldn't allow no church service for Mama, and he wouldn't wait for no relations to get there from back home neither. I don't know if they could have, but Daddy didn't give them no chance to. It was awful hot, but I reckon he could have put her in the ice house Alta Bea and them had. He just didn't want to, plain and simple.

He had a preacher to say words over the grave, which was in the graveyard two miles from our place. It was on a rise, like they often is, and from there you could see half the county. It was another hot day, with bright white popcorn clouds sliding across the sky, casting shadows along the ground. From a little ways off you could hear the racket of a steam thrashing machine—a regular *knock-knock-knock-knock,* an underneath grinding sort of a bellow, and ever little bit a screech—and men hollering. I shuddered. I never could abide big machines. Seemed like somebody would get tore up in the gears or burnt up in the fire or get their leg ran over by them spiked iron wheels. Seemed like when men took it into their heads to do chores with a machine, they felt like they had to do it or die trying.

I remember us standing there all in a row—Daddy, Buck and William, me, Opal, Dacia, and the twins. Of course Alta Bea and her mama was there. Alta Bea had on a black band around her arm. The schoolteacher Miss Snow, she was there, and old white-haired Mr. Tibbets that owned the dry goods store in Obsidian where we traded—sometimes I sold him eggs—plus two ladies from the church who I don't know their names, and two gravediggers standing a ways off. One of them was sucking on a pipe, and you could see the smoke rising out of his lips and pipe both. We was standing there, and the clouds was chasing after their shadows, and the thrasher was thrashing, and the men was shouting, and the gravedigger was smoking, all of it just like Mama wasn't dead.

When the preacher finished, Dacia took a step toward the grave. I grabbed aholt of her arm—wasn't no telling what she might do—but she shook me off and started in singing "soft as the voice of an angel." A few people started singing with her. I tried to, but my throat closed up. She knowed the words by now, of course, but she got some of the lines mixed up, and people just dropped out and let her sing. She had a strong voice for a child.

When she finished, the preacher give the bene-diction, and Daddy took to sobbing. His voice went high like a girl's. He moved his mouth like he was talking, but it wasn't words that come out, only squalling. Opal and Dacia and the twins, when they seen he was bawling, why then they started up, too. Dacia howled like a coyote. Me, I stood there dry-eyed. I didn't feel like I could afford to let go. Maybe later out back of the barn.

Afterward the people that was there, one by one they come by and spoke to us. Alta Bea's mama, I heard her say to Daddy, "I hope I never get as tired as she was." She squeezed my arm till it hurt and I pulled away. Then people wandered off to visit the graves of other people.

I knowed Daddy wouldn't leave till Mama's grave was filled in. Any funeral he went to, he always stayed till they filled in the grave. William and Buck, they waited with him.

Directly I gathered up the children, and we all started walking back to the house.

With ever step, I felt like I was walking futher away from Mama, now that she was done with. In my heart I'd always hoped she would go back to her old self, like she was back in Kentucky, when she'd put the fear of God in me, when she'd laughed with the other women, when she'd stood up to Daddy with a hammer and called me *her girl*. Mama never once in her life told me she loved me, but ever little bit, she praised me for doing house chores like I done, and me the oldest girl. That always give me a contented feeling.

Even in the long months—the years—when I couldn't count on her to help out, I counted on her to know things. More than how to lance a boil, how to tell if an egg has gone over, how to cut hair—all that was important, but what she knowed was, she knowed stories about the Sweets going way back, Bible stories, songs, jokes, games, prayers. None of that was wrote down, of course, and with her gone, we only had what we could remember, which I knowed we would forget with ever day that passed. Just like with Timmy, I knowed how utterly you could forget. Time was streaming away from me and Mama, rushing away from us like a flood, and not toward us no more. It was hard to see down through time what my life would be like without her.

Something landed with a thud next to me, and I looked up. The twins was pulling weeds off the side of the road and throwing them up in the air, whooping and chasing each other like pups. Dacia hollered at them, but I told her to leave them be, they was just boys. I took aholt of Opal's hand, and we never let go all the way home.

The minute we got home I fetched the buttonhook and undone my shoes and run to the back porch. Dacia tagged after me. It was afternoon, and the porch was mostly in the shade of the trumpet vines.

"Bring me the pitcher off the table, will you?" I lifted up the pump handle and poured in the bucket of priming water.

"You ain't my mama," she said.

"Ain't you thirsty?" I grabbed the handle and started pumping, and it made the grinding, swirly sound it always made when the water started to rise up. The porch boards had soaked up heat all day, which I felt now through my stockings even in the shade.

"I ain't gonna call you 'Mama' if that's what you think," Dacia said.

"Who said you had to? Go get me the pitcher." I swatted at a fly buzzing around my head.

"You ain't my mama," she said again. "Mama's in Heaven with the angels." She twirled around and waved her arms in the air like a child would, one younger than her. Seemed like she done it just to rile me.

"If I lose my prime—" It was hard work, priming that pump, and you didn't want to have to do it but once.

"I'm calling you Birdie, just like I always has," she said.

"It's 'Bertie,' Day-*see*-uh."

Now the water started flowing out of the spout. It was so cold, it felt like sparks on my arms. I cupped my free hand and sucked down a swallow, and it spread cold all the way down to my belly.

"You know better!" she hollered. "Mama was right! She always *said* you was hateful!"

Without hesitating, I reached out and slapped her hard on the face, and instantly you could see where my fingers had been. There they was— my jealousy and pride and wrath—right there on Dacia's face. I was shocked. I felt a cold chill up and down my spine. My pride was telling me I done the right thing, just like Mama would have, but my envy and wrath was telling me something different.

Dacia screamed and jumped off the porch and took off running, and pretty soon she disappeared over the south ridge.

I looked at the red smudge on my hand. Hateful? Had Mama really told Dacia I was hateful? Would Dacia tell a lie this evil—one that tarnished Mama's memory, never mind how it hurt me? My heart pounded, and my throat closed up till I could hardly get my breath. It felt like Dacia would kill me and stomp on my corpse, and I had no notion what to do about it.

I heard Opal sniffling, and I seen she was setting on the far edge of the back step next to the trumpet vine. I reckoned I'd been hearing her in the back of my mind all during this commotion but didn't pay it no mind. She was sucking her thumb, which she hadn't done for a while. I hated Opal seen me slap Dacia. I hated to think that sweet child would be afraid of me.

I grabbed the pump handle and kept it going. "Opal, go get me the pitcher."

When she brought it I filled it up, along with the prime bucket, and let the pump go slack. I drunk down swallows and swallows of cold water and give some to Opal. Then I set down on the steps and took her on my lap and petted her and cooed to her. She was quivering like a bird.

Daddy never got home for supper, though Dacia did. I put out the leftover short ribs and noodles, and afterward I put Opal and the twins to bed. Directly they closed their eyes, their heads fell back, and they looked dead, like children will when they're clear wore out. Dacia, she went into Mama's room, and I never stopped her.

I myself set down at the table and untied the string from around Mama's Bible, which was like to fall apart. I turned to Matthew and read the words *Blessed be they that mourn, for they shall be comforted.* I had heard them words before, back home. I wished they told me how on God's earth I was going to be the mama of these children, especially Dacia, but the words didn't mean one thing to me. They was just words. *Don't you do this to me* come back to me. Them was the words on my mind. I felt like I was hollowed out and, at one and the same time, like I had a belly full of fire. I hadn't never felt like that before. I wanted to climb up on the roof and scream, but I wasn't about to wake up the children. I closed the Bible and tied the string around it with a knot, and I put it away on a high shelf.

Daddy, I don't know when he got home. He was passed out on the front porch when I got up in the morning to build the fire to get breakfast so William and Buck could get an early start back to Kansas, where they was hired out. I poked Daddy in the ribs with my foot, but he just laid there snoring.

When William and Buck come up to the house, bleary-eyed, I reckoned them and Daddy had shared a bottle or two at the grave.

"You make your peace with Daddy?" I said.

William shrugged. "He's the one ain't made peace—with the whole Goddamn world."

Buck blowed on his coffee. "You gonna be all right?" he asked me.

I slid eggs onto their plates. "Or else what?"

He winced. "Damn, we hate to just . . ."

"We'll be sending money regular still," William said. "Don't let Daddy get his hands on it."

I turned back to the stove and stirred the potatoes. "You think I don't know that?"

"See to it, then," William said.

The second night after Mama's funeral, I dreamed she stood next to the bed and tried to say something to me. But when I woken up, the dream disappeared.

It was still dark out. I was in Mama's bed. William and Buck had left, and it was just me and the children in the house. Daddy was off to wherever he was at.

I felt like I'd been hit square in the face with a rock.

From far back in my childhood come the words *sacred task*. Mama, she'd give me a sacred task, sure enough. I never wanted it. I never asked for it. I didn't feel like I could do it. Looking after children, which I'd done, ain't the same thing as being their mama. There wasn't nobody I could send them to with the stomachache—it was on

me. I couldn't say *I can't* no more. *I can't get up,
I'm too tired. I can't make supper, ain't no fire.
I can't wash the clothes, my arms is like lead. I
can't take care of these children no more.*

And then a picture come into my mind of my
little brother Timmy. For a minute I just laid
there and marveled, since I hadn't been able to
picture him for some years. There he was, clear
as anything. I seen his hair falling raggedy past
his collar, his pretty lips, his shoeless feet, his
blue-and-red-checked shirt with the pig's blood
on it. Electricity went through me. There he was.
Then I strained to remember his voice, and the
funny thing he used to say all the time, something we all laughed at—what was it? Some word
he said wrong? Some saying he copied from a
grown-up but didn't get quite right? Whatever it
was, it wasn't nowhere I could call it back from.
Wasn't nothing there. Then I tried to recall what
he smelled like, what his hand felt like curled up
in my bigger one—and as I strained to recollect
these things, it all vanished. All I could remember
was, on his last day me and him played leapfrog,
and they found him wedged in the rocks, and he
was there all alone in the water all night long
because I never looked after him like Mama told
me to.

Now I relived the shame of it, felt those feelings
all over again like it'd just happened. I laid there
on my back and felt like I was sinking into the

bed and suffocating. Like I halfway wanted to.

I remembered Mama saying, long ago, *God is our refuge and our strength, a very present help in trouble.* I waited for that refuge and that strength, I longed for it, but it never come. Nothing come. I felt like the Lord wasn't no more real than Rumpelstiltskin, else he would be standing next to the bed giving me refuge, giving me strength—and where was he at?

Where you at? Where was you when Mama was gurgling her life out?

I wanted to lay there and cry and throw things and break them against the walls, but it was past time to make the fire. I could almost hear Mama saying, "No fire never made itself." I got up and pulled on my skirt and my shirt and my apron. Before I even got to the backhouse I heard the twins tearing around in the front room. I never felt so tired.

I fed the twins and sent them out on the porch, where they started rolling their one-wheeled toy wagon around and around. I seen Daddy out there sleeping, and I didn't care if the boys waked him up or not. Serve him right.

I called in the girls to breakfast. "You wash up?" I said to them.

"*I* did," Opal said.

"Dacia?" I made my voice, as much as I could, sound like Mama. Certain.

Dacia leaned her elbow on the table and her face on her hand and stuck a bite of egg in her mouth. She narrowed her eyes and looked at me like I was Satan himself.

"I asked you a question."

She chewed on her food and acted like she didn't hear me.

Her silence give me courage. I reached down and took her plate off the table and pointed with it. "Go stand in the corner."

"I'm hungry," she said. "You can't keep me from my food."

"Go stand in the corner till you're ready to act decent."

Opal put her hands over her face.

"You ain't my mama," Dacia said.

This time I was ready for it. "You ain't my daughter neither. Now do what I said."

She squinted but didn't say nothing.

"You want a whipping?"

"She washed up, I seen her," Opal said.

"You hush, or you'll get what she gets." I gritted my teeth. I'd have sooner took a whipping myself than raise my hand to Opal.

Well, Opal busted into tears. I knowed what that felt like, when you're crying with food in your mouth, and the crying makes salt that gets into your spit, and the salt gets mixed in with your food. Makes a taste in your mouth like blood.

Dacia throwed her fork across the room. Then

she got up and sashayed over to the dish bowl and stuck her face down into the cold water. She kept it under a long time, and of course I held my breath right along with her, couldn't help it. I felt dizzy by the time she finally lifted up her head. She never dried herself off. With her nose in the air, she walked, dripping, back to the table and set down.

I put the plate and the dirty fork in front of her, and nobody said nothing while she finished her breakfast. Opal, she never eat another bite.

In the next days it seemed like I was falling headlong, like I'd just tripped over something and was dropping into some strange new place. I went over and over what I could remember about Mama. I recalled asking her how her and Daddy met, and she told me that tale about the two of them drifting together, and then she laughed. She was like to tease me that way, like we had all the time in the world. She'd showed me how to cook okra and get out spit-up stains, but I hardly knowed nothing about Mama herself, what she was like. It was as if Mama was what she *done,* and not who she *was.* It wasn't nothing I'd thought about before, her being somebody like everbody else, and now I'd never know her, not that way. It made my skin cold to realize how long eternity was.

Daddy, you couldn't ask him. You couldn't

believe nothing he said. It was all stories. What he wanted you to hear.

But I didn't have no time to set around and grieve for Mama. There was chores to do ever minute and meals to get. You do what's in front of you, hour by hour, and you hope to fall asleep at night before you think too much about where you're headed.

Chapter 7

One day about a month after Mama died, with fall coming, me and the girls was sorting through school clothes when little James come running in all out of breath. "Slow down," I said. "You're like to—"

"Come quick! John's a-hangin' from the tree!"

"What?" Opal cried, but me, I was out the door and running fast as I could to where James was pointing to—where the road met our place, next to the bent cottonwood. Halfway there I seen John hanging in the tree by the neck. I screamed fit to die. Dacia and Opal, behind me, they started up screaming, too.

When I got there, I throwed myself at John and started pushing him up by the legs. "Dacia! Help me! Opal! Run to Alta Bea's house! Get somebody! Fast as you can!"

I looked up and seen John's eyes was closed, and without a thought I started in praying. "Lord, save this boy! Save this boy! Dacia, grab his feet!"

Me and Dacia, we neither one was quite tall enough just to raise him up and hold him free of the rope, so we inched him up the tree trunk. We got him up high as we could, with our hands on the very bottoms of his feet. It felt like his neck was free a little bit, but we neither of us could see good enough to tell for sure.

"Bertie, Bertie, save me! Lord, save me!" come a high-pitched voice, and my heart about busted out of my chest.

John's body started buckling, and Dacia let out a terrible scream.

"Hang on, don't let him go!" I said to her. "We got him! Just hang on! Help's coming! Opal's getting help!"

Then I heard giggling. "Dacia!" I hollered. "Have you lost your mind?"

"Wasn't me," she said.

"What?"

"Wait a minute," she said. "Wait just a God-damn minute."

Now I heard more laughing, and I knowed that whinny. "Daddy?"

" 'Hang on, don't let him go! Help's a-comin'!' " Daddy stepped out from behind the tree.

I choked back the curse words that come to me. Me and Dacia, we was still leaning there, holding John by his feet. I felt the bark digging into my arms.

Now Daddy started laughing his fool head off. I felt John laughing, too, at least I thought it was laughing, I felt it in his feet. James, I heard him back behind us sniffling.

Daddy laughed a good long time. Several times he started to say something and then laughed so hard he couldn't get the words out.

Dacia, she let go of John and pulled back. I felt him slip a little bit and held myself where I was. I felt a moan go through him. I smelled where he had wet his pants.

Finally, Daddy grabbed aholt of a fruit crate hid in the grass, and he leaned it up against the tree. When he stepped up onto it, it wobbled. I thought he might fall—I halfway hoped he would—but he steadied it, pulled the knife out of his pocket, and cut the rope. John come down on top of me, and we both skinned up our knees and elbows in the loose sand.

I got John on his back and knelt next to him. I lifted up his shirt and seen that the rope was tied around his chest, and there was some slack in it before it looped around his neck. There was a red rope burn from his underarms up his shoulders where his weight had pulled on him. His eyes was big with fright, and he was crying. James, he was standing there bawling, too. It wasn't hard for me to imagine how Daddy'd painted them boys a picture of how funny this trick would be. But if they ever did think it was funny, which I doubt, they didn't no more.

Daddy was laughing so hard he like to lost his breath. Tears was on his face.

"What happened? What happened?" Alta Bea's

mother come running up with Opal, and one of the hired men followed, carrying a hay fork. Her and Opal was out of breath, and the hired man looked pale and shooken.

I petted John's face. I seen the heels of my hands was skinned and bleeding, with bits of sand buried in them, and now I felt it.

Daddy leaned over and closed one nostril with his finger and blowed snot onto the ground. "You!" He pointed at me. "You should see your face!"

I got to my feet, speechless with wrath.

"What happened here?" Alta Bea's mother said. "Is everyone—"

Now Daddy left off laughing and bent over coughing for a while, finally letting go a glob of spit. He straightened up and wiped his face with his hand. "This 'n—this 'n—she ain't never in her life knowed how to take a joke!"

"Daddy, he hung John for a joke," Dacia said to Alta Bea's mother, who got a bewildered look on her face.

Daddy looked down at the ground and shook his head. "Her mother, now, that one, *she* had a sense of humor."

Shame, burning shame, swept over me, and fury. I run and grabbed the hay fork from the hired man and turned toward Daddy. He took a couple steps back, and I held up that hay fork like a spear and run at him, aiming it at his heart.

160

Drunk as he was, he still managed to step aside, and it got him on the arm, leaving a long red gash. You could see the bone and the meat, and I was surprised how much blood. Daddy yowled and fell down, grabbing at his arm like it had a two-day tick on it. He kept on yowling.

"Die, you old fool! You Goddamn goat!" I hollered. "Die!" I screamed like a banshee, rageful.

The children hollered, Alta Bea's mama hollered, and the hired man wrapped his neckerchief around Daddy's arm.

Daddy started bellowing at me, and I bellowed back, and Alta Bea's mother took aholt of me and drug me down the path into the house and pumped up a pitcher of water and had me to drink some, me and Dacia and Opal all three. Directly the twins come in, hanging their heads and bawling. Alta Bea's mother wetted a towel and wrapped it around John's chest. Dacia, she told her the whole story of what happened, and then she told it again. When she started to tell it a third time I told her to hush, and she give me a hateful look and went into the bedroom.

Grateful as I was for our neighbor's help, I suffered wave after wave of shame. Not for stabbing Daddy—I despised him, and I felt like I could never in this life forgive him—but for how bad things had gotten for the children who Mama had give me charge of. I knowed I had fell short of my duty to them. I was relieved when Alta Bea's mother left the house, which I never would have imagined I would feel. I was glad, too, that Alta Bea wasn't home and never seen what happened, though I imagine she heard plenty about it.

The hired man, he took Daddy into town and got him sewed up. Fifty-two stitches, I heard. One thing I knowed—I couldn't leave them children with their own daddy. No telling what kind of fool drunken thing he might do.

We didn't see Daddy around the place for four-five days. When he come back, he had William and Buck with him, sent for from Kansas. Out the front window I seen them walking up to the house, and I went out on the front porch. I stood there with my arms folded. Daddy stopped a ways from the porch and said he was sorry, it was the drink made him do it, he was still grieving Mama, he knowed better, he wasn't going to drink no more. He never looked me in the eye.

"There's work needs done around this place," I said. "You mean to do any of it?"

"You got a mouth on you. I'll thank you to remember who—"

Buck stepped in front of Daddy. "He said he ain't going to drink no more. All's he can do, Bertie."

William, he just frowned.

"Me and William, we'll be staying home for a while," Buck said. "We talked it through. Daddy can sleep out in the barn with us. We'll keep an eye on him."

I looked at William, but his eyes was cast down.

"He gives you any trouble, he answers to us," Buck said.

"William?" I said.

He nodded, still looking down.

"He gives me any trouble, he better hope he don't answer to *me,*" I said.

Daddy, he squinted in my direction and snorted like a bull, but he didn't say no more.

"You hear me?" I said.

The look he give me was pure bile, and I give it right back. Couldn't help it, seemed like.

Chapter 8

Alta Bea's mama, she sent over a pork butt for us to have on that first Thanksgiving Day without Mama. I roasted it with turnips and onions and made biscuits. William and Buck, they made sure to be there. Buck had went to town and brought home a bag of horehound candy for the children. I give them each a piece before dinner to keep their mouth busy, what with all the good smells in the house. Horehound wasn't their favorite kind, but they took it anyhow. I was glad to have it—it's good to have in the house for coughs. Me, I had squirreled away some oranges, one each, for a surprise. I set aside my grief for the day. I wanted the children to have good memories of Thanksgiving.

Daddy showed up in time for dinner. We hadn't seen him for a while, and here he walked in with his hat in his hand. He'd took a bath and combed his hair, and he smelled of Bay Rum toilet water. He brought a bucket of apples, which he claimed he picked himself. "Wonders never cease," William said to me in my ear. Daddy and Buck, they went and set out on the front porch, talking.

We had the door open to let in some air, and you could see their breath.

William drug Mama's trunk in from the bedroom and put a cloth over the top of it for the children. He brought in some fruit crates for them to set on, and he'd borrowed two extra chairs from somewhere for the table, so everbody had a place. I'd cooked some of the apples in the pan with the pork, and it was sweet and juicy. We had a feast like we hadn't had in a good long time, since before Mama died.

Halfway through, Opal said, "Dacia, do Alta Bea." I don't know what made her think of Alta Bea. With Opal, you never knowed what she was thinking.

"Alta Bea! Alta Bea!" The twins got to chanting, like children will at that age.

Dacia put down her spoon. Seemed like she loved it when we asked her to do her imitations. Now she put her nose in the air and looked around the table. "Well, well, well," she said. "Who might all *you* folks be?"

James and John, they started up laughing. Not that they really knowed what was going on, but they could tell it was supposed to be funny.

Dacia broke into a smile and then stuck her nose in the air again. "When's the *hired* man gonna get here to do up these *dishes?*" she said, and everbody busted out laughing, even me.

"And I need *somebody* to wipe off my bottom!"

Well, of course the twins screamed at this, but the rest of us, our smiles faded. We all thought the world of Alta Bea. She was always friendly even if she did have some strange notions. She couldn't help how she was raised no more than nobody else. It was all right to make fun of her, but now Dacia was being mean.

"Wipe off my bottom!" James screamed, and then John.

"Ha ha ha," I said. "Eat your dinner now, else you won't get no orange."

"We got oranges?" Opal said, almost in tears.

Now the twins jumped up and started dancing around the room shouting, "Oranges, oranges, oranges," and I myself got to laughing so hard I come to tears.

After dinner, Daddy said he had someplace to be and left the house. We put the twins down in Mama's bed and shut the door. Dacia, she went outside to play with the dogs and get out of doing dishes—not that she said nothing about the dishes, just the dogs—and Opal set her foot to the treadle, like she had been teaching herself for months. I didn't know what she was working on, but I reckoned it was a Christmas present. The twins didn't have no fancy Santy Claus stockings—we just hung up their regular socks—and maybe she was making them some. Come Christmas, she give the boys stockings with embroideryed lambs, stars, and angels on them.

So me and William and Buck cleared off the table. I washed, William wiped, and Buck put away.

"How come you ain't singing?" Buck asked me. "You always used to sing when you done dishes."

I scrubbed a fork and didn't say nothing.

He started in singing but soon trailed off. "Don't you like singing no more?"

"Don't like much of nothing, tell the truth."

"Ain't you bearing up?" He flipped the towel over his shoulder and put his hand on the back of my neck.

I shook it off. Then I throwed the dishrag in the water, and greasy drops flew up on the wall. "I'm bearing up! Don't nobody say I ain't bearing up!" It just boiled out of me. "Who said that? Dacia? What'd she say? Can't nobody say I ain't a good mother to them children!"

"Oh, Bertie," Buck said. "You're having it the worst of any of us."

"Quit saying that! Everbody just quit creeping around me like I'm some kind of a china doll! I ain't!" I felt like a fool, hollering at him, when I was trying to prove how good I was bearing up. I felt my shame, tell the truth, and I took off and run out the back door. I heard Opal say something, sounding worried like she was like to do, but I run out on the porch anyhow.

168

I leaned my hands on the pump and started bawling like a baby. William, he come out and put both of his big arms around me and held tight on to me while I cried. He never told me not to, he just let me. Buck, I seen him standing back by the door.

It took me a long while to wind down. A couple times, when I thought I was about to get control of myself, it started back up again. But the time finally come when I was just standing there gulping air and shivering. Buck come and wrapped my shawl around me. The two of them, they was in their shirtsleeves.

"Me and Buck been talking," William said.

"We was going to wait, but seems like the time's come," Buck said.

I pulled out my hankie and blowed my nose. "For what?"

"The children, they's too much for one girl," William said.

"Even you," Buck said.

I took in a ragged breath.

"And Daddy, he ain't much help." This from Buck.

"Worse than no help," William said.

I filled up my chest with cold air and got to coughing. They waited.

William took aholt of my elbows and turned me to him. "I been seeing this girl, Dora Darling. We're fixing to get married come spring."

I opened and closed my mouth like a fish. "How'm I supposed to pay bills?" I wanted to feel glad for him, but I didn't have it in me.

He took a deep breath and said it all at once: "Dora, she said, her and me, we can take in the twins."

All the tears went out of me, and all the breath at once. I swallowed. "Oh, is that a fact? The two of you's deciding things now?"

"You got to hear us out," Buck said. He looked serious, which he hardly ever done.

"I don't *got* to hear *nothing,*" I said. "Who do you think's been looking after them boys since the day they was born? Ain't nobody going to—"

William gripped my arms till they hurt. "I got me a job—I'm taking over the grain elevator in Trenton," he said. "It's only fifteen mile. You can come and see them whensoever you feel like it."

"You listen to me, the both of you." I looked from one to the other. "Nobody's taking my twins—not you, and not this Dorie, or whatever she calls herself." After months of confusion and dread, it was a pure relief to have no doubt about something. I knowed my brothers wasn't going to get the best of me. I never felt so sure of nothing before.

"Bertie," Buck said.

"You know Buck's been wanting to open a barber shop in town," William said.

"You think I don't have things *I'm* wantin'? This ain't about wantin'."

"I took a place, corner Fifth and Adams," Buck said. "It's got rooms over."

"Did you now."

William said, "Daddy can live up there. Old man can visit with the customers while they's waiting."

I give a bitter laugh. "And you think Daddy's gonna go along with this wild hair? You got the same daddy I've got? You ever knowed a man had more pride? And live in *town?* Where's he going to keep his horses?"

Buck shivered. "We stick together, won't have no choice."

"Far as his horses, he's pissed that away pretty much," William said. "And it's not like he's doing you no good around the farm. He's got to see that."

"Oh, you ain't forgot about me, then. What've you got planned for me? Walk the plow with Opal pulling it? Sell my favors to pay the rent?"

William let go of me so fast he like to throwed me on the porch floor.

"It ain't *like* that," Buck said. "We got to think of the children's sakes. It can't go on like it's been."

"We thought—well, we thought you might find an old lady in town needs took care of, get room and board for the three of you girls," William

171

said, like he was coaxing a willful calf. "Me and Buck, we could help with expenses, too."

Nobody said nothing. We stood there blowing steam out our mouths.

"I don't want you here no more today," I said after while. "I want you to go to wherever Daddy's gone off to, or wherever the hell you want to, but leave my house."

"You got to hear us out," Buck said again, but William, he'd already jumped off the porch, and he was walking away stiff-legged as fast as he could.

"You mind me, Buck," I said. "Ain't nobody taking a one of my children, not a one. You do what you want to—I don't care if I don't never see neither one of you again. But don't you think nobody's going to raise up them boys but me."

He opened his mouth, but then he shoved his hands in his pockets and walked off after William.

"Nobody!" I hollered after him.

Then I set down on the steps and wadded up my shawl and pressed my face in it and screamed till my throat give out, because I knowed they was right. I seen my future, and the children's, and I knowed we couldn't all stay together.

But the notion of losing the twins, after Mama give me the sacred task of raising them, it hollowed me out. I'd knowed them since they took their first breath in this world. I knowed their boyish ways, their fascination with natural things, their pure joys, their bright, wild hearts—I knowed them like they was my very own. If I had to put up with Dacia, how come I couldn't at least have the boys for consolation? Of course, this thought shamed me. I had to let the twins go for their own sakes, not mine, or what was love for? And in that moment, I realized I did love them, which I'd never thought about before, or thought about what it meant. And my sorrow was greater than my shame, and I cried into my shawl for a long time.

That night, I felt like my eyes was swole to bursting. Sleep didn't come, so I wrapped up in a blanket and went outside and set on the front porch. The air was cold and clear, and the stars felt close. When I seen a falling star, I thought about something Alta Bea had told me—how it took millions of years for us to see a falling star after it happened way out there. I remembered the yellow-white light beams I used to see in the woods back home—sparkling with insect wings and crumbs of leaf and dust—and I tried to picture light beams so far away they didn't reach the earth for millions of years.

"What're you doing out here?" come Dacia's voice from behind me, and of course I like to jumped out of my skin.

"Jesus Christ!" I said.

"You swore." She hadn't lit a candle nor made a sound. She was standing there in the dark.

"You like to scared the daylights out of me." I turned around, but I couldn't hardly make her out in the shadows.

"You said 'Jesus Christ.' You ain't going to Heaven."

I turned back around. "That's not something—"

"You won't see Mama. She's in Heaven, which you know good and well."

I didn't want to get in a fight with her. "Why don't you come and sit by me for a minute?" I patted the spot.

She didn't answer.

"You'll catch your death of cold. Come on."

Again she didn't say nothing, and I looked around to see was she still there. I seen the toes of one foot on the porch floor. I turned back. "If you ain't going to come and sit by me, then go on back to bed."

"No."

I don't reckon she could have said nothing that would shock me more. "What did you say to me?"

"You can't tell me what to do no more."

"Dacia. It's late. Don't make me—"

"You ain't my mama."

I stood up and brushed the dew off my skirt. "No, I ain't. But I'm the one that's stuck with you." I hated how bitter that come out.

174

Now she stepped forward. "I know something about Mama you don't."

"What." My teeth was on edge. I heard it in my voice.

"She wanted to go to Heaven for a long time. She never wanted to take care of us no more. She wasn't bearing up."

"Hush, that's . . ." The word that come to me was *blasphemy.*

"She *told* me."

"That's a lie." I took a step around her to go back in the house.

She reached out her hand, and I stepped back. I realized Dacia had hardly never touched me in no kind of a way.

"Ain't no tears in Heaven, Mama told me," she said.

I put my hands over my ears. I slipped around her and run into the house. I don't know if she followed me or not, but I heard her say, "She didn't want none of us no more. She told me."

Laying there in Mama's bed that night, I had a vision of holding Daddy's pistol in my right hand. I reached over with my left hand, cocked it—it took both thumbs—raised the pistol up to the right side of my head, and pulled the trigger. Then I cocked it again, swiveled my head right, lifted the pistol to the left side of my head, and fired again. Then I shot myself in my forehead, and then I held it over the top of my head and pointed straight down into my skull and fired again. Then I pointed it in one eye, *bang,* and then the other, *bang.* My thought was, more or less, *There. That oughta do it.*

I just laid there and watched myself. It was peculiar, of course—almost comical—to think a person could shoot theirself over and over. But as it played itself out, why, as I shot myself everthing flowed away from me, all my troubles. My eyes was open, but I wasn't seeing nothing.

My thoughts swirled around and around. What Dacia'd said about Mama, it was the worst lie she'd ever told, the worst I'd ever heard. Didn't make no sense—why would Dacia lie like that, something she had to know I wouldn't believe for a minute?

After a little bit I thought about my brothers' idea for me and the girls. I tried to picture how things would be if we took us a room in some lady's house. I couldn't get no picture in my mind, only a smell. There's a certain smell in a house with only old people in it. When the weather's hot, or in the winter when the fire is high, that smell pushes itself inside your skin. My mind roused up and asked me, where did I know that smell from, whose house had I ever knowed that only had old people in it, but I smacked back that thought. Didn't matter. I knowed that smell.

Then out of nowhere, seemed like, a thought come to me—I could get married. I could find me a husband. Mama and the aunts, they was all married by the time they was sixteen or seventeen. Why not me?

My heart started thumping. I could get married, and me and the girls, we could move into his place. I could make us a home, do the cooking and clean house, dress chickens and take in ironing, have me a little garden maybe. Sundays, we could pack up a picnic and go visit William and his wife and the twins. Opal, in my mind's eye she would make some muslin curtains to hang at the kitchen window. I pictured them curtains, how crisp they would be, how sweet they would smell.

These pictures come easy to me, though where the husband should be, of course, there was a blank. I'd had a few little sweethearts in school—held hands walking across the schoolyard, passed a few notes—but I knowed that wasn't the same thing as a husband. And I didn't know of no man looking for a wife, and I didn't know how to find me one or, if I found one, how to get him to marry me except like harlots done, and I didn't know exactly what that was.

After while, laying there, my heart slowed back down. I knowed the what, though I didn't know the how. Just as I was dropping off to sleep, I seen Alta Bea in my mind. Seemed like if anybody I knowed could figure this out, it was her.

I never pictured shooting myself again, at least not that night.

Chapter 9

The next morning there was a cold, thick fog around me as I walked over to Alta Bea's house. The fog had a grassy smell to it, and it made my face feel tacky in a good way.

Alta Bea led me into the room with the bookshelves, and we set at the same table where we'd played paper dolls years ago. The gloom outside give the room a gray-blue tinge through the bay window.

She asked me where was the children, and I told her I'd left them with Dacia. "She's nine already, it's about time."

Her mama come in carrying a silver tray with a pot of coffee and a cake. She said hello, how was the children, and I said fine. I'm glad, she said, and she left, closing the door behind her.

Alta Bea poured us some coffee, and I doped mine with cream and sugar and took a big swallow. Then she cut us each a piece of the cake. "Have you read the new book?"

"Ain't had time, tell the truth."

We visited for a while, I forget about what. Pretty soon she reached into her pocket and, cool and smooth, pulled out a little silver flask about the size of your hand. I watched as she poured the liquor into her coffee and took a couple sips. You could tell it wasn't the first time she done it.

I was shocked. I'd never saw no girl drink liquor—or woman, come to that—and Alta Bea's mother just in the other room. It seemed unnatural, like a tree growing upside down. I couldn't think of what to say.

Alta Bea, she didn't look in my direction, only stared down at her hands.

After a silence I said, "That pork butt your mama sent, that was a blessing, sure enough. I cooked it with apples. You never seen nobody eat like the twins done. That was real nice, that pork butt." I felt like I was babbling, and I drunk some coffee to shut myself up.

We picked up the conversation, and after a while I took a deep breath and told her I was looking to get married if I could find me a decent man.

"Oh, please," she said. "You're what, sixteen?"

I was fifteen yet, but I never said so.

"Next thing you know you'd be having a baby," she said.

I blushed.

"And what about your brothers and sisters?"

I picked up my fork and started rubbing the crumbs off of it. "Well, looks like we've got to break up the family."

She lifted up her eyebrows. "What?"

180

I told her William's plan to take in the twins, him and his new wife. I was looking down at my hands, but I kept her in the corner of my eye. I was trying not to cry in front of her. I had my pride.

"The twins?" she said, blinking. "How do you feel about that?"

"Ain't about how I feel. About what needs done." Now I was rubbing the mouth grease off of my fork. Pressing in between the tines. "Buck, he's wanting to take up the barbering trade. Got him a place in town where Daddy could go live, if Buck can talk him into it."

"But what about you and the girls?" she said. "Surely you can't manage the farm by yourself?"

I didn't say nothing. I don't imagine Alta Bea'd ever knowed nobody that had to figure out how they was going to make out in the world. Now I seen it dawn on her, and she finished her coffee and poured another cup. "Oh, I see." Out come the flask again.

"I can't picture no other way."

She opened her mouth to speak, seemed like, but closed it back. She took a sip directly out of the flask.

"I don't want to marry no farmer, truth be told," I said. "Too hard of a life for children. Opal, she . . ." I got lost in the picture in my mind.

"You have to think of yourself, too, Bertie," Alta Bea said. "Nobody else is." There was the

181

slightest little slur on *else,* so it come out *elsh.*

I took my chance, though I didn't hardly know what to say. "Could you—do you—I hoped—"

She give me a puzzled look.

I swallowed. "I thought maybe, with your folks—with your mama, she's friends with so many people—"

"Oh," she said, drawing it out. "You want me to help you find someone."

My face was burning.

"Lordy," she said. That was a new one on me. She didn't say it like a curse word, though.

She stood up and put the flask in her pocket, and then she walked over to the bay window and looked out at the fog. "A decent man, like you say. A widower maybe. But not too old." There was steam gathering in the glass in front of her face. "With a steady income. Stable. Good-looking—that would be nice." She laughed softly. "And no farmers."

"Somebody that'd take in the three of us," I said.

She frowned. "Yes, that." She turned and come back to the table and set down.

"I keep a good house," I said. "And Opal, she's awful sweet-natured."

"Wait." Now Alta Bea stood up again. "I know someone. Benjamin? What's his name? Raymond? Marion? No, it starts with a B." She begun pacing. "I saw him once, though we didn't actually meet, but everybody knows him. He's from Millard—he's a schoolteacher. A friend of Mother's knows his uncle, I think, or his cousin."

"Oh." A man teacher would be nice, but what man teacher would have me, ignorant like I was?

"He's a catch, actually. Everybody says so. No one can figure out why he's not married already." She was flushed now.

"Don't sound like the kind would be interested in me, though."

She leaned over and reached out her hand and touched my cheek. I smelled the whiskey on her breath. "Why not? You're a pretty girl."

I'd heard that a few times as I'd got older, but I never thought about my looks much. The only mirror we had was in Mama and Daddy's room, high up. I don't reckon I saw my reflection more than a dozen times living in that house. I done my hair by feel.

"Lordy," she said again, shaking her head. "Lordy Lord." I wondered, did the drink make it easier for her to talk to people? And was I just "people" to her, after all this time? After we washed Mama together? I wondered, was I as peculiar to Alta Bea as she was to me? Truth to tell, I wondered would we even have became friends if there was any other females near our age inside of five miles, which there wasn't. I recalled Mama always said, "Beggars can't be choosers," and for a moment I was lost in thought, back home where everbody's your cousin and you never wonder if somebody's looking down on you, and even my flat-headed cousin Frank was treated the same as everbody else. Seemed like me and Alta Bea could never be the same like that, and I felt in my heart how it must have tore Mama up when we moved away from everthing she knowed. She didn't have a friend in the world. No wonder her and Dacia had growed so close.

"Bernard!" Alta Bea cried. "That's his name, Bernard. Bertie and Bernie!" She smacked her hand on the table and got to laughing, and after a minute I started in laughing, too. Didn't seem like I could help it.

The day I went to meet Bernard at the Triangle Cafe, I knowed who he was directly I walked in. He was setting there in a black suit with a high white collar and a thin black tie. His hair was like a preacher's but more greasy than oily, and there was a sharp part on his right side of his head. He wasn't a bad-looking man—he had a long nose and curly lips. Alta Bea's mama's cousin, or whoever it was Alta Bea talked to, they'd said he was about thirty.

He seen me and stood up. I liked it that he walked over without waiting for me to come to the table. I smelled sweet pomade on his hair. "You must be Miss Winslow," he said, friendly.

He shook my hand with a light grip. "Bernard Whitson."

I smiled back at him, and we walked over to the table. He already had a cup of coffee going. I noticed the sugar bowl was open. I started to sit down, and he like to pulled the chair out from under me. I laughed a little bit, and he smiled.

I tried to not think about what was at stake for me and the girls. I tried to keep my mind on him, what he was like, what kind of a man he was. It wasn't easy.

He asked me did I want coffee or what, and I said I did. He asked me did I want a piece of pie, but I thought it would be better not to obligate myself that much. The girl brought me coffee and a little pitcher of cream, and I poured ever drop in. I seen him looking at me, and I said, "I've always been partial to cream—that, and clabber milk. I thought I wouldn't like it, but I did the first time Mama had me to try it."

"I don't believe I've had clabber milk."

"You must not have been raised in the country."

"No, I grew up in Kansas City," he said.

"Clabber milk, it's easy to make. You just set it out on the table for three-four hours, or maybe an hour if it's hot in the house. Gets lumpy and has a nice sharp taste."

He nodded. "Is that right. I'll have to give that a try."

"Best thing there is for the stomach. Just don't

leave it out all day long." I felt like I was talking too much, but I got the feeling he liked to talk and hear you talk, too, not like no man I ever met before. Except Daddy, who liked to talk but not listen.

Me and Bernard got to visiting about what kind of food did we each like, and then we got on the subject of things going on around town. Seemed like besides Obsidian and Millard, he knowed everbody in Harris, Trenton, all over the county. He told me he liked traveling, particularly in the summer when school was out. He liked meeting new people.

He was easy to talk to, and he looked me in the eye. I liked it, but at the same time it made my scalp prickle. The way I was raised, if somebody looked you in the eye it meant you better be ready for something—maybe good, maybe bad, or maybe they just wanted something. After while, though, it seemed like Bernard didn't mean nothing by it except being friendly.

Directly he said, "I surely was sorry to hear about your mother."

I looked at his chin. "She went awful young."

"I lost my own mother three years ago," he said, and there was tears in his voice.

"It's a trial, sure enough."

"I miss her every minute of every day," he said. I nodded.

He clenched his teeth and then cleared his

throat. "Do you find it difficult to care for your brothers and sisters?"

Seemed like this question had a hidden thorn in it, though I wasn't sure. "Has to be done."

"I expect it takes all your time." Again he cleared his throat and swallowed two or three times.

I took a drink of my coffee. I felt like I needed to tread lightly.

"I'm sorry," he said. "I didn't mean to bring up a sad subject."

"It's only natural."

"How much schooling have you had, Birdy?"

"Bertie," I said. "Short for Albertina."

He smiled. "Pretty name. May I call you Albertina?"

I felt my shoulders relax. "Up to you."

"Do you like school, Albertina?"

"Like it all right."

"Are you in high school now?"

Him being a schoolteacher, I knowed he would ask me that. Well, nothing to be done but tell the truth. "Ain't been to school much since eighth grade. Mama was sick a long while, and I had to mind the children."

He nodded. "Would you like me to teach you proper grammar?"

For a moment I couldn't breathe. We all of us Winslows talked improper, sure enough. Timmy had, and Mama, and seemed like what I missed the most about them was just talking to them. I didn't give a diddly darn about proper grammar. Now I seen myself like a monkey on a string, dancing for this man teacher, and my face turned red. If I married him, would I have to do like his ways? But if I didn't marry him, what would happen to me and the girls?

"I wouldn't mind it," I said finally, "though the people I come up with, they was decent even if they wasn't proper."

To my relief, he smiled. "I know what you mean. I'm the first one in my family to finish high school." Saying this, he looked at his hands, and I followed his eyes. He had man hands, naturally, with coarse black hairs on the back and in between the knuckles, but his nails, besides being real clean and pink, was curved on the ends like a fine lady's or a harlot's. I never seen the like. I must have stared at them—he pulled them under the table.

"After I left home, someone taught me how to speak well," he said. "A very dear friend." It seemed like there was tears on his eyelashes again. I opened my mouth but didn't know what to say.

He give me a kindly look. "Speaking well opens up your life to more opportunities. You can meet anyone at all and feel confident in talking to him."

This felt like he was trying not to insult me, but

it did. Then it come to me what to say. "I can see how it would be good for the children to know them things."

He nodded. "You're right about that. The world is getting smaller all the time."

"What?" I said. "I never heard that."

He smiled. "I don't mean it literally."

I probably had a look on my face.

"It's not *actually* getting smaller. It just *seems* as if . . . Well, think about magazines, for one thing. There are thousands of them, and dozens that are read in every part of the country. *The Saturday Evening Post, Harper's Weekly, Ladies' Home Journal.*" He sounded like a teacher, sure enough.

"Uh-huh." I seen them magazines, but we didn't take them.

"So for the first time, we have a truly national culture being created." He was sweating and looking close into my eyes. "Not just the wealthy and the educated, but everyone. For five cents you can read the ideas of the most brilliant people we have. And the idiots, too, of course."

"We get the Sears catalog," I said.

He laughed. "That too! So pretty little Albertina, in Obsidian, Missouri, can buy the very same bedroom suit as citified Albertina in Chicago."

Now I laughed. "Hairpins and Mason jars, more like." I noticed he called me pretty.

He looked sheepish. "I get carried away, I

know. All I'm saying is, the more that people get to know the whole country, the more we will all be expected to talk—well, you see what I mean."

"I expect you're right. But I'm stubborn, tell the truth." I held my breath.

He started off giggling. "Oh, I like you, Albertina. If you could see some of the ladies I—" Now he opened his mouth wide and laughed.

I felt people looking at us, but I couldn't help but smile. I started to say I liked him, too, when he pulled out his watch and said, "Look at the time."

I drunk the last of my coffee. "This is awful good. Course, anything goes in my mouth is awful good if I don't have to make it myself."

"Really? I *like* cooking," he said.

"I never heard of no man liked to cook," I blurted out. It sounded hurtful, so I added, "Must be aplenty, though."

He laughed and then pulled out a white hankie and patted his face. He put it back in his pocket and took out a dime and a nickel and put them on the table. Coffee was a nickel, but I knowed he could add two nickels together, so I never said nothing to him about leaving too much money.

"Albertina, would you like to take a walk?"

When we got outside, the day had turned colder. I shivered and pulled my shawl around me. A wind come up, sharp, and my eyes got to watering.

Bernard looked at me. "Thinking about your mother?" he said, and before I could answer, "You needn't be ashamed of your grief, my dear."

I like to busted into tears. Nobody except Mama herself talked to me tender like that, and not very often, in fact hardly ever. I felt like I was in a dream. It hit me all the sudden what it meant to fall in love, and I felt like I could fall in love with this man. I felt light-headed. I swallowed back tears.

"Should I take you home?" he said.

I shook my head. "Do me good to walk." I blinked my tears away. Was this what it was like, being looked after?

After a little bit he said, "There is something I'd like to talk to you about. See how you feel about it."

"Well then," I said.

He stopped and looked at me. "I know your situation. I understand you will soon need—well, a home. For you and your two sisters." He laid his hand on my arm.

I looked down at my shoes. There it was. And now that it was in front of me, why, I felt like I wanted to take off and run. Getting married seemed like a harebrained notion. He seemed nice, sure enough, sweet even, maybe the sweetest man I ever met, but I didn't hardly know him. His hand on my arm felt peculiar.

"I have a small inheritance, including my home in Millard," he said. "On my income, you would not live in luxury, but I can provide some comforts." He pulled back his hand. "Albertina?"

I thought about Opal and Dacia. If I got the willies thinking of myself married to a nice man I liked, how was I going to marry anybody?

I made myself look him in the face. "You a drinker?"

He smiled then. "Only a glass of sherry. In the evening. Not to worry, my dear."

I didn't know what sherry was, but I reckoned— only one glass.

We took up walking again. I heard him stop his breath several times like he was going to say something, but he hesitated. Finally, he said, almost whispering, "I would not trouble you."

"Trouble?" I whispered back.

"You know."

I felt a catch in my throat. "You mean . . . ?"

He kept on trudging, leaning forward like he was walking against a storm, but the wind wasn't blowing that hard.

"Oh," I said. "Oh."

Just then a man in boots and overhauls walked by and brushed his leg against my skirt. When he was well by us, I said, half to myself, "No children?"

He smiled. From what he'd likely been told, maybe he reckoned I didn't want none. Lord knowed, I'd had a hard time of it, and likely it wasn't over yet, especially with Dacia still to finish raising. But never once had I thought I didn't want no children when the time come. Tell the truth, it never occurred to me. Now I tried to picture it, me getting on in years, my twenties, my thirties, Dacia and Opal grown and gone, and me without no children of my own. I just stood there, taking it in. Not wanting children would be like not wanting food or water or air. To me, it wasn't natural.

Now as far as the coupling, that part I didn't know much about except for watching the livestock. The way the Bible talked, though, it seemed like people, even women, took pleasure in it, the way they defied the Commandments to lay with the one they desired. Thinking this, I blushed deep red.

"Ah, Albertina, all this is a bit much for you, isn't it?" Bernard said. "We can talk again. Let me get you home."

I was too shocked to ask him how come he wouldn't lay with me, or couldn't. I didn't know was he born that way, did he have an accident, or what.

We parted without me saying one way or the other would I marry him. But I did let him put his cheek on mine when we said good night, and it was soft and sweet, and his hair smelled good.

• • •

As I laid in bed that night, sleepless, my thoughts went back and forth. There would be comforts for the three of us girls—comforts, what a wonder!—and Dacia and Opal, why, Bernard could teach them things I never could. And he acted so kindhearted. I thought about Mama and Daddy and whatever it was Daddy done that made us pack up and leave Kentucky. I thought about the hollering that'd went on between them, and how Daddy liked his drink, and how Dacia'd told me Mama didn't want her children no more. I didn't believe what Dacia said, of course, but maybe if Daddy'd treated Mama more kindly she might've felt different and done different in some kind of way.

Against all that, no children of my own.

When I woken up in the morning, I knowed I couldn't marry Bernard, and it was foolish to even consider it. Of course I wanted children— everbody did—and I reckoned I would want relations with my husband, too, once I got used to it.

But Bernard had taught me something. What he taught me was, besides taking in my sisters, the man I married had to look me in the eye when we talked, and me not feel prickly. And I had to feel like there was a chance I could fall in love with him. I wasn't going to settle for no less.

I didn't have no idea how or where I was

going to meet this man, or even if there was one. And I didn't have much time. William and that woman—Dora was her name—why, they was planning to get married in the spring, and it was coming up Christmas already.

Chapter 10

Alta Bea come over to the house one morning long about mid-March. It was a breezy day, so I was taking down the curtains to hang out on the line and beat the dust out of. I was standing on a chair when she come in.

"Don't stop on my account," she said. "The girls in school?"

I nodded. "Bring me that basket, would you?"

She pushed it with her foot. "Did you like either one of those farmers William set you up with?"

"Only met the one so far." I pulled the rod down and started sliding the curtain off into the basket. "He didn't have much to say."

The twins was standing in the corner, leaning on each other, staring at Alta Bea.

"Where is his place?" she said.

"South of the river. Good bottom land. Grows alfalfa hay, besides wheat, and runs cattle." I dropped the other curtain into the basket and sneezed from the dust.

"How did he seem?" She was talking to me, but I seen she was smiling at the twins. They didn't say nothing.

"Where's my manners?" I said. "Let me get you some coffee."

"I can't stay."

I climbed down off the chair. "James, John, go outside and play. Go on now."

"Cold out there," one of them said.

"Go on now. Do you good." The boys put on their extra shirts and slumped out the door.

"I really can't stay," Alta Bea said. "I just came by to ask you to go to a dance with me Saturday night."

I carried the chair over to the other window. Dacia'd heard at school that Alta Bea had started gallivanting around, and her mama was trying to get her to settle down. I wondered did she drink when she went out, and what-all went on. I was troubled for her reputation. "Don't like to leave the children alone of an evening," I said.

"Dacia's old enough to watch them. You said so yourself."

There wasn't nothing to say to that. I climbed up on the chair and loosened the curtain rod.

"You'd be doing me a big favor," she said. "I'm supposed to meet this man there, this son of a friend of Mother's, and I don't know him. You know what that's like."

I sighed.

"If you're with me—you know," she said.

"Where's it at?"

"You'll go? That's wonderful. I'll pick you up."

She gathered up her things and left before I could say any more.

"A dance?" Dacia said. "What for?"

I opened a hairpin with my teeth and poked it in my hair. "Me and Alta Bea. I'm keeping her company." I eyed the cup of coffee I had there on the table, but I reckoned it was cold by now.

"What about me?"

"You can watch the children. We won't be late."

"Alta *Bea*," she said, wrinkling her nose. She took aholt of the hairbrush and pulled a handful of hairs out of the bristles. Then she stretched out her arm and let them float to the floor, following them with her eyes like a cat.

"You're just gonna have to sweep that up tomorrow." I felt around my head and added another pin.

"Daddy says there's something *wrong* with her. Crazy as a hoot owl." More hairs.

I drunk a sip of coffee. Cold, like I thought. I got up and went to the stove, and when I come back with the coffeepot, there was a couple hairs floating in the cup. "How'd them hairs get in there?"

She set back and folded her arms. "Damn if I know."

Just then come a knocking at the door. "I don't

have time right now to rebuke you, Lucky," I said to Dacia.

"You've got a big stain on the back of your skirt," she said. "Looks like you wet yourself." She lifted the hairbrush and fluffed her side hair with it.

I suspicioned she was lying, but I twisted myself around and checked it anyhow. Wasn't nothing there.

Alta Bea opened the door and walked in. "You ready? Hello, Dacia."

Dacia stood up and walked toward the door. "I gotta go to the backhouse," she said. "Don't leave till I get back." She stopped and said to Alta Bea, "I gotta watch the children. *Somebody* in this house has to take care of them."

Alta Bea give her a half smile. "You're so sweet to oblige your sister."

"Huh." Dacia tossed her head and went out the door.

"You look awful pretty," I said to Alta Bea.

She shook her head. "That girl."

"She's a pistol, sure enough," I said. "Let's go."

Me and Alta Bea walked arm in arm into the Sullivan County Men's Fraternal Hall. I'd heard about these dances, but I never had been to one before. After the cold night air, it was hot inside, smoky, and the music and people talking made a racket. There was people dancing, and the old wooden floor creaked and cracked, and there was a hissing sound as people shuffled their feet.

My lips felt dry. I was looking around for the punch bowl when I seen this man playing the fiddle onstage. I watched him for a minute, and something happened inside me that'd never happened before. I told Alta Bea, "That one's mine even if I never get him."

"What?" she said, though I knowed she heard me. Her mouth was wide open.

"The one playing the fiddle." He looked to be in his late twenties, and he was scrawny and nearly bald, but he had a smile that went all over his face, and he closed his eyes while he was playing and seemed like he was transported.

Alta Bea told me she happened to know the man's name—Sam Frownfelter—because he played for weddings around town. Alta Bea's mother loved weddings, and seemed like she never missed one. She often talked about the fine wedding she'd put on for Alta Bea when the time come.

"He available, do you know?" I said.

"Well, he may not look like much, but I've heard he's a ladies' man."

I took her arm. "Where's the punch? I'm thirsty."

After a little bit the band took a breather, and I followed the fiddler out a side door. My heart was pounding.

I seen him standing by himself smoking a cigarette. I walked right up to him and asked him did he have another one. He looked me up and down, and dug in his shirt pocket. "I never knowed a little girl that smoked," he said, but he lit it for me anyhow.

I pulled the smoke in my mouth—I knowed better than to draw it into my lungs—and blowed it out. It tasted awful. "I ain't no little girl, I'm sixteen." Just turned.

"Don't look but thirteen."

"I been around." I tried to make my voice low and womanly.

He laughed. "No, you ain't."

I throwed the cigarette on the ground and mashed it. As I was walking away, he said, "Don't go off in a huff now. What's your name?"

"Wouldn't you like to know." My heart felt squeezed. I wasn't the kind to act smart-alecky, and I didn't even know, was I doing it right or just looking the fool.

Later on, back inside, Alta Bea said to me, "He's watching you," and I knowed who she meant. But I only glanced at the stage ever little bit.

Me and her, we stayed till the last song, and we tarried a while by the door. He come out carrying his fiddle in its case. Another man, with light-colored hair, kind of stocky, was with him—the banjo player.

"Hello there, Bertie," the fiddler said. To this day I don't know how he found out my name. A thrill run up and down me.

"This here's my friend Alta Bea Snedeker," I said.

He nodded and reached out his hand to shake hers. "Sam Frownfelter." He stood there staring at me.

Then his friend shook our hands and introduced himself as Harold Satterfield. Now Harold, he had a deep dimple in his chin—first man I ever saw that had one—and I thought of a saying Grandma Sweet had: "Cleft chin, devil within." I didn't like the way he looked at me, like he was calculating. He struck me as the kind of man makes a good salesman. Kind of man you got to watch yourself around.

After me, he looked at Alta Bea. He said to her, "You ladies have a way to get home?"

"You have a way to get us home?" Alta Bea said quick. She used a tone of voice I never heard her use before.

"One buggy and two mules."

"That should be enough," she said. Me, I stood there like a stone. So did Sam.

It was Sam's buggy, so him and me set on the springboard, and Alta Bea and Harold got in the back. Sam told me he had a draying business, hauling sundry items in town and between towns, with a wagon and a team. Besides his music.

Before we got home, he managed to ask me out for a date the next day. If Alta Bea heard, she never give no sign of it.

I never found out who the man was she claimed she was supposed to meet at the dance. I reckon that was a tale she told.

The next day I left Dacia in charge of the children, saying I was going to wash a lady's windows in town. Then I met Sam behind Karlsson's dry goods store, where he rented three rooms in the back. Karlsson, the man who owned the store, he was Sam's biggest dray customer.

I didn't want nobody to know I was seeing Sam. I reckoned my big brothers, why, they would find some reason not to like him since they never picked him out. They wasn't boys no more, and they imagined they should run things. It felt like I was doing wrong, seeing Sam behind their backs, but I done it anyhow. Daddy, I never paid no mind to his feelings no more, not since the day he hung John for a joke and I stabbed him with the hay fork. But me being sixteen, he could get the law after us if he took it into his head.

Sam was setting in the buggy when I walked up, and soon's he seen me, he hopped down and took my basket of food and put it in the back. Then he helped me up, set down, and tipped his hat. Now we was setting side by side on the springboard, and when he tipped his hat, he tipped it to the front like he was tipping it to the mules. "Good morning, Miss Bertie," he said. I could tell this was his way of doing something a little bit funny to ease my mind, seeing's as how we didn't hardly know each other yet. I liked he did that. Alta Bea was right—he wasn't very good-looking. But he had a way about him that wasn't like nobody I ever knowed before. Maybe a little like I pictured Daddy if he wasn't drunk all the time.

Now Sam turned to me and smiled. Deep lines spread out from the corners of his eyes—seemed like they went all the way to the top of his forehead and down the sides of his cheeks to his mouth. I never knowed nobody had a smile like Sam's. It was like the sun come out.

He put on his hat and clucked to the mules, and we set off.

The cold wind had let up in the night, and it was a sunny day for March, with a little heat in the breeze. A beautiful day for a picnic.

Me and Sam, we got to talking about our kin, and I told him I had charge of my little sisters. I started off with Dacia. "You should hear her when I go out," I said. " 'Where you going? Is that what you're wearing? You putting on powder? You gonna comb your hair?' " I realized I was making it sound like I went out all the time, which I had only done two times—once with that farmer—but Dacia made a fuss about it. When I got back, she also peppered me with questions. "He smell good? What'd he say? What'd you say? He hold your hand? He kiss you?" But I didn't see no need to tell Sam about that.

"What about the little one?" he said. "She like the boys, too?"

It took me aback, what he seemed to understand about Dacia already. "Oh, Opal, she's a caution," I said. "Always making something. I said, if she had two sticks and a sand burr, she'd make something. But sewing, that's what her heart inclines to. She'll set down and cut up material without no plan nor pattern, seems like, and it'll come out. Never seen the like of that child."

"Whoa, mule, hold up." One of the mules was shying away from a tall Jimsonweed, and Sam reined him back in.

I wasn't there to ask him, "Would you be a good father to my sisters? Would you be a good husband to me?" I was there to find out them things, but you don't find them things out by asking directly. You have to sniff it out like a dog does.

Pretty soon he said, "River suit you to eat?"

I nodded. "Opal, one day I come into the room, and she was setting there talking to the material. 'Now don't you bunch up like that, I don't want to see no puckers.' "

We both laughed.

"I'll say one thing," I went on. "If she darns your sock, you'll never raise a blister where the mend's at."

"That recommends a girl," he said.

"How about you? What's your family like?"

"Well now, I'm the third youngest of thirteen," he said. "I got more nieces and nephews than you can count on two hands and feet."

That made me laugh.

He told me he'd moved away from home—his folks lived in Nebraska—more than ten years ago. He tried to get up there once ever year or two. "My sisters, they'll make up a big dinner. 'Don't forget your fiddle.' Them kids can't get enough fiddling—set still for an hour sometimes." He clucked to the mules. "They love songs that tell a story. You know, 'Do "Frog Went a-Courtin'"," do "Clementine," do "Clementine!"' " The way he said this, in a child's voice, went a long way with me.

Wasn't long before we got to the river. We eat our sandwiches and set on the blanket afterward and talked some more. We never hardly took our eyes off of each other, seemed like.

I asked him about his religion.

"I'm a believer, I reckon," he said, "but as far as church, I ain't been since I left home."

"Me neither, for a while now."

"With us, it was the wife took the children. The men went Easter and Christmas."

I knowed what he was saying. I nodded, and he never said no more.

After while he took me by the hand, and I let him. My sweat broke out, and my hand felt like it had electricity in it. I hadn't never felt of electricity at that time, of course, but that's what it felt like. That feeling I had in me was desire, sure enough. *Thy desire shall be to thy husband, and he shall rule over thee.* And soon's I felt that desire inside me, in my mind I pictured ever woman whose talk I'd ever listened to around a kitchen table or over a tub of washing, all the way back to my earliest memories as a girl, and now I heard all that talk anew, with new understanding. I pictured ever last one of them, and especially Mama, and I felt a whole new kinship with them that like to stole my breath away. I ached so bad for Mama, I started up crying, right there setting next to Sam on the blanket.

He took me in his arms and said, "Little bird, what's wrong? I won't hurt you none. I won't never hurt you." He always, even from the first, called me his little bird since I was so short and tiny. He told me I was pretty, too, like the man teacher done. I thought about how Mama always said that, being's as how I took after the Winslows, I had eye-colored eyes and hair-colored hair, and I wondered what Alta Bea and the man teacher and Sam seen in me that Mama never done.

We stayed out by the river till mid-afternoon. As we drove toward home, I asked Sam to let me off at the road, ahead of the bend.

He pulled up the mules. "You don't want your dad to meet me? Or even see me, evidently."

"He's an old fool, and he thinks he runs the world."

Sam winced. "I hate to hear you talk that way about your dad."

"It's the Lord's truth, though."

He studied his hands for a minute. "Maybe so, but it don't show you in a good light. Or me neither."

I reached back to fetch the picnic basket, but he took aholt of it first. "I don't like this," he said. "I ain't no slinker."

"I know you ain't." I took the basket from him, miserable.

"I don't see how I can keep on seeing you this way."

My chest buzzed, and I put my hand in his. "He'll come around."

"And if he don't?"

There wasn't nothing to say to that. For a minute we neither one said nothing. Then I told him about a little cabin on the Snedeker property about two miles and a half from the house—one of the places me and Alta Bea used to explore when we was younger. "If you want to meet me, come to the cabin late in the day tomorrow. If you ain't there . . ." Then I leaned over, kissed him like a brazen woman, and leapt down from the buggy. The mules shied, and I took off running and never looked back. That kiss burned my mouth all the way home, being the first time I ever had that kind of a touch anywhere, let alone my lips.

Halfway to the house I seen Daddy standing in the front yard, his feet planted wide apart. "Where the Sam Hill you been?" he hollered.

I never answered him. I felt defiant, though I wished I didn't have the picnic basket with me.

"The whole town seen you!" he bellowed. "With a man! Headed to the river!"

This stopped me. But then I walked up to him and looked him in the eye. "You're drunk."

"I said where *was* you," he said, but he did back off a step. He rubbed himself where the hay fork had gashed his arm.

"You never told us you was going *out,*" come Dacia's voice. She was on the porch, swinging by one arm on a post.

Daddy give me a look of disgust. "You made yourself a *hussy* in *front* of people."

In my mind, rage wrestled with shame, and it felt like the air went out of me.

"Are you intact?" he whispered, breathing alcohol on me.

Instantly I let out a sound I'd never uttered before, a kind of an animal scream, my arms flew up in the air, and I run toward him. I don't know what I expected to do—it wasn't like I had a hay fork this time—but he shrunk back a few steps, and I stopped short of him and stood there with my fists clenched. It seemed like my bellow echoed for a while, and when it got quiet again he said, "I forbid you to see this man again, you hear?" Now his voice was whiny like an old man's.

"Go to hell," I muttered. I turned on my heel and started walking off toward the road.

"Or any man, you hear me?" he called.

I needed to talk to somebody that knowed something about life. I went over to Alta Bea's house. Wasn't nobody else.

Alta Bea was in her bedroom having a dress pinned on her by a lady named Mrs. Benson. She was a seamstress and tailor, somebody everbody in town knowed, and a hero to Opal.

Alta Bea told me to come on in and not to mind the mess, and I come in and set on her bed. Mrs. Benson never looked at me nor said nothing, just worked. I never seen nobody could pin as fast as she done.

Alta Bea and me visited till Mrs. Benson finished and packed up the dress in a big round box. She gathered up her things and said to Alta Bea she'd come back next Tuesday for a fitting, and she left.

Alta Bea pulled on a skirt over her chemise. "What'd you come to talk about? You were sweating when you came in." Now she reached for a blouse and put it on. I never smelled no whiskey on her.

Well, I told her the whole story. She asked me did I like Sam, and I told her I did. I told her he was the one, sure enough, and my heart fluttered.

She was setting in her chair at her desk, and now she begun pinning her hair back in place, eyeing herself in a mirror propped against a stack of books. "You scarcely know him," she said. "You only met him last night."

This took me aback. "But I *like* him." I seen her roll her eyes, and I felt burned. "And I ain't got till kingdom come."

She stopped messing with her hair and looked at me in the mirror. "I've been thinking about it." She turned toward me. "You're too young to get married, Bertie—you are. Maybe you should board with some widow in town, like your brothers said."

"But—"

"It doesn't have to be forever—a year or two, maybe three," she said.

"But I thought—"

She turned back to the mirror. "It's too risky to get married—don't you see that?" Her voice sounded like she was speaking to a child.

I fought back tears. "How comes you to do

me this way? You was helping me. You said—"

"I say a lot of things—don't you know that by now?" Seemed like she was trying to sound superior, but it come out shaky.

I felt confused and, strangely, more humiliated than when Daddy bawled me out in front of Dacia. Most of all I felt betrayed. I didn't trust myself to say nothing to Alta Bea. I just hurried out of her room and down the stairs and out the door.

When I got to the bent cottonwood tree, I slowed down. I pictured Alta Bea on the day we played paper dolls, the first time I was in her house. I recollected how strange it was there, how odd her daddy acted. Alta Bea, she was smart, she knowed people, she understood things I never had no notion of—but, I realized now, she was somebody didn't have no nerve. She wanted to, that was the hell of it. But when things got serious, she turned tail and hid, just like she told me she used to hide behind the paint on the wall. I myself had plenty of things to be afraid of—a sight more than her, truth be told—but there was something inside me give me nerve, and something inside her didn't, whiskey or no whiskey. Me and her needed each other, seemed like, but I couldn't count on her but only so far. It give me a feeling of deep loneliness.

When I got home, Daddy was gone, which I figured he would be. I cooked me and the

213

children some salt-meat and gravy, thinking about Sam the whole time. Only thing I was worried about was, did he like me as much as I liked him. If he did, wasn't nothing going to stop me from marrying him.

Dacia, she never said nothing. She just chewed her food and studied ever movement I made.

Chapter 11

That night I put Opal and the twins in Mama's bed—that was a rare treat—and asked Dacia to set with me at the table. I told her I had something to talk to her about.

"I want popcorn," she said.

"Ain't enough fire left." I got up from the table. "How about cornbread? I got some strawberry jam set by." We had a rule, no piecing, which I was breaking. I wasn't one to bribe a child, but this wasn't no time to be particular.

I set the food in front of her. "We're in debt, and we got to fix it."

She didn't say nothing. I doubt she knowed what that meant.

I set down at the table. "We owe near forty dollars to the store, and we ain't paid the rent in two-three months." She licked syrup from her fingers. "Ain't made the payment on Mama's coffin."

"I don't know nothing about none of that," she said.

"Time you did. I was your age, I dressed chickens and took in ironing."

She wrinkled her nose. "I need a glass of milk."

215

I set my hand on her arm. "Listen to me."

She stared at my hand till I let go. "You ain't my mama."

Picturing Sam, with his whole face smiling, helped me hold my temper. "Dacia, we're about broke, is what I'm telling you."

She narrowed her eyes. "That ain't right. William and Buck, they send money, I know they do. And Daddy—"

"William and Buck can't support this whole family, they've got their own plans to think about. And Daddy—how long have we had them three horses out there in the corral? That paint and them two bays? Feeding them?"

She rolled her eyes. "How would I know?"

"Before last Thanksgiving," I said. "Daddy ain't sold a horse in months." I waited till she looked me in the eye. "If it wasn't for Alta Bea and them, I don't know what we'd even eat."

"What plans?" she said.

It took me a minute to understand. "They're growed men. Things is different when you're a growed man."

I was tiptoeing around some things—I reckoned if she knowed what-all was coming, she'd have a fit and fall in it. She seemed satisfied with this answer, though, so I went on. "I can't get a job and leave you out here ever day to look after the children—that wouldn't be fair."

Her eyes got wide. "By myself? All the time?"

"I said, I ain't—"

"You can't do that!" she cried.

"Hush, you'll wake them up."

"We ain't going to the poor farm? We going to the poor farm, Bertie?" she said, tears in her voice.

Now there wasn't a child nowhere, except maybe Alta Bea, that wasn't scared to death of being sent to the poor farm. We heard a lot of tales about children worked to death at them places. Truth was, a lot of them, if they got sent there without their people, they never come back home, but I doubt any of them died from over-work. They just growed up and left. Still, wasn't no worse threat you could use on a child.

"I'm trying to talk to you like a grown-up," I said.

"I ain't going to no poor farm," she said, sticking her chin out.

"Listen to me," I said. "I met this man."

"The one you *sinned* with?"

It took all my strength not to snatch her by the hair. My voice, when I spoke, I heard the wrath in it, quiet though it was. "I never sinned with him nor nobody. Understand that."

"But Daddy—"

"Christ," I said. "Daddy." It wasn't no use. Even ten year old, she was too little to comprehend Daddy's ways. To her, he was funny when he was drunk. Her and him, they was all the time laughing and joking, just like her and Mama. Everybody always said Dacia could charm the spots off a leopard, and she could, when she wanted to.

"Look," I said, "this man I met, he's going to fix things so we don't have to go to the poor farm."

She leaned toward me.

"But we have to pull a joke on Daddy," I said.

"We do?" Her eyes got bright.

"We have to keep a secret. Just between you and me. You can't tell nobody."

So that's how I got her to lie for me and Sam when we was together. I bribed her, I threatened her, I made her think it was a game. Worst of all, I made her think she was older than she was, that I was letting loose of her, that she was going to have freer rein than I ever planned to give her after I got done what needed done.

I ain't proud of it. We all needed Sam, but the truth is I wanted him, too, and I wasn't above corrupting my sister—lying to her and threatening her and getting her to lie—to get what I wanted.

When I got to the cabin late the next day, Sam was there waiting for me. It was cold in there and smelled clayey, like dirt ain't seen the sun in years and years. There wasn't no place to set, so we just leaned against the wall.

I asked him about his music, how come he was so good at it.

"Not near as good as I hope to be," he said. "Good enough to make pocket money, is all." He pulled out a cigarette and offered me one. I shook my head.

"You wanting to go to Nashville or some-place?" I remembered the other Dacia in the family, who sung there.

He drawed in the smoke. "It's just something I do. I want to get better."

"How many songs do you know by heart?"

"Couldn't tell you."

"You know 'Whispering Hope'? That's my favorite."

He nodded. "Nice tune."

"Mostly I just heard people sing at home. Never been to dances much."

He nodded again and kept smoking. Pretty soon he said, "How come you don't want your dad to meet me?"

"He's a drunk, Sam. He don't pay bills." I held my breath.

He bent his knee and stubbed out the cigarette on the sole of his boot. "That ain't no secret around town."

I felt hot and cold at the same time.

"How this is gonna go, that's up to you," he said. "But you've got to know, it ain't no good to try to fool people." It was getting on dark, and the only light in the cabin was through a tiny window half caved in. I seen Sam's outline, and I seen his eyes, and I heard his voice, ghostlike.

"I ain't trying to fool you," I said.

"Then tell me what you want from me."

"Ain't what I want. Well, I do, but . . ."

"But?"

"It's what I need," I said. "Me and my little sisters."

"Need," he said, and hearing that word in his mouth like to killed me.

I took a step back and told him the whole story. He'd heard about Daddy's reputation, but he didn't know how bad things was. He didn't know about my brothers' plan to break up the family. He didn't know I'd been looking for a husband to take us in. He didn't know about my date with Bernard or the one farmer. It like to shamed me to death, telling him all this.

When I finished, he picked his words. "Bertie, I ain't fixed to where I can marry nobody, especially one comes with children." He was staring at his boots.

I sucked in so much breath I near choked on it. I nodded and backed away from him.

"I got some money put by, but . . ."

"No, I understand," I said.

We stood and looked at each other for a long time. "This ain't what I reckoned on," he said finally.

"Nor me neither." I walked over to the window and looked out. "It's getting on dark. I better get home and make supper."

He walked over to me. "I still want to see you."

"What for?"

He blinked. "Shit—you're a hard one." By the light of the window I seen he had a moony look on his face, and I felt certain he loved me, or at least he was took by me. I felt a surge of hope.

"All right," he said, like something was settled. "Meet me here day after tomorrow, in the daylight."

"Reckon I could."

This time he kissed me, and my heart went wild. I kissed him back and leaned into him, and when I felt his response I got light-headed and pulled back away. I couldn't hardly get my breath. For the first time in my life I felt my power as a woman, and it thrilled me. I couldn't picture what it would be like, only felt it, but it excited me. Then the smell of Mama and Daddy's sheets come to me unbidden, and it made my eyes water.

After while me and Sam walked outside, and he give me a ride as far as the big bend leading up to the house.

"Coming up a bad cloud, looks like," Sam said when we met again. "We better not dawdle."

I nodded, and we went inside the cabin.

He wiped his hands on his pants. "I never reckoned on marrying no sixteen-year-old."

I nodded. "I been keeping house, looking after the children, for a long time. It ain't like you're starting from scratch."

"I know. It's just—it's—"

"It's a lot to ask," I said.

"No, it ain't that. It's—everthing costs more than you think, when you get down to it."

"I can dress chickens and take in ironing," I said. "I reckon we'll make out." I looked all over his face. Seemed like I couldn't get enough of just looking at it, every inch of it.

Now he smiled big, like he done. "I believe you. Don't know why, but I do."

I put my hand on his arm. "It ain't just—this ain't just about . . ." I felt my face go red, but I wasn't afraid. "When I seen you at the dance, up there singing and playing, I told Alta Bea, that's the one I want, right there."

He cocked his head like he didn't believe me.

"Ask her," I said. "You think I ever rode out to the river with nobody else? Well, I never did. I never felt this way about nobody. There's something about you—I don't know what."

He fidgeted, and I pulled my arm away. "I feel like—I feel like, if you and me get married, it will be lucky for me, and you, too. I was looking for just somebody, but I found *you*." I took his hand and raised it up and kissed it. I felt a rush of desire, and I put my arms around him. He took a breath out loud and pulled back. He stared at my face, and I seen the rims of his eyes was pink.

He blinked hard a few times. "Well, if you're bound and determined—"

"The girls, they'll learn to love you," I said softly. "Us three, I know we're kin, but you'll be a better daddy to them than they ever knowed. We'll be happy together. You'll see."

Now he pulled out his hankie and blowed his nose. "Oklahoma," he said.

"What about it?"

"Down there, you can get married without your folks signing for you." He put his hankie back in his pocket. "If you're bound and determined."

"You know I am." I felt light as light itself. I felt I could float away.

"Only problem is, the money." He pulled out a piece of paper with numbers on it. He'd wrote down the train tickets, a hotel (we'd sleep on the train coming and going, but we'd need rooms for the wedding night for him and me, and for the people standing up with us), and meals (nine or twelve meals apiece, depending). Then there was the marriage license, along with bride's and groom's expenses (he'd put down six dollars for me, twice as much as him). It all added up to $127.00. I was shocked, tell the truth—happy he'd done the figuring, but shocked at how much it was.

"I can cover the twenty-seven dollars," he said, "but that leaves us a hundred short. And that don't count no gewgaws you'll be wanting for the house." He stared at the paper miserably, like a man will, like numbers has a meaning all on their own besides what they stand for.

"Could we borrow it?" I said.

He folded up the paper and put it in his shirt pocket. "I don't owe nothing to nobody, and I don't intend to start." His mouth was set. He sounded wroth.

"I don't see no other way, do you?" I said.

He put his hands on my elbows. "You could make up with your dad. If he'd sign for you, we could get married here, wouldn't cost much atall."

I pulled away from him. "I ain't asking *him* for nothing."

"Well, if you're going to be pigheaded—"

"*Me* pigheaded?"

This argument went on for two weeks. Turned out I was the most pigheaded. Sam finally said he'd borrow the money if we could find somebody to loan it to us.

Of course the only person I wanted to stand up for me was Alta Bea, and she was also the only person I knowed who could get their hands on a hundred dollars. The next day after Sam agreed to borrow the money, I asked Alta Bea over to the house, and we set out on the back porch. It was April by now, and we'd had good rain for a couple days. As me and her looked up at the slope into the south pasture, you could see patches of green among the black dirt. You could smell things waking up.

I thought she might bolt when I told her me and Sam was wanting to elope, but she just set there with her arms wrapped around her knees.

"We been seeing each other," I said. "We neither one of us is the kind to sneak around—you know me. It's been hard."

She raised her face, cool and composed. You could see it took an effort.

"I love him, Alta Bea." It was the first time I said it out loud. "I'd marry him even if I didn't have to."

Her eyes widened. "You *love* him? When did you decide that?"

I pictured me and Sam in the cold cabin that first time. "At first he said . . ." I sniffed back tears, and then I felt a smile break out on my face. "But then he looked it *up,* Alta Bea—he found out you can get married in Oklahoma without your folks signing if you're sixteen. He asked around, all on his own."

She leaned her head toward me. I couldn't tell if she was mad or she thought I'd lost my mind. I wanted to make her understand. "Don't you see? Before I even—"

"How are you going to get to Oklahoma? Do you even know how far away that is?"

My face went red. "Well, that's just it."

She opened and closed her mouth. Then she slumped down and laid her elbows on her knees and her face in her hands. "Oh."

There was a lot in that "oh." Everthing, all the seven years we'd knowed each other. For a moment neither one of us said nothing.

Then she dropped her hands. In an even voice she said, "How much do you need?"

I told her what Sam had figured up, the train and meals and hotel. Then I asked her would she go with us and stand up for me. She listened to the whole thing, and by the time I was done she had tears in her eyes.

"I thought maybe your mother, she'd help us out," I said finally. "She's always been so kindly to us."

Tears come down her cheeks. "The truth is, I'm jealous, Bertie. I wish I loved someone."

This touched me. I didn't know what to say.

Then she set up straight and wiped her face with her hands. "I'm sure Mother would give us the money if she could, but she can't. She hasn't any cash, never has." Turned out, Alta Bea's dad had everthing in his name and never let her mama have more than a few dollars at a time. But Alta Bea herself had near twenty dollars squirreled away, and she had a notion of how to get the other eighty. Her daddy, he always left the bank where he was president at three o'clock on Wednesdays to get his hair cut and his shoes shined, and then he played dominoes with the men from his lodge. The night man, name of Walter, he stayed and balanced the accounts. Now Walter, he was sweet on Alta Bea, and, from her being at the bank off and on since she was a little girl, she knowed where the window was at where you could tap on it after hours and he would see who it was. She figured she could sweet-talk him into giving her the money, acting like it was for her dad.

I set there with my mouth open. "When did you think up this-all?"

She was silent for a moment. "I've been thinking about things for a long time. Since I'm not going to college . . . Well, it's time I left this godforsaken place."

"But your daddy, he—"

"And Bertie, I've been seeing Harold Satterfield. No one knows."

"The banjo player? He's the one's going to stand up with Sam!" I pictured Harold in my mind, and I recollected how I was leery of him when we met the night of the dance.

She dropped her eyes. "He didn't tell me about your plans. I guess he was waiting until things were—"

"You two serious?"

She hesitated. "He is."

"But you ain't?"

She smiled. "Not everyone falls in love as fast as you do, Bertie."

We was silent for a while, till finally I said, "But your daddy, he's liable to get the law on us, ain't he? It's stealing, ain't it?"

She shook her head. "He'll be furious all right, but he values his reputation too much to do anything so public. He'll just write it off. And Mother . . ." Quick tears come now. "Mother wouldn't let him do anything to harm me. That I know."

I took aholt of her hand.

"Though he might disown me," she said.

"Oh!"

She looked me square in the face. "I've thought about that for a long time, and I've made up my mind. I can't live with him holding that threat over me and everything I do." From somewhere, Alta Bea'd got her some nerve, sure enough.

I decided not to tell Sam how exactly Alta Bea was getting the money. He was already edgy about even borrowing it. Me, I was worried, too—you'd be a fool not to be—but I swallowed back my disquiets. Mama always said, "Worry is interest paid on troubles you ain't had yet."

That night I dug through Mama's green trunk and found the nightdress she'd made me for my wedding night. She had tatted the lace herself around the neck, and it was brittle from being packed away. The gown was mouse-chewed in a couple places, and I mended it. I didn't have no fancy dress to get married in, but I had a pretty white blouse with embroidery at the cuffs and a clean brown skirt, faded to almost lilac.

Me and Sam, we went and told my brothers. We was going to be gone three days—more, if the train run late—and somebody had to check on Dacia and the children while we was gone. Sam, he give a good account of himself, which I knowed he would, and William and Buck, they shook his hand and give me a hug.

"I reckon you know what you're in for when you get back," William said.

"It'll be over and done with," I said. "He won't be able to undo it." Him and Buck, they even give us seven dollars and a half for a wedding present. We all bawled a little bit.

The next Wednesday, Alta Bea went and got the money like she'd said, and early the next morning, April 14, 1916, the four of us got on the train in Milan, bound for Oklahoma.

Chapter 12

Sam, Alta Bea, and Harold, they'd been on a train before, but it was my first ride. The footstool wasn't hardly tall enough for me, so the porter grabbed aholt of my elbow and helped me climb up into the car. I felt a spark fly up my spine, having a strange man touch me like that. I hadn't hardly been touched in my life, except for punishment, before the last two weeks.

Buying our tickets at the last minute like we did, we had to take the long way down through Kansas, and we had some layovers where we had to wait. But I never minded it. All them hours with no chores was like a dream to me.

The four of us, we had seats facing each other—me and Sam on one side, and Alta Bea and Harold on the other. At first it was odd seeing them two together, but after while I got used to it and seemed like they always had been a couple. Alta Bea, she was near as tall as Harold, and she had grown into her womanhood. She had a nice long face with high cheekbones and full lips, and of course her hair, which any woman would love to have half that much of, had a nice natural wave in it.

Harold, he never let a minute go by without filling it up with talk. Right off he talked about his job. Like I thought, he was a salesman.

"Right now I'm calling on retail stores in eastern and northeastern Missouri—that's my 'territory,' as we say." He was talking to me mainly, since Sam and Alta Bea already knowed what he done. "Cleaners, patent medicines, mouthwash, waters, ladies' elixirs, that sort of thing. Sundries, too. If you've bought Brasso or Listerine in the past year, I probably sold it!" He combed his fingers through his hair, something he done a lot.

Alta Bea, I seen her put her hand on his wrist, and he lowered his voice. "But I never stop investigating other opportunities that I have every reason to believe will be even more remunerative." Harold's talk was like the man teacher's but different some way I couldn't put my finger on. Harold and Sam, they made an odd pair, Sam being quiet and plainspoken like he was, but wasn't none of us had a lot to choose from in friends, coming from where we come from.

Now Harold, wasn't hardly nothing he talked about—and he talked about a lot of things—but what he mentioned how much it cost, how much you could get it for if you knowed people, how much commission he got, how much the stores marked things up, and on and on. Now the people I knowed, they'd as soon talk about their bowels as their money. But Alta Bea, she never said nothing, only put her head back and half closed her eyes.

After while Harold dozed off. Sam, he pulled two pieces of paper out of his vest and give them to Alta Bea. He leaned over and talked low to the both of us. He'd wrote up a note for the eighty dollars she loaned him—he had managed to save up another twenty dollars himself. The note promised to pay Alta Bea seven dollars ever month for eleven months, then fifteen dollars, total ninety-two dollars.

"That's too much interest," she said softly. "You could get it for a lot less from any bank."

"Couldn't get it from no bank at no rate," he said, frowning.

She signed both copies and give one back to Sam, and nobody said nothing much for an hour or so, till Harold woke up and said, "Who's hungry? Let's break out those sandwiches."

After we eat, Harold brought out cards and we played pitch for a while and then hearts. These was games Mama'd showed me when I was a little girl, to teach me my numbers. Then the three of them got to playing pinochle, which I never learned, and I set back and looked out the window at the scenery passing by, though I hardly seen anything. I thought about Sam, about getting married tomorrow, about what was going to happen tomorrow night, about the years to come. I couldn't get a clear picture of none of it.

233

I could picture Mama, the children, the places us Winslows had lived at, but I had a strong feeling things was going to be different for me and Sam. I wondered, did Mama think about the future when she was first married? Did she picture the new things in the world that wasn't there when she come of age? And Daddy—did she have any notion how he was going to turn out, or was that a miserable surprise?

I didn't like the turn my thoughts had took, so I went back to when I was real little, far back as I could, before Dacia come. I don't know if Timmy was even born yet. All I could recall was scraps and snatches, but I did remember Mama laughing one time with her head throwed back and her mouth wide open—a happy laugh, not mocking—and she rocked back and forth and closed her eyes and squeezed out happy tears and rubbed her eyes and laughed some more. I remembered her hair—back then she had it did once in a while—and it was dark brown and curly and smelled sweet. Seems like she had on red lip rouge, and we was outside in dappled shade setting on a quilt, though I might have made that part up. I didn't have no notion what she was laughing at, but remembering this moment, I shivered and felt alive and new all over again, like I was still four year old.

That may be my oldest memory—either that or the bad dream I often had about heavy drapes rippling next to my bed, casting shadows where devils might lurk.

Next thing I knowed, the train whistle was shrieking and we was in Kansas City. We had to wait an hour there to catch the westbound train to Topeka, so we walked around in the train station. You never seen a building so big, all made out of white stone. They had a clock must have been six foot tall.

Alta Bea and Harold, they went into a place and tried to order a drink, but they found out there wasn't no sales of alcohol allowed in Kansas. They was laughing when they come back—it turned out they'd both brought a flask. Sam, he took a sip out of Harold's, but I didn't have none. Alta Bea and Harold kept on drinking after we got back on the train.

Wasn't long before Harold started telling jokes. He told one about a man in a hotel went to complain about mice fighting in his room, and the hotel man said, "What do you expect for a dollar? A bullfight?" I reckon a salesman's got to know them kind of stories. After while, and after he drunk some more, he said, "You know what a lady says—'You loved me before we were married'—and the husband says, 'And now it's your turn.' " He looked from me to Sam and winked, and Alta Bea giggled and took a drink out of her flask. Then Harold told a couple more off-color stories like that.

I excused myself to use the bathroom. As I squatted there over the hole, with the crossties flying by, I welcomed the swirling air underneath me. I didn't hardly want to go back, tell the truth. Harold give me a feeling like being wrapped up tight in cotton batting, smothered.

From Topeka we went south through Emporia and El Dorado. When we got to El Dorado, why, Harold pointed out there was a big oil derrick right in the middle of town. He'd been looking into the oil business in this part of southeast Kansas, he said. They'd had a huge strike the year before, and they was putting up derricks all over. Sure enough, when we got to the countryside again, why, there was bunch of them—maybe thirty or forty—sticking up like Christmas trees in a one-square-mile section. Harold, he got excited when he seen them oil derricks. To me they looked ugly. Didn't belong there in the prairie grass, seemed like.

After a little bit, it got dark outside. There was sleeping berths on the train, but we'd bought the cheapest tickets and didn't have no place to sleep. We laid back our heads and dozed as best as we could. I reckon I fell clear asleep sometime after midnight.

We got to Turner Falls, Oklahoma, about mid-morning. When I climbed down off the train, the air hit me—breezy, warm, dry, and sweet-smelling, with things in bloom. After the smoky train car, the outside air felt so good you could taste it, seemed like.

We walked three blocks to the justice of the peace's house. His wife, only thing I remember about her is she had her hair coiled up like a snake. She give us papers to fill out, which we done. I wrote my name, Albertina Sweet Winslow—Sam didn't know Mama'd give me her maiden name for my middle name. That tickled him. I give my true age of sixteen, and nobody said nothing about it one way or the other.

The justice of the peace, I don't remember him at all, except he smelled like cigars.

It cost two dollars, and I believe Harold give him fifty cents extra for his trouble. We didn't have no ring, which I didn't care about, long as it was legal.

When the four of us walked out of the house, I remember thinking Oklahoma was the prettiest place I'd been in since I was a girl in Kentucky. I felt like I didn't have no cares at all.

While the men went to rent a horse and wagon, me and Alta Bea went in the store and bought some light bread and lunchmeat and a box of little lemon cookies. "Do you feel different?" she asked me, but I just said, "I forgot to bring aspirin powder, I got a crick in my neck," and walked over to where the medicines was at.

Harold come into the store and asked the

lady where could he get some cold beer, but it turned out Oklahoma was dry like Kansas. He grumbled and bought us some pop, the first time I ever seen pop in a bottle. Sam got a pack of cigarettes.

Outside, Sam jumped up in the wagon seat and then reached down to help me up. He wasn't paying much mind, and when he grabbed aholt of my arm just above the elbow, he squeezed so hard it hurt like the very devil. I don't believe he knowed his own strength. Either that or he'd been working with horses and men for so long, he wasn't used to handling a woman's flesh. Anyhow I yelped like a pup and jerked my arm away.

Seemed like everthing stopped. Alta Bea and Harold froze where they was. Sam turned his face to me and give me a look like I was blaming him for hurting me apurpose, which I wasn't. It felt like I needed to say something, or he did, but I didn't have no idea what.

The moment passed, like they all does. Harold made a joke, and I grabbed aholt of the wagon seat and climbed up. My arm felt like it had a rope burn.

We drove out to the falls to eat our dinner. Where they had dug ditches along the road, you could see the dirt was red as rust. I never seen nothing like it.

The falls, now, they was real pretty, with the

water all boiling up and foamy. There was one channel in the stream where the water flowed ankle-deep over flat rocks, rippling the moss like hair. Harold dared me and Alta Bea to go wading, and we pulled up our skirts to our knees and stepped in, but only for a minute. The water was ice cold. Me and her, we got tickled and laughed till we couldn't hardly breathe.

That night in the room I put on my nightdress and crawled into bed while Sam washed up in the washbowl. He'd pulled off his shirt and had his suspenders hanging from his waistband. He rubbed his face and run his wet hands through his hair. Then he slipped off his trousers and come to bed with his underdrawers on.

I recollected something Memaw had told me when I was a girl—"The only thing uglier than a naked woman is a naked man." But then she always had a hard time taking pleasure in life, seemed like.

"Big day," Sam said.

I nodded.

He give me a smile and leaned over. I held my mouth up to let him kiss me, but when I felt his tongue, which he hadn't done before, why, I pulled back. I reckon it was just nerves.

He slipped off the bed and reached into his bag. "Here, look at this."

I could see it was a photograph, but the light

was dim and I couldn't hardly make it out. There was a window on the wall beside me, so I pulled back the curtain to let some light in. It was blue twilight.

When I seen what it was a picture of, I like to died—a woman with her skirt pulled up. Her hands was holding her legs apart, and you could see everthing she had. I hadn't never saw a woman's parts so close. Even when Mama had the babies we kept her covered up with sheets. And then off to one side a man was standing there, naked as a jaybird. All you could see was his front half. Couldn't see his face.

I never had imagined such a picture existed.

"Lord *God.*" I dropped the picture, and it fell into Sam's lap. I dug my heels into the mattress and shoved myself backward as far as I could into the corner.

Sam's eyes got huge. "Oh. Oh, Bertie. Oh."

I pulled my nightdress tight around my ankles. I couldn't tell which I was the most—shocked, mad, disgusted, scared, or just bewildered.

"Oh, Bertie." Sam's shoulders slumped down. His face had a dejected look, and he sounded like he was about to cry. "I got shit for brains."

The words that come to me was, "You won't get any argument from me on that," but to tell the truth I couldn't hardly get the breath to speak.

"I don't know how to treat a nice girl," he said. "Or any girl, come to that."

A shiver run through me. "You been treating me fine till just now."

He looked at the floor. "I'm gonna go outside and smoke." He got up off the bed, and it swayed. The picture fell off the mattress and rocked like a leaf to the floor.

"You coming back?" I said.

He pulled on his trousers. "You want me to?"

I wanted to say something—I started to—but he put on his hat and walked out the door. His feet was heavy on the floor planks.

After he left I picked up the picture and looked at it again. I covered up her parts with my hand so's I could see her face. She had a wrathful expression on her face, and she looked a lot older than me. Who was she, I wondered. Where was this picture took? Was she married to this man? Did they have children? I thought about it awhile, and then it occurred to me she must be a harlot. There was a woman back home that people said was one. Annis Drosselmeyer. People said she didn't have good sense, so I don't know. Maybe it was the only way she knowed.

More I thought about it, more I felt sorry for the woman in the picture. The man, him I wasn't so sure about.

It was a pure mystery to me why Sam would have such a thing. Seemed like there was a lot I didn't know about men, and a lot Sam didn't know about women.

In the morning he was there in the bed, snoring. I reached over and touched his bare shoulder with my fingers, and he moved a little. His flesh felt hard and cool, with a few coarse hairs, not like a woman's or a child's flesh, not like nothing I'd felt before. Then I smelled him, a horsey man smell, and I felt desire rise in me. I was shocked and surprised how like it was to hunger, how much it made my muscles twang and at the same time filled my heart. It felt like the whole world, everthing that mattered, was in our bed, the whole future, the whole past—everthing I ever wanted but didn't know I wanted. I understood then how come people sinned in that way. We was married, it wasn't no sin, but still it felt like it somehow, and somehow that didn't matter. I scooted up against his back and whispered to him was he woken up.

Now I'd seen animals mate, but I never knowed exactly how it worked. I thought the man just laid himself between your legs someway. I never knowed he put himself up inside you. I never knowed there was such a place in a woman, tell the truth—in our house, it was just "down there," and nobody talked about it, not Mama nor nobody. I was that ignorant. I closed my eyes and let him do it, and afterward I laid there and tried not to cry. Sam, he held me tight and rubbed his face on my neck. He kissed me and kissed me, all over. After while I felt like I wanted to open up my very skin of my whole body and wrap him up in it and never let go.

The train depot had a water closet for ladies, and me and Alta Bea went in there before we got on the train to go home. She grabbed me by the wrist. "Bertie!" She pointed to the bright purple bruise on my arm.

"Don't know his own strength," I said.

When me and Sam drove up to the house, why, Daddy was setting on the front porch with his arms folded. Soon's we got within fifty foot of him, he said in a loud voice, "If you're a married woman, you can just turn that buggy around right now. Won't have you on the place." He said "married woman" like it meant "hussy."

Sam pulled up the mules. "Sounds like he's been drinking." He handed me the reins and started to climb down.

"Where you going?" I said. "Let's—"

"What's he gonna do—shoot me?"

"He just might."

Sam smiled his big smile like he done. "I'll talk to him."

"He's got a long rifle," I said, but Sam was already halfway to the house. He took off his hat and stood back a ways. I seen Daddy reach down between his knees, but all he pulled up was a whiskey bottle.

Sam started talking real low. I couldn't hear what he was saying, but directly he walked slow up to the porch, still talking. Now Daddy, he dropped his head down, and his shoulders started shaking like he was sobbing. Sam stepped over to him, leaned over, petted him, and pretty soon Daddy and him was both setting there talking, and then after a little bit they was leaning back against the wall, drinking and crying and carrying on. If it wasn't for the drink, I might have laughed. They put me in mind of a couple of old biddy hens.

After while I clucked to the mules and drove on up. "I need to use the backhouse," I said, and Daddy shrugged and tipped up the bottle.

Sam, he had more of a silver tongue than I knowed. He wormed his way into that old man's heart, sure enough. He never told him yet we was breaking up the family, of course. That had to come from blood kin.

Later on I got a little supper, and Sam treated Daddy and the children to tales about the wedding trip. "We drove the wagon as far as Milan, and then we caught the train down to Turner Falls, Oklahoma. Went all through Kansas."

"You own a wagon?" Daddy slurped his coffee.

"Well, sir, that's how I make my living, hauling goods," Sam said.

"What's 'goods'?" said Opal.

"It's 'bads'!" Dacia cried. "He hauls *bads!* He's

a bad man!" You could tell she thought this was funny.

"He's a bad man!" one of the twins hollered. The other one made a face.

"You're the one that's bad," I said to Dacia from the stove. "If you're not going to behave—"

"You're not my mama!" she hollered. "My mama's went to Heaven!"

"You're not her mama!" the twins cried.

"Hush," I said. "We all know that."

"You don't!" Dacia hollered. "You think you do, but you don't! Mama, she—"

"Dacia, my girl, my sweet little sister-in-law," Sam said. "Looky here what I found." He reached over behind her ear and pulled out a shiny quarter-dollar, which she grabbed out of his hand. She folded her fingers around it. She was too old to be fooled by this trick, but seemed like she was content to have the money. Then he done it to Opal, who almost bawled, and the twins, too. Them boys whooped and hollered and run around the house like banshees.

"Wait till you see what I got you in Oklahoma," Sam said to Dacia. "You too, Opal. After supper." Both girls started up squealing, and there wasn't going to be no waiting till after supper. He raced them outside, and they come running back in the house carrying human-hair dolls dressed both alike in pink petticoats. They had bisque heads with glass eyes and painted-on eyelashes and lips. Dacia had the brown-haired one with the blue ribbon, and Opal had the one with the yellow hair and the red ribbon. The dolls' eyes opened and closed as them two girls run all over the house with them. You never seen the like.

I don't have no earthly idea when or where Sam boughten them human-hair dolls. It wouldn't surprise me none if he took them dolls with us just to have them for the girls when we got back home.

James and John, he'd got them each an iron truck. Them two flew out of the house and drug them trucks in the dirt till the chickens started following them to eat the bugs and worms they laid bare.

Things went bad for Alta Bea, just like she figured. While we was gone, her daddy'd had her things packed in trunks and set out by the road. Nobody said nothing about the money she took. It was enough of a scandal she went on the train overnight with a man.

Well, what did she do but move in with Harold, who lived in a boardinghouse in a town about ten miles from Obsidian. When I heard it, I was shocked and mystified.

She wrote me and asked me to meet her at an eating place on the road between the two towns. I drove our little buggy. When I got there, Alta Bea was setting in an enclosed automobile, black, which I gathered was Harold's. I walked up to the passenger side, but I couldn't figure out how to work the door handle. She leaned over and pushed the door open, and I climbed in. I was surprised how bouncy the cushion felt.

When I got a good look at her, I seen she had had her hair cut short and marcelled into finger waves, like the fashion was, and she had on pants like a man. She wasn't the only woman that wore them, of course, but I still wasn't used to how odd it looked. "You don't hardly look like yourself," I said.

"Oh, not you too." She made a face.

"Me too what?" I reckoned she meant Harold. I never knowed a man liked short hair on a woman.

"Never mind." She took out a cigarette and lit it. I was shocked she was smoking, but not surprised. She leaned back and gazed at me with her eyes half closed like a woman in a Lucky Strike ad. The smoke curled around her face and then floated out the window. "You're wondering when Harold and I are going to get married," she said. "Well, I'm not in any hurry."

"You ain't?"

"Why should I be?"

"But what if you . . ."

"There are ways, Bertie," she said.

I'd heard there was ways, but they didn't always work. I never said nothing about that. Instead I said, "But don't you *want* to get married?"

She took a deep drag. "Will you come and call on me?"

"It's hard for me to get around, what with the children. But I will if I can."

She narrowed her eyes and then nodded.

We talked some more, but it was strained. I couldn't get used to how much my idea of Alta Bea had been turned upside down, and how fast. And I didn't believe she was as calm and cool as she acted like. She didn't drink in front of me that time, but I reckoned she still was. I never knowed nobody that quit drinking once they got used to it.

When I got home, Sam wasn't a bit happy. "I don't think you should be seen with her."

I took off my hat and put it on the hook. "She's my oldest friend. And Harold, he's yours, ain't he?"

He winced. "It ain't good. That's all I'm saying."

"Are you forgetting we was there, too? Eloping?"

"It ain't just that. She's flighty—you know she is. And a drinker."

"Who's flighty?" Dacia, she come sneaking up on us.

"You are, that's who," Sam said, and he pretended like he was about to grab her up. She run off, laughing.

Sam turned to me. "I wish the best for

them two, but I don't see it coming to a good end."

"All the more reason to stand by them," I said.

He shrugged. "I better go unhook the mules." He put on his hat, and he kissed me on the way out.

I put on my apron and got out the skillet. I was halfway done with scraping the potatoes before I realized me and Sam'd just had our first argument as man and wife. I wondered, did Mama and Daddy ever fight like this and have it end without hollering? But fact is, even though it ended, the argument wasn't settled. I didn't like that feeling. I knowed it would stay there like a knot in a neck chain, rubbing your neck ever time you wore it.

Now Daddy, after the hullabaloo died down, he just assumed things was going to go along as they had been, only with Sam moving in and taking care of the farm while I minded the children, and nobody didn't tell him no different. It was less than two months before William and Dora was to be married, so Sam just kept paying rent on the rooms behind the dry goods store and hauled a few of his things out to the farm. Daddy moved into the barn permanent, and me and Sam slept in Mama's bed. That's where we made our first baby, there in that bed, if not in the hotel in Turner Falls.

Sam, he likes to tell the story of driving up in the buggy and Daddy setting there on the porch. *What's he gonna do—shoot me?* I've heard it a thousand times. Never gets old.

Chapter 13

Sunday week before William and Dora's wedding, we had a dinner at the house. The bride and groom was there, and Buck, the children, me and Sam, and Daddy. We'd told Daddy we wanted to have a final meal all together before the wedding, which Dora's kin was putting on at a church in town. Truth was, it was just an excuse so the three of us could tell him we was breaking up the family. I reckon we was twitchy as cats.

Now Dora, it was the first time I'd spent much time with her. She was the same age as William, but she looked like a girl. She was a little thing, smaller than me, and she had light-colored hair she wore in a pigtail down her back. While I was making the gravy, she set down on the floor and watched the twins playing with their trucks. After while she asked them did they like fishing, and they told her they'd been to the creek, but they'd only ever fished for crawdads. Dora mentioned her and William's place in Trenton had a pond full of pumpkinseeds. They asked her what pumpkinseeds was, and she leaned in close and told them they was also called sunfish or bluegills. She looked from one to the other like they had a secret, and she pulled a pencil and a piece of paper out of her pocket and drawed one for them. Then she asked them did they know what a tadpole was, and she drawed a tadpole, and then she made the frog legs on it, and the twins laughed and said that wasn't no frog, and she said, "Really? Because I have some in a Mason jar out in the truck, want to see them?" and they all three jumped up and run out of the house.

I was glad she come. I was used to the idea of losing the twins, much as I hated it, and it was a load off my mind to see how their new mama liked them and their ways. William, he could be stand-offish, and his squinty look could give children the willies.

When the twins come running back inside with the jar, I let them put it on the table to keep us company while we eat, though normally I wouldn't allow nothing filthy like that on the table. It was a noisy meal, so most likely Daddy didn't notice how quiet me and William and Buck was. We never hardly eat nothing. Most likely it wouldn't have set well on our stomachs.

After dinner, Sam pulled out four cigars, one for himself and one apiece for the other men. Buck, he had a bottle of whiskey. Then the men stood up and walked out to the back porch. Daddy didn't seem suspicious, though neither one of my brothers had ever drank in front of him since Mama's funeral that I knowed of.

Dora helped me clear the table, and then her and Opal and the twins took out the scraps to feed the chickens. Dacia dried three dishes. Then she flopped one back in the washbowl, splashing me with greasy water, saying, "This 'n's still got gravy on it." I told her to leave me be, and she went into Mama's room. Played cards by herself or set there daydreaming, most likely.

After a little bit I went out on the porch where the men was. The sweet, cool air raised goose bumps on my arms. It was the finest spring day we'd had so far that year, the kind of a day you want to run outside till you can't run no more and then lay in the grass and just open up your nose and smell. Seems like you can hear little plants and grubs pushing up through the dirt to their life. Time was, a day like that made me feel grateful to the Lord to be alive. Seemed like I still had a feeling for the Lord deep in me somewhere. Couldn't help it. I'd knowed about the baby for a while, but I hadn't told Sam yet.

First we had business with Daddy.

The men was crowded together, standing around on the small porch. When they seen me they moved apart, and I walked through the smoke and set down on the steps. Cigarettes was bad enough, but the smell of cigars like to made me throw up, which I was like to anyhow on account of the baby. But I felt like I had to be there. William and Buck, they was doing what had to be done, and Daddy needed to see we was all in on it. I felt like the girls and the twins, they had to see we wasn't making him do nothing but what had to be done. They was too young to understand this separation, but I knowed they would remember it all their lives, and I didn't want Daddy's sorrow or wrath to be the thing they remembered. My knees was knocking together, tell the truth. How did we know, really, that we was doing the right thing? I hoped we was. I hoped I was, and it wasn't just about me getting shet of Daddy.

William cleared his throat, and Buck said, "Daddy . . ." But he stopped.

William give him a look, and Buck started again. "Daddy, we think—I mean, we've decided—"

Sam put his hand on Buck's arm, and then he clapped Daddy on the shoulder. "Two of them married off! How's it feel, old hoss!"

Daddy seemed took aback for a minute, and then he grinned. "I know how to pick son-in-laws, don't I?" He had took to Sam, sure enough. He never bothered to hide how much he liked him, even in front of my brothers.

We all laughed. I slipped off of the steps and stood up in the grass.

"Who do you suppose'll be the next one to fall into the pit, after William?" Sam said.

Daddy sucked on his cigar. "Well, I reckon it'll be Buck'll leave the nest directly."

Sam said, "I reckon so."

Buck said, "See, Daddy—"

"How many more you got to go through?" Sam said. "After Buck, then there's Dacia, Opal—they'll go young, most likely, girls—but how long till the twins go? Twelve, thirteen, fourteen more years?"

Daddy upended the bottle and drunk.

"You're still a young man, Albert," Sam said. "Fourteen year, long time to wait."

Daddy closed one eye and peered at him. "For what?"

Sam looked around at the other men and then at me. "Bertie, will you excuse us?"

I truly had no notion of what was going on in Sam's head, and, by the looks of them, nor did my brothers. But me and Sam, we both trusted each other. I walked back into the house. I washed the roasting pan and put it away, and then I got out some ironing. I heard them out back, laughing and talking.

After while, everbody left except me and Sam and the children. Dora, she surprised me by grabbing aholt of me and hugging me close. Me and my kin, we wasn't huggers.

Buck drug Daddy out to the barn and put him to bed.

That night when Sam and me went to bed, he told me what happened out on the porch after I left.

"I said how sad it was, him losing your mama," he said. " 'She was sick for a long time, you was so patient, Albert, you helped her best as a man could.' Now your brothers, they like to choked on that, but Buck, he chimes in, powerful good husband and father, and so forth." Sam had drunk some whiskey himself, seemed like—I smelled it on him. I shivered in the bed.

"Well, next thing you know, your daddy says he's sorry how much he likes his drink—don't pinch me, he said it—and I says, 'Well, who don't?' and we all laugh. We was passing around the bottle, but it was him done most of the drinking."

I reached over and petted his arm.

"I told him, 'It's going on a year since Polly went—ain't it time you started back up?' And he looks at me fishy-eyed. So I says, 'You're a young man still, Albert.' " Then Sam, he painted a picture of Daddy living the life of a man-about-town, cock of the walk, women hanging off of him.

"He must've been drunk to believe that line of malarkey," I said.

"Who's telling this story?" he said. "So we bring up the children, how they love their daddy more than anything in this world and so forth, but, I asked him, 'What kind of a woman's gonna want a man with a brood already? Marrying kind, is what—last thing you're looking for.' And I poke him in the ribs, and he laughs. And then I say, 'Wouldn't it be a fine idea if us older ones was to take over the children's daily care at our own place?' "

"How'd he take it?" I whispered.

"Before he said anything, why, Buck says, 'I've got you a nice clean room over the barbershop,' and I said, 'Private! You can sleep late! Have your friends over, no squalling children around!' And Buck says, 'Two saloons close by, Daddy.' And William says, 'You can come and see them whenever you take the notion,' and your daddy says, 'See who?' And we all laughed like heathens."

I took the Lord's name in vain then, and Sam was silent for a moment. Finally, he said, "He whimpered some, and he hung his head for a while, but directly he seen the light."

"He give his blessing?"

"Not exactly," he said. "But he asked Buck, did that room have a rope bed or a spring bed, 'cause he wanted a spring bed."

"So it's over with."

He sighed. "It's over with."

I felt a surge of relief, sure enough, but somehow at the same time I was wroth Daddy didn't put up no fight. Maybe *wroth* ain't the right word, maybe it's more like *sad* or *let down*. But I didn't have no right to whatever feeling it was, I reckoned. After all, he'd done what I wanted him to.

Then Sam said, "There's more than one way to kill a cat besides choking him on butter," and in the darkness of our room I could almost hear the smile on his face. It made me smile, too, and then I felt like I knowed what it meant to be married—the world didn't have nothing for the two of us to be afraid of, and our life was going to be filled with wonder. I felt the strength that comes from cleaving together as one flesh, and I turned to him in bed full of heat and promise, and afterward we both cooed like the angels do, and in the darkness I told him our news, and we wept for the joy and marvel of it. We hadn't been trying to have a baby so soon, but we wasn't trying not to, either, and it seemed like things was turning out as good as we could have hoped for.

A week later, William and Dora got married, and we all started moving off of the farm, one by one. Daddy, he went first. Buck come to pick him up in his automobile. Me and Sam stood there, Sam with his arm around me. Before Daddy got in, he looked around the farm and said, "Seems like this family died when your mama went." He stared at me. "Too bad you ain't half the woman she was."

I opened my mouth, but Sam tightened his arm around me. "Don't be a stranger, Albert," he said, his voice cheerful. "It's only five blocks." He meant from our rooms behind the dry goods to Buck's barbershop.

As for me, Daddy's words, ever one of them, was branded in my heart. He was right—I wasn't half the mama that Mama was. When she died I had felt like I'd been hit in the face with a rock, like I couldn't do right by the children, I felt tired down to my bones, abandoned. And in the end I had failed them, especially the twins, and it ate at me, sure enough. But I didn't need to hear it from that old drunk, that liar and storyteller, who never loved me for a minute and who I once loved but now despised, and what the hell had he ever done for Mama but cheat on her, spend our money, and come home and get her pregnant again.

As I watched the car disappear over the ridge, it was like a fifty-pound sack of flour was lifted off of my back. That old cottonwood where Daddy'd hung John was still there, but Daddy was gone. One thing I knowed—it wouldn't be me walked them five blocks.

The next day William and Dora, they come by to take the twins home to their place. I served cookies and coffee, and while the four of them eat I gathered up the twins' clothes and toys in a cardboard box and carried it out to William's truck. When I got back, Dora was telling them there was a kite to play with when they got to Trenton. None of us told the boys they wasn't coming back to the farm, so when they left, they was bouncing around and hollering like it was a party.

Me, I held my tears till they was gone. I had Sam, Opal, and Dacia, and one on the way, but one child don't make up for no other one. It hit me I was losing the twins' whole rest of their childhood. Fifteen mile might as well have been fifty, and them living in another woman's house, no matter how much I liked her.

Sam, he seen me crying and come over and held my hand and just let me cry. Never tried to talk me out of it, like most men will. I was too young, and married too short of a time, to know then how lucky I was to have him.

The next day after that, why, me and Sam packed up the girls for the move into our rooms. Come time to go, I couldn't find Dacia nowhere—the house, the barn, nowhere. Finally, I remembered the smokehouse, and sure enough there she was, setting on a fruit crate among all the junk she'd drug in there. She was too tall now for the crate, and her knees stuck up in the air.

"Smells like dirt in here." I went around and picked up cups and saucers and silverware she'd took from the house, gathering them in my apron. They was coated with grime and dust. "So that's where my berry bowl went."

"You think you and Sam can make me go with you, but you can't," she said.

260

I walked over there and stood over her. "Dacia, we can. But that ain't the point."

"No, you can't."

"We'll be happy, we will," I said. "You'll see."

She put her hands over her face.

I wrestled with myself over my feelings—pity for her, pity for me, anger, impatience, defiance, fear. Finally, I said to her, trying to keep my voice even and calm, "This ain't my doing, Dacia. It had to happen."

She dropped her hands and narrowed her eyes like she was like to do. Cold as ice, she said, "You might fool Daddy, you might fool Sam, but you ain't fooling me."

I took in a sharp breath. There was so much wrong with what she said, and a tiny kernel of truth. I must've jerked my hands without realizing it—the dishes rattled in my apron.

She stood up and brushed off her skirt and walked out ahead of me to the wagon. As I followed her, trembling a little as I walked, I figured something out. In her eyes, we wasn't making her go. She was choosing to. I admired her backbone, though I feared the complexion her defiance might take, down the road.

Chapter 14

The rooms Sam'd rented, they opened onto the alley behind a block of businesses downtown. There was Karlsson's dry goods, then there was an empty storefront that used to be a millinery before the lady died that had it, and then there was a creamery. On the corner was a livery and auto repair shop. In Obsidian you'd see a dozen automobiles during the course of a day if you was out on the street. I say street, but it was just a wide dirt road.

We had three rooms—a front room and two little bedrooms—on the ground floor. There was "a path" in the alley, like we said in them days, meaning a path to the backhouse, and there was a pump. We shared both of them with the stores. Our rooms used to be storage, evidently—the windows was high up near the ceiling. We had three windows, and sure enough, Opal made up three sets of ruffled curtains, a child her age. And matching dishtowels, which she called "tea towels." Learned that from a book, I reckon.

It was different, being in town. Noisy compared to the farm, and you run into people a lot more. Everbody scurried around, seemed like.

Reminded me of a saying of Mama's—"Ain't nobody happy where they're at."

Now that things was settled, Sam went back to fiddling for dances ever little bit. He was a caller, too—all the square dancers knowed him. It's hard to find a good caller like Sam.

Seemed like whenever he had a minute, he was making music or thinking about music or talking about music or listening to music. He purely loved it, and he was good at it. He had a strong singing voice—gravelly, though he could bring it down soft in certain parts. It was hard not to like his singing, and you sure felt the lack of it whenever he finished a song. You wanted him to start another one soon's he got his breath. It wasn't just me, everbody loved to hear him, and he loved playing and singing, especially if there was people there to listen. He wanted you to sing with him. He'd say the words before each line so you could join in. He wanted you to laugh, and he wanted your heart to get lifted up. Even sad songs made him smile all over his face like he done. It was a wonder.

He knowed ever song anybody'd ever heard of. He made them up, too, by the dozens. He liked silly songs about frogs and grasshoppers, and he liked serious songs about broken hearts and salvation. If you sung a tune, he could play it, first the melody and then the chords. He never could read wrote-down music.

Besides the fiddle, he played the mouth harp. He was passable on the ukulele and banjo, and whenever he was in a room with a piano, he'd play that, too. He could drum, in a pinch.

Of course, we didn't have no radio nor electric yet, and at home it was just him playing for me and the girls, practicing like. Whenever Sam would get out his fiddle and start in, it give me that same feeling I had that first time at the dance. I always said, it felt like Sam's music went right into my heart without even going through my ears. And him always smiling, and his strong voice. Having music in the house made it seem like someplace you wanted to be, not just someplace to eat and sleep. Someplace special. Before Sam, I never knowed that would happen, or could happen. One day I was doing up the dishes, humming a song, and I felt something flood me and the thought come to me, *I'm happy. This is what it feels like.* Then I pictured the twins, how much fun it would be if they was there, too, and next thing I knowed I felt a couple tears trickle down my chin.

It's a wonder Sam had the breath to sing, he was working so hard. There was a lot of hauling to be done that summer, and he worked six days a week, sometimes seven. After while he sold the mules and got four draft horses and a spare, which he kept at the livery. He loved them horses, and he was partial to the work and there was plenty of it, but seemed like no matter how many hours he worked, he couldn't hardly make out. We was running a bill at the store, for one thing, and it was hard to always keep up with it. And getting ready to put the girls in school, I was shocked how much clothes and shoes cost, even with Opal making over my old dresses for the two of them. And doctor bills. Dacia was plagued by sick headaches. I give her cinnamon in milk, and if that didn't work I had her drink quinine salts—she hated the bitter taste—and if that didn't work, I built a big fire and heated water as hot as she could stand it and put her in a hot bath. I also bought aspirin powder and had her to sniff it in through her nose. Sometimes nothing worked, and she shut herself in their room and had me to hang a quilt over the window to keep out the light. She set in the bed with a bowl in her lap to throw up in.

And of course on the sixth of the month Sam wrote Alta Bea a check for seven dollars and mailed it to her in care of Harold's boarding-house to pay back what we owed her. He never failed to make that payment. And there was feed and doctoring for the horses, a new axle or wheel for the wagon. Things added up.

Then the day come when I found out how come we was having such a hard time. Out on errands I run into a man we knowed, Abel Kressler, who

Sam hauled with sometimes. Kressler was the kind of man that swung his hips when he walked like he owned the world.

When he seen me, he nodded. "Mrs. Frownfelter."

We was standing in the doorway of the lumberyard. I caught the insect smell of sawdust. "How's Orpha?"

"Tolerable." He pulled a knife out of his pocket and started in paring the nail on his middle finger. A bit of nail come loose, and he blowed it away with his mouth.

A dog barked nearby, and Abel turned to look. "That Herman Doering's dog? Sounds like her." He looked at me like I knowed all the dogs in Obsidian, or ought to. "Queenie," he said. "She does holler. Needs to be taught some manners."

He took off his hat and run his fingers along the brim. "Say," he said, "would you give your husband a message?" He put his hat back on. "Would you remind him he owes me near sixteen dollars?"

My face went red. "That's your business. You can tell him yourself."

"Oh, I *beg* your pardon," he said in a false voice. "I never knowed you was so—"

"Excuse me," I said, and I admit I flounced my skirt at him as I walked away.

"If he collected his *own* bills, he could pay

what he owes." His voice caught up to me, but I didn't look back nor answer.

Now I'd knowed Abel Kressler for a while, and I knowed he would sooner jump up to tell a lie than stand on the ground to tell the truth. But soon's he said this, I reckoned it was a fact. Sam was a soft-hearted man, and a lot of his customers was folks like us. If they couldn't pay him what they owed, I was sure he wouldn't hound them.

That night when he got home, I pulled him out into the alley and asked him was it true what Abel Kressler said.

"What're you talking to Kressler for?"

It irked me he answered a question with a question. "Passing the time of day."

He frowned. "You don't have enough to do around here?"

I had it in my mind to answer him sharp, but I just said, "Good and plenty."

"The man's a born liar, and my business ain't no business of his."

"Bertie!" Opal called from inside the house. "Me and Dacia's hungry!"

"There's biscuits in the cupboard," I called back. "Go ahead and eat one. We'll be in there shortly. One, mind." To Sam I said, "That's what I told him—talk to you."

"Son of a bitch beats his horses," he said. "Ain't got the sense he was born with."

"Opal's taking two!" come from inside the house.

"No, I'm not! *She* is!"

"I have to come in there, I'm gonna blister you both!" I hollered.

"Has this nice bay, sixteen hands," Sam said. "Balky, but he don't rest her like he ought to. So I'm hauling on contract with Lloyd Rice—bunch of skinners, ten or twelve wagons, Kressler's the lead wagon—and we're on the way to Milan, and I guess she balked. So he takes her out of harness and ties her to the wagon and starts beating on her with a board. Wagons go by, he says, 'Help me teach this horse,' and some of them's got no better sense than to grab whatever they got—chain, rope, two-by-fours, I don't know what-all. When I got there, her flanks was running red. I can't abide a man beats a horse."

This was a long speech for Sam. "You never told me this before," I said.

"Never come up."

One of the girls yelled something from inside the house.

"I better go feed the girls," I said. "And then I got to run to the store."

"Don't be all day," he said.

I looked at him to see was he smiling—Sam liked to tease me sometimes, and mostly I didn't mind it—but he wasn't. "I'll be as long as need be," I said sharp.

He set his mouth and looked away from me, down at the ground.

The look on his face give me a chill, like I didn't know him at all. I swallowed. "Something you ain't telling me."

Now he spit in the dirt.

"Sam." I reached out and tried to take aholt of his hand.

He pulled it away. "I told you before, I can't stomach being in nobody's debt."

"And I told you, we'll get it all paid off." These was tones of voice we hadn't used with each other—almost hateful. I gritted my teeth and said to myself, *Stop talking this way. Find some other way to talk.*

He said, "You think so, but that don't make it so."

This got my dander up even more, but for once in my life I never said the angry words that come to my mind. Instead, I said, "I think you're wroth with me, and I don't know how come."

He pulled out a cigarette and held it in his fingers. Almost breathless, he said, "We was on the county, off and on, when I was coming up."

For a few seconds I was too shocked to say nothing. Then I said, "Ain't no shame in that."

"Right," he said, sarcastic. "Your kin, you was on it, too."

"No, we wasn't." This come too fast, just like the other had come too slow.

He shrugged. "Well, now you know."

"Daddy'd sooner let us starve," I said.

"That's the point, ain't it?"

"You know him. Pride, he's got—for all the good it ever did a one of us."

It was getting on twilight, and Sam's face was in a shadow. "At school—well, you know how children is," he said.

I nodded.

He puffed out his cheeks. "Well, we had these chickens, couple dozen, maybe three weeks old. Chicks. Had their first feathers. Size of your fist, I reckon, but bony. We'd already eat the hens. Then something happened—I don't know what—and there wasn't no money. Daddy said they was too little to eat and they cost too much to feed." He lit the cigarette and sucked in the smoke. "He told me, 'Come sundown, shut 'em out of the coop, let the possums get 'em. Coyotes.' "

I winced.

"I started up bawling," he went on. "I must've been six, seven. 'They's half-starved already—now do as you was told.' " He shook his head and then laughed a little bit. "No six-year-old boy has feelings for a goldarn chicken. But Christ."

"No," I said. "Yes."

He blowed out some smoke. "Well, so, I never shut the gate. Nightfall, here they come, *cheep-cheep-cheep,* and one by one I wrung their necks. Dug a hole and buried them in it."

It was quiet for a long time. I pictured him, a little boy, digging a hole as night come on. How black that hole must've been. I wanted to ask him, *But can't you collect from your customers that owe you?* I almost did.

"Dad said to me, 'Don't never go in debt. They kill you with the interest. You can't never get ahead of it,' " he said. "Kind of a thing you don't forget."

"I reckon so."

"You better get to the store," he said. "I'll feed the girls." He turned and walked toward the door.

A couple days later, he come home and said he'd paid Abel Kressler his sixteen dollars and would I kindly not mind his business again. I never asked him where he got the money, though I fretted about it. I knowed how come he felt like he done, but I was worried his pride would bring a cloud over what we had and make it shrivel up and die.

Wasn't long after that, Sam come home with a big grin on his face, but he wouldn't talk about it till after the girls was in bed. By that time I was near wore out. I pulled out the bag of mending I kept under the bed and carried it into the front room. I got out a shirt of Sam's that was missing a cuff button, and I fished through the button box for a match.

Sam had his fiddle out, buffing it with a rag.

"Remember when we went through Kansas on the wedding trip?"

"I reckon I can remember something for three months," I said.

Either he never noticed I was mocking him, or he ignored it. He set the fiddle down and eyed the bow along the horsehair. "Seemed like a nice place."

"You know somebody lives there?" I found a white button the right size, and I lined it up where it needed to go, spearing it with a pin.

"Can't think of nobody offhand." He loosened the bow and put it in the case.

"But . . . ?" I threaded a needle and tied the knot.

"But what?"

I dropped my arms on my lap and just set there. Who brought up this subject anyhow? He was talking sideways, is what. He had a habit of it—trying to make you carry the conversation where he wanted it to go. Talking sideways.

He picked up the fiddle and run his hand over the fingerboard, holding it up close to his ear. "May need redone. Starting to buzz."

I never said nothing. I was tempted to sew the button on tight just to aggravate him, but a tight button's more like to pop off. Mama all the time told me, said, "Don't cut off your nose to spite your face." A lot of women's work is like that.

Next thing I knowed, Sam laid a newspaper on

273

my lap. I seen it was from El Dorado, Kansas, but I didn't look at what it said. I moved my legs till it fell on the floor. "You're in my light," I said.

He sighed. "They found oil in Kansas, Bertie. Year ago. Big strike."

"I know. Harold told us. On the train."

He set down next to me and put his hands on top of mine. "Teamsters is making three dollars a day there, more if you got your own rig."

"Doing what?"

"Hauling! Machinery, spare parts, pipe. Ten-, twelve-horse teams."

"Is that a fact."

"Oil hands is working round-the-clock, three shifts," he said. "They's got more hauling than they can get hauled."

I looked on the floor. "Where'd you get that paper?"

He let go of me and pulled back. "Three dollars a day! They's begging for men."

"Who's putting you up to this? Harold Satter-field?"

Sam got up and started pacing. "You *like* chasing the bills ever damn month? You *like* scrimping and scraping?"

"Never knowed nothing different."

"Well, me, I'm sick to death of it," he said. "I keep working twelve hours a day hauling for dirt farmers and grocery stores, ten years from now we'll still be living in these three rooms."

His arms flew up from his sides. "It's oil, Bertie. Steam's over and done with. Ever machine you ever heard of—cars and trucks, tractors—"

"We've got kin here," I said. "William, Dora, Buck, the twins. And there's the baby." I had my hand on my belly.

"I'm *thinking* of the baby," he said. "We can't get ahead here, I'm telling you."

Get ahead—that was Harold Satterfield talking. I never heard "get ahead" before in my life.

He was standing over me now. "And if we stay for this one, next thing you know there's a houseful, and you're stuck."

"Stuck? That's what children is to you—being stuck?"

He scowled. "No, hell no." He jerked out a chair and set at the table with his head in his hands.

"We don't know nobody there," I said.

"People's people, wherever you're at. Ain't no different than us." He was talking to the table, seemed like. "Think about the money. We could get ahead there. Think what that would be like."

If I was honest, I'd knowed something was coming ever since me and him talked that night in the alley and he told me about killing them chicks. I knowed something was coming, and this was it. I pictured the towering derricks I'd saw through the train window, how they seemed like a dark forest in a bad dream. And just now I recollected the smell that had filled the train car, a smell I hadn't even noticed at the time, seemed like. Now it come to me, an odor of death, long buried, forced out into the living earth from deep in the ground, a terrible stink, worse than when Buck found an old dog of ours dead under the granary and Daddy dragged it out, in pieces, and it was boiling with maggots.

Now I jumped up and run to the washbowl and throwed up. I retched till it felt like I was turned inside out. When I was done I broke the string of drool with my fingers and stood there hunched over and panting.

Seemed to me it was stark—Sam's fears, and his pride, they come from a deep place, sure enough. But so did mine. I understood how come he needed to feel like he could make money, but I dreaded the idea of leaving everthing I knowed, only to go someplace strange, where it wasn't no sure thing we would even make out. Dacia's words come to me—*you can't make me*—and my insides ached like I'd been kicked by a mule. I felt a groan go through me. I laid my head in my hands.

Then I felt the air move a little as Sam walked by. He got down a pan off the shelf and left it on the table, and he took the bowl of vomit outside. I heard him rinse it under the pump. He come back with it filled, and he had me to set down at the table, and he took a rag and dipped it in the cool water and wiped off my mouth and then my whole face. He rinsed out the rag and squeezed it and patted my neck with it. I must've had some pieces in my hair—he took a lock of it and run the rag along it and shook out the rag and done it again.

Now it's true I hadn't knowed very many men, but for sure I'd never knowed a man that knowed what to do when there was vomit or blood or them kind of things in the house and just went and took care of it without you saying nothing. Women, they knowed, but not men, as a rule. Sam, he just done it without one word. I wasn't used to nobody looking after me.

I don't reckon there was nothing I wouldn't do for him after that. I told myself, *After all, it ain't Russia, it's just Kansas.*

"Do people live in the oil fields?" I said.

"Single men mostly," he said. "Ain't enough rooms, and some of them's doubling up or sleeping outside in bedrolls."

"Outside?"

"Not us—not you, in your condition. We'll get us a place, don't worry. There's a little town I've got my eye on. Wiley, they have a hotel there." He took up patting me with the rag again.

"You been planning," I said.

"Well—in case. You know." He give me a big smile.

I sighed. "Reckon it wouldn't hurt to go down

there and see if we like it. If we don't, we can come back."

He let out his breath and laid the rag in the bowl. "You'll like it, I bet you will." He smiled his big smile. "My dad used to say, 'All's fish that comes to the net.'" He laughed, and then he stood up and danced around the room. "Three dollars a day! Three dollars a day! We won't know how to spend it all! Three dollars a day!"

Wasn't till I got ready for bed that it hit me— today it was a year since we'd buried Mama. No wonder my thoughts had went to such a dark place. I reminded myself, Daddy always said, us Winslows could fall into an outhouse and come out smelling like a rose. I hoped he was right for once in his life.

I couldn't get to sleep that night, so I got up and lit a candle and read the El Dorado paper. That's the first time I ever heard of a thing called a tarpaper shack. It was a little house built on a wooden frame, but for siding they used thick paper coated in black tar. It didn't do a whole lot to keep out the wind, the cold, the heat, nor the rain, the paper said, but it was cheap and lightweight and quick to build. They built some of these shacks on skids, so when one field petered out, why, they just hooked up a team of horses and drug the house to the next one. Tarpaper shacks was for people that was lucky. Otherwise you slept outside, like Sam had said.

Then I wrote a note to Alta Bea, could I come calling on Tuesday morning. There was something I wanted to talk to her about. Seemed like she always helped me think things through.

When I got to the boardinghouse where Alta Bea and Harold lived, I wasn't surprised he'd give the impression he was living higher than he was—Harold was like to puff things up. The house was at the end of a treeless, dusty street. There was boxes of trash scattered in the weeds, and a possum hissed and run off when I walked up the steps. Kind of a place where me or my kin might live, but Alta Bea, she was used to a lot better than this. I wondered what did she do all day.

The front porch had two doors on it. I knocked at the one had *Satterfield* wrote on a piece of paper in the window. Alta Bea come to the door directly.

"Where are the girls?" she said.

"At the barbershop with Buck and Daddy," I said. "They like to play like they're cutting each other's hair." I unpinned my hat. It was awful hot in that house.

She motioned for me to set on a cushion chair under the front window, and then she poured a glass of water from a pitcher on the table. It felt dark in the room, and I realized all the curtains was closed. I seen the ones on the window behind me was fastened with straight pins up and down.

I remembered the letter her mama'd give me for her, and I fished it out of my pocket.

At first she just looked at it in my hand while she poured herself a glass of water and gulped it standing up. Then she poured another glass and set down with it. She took the letter, glanced at the handwriting, and put it in her pocket. We neither one said a word about it. I was curious, but it didn't feel like it was none of my business.

"You look tired," I said. There was big circles under her eyes and a greasy shine to her face. Her hair was combed, but the waves was frizzy.

"How's Harold?" I said, to be polite.

"Work," she said. "Work work work." Her voice was breathy. She gulped more water.

It hit me, she was hung over. I seen it many times with Daddy. I felt a chill.

"We had so much fun on the train, Harold and I, remember?" She glanced around the room like she was looking for something. "He wants to get married, but I don't know. It's not what I expected. I don't know." She got up, poured herself another glass of water, and set back down.

She sounded so downhearted, I never said nothing. I wondered was it a mistake, coming here. Things seemed off here, just like they was at her folks' house. I felt an ache start up in my jaw. I couldn't think of nothing to do or say to make things right for her.

"Now he's got it into his head he wants to be

in the oil business." She took out a cigarette and stuck it between her lips. "He's like all sales-men—believes his own line of blarney."

"I know. Sam, he—"

"And move to Kansas," she said. "The middle of the desert." She lit the cigarette and sucked in three deep swallows, blowing the smoke in a stream out of her nose, looking up at the ceiling.

"That's what I come to talk to you about," I said. "Sam wants to go, too. I told him I'd go, but now—I'm worried the girls'll get homesick. Dacia like to had a fit when we moved off the farm."

Alta Bea brought her head back down and stared at the wall just past my head like she was reading something in the wallpaper. Her mouth went down at the corners, and her lips took on a swole-up, ragged look.

"And most all my family I got left is here." I took a long drink out of my glass. The water was warm, and I seen the glass had a film of some-thing in the bottom.

She made a sound through her nose. "I guess neither one of us wants to go."

"It's like when the folks moved us here from back home," I said. "You pull up roots, you feel like—Mama, she—"

"You and I would never have met, though." She stubbed out her cigarette, but a little curl of bitter smoke trailed upward. "I hate to think . . ."

We neither one said nothing for a while.

"Sam, he's bound and determined," I said finally. "Says he can't get ahead if we stay here. I expect he's right."

She leaned forward in her chair. "Me, I don't have anyone to stay for."

"Not even your mama?"

She frowned and shook her head. "It's hard for her. She's used to things—a certain way." Again she looked around the room. "She could just as easily write to me in Kansas as here."

I felt a stab for her. I knowed what it felt like not to have your mama.

She said, "Harold . . ." but didn't finish.

I said, "If a man thinks he can make money, seems like won't nothing stop him."

Alta Bea got out another cigarette and lit it. "Oh, I could stop him all right, but I have a feeling I'd live to regret it." She give a bitter laugh. " 'Live to regret it'—that's Mother's voice in my mouth." Now she set down her cigarette and looked me in the eye. "I think we should go. All of us. Get a fresh start." She blinked and rubbed her eyes with her two pointer fingers.

A fresh start—that notion appealed to me.

She took up her cigarette again. "And if I marry Harold, who knows. Maybe even Dad will overlook my indiscretion, especially if I'm far away."

We visited for a little while longer, wondering

what Kansas was like, though Alta Bea never said for sure if she would go or not. When I walked out on the porch, I took deep breaths. Hot and dusty as it was, it felt good to be out of that dark and smoky house.

I climbed up into the buggy and clucked to the horse. I wondered, if Alta Bea moved to Kansas, too, would it be sort of like having kin there? Would I keep from being lonesome? Strange as she was and much as she aggravated me sometimes, there was something about her, I didn't know what, that beguiled me, too. Always had been.

After while the *clop-clop, clop-clop* of the horse on the sand road made me drowsy, and I nodded off. I had a vision I was asleep on the ground underneath of an oil derrick, and Sam was hollering at me, trying to wake me up. I turned my head and seen a bear was lunging for me, a black bear with big yellow eyeteeth and its mouth full of maggots, and then I woken up for real. Startled, I took the reins and looked around. For a moment I never knowed where I was at, but then I seen I was on the road to Obsidian, and there was a girl walking toward me hollering at me to watch out where I was going. When I come upon her, I said, "Good thing he knows the way home," meaning the horse. The girl scowled and pulled her skirts to the side as we passed.

The thought come to me—much as I dreaded

moving, even if Alta Bea never come, at least I was going with a man I loved and wanted to be with. Sam, he was my kin now, him and the girls and the new baby to come. If other people lived in tarpaper shacks, I reckoned we could, too. I thought about Alta Bea in that dark room, and I couldn't help but feel a surge of thankfulness for my great good luck.

BOOK TWO

Chapter 15

When me and Sam come rolling into Wiley, Kansas—east-southeast of Augusta and pretty much straight east of Rose Hill—the sun was low, and there was dry clouds spread out along the edge of the world like wavy threads, stripes of pink and orange and purple. The last of the light flared behind the clouds, giving each one a white halo. The prairie grass took on a green-yellow glow, and the bark turned gray on the few little trees that was scattered around. The grass give off a dry, crackly smell.

A light wind come up out of the south and stirred everthing—the grass, our clothes, our hair—and I shivered inside and out. It felt like something big was about to start, like this was what my life'd been leading up to.

In the afterglow I looked over the town. There was a wide road down the middle, and to the south there was a store, a hotel, and a bank. A livery stable fronted the railroad tracks to the east. On the northeast side across the tracks was a pen with cattle, along with a small, flat building we found out later was John Naab's sorghum mill. Roads took off both ways, and I reckon there was fifteen-twenty houses. A ways off, half a mile or less, you could see farmhouses, with barns, horses and cows, some pigs and chickens. To the north and east was the Flint Hills—wave after wave of smooth-topped, flattened bumps of earth as if a giant had spilled globs of porridge. You never seen the like.

Everwhere else was flat. You could see futher than you could in Missouri, way futher than you could in Kentucky. Miles and miles. The prairie was flatter than it had looked from the train window when we run off to Oklahoma. I never knowed there was no place so flat. I thought, how am I going to make them believe, back home, how flat this is?

A handful of horses was tied up next to the buildings, and there was a few teams and wagons, a couple motor trucks, and a half a dozen automobiles. A woman was walking along the main road, carrying a round box. Two men was setting in the back of a motor truck with a dog. They stared at us for a second and then went back to visiting.

We rolled up next to the hotel, the tallest building in town, three stories. Sam clucked, and the horses come to a stop. "Reckon this is it," he said.

I stretched my back real hard till it popped.

He put his hand on my leg. "You'll like it here, Bertie, I bet."

"Nice-looking store." The last of the sunlight slipped away.

"See there?" He grinned with his whole face, like he done, and he hopped off the wagon and put his hand up to help me. Softly he sung, just like it was a real song, "Three bucks a day, sweetheart, three bucks a day." Seemed like Sam could always make me smile.

He got us a room on the second floor, hardly bigger than a broom closet but with a nice window overlooking the street. It had a spring bed, and when I laid down I felt like the Queen of Sheba. Me and Sam'd been on the road for two weeks, and my back was mighty tired.

The girls, we'd left them with William and Dora. We was going to send for them once we got settled.

Next thing I knowed, Sam was leaning over me, whispering. "Don't get up. I got hired on by a man at the livery. Gonna help 'em haul a boiler to Oil Hill."

"A what?" I hardly knowed where I was at. It was still dark.

"You can get breakfast downstairs if you don't sleep all day. Dinner too. I reckon I'll be back by suppertime." He leaned over, put some coins in my hand, and kissed my forehead.

When I woken up again, the only way I knowed it wasn't a dream was them two quarter-dollars in my hand. I laid there for a minute just to feel how good my back felt. Then I washed my face in the bowl and got dressed. I was awful hungry.

"Eggs and coffee is ten cents," the woman said to me when I set down at the table downstairs. "Fifteen if you want the ham." She was a stout woman with a mouth that sagged down. I felt sorry for her, though I couldn't think how come.

"Eggs and coffee." I dug into my pocket for the money.

"We'll put it on the room." She turned and headed out the doorway to the back.

"Put it on the room" didn't make no sense to me, but it was her dime.

When she brought it out, it was two fried eggs and potatoes and red-eye gravy. I hadn't never saw so much food for one person, or anyhow one woman, but I eat ever bite.

After breakfast I set out walking to look around town. In the bright sunlight I seen there was more buildings than I thought, and I noticed that the livery had a sign said AUTO REPAIRING. Ever block had at least one path.

I seen a big sign hanging sideways that said ARBOGOST STORE, and I walked toward it. The grass was beaten down where people had tread, but as I walked I scared up a grasshopper now and then. Off they flew with a whizzing sound. There was a little breeze and the smell of horse droppings. You could hear the tick of heat flies—

what some people call cicadas, or some people call locusts—getting ready to start buzzing soon's it got hot enough. When I got there, I realized it was the same store I seen the night before.

I was surprised how dark it was in the store after the sunlight.

"Hot out yet?" a woman said, and I like to jumped out of my skin. "Didn't mean to spook you."

Now I seen her standing behind a glass counter. "Tolerable."

I looked around the store. My eyes was drawn to a big metal can that said SWEET PICKLES, and there was bushel baskets and bins of onions, potatoes, and beans. The back wall had a couple shelves of can goods (store-boughten tin cans, not fruit jars), and there was a big box on the counter that had cookies, of all things.

The floor creaked as I wandered around, and I smelled dust in the air. I felt the woman looking at me. After while I come over to the glass case where she was standing. Close up, I seen she had a fine head of curly gray hair and a long, thin face.

"You passing through?" she said.

I leaned over and pointed in the case. "How much is the blue calico?" It come out raspy, which surprised me. Didn't sound like what I was used to.

"You look peaked," she said.

Now I seen the floorboards coming up to hit me in the face, and I thought what an odd thing that was. It felt like the world was going cockeyed.

When I come to, there she was with a flour sack towel, wiping my neck. She poured me a cup of water out of a pitcher, and I swallered it down.

"Here's a bucket if you need it," she said, and sure enough I bent my head down and throwed up my breakfast. I scooted away from the slop bucket and pushed it under a table with the toe of my shoe. The smell was fixing to make me retch again.

She poured another cup and handed it to me. "Drink it slow this time."

While I sipped, she told me the pump was west half a block, on the alley, if me or my animals needed water. After while she said, "Your cheeks are pinking back up."

She helped me get up off the floor, and she pulled out a rocking chair from the corner. I lowered myself into it.

She set down in a chair next to the table. "Whereabout's your husband?"

I told her.

"Did he say where they was taking the boiler?" she said.

"Don't recollect. Someplace where they're digging for oil."

"Oil Hill, maybe?"

"That's it."

"Dry as it is, he may be back by suppertime if he don't run into trouble," she said.

That word *trouble* lingered in my mind.

"They don't *dig*—they pound," she went on. "They take a giant post and pound a hole in the ground. The boiler makes steam, which is what they use to pound the post with. God-awful racket."

I tried to picture what she meant, but I couldn't. In my mind's eye I seen Sam, scrawny as he was, how he might be driving by in the wagon and get pounded into the ground by a giant post. Next thing I knowed, I pulled out the bucket and vomited again.

She come over and rubbed me on the back. She told me her name was Tillie Arbogost and she had six grown children and five grandchildren so far. Her husband'd up and left two years before on the train to California.

I felt like I needed to go back to the room and lay down. I rose up slowly from the chair, told her my name, and thanked her for her kindness, and then I stepped out again into the sunshine.

I was walking along the road toward the hotel when a man whispered, right next to me, "Are you saved, little mother?"

I looked up. His beard hung halfway down to his waist, and his clothes was wrinkled and raggedy. His skin was burnt brown. He wasn't much taller than me, and real thin. His eyes was pale blue.

"Excuse me." I took aholt of my skirt to pass him by.

"It ain't what you expect," he said.

I kept walking.

"You will need the strength of ten thousand angels," he said.

He was ten foot behind me, but it felt like he was still whispering in my ear. There was a chill along my arms. I recollected how people back home would say if you got a chill, it meant a rabbit just run over your grave. I wondered where would my grave end up. Would they bury me on the Sweets' property like Timmy, or next to Mama in Missouri, neither one with a marker? Or around here? Or someplace I'd never been to yet?

About that time I remembered I left my mess back in the store for Tillie Arbogost to clean up, but I didn't have the heart to go back.

Even with the window open, our room at the hotel was ungodly hot. I couldn't hardly get my breath, the air was so close. I took off my clothes but for my slip and washed my face and arms in the washbowl. Then I laid down on the bed.

I fell asleep quick, and I dreamed I was looking at my mama dead in her bed, but when I looked at her face, it was me. I woken up soaked in sweat. The room smelled rank.

I rose from the bed and walked to the window. The sun was almost straight overhead, so I figured it was about noon. Down below I seen some people walking by, but the man with the white beard wasn't nowhere in sight. I wondered, did I imagine him, like Daddy and his brothers imagined their dead uncle Seth riding up to the house on a mule named Jackie. I hoped so. I looked out beyond the town to the Flint Hills. Seemed like the sun was so fierce it washed out all the colors to white and shades of brown. I wondered, did the sun burn down like that ever day?

When Sam got back to the hotel, he was flushed with excitement. He'd met up with a man name of David Whiteside, who told him about a place for rent five miles from town. It had a barn and an orchard, and you could have the use of two or three acres for garden. The house, which belonged to the man's folks, was the original place they'd homesteaded in the seventies before they built the big house north of it a ways. Sam took it sight unseen and give Whiteside the four dollars cash he'd made that day. We was the luckiest two people in Kansas, was Sam's opinion. He treated me to a fried chicken dinner to celebrate. I didn't eat a whole lot, but it wasn't very good cooking anyhow. Seemed like they never done it like they done it back home, so that the goody stuck to the skin and got crisp. This breading tasted floury.

Sam asked me about my day. I told him I met Tillie Arbogost and she seemed nice.

I was tired when we went to bed, too tired to sleep. It was a long time before my mind quieted down.

We drove out to the house early the next morning. You couldn't hardly see the house from the road. It was set back a ways, partway up a slope, and there was trees clear around it.

"Nice shade," Sam said.

He found the gate and brung the horses to a stop. Wasn't no proper gate. You just pulled loose a wire loop that held two posts together, and then you drug the section of fence till there was room to drive through, which he done.

Then he looked around on the ground for a while. "Guess we'll make our own road." There must've been a road up to the house at one time, but evidently it was growed over.

Sam led the horses through the fence, closed it back, and then led them up toward the house. Now pasture ground is awful bumpy, and at the first jolt, I said, "Let me get down and walk."

"Better not," he said. "Whiteside says the Indians used to call this Rattlesnake Hill."

"Lord Amighty." I grabbed aholt of the spring-board and hung on, though it rocked awful hard.

When we got to the house, my heart sunk. Hadn't nobody lived there for years, from the looks of it. Bushes and trees had growed their-selves up through the siding on the south and west sides, and branches had broke through the roof in several places. Wasn't no window that still had all its glass. You could see daylight where the front porch had got loose from the house, and there wasn't no way to step up to the front door.

Me and Sam walked through waist-high weeds to the back, where there was a lean-to nailed to the siding. Looked like they'd used it for a summer kitchen at one time. We walked through the lean-to to the back door, which was stuck open.

I turned to Sam. "I expect animals been living in there."

"I reckon." He looked scared, tell the truth. Scared of me.

"Find the well," I said. "If the pump don't work, fix it. We've got to have water first thing."

"Don't you want to see inside?"

"No need to." I turned and walked out front to the wagon to get my bucket and my broom.

Long about noon, why, I was sweeping cobwebs in the northwest corner of the bigger bedroom when I heard knocking on the back doorjamb. "Anybody to home?" come a reedy little voice.

The white-haired lady at the door was bent over so bad she had to crane her neck to see in front of her. I seen she had a fruit jar of water and a bundle wrapped up in brown paper. There was wet spots, so I reckoned it was food. Looked like she was about to drop them.

"You must be Mrs. Whiteside," I said. "Here, let me get these things."

"Mrs. Frownfelter."

"Call me Bertie." I looked around for some-place for her to set, but we hadn't unloaded no furniture.

"Let's go sit on the wall," she said.

"The wall?"

She never answered, just got herself turned around and limped away—she used a big black cane—and led me to a little rock wall maybe fifty foot behind the house. It was made out of light-colored stones I found out later was limestone, which the Flint Hills was full of. Besides walls, they used limestone for building foundations, and even fence posts. The stones, they're awful pretty. Rough and chalky, ranging from browns to yellows to whites, all shades.

The little wall was maybe fifteen foot long and a couple foot tall, and there was a big hackberry tree giving shade there. Mrs. Whiteside, she eased herself down on it and rocked herself sideways a couple times to settle in, and she leaned her cane against her thigh. I set next to her.

She asked me where was my husband, and I told her he was in town getting supplies.

She nodded and then closed her eyes. Took me a few seconds to realize she was praying, and by the time I did, she opened them up again. "Egg salad," she said.

I unwrapped the sandwiches and handed her one. When she reached for it, I seen her hands was gnarled. Her knuckles was swole up and red, and the fingers was all turned sideways. She took aholt of the sandwich between her two hands, using the first knuckles. It hurt to look at them hands. I tried not to stare, like Mama'd taught me.

Mrs. Whiteside took a bite of her sandwich, and I started eating, too. Truth to tell, I'd never tasted nothing so good as that sandwich, rich with cream or something—I couldn't tell what—that I never knowed egg salad to have, and maybe sugar. I ate it like I craved it.

After while she turned her head and looked at the house. "Land, it's gone to rack and ruin. I told David, we have to get some people in there, or tear it down. You tried the well?"

"Pump's broke."

She shook her head. "I'll get Kenneth down here. If he can't get it going, I'll send water. He's my other boy. You met David."

"My husband did."

"And the roof! And the windows! I didn't

know it'd gotten so bad. My stars." She sighed. "Disgrace to humanity." She brought her sandwich to her mouth and took another bite.

We both eat for a while. "Your husband ain't well?" I said.

She frowned. "Stroke."

"I'm sorry to hear that."

"We've got ten, twelve men working for us now. Oil well." She pointed her head to the north, and I heard her neck bones creak. "Worse comes to worst, they can sink you a new one—water well, I mean."

She looked again at the house. "I grew up in that house. Disgrace to humanity." I looked at the house, and when I looked back at her, I seen her lean forward with her weight on her knuckles and struggle to get up. I reached out to help her, but she frowned and pushed me away with one crippled hand. She scooted over the rough rocks and somehow got herself to stand up, and you could hear her hipbones as she rose. The sound of it—raw bones rubbing together—run a chill up my spine. I'd seen crippled people before, but nothing this bad. I pictured her up in the big house, with her husband sick and her boys growed up.

She stood there for a moment leaning on her cane, gasping. I rose and put my arm on her elbow, but she shook it off.

"You need anything," she said, and she started

off limping through the weeds, heading up the slope to the big house.

"Thank you for the sandwich," I said, but she never turned around nor said nothing else.

I opened the jar and drunk down half of it, watching her. It was going to take her a long time to get to the big house, a long, painful trudge. I wondered, how come she didn't have one of the men bring her down here in a buggy? How come was she putting herself through that? Then I remembered I meant to ask her what the limestone wall was for, but I never had the chance.

Wasn't a couple hours later, her son Kenneth come down with two cream cans full of water in the back of his truck. He had the look of a school-teacher, with spectacles and his hair greased and combed back, but he was wearing boots and overhauls like regular men done. He looked about thirty, younger than I expected from his mother's age. Maybe she was younger than she looked.

Kenneth took one look down the well—it was in the lean-to on the back—and told me it was half-full of dead animals and they'd start digging a new one in the morning. Meanwhile, he'd bring water twice a day, and would I mind putting the empty cans out back.

Then he took out a notebook and pencil and walked over to the porch, and I followed him. He looked at the place where the porch had split off the house and wrote in the notebook. He never said nothing, so I asked him, "You and your brother, you take care of the folks' place?"

"David's in charge of the oil business, which I guess is what we're in now. Don't farm much anymore." He took out a pocketknife and poked the sill of the house. "Me, I do what he tells me to, always have." He laughed and moved along the foundation, where he poked the sill again. "No dry rot, that's good."

He circled the house, writing things down, and then he walked over to his truck.

"You know what that wall's for?" I pointed to it. "Don't seem to go noplace."

He blinked like he'd forgot I was there. "That wall?"

I nodded. What other wall did he think?

"Huh." He squinted at it. "When we were boys, she made us carry stones down here and build on it whenever we got in trouble." He laughed. "Who-eee. Spent many an hour tromping up and down that hill, hauling rocks." He climbed into his truck, nodded to me, and drove off.

One day in late August I got two letters in the same mail. I read the one from Dora first. It was easy to picture her when you read her letters, they sounded just like her. Wasn't much news in this one, just that Dacia was growing fast, Opal was about the same, they was all well, hadn't

302

rained in two months, the twins was thriving, the neighbor had a new automobile, Dacia claimed she seen an aeroplane one day hanging the wash out, it was a sight, Buck's barbershop was real busy, how was the house coming along, did we have water yet, and so forth. Write soon, we miss you both, we love to get your letters.

The other letter was from Alta Bea. She'd made her mind up, her and Harold was getting married in a couple weeks and settle near Oil Hill, had I heard of it? Was it decent? And they'd bring Dacia and Opal on the train with them, if we was ready for them.

She said she was sorry for how sick she was the last time we seen each other that day at the boardinghouse. "Sick" was what she wrote, and her hung over. She was feeling better, now that things was settled and she was going to be married. She reminded me she'd loaned me and Sam the money to elope—I knowed Sam had never missed a payment, she just wanted to remind me I owed her—and she said, "Do you remember that day at Turner Falls, when we went skinny dipping?" Which of course wasn't true at all. We'd only waded in up to our ankles, and we'd kept all our clothes on.

She closed by saying she missed me something fierce and couldn't hardly wait to see me again and to let her know about Dacia and Opal.

I read Alta Bea's letter with trepidation. Her

getting married and coming to Kansas, that was one thing when we was back in Missouri, but now it felt different. It felt like me and Sam was tangled up in something I never seen coming. I thought about how Alta Bea was turning into a drinker, and how she was marrying a man she wasn't sure about and a sneaky one at that, and how after they got here we'd be the only people she knowed, and with us being beholden to her—it all give me a queasy feeling in my stomach. But I also remembered how Alta Bea and them, they'd been awful good to me and the children when we needed it.

When Sam got home, I met him in the lean-to—only strangers used the front door—and told him the news. "Is that right," he said. "Well, good for him. About time." He dipped his hands in the washbowl and rubbed them over his face.

"I reckon we're ready," I said. While the men was hammering on the house, I'd scrubbed and whitewashed the walls and floors till they was practically raw. Ever little bit I'd feel a pang of lonesomeness, but it never lingered because there was too much to do.

"Maybe we can get a band going, banjo player. Just need a second fiddle, maybe a piano. I reckon they dance around here, don't you?"

Sam, he was always thinking way above me. Now he looked at me and said, "Everthing's working out, ain't it?"

"It'll be good, having Alta Bea and Harold with the girls on the train," I said. "I was worried about sending for them, all alone."

He took me in his arms. "You're the one always says, worry's interest paid on trouble you ain't had yet."

"Let go, your arms is wet."

Well, he wouldn't let go. He said that old lean-to reminded him of when we used to meet in the cabin on the Snedeker property when we was courting, and how much he wanted then to take my virtue, and why didn't we spend a little time in our bedroom we had all to ourselves while we still could. He always was a smooth talker, Sam was.

That night I wrote Alta Bea back and wished the two of them well. I teased her about changing her name from Snedeker to Satterfield. I wrote to her how Memaw used to say, "Change the name and not the letter, change for worse instead of better. Ha ha." I caught her up on the house—besides the new well and the roof, the windows was done and the bushes was cut back, and the second bedroom was ready for the girls, though she and Harold was welcome to sleep in there till they found a place. And I told her we couldn't hardly wait to see everbody.

Chapter 16

The day Alta Bea and them come was a hot one, and there wasn't no shade to stand in by the tracks, and the train made an awful racket slowing to a stop. Soon's I seen Opal wave from the window, I started up bawling. Till that moment I hadn't let myself miss them two, especially Opal, and now it hit me. Them, the twins, Mama, my brothers, even the kin back in Kentucky, even Daddy. I missed them all. Then I reminded myself I was lucky to have my sisters, and I swallowed back my tears.

The first one down the steps was Dacia, and I was surprised—it looked like she'd growed half a foot since we'd saw her last, though it had only been a couple months. She was just eleven, and here she was getting bosoms and hips, and her face sharpening up.

She said to me, "Well, I hope you're happy, making us come all this way." The words of a girl, but her manner and voice seemed like a woman, or soon-to-be one.

Alta Bea was close behind. "Dacia!"

"I'm so glad you come," I said to Alta Bea. "You too, Dacia." I tried to touch her on the cheek, but she pulled her face away with a frown.

"Harold," I said, nodding to him.

"Bertie." He looked around. "Where's Sam?"

"Hauling to Wichita. Back tomorrow, most likely."

He looked disappointed. To Alta Bea he said, "I'll see that the bags get to the hotel."

"Ain't you staying with us?" I said, but secretly I was relieved they wasn't.

Alta Bea just shrugged and pointed her head toward Harold, like it was his idea.

Now Opal come down the steps, and I grabbed her up. "How was your trip?"

"Got a lot of mending done," she said, serious.

"The poor thing," Alta Bea said. "She couldn't keep anything down, the whole way."

I looked at Opal, alarmed. "You all right?"

She smiled. "Just hungry a little bit, is all."

"Is it always this hot?" Alta Bea said. "Let's go inside." She started for the little depot.

"I hate this place!" As soon as this was out of her mouth, Dacia took off running. I seen her duck behind a tree.

"I'll get her," Alta Bea said.

"Let her go," I said. "Ain't no place she can go." But Alta Bea was already after her.

I took Opal's hand. "Nice clean sheets tonight, won't that be nice?"

Harold come back, slipping his wallet into his jacket pocket. "Where'd they get to?"

"I expect they'll be along," I said, and then there they was.

I'd borrowed the Whitesides' wagon, and now I climbed up on the spring seat and took the reins. Alta Bea set beside me.

"We're off, like a dirty shirt," I said. One of Mama's sayings.

As we rode along, Alta Bea remarked how pretty the Flint Hills was.

"Mrs. Whiteside, our landlady?" I said. "Her son David, he has a book says there's rocks under the ground that go back to before there was people. You think that's true?"

She wiped off her neck with her hankie. "Rocks and oil both."

"Just imagine what-all them rocks has saw."

Alta Bea nodded. "It's a wonder." She got out a cigarette and lit it.

"Ugliest rocks I ever seen," Dacia said.

The minute we pulled up to the house, Dacia said, "If you think I'm living in that shack, you got another think coming."

"It ain't so bad," I said. "You'll get used to it, I expect."

"Bigger than the home place," Opal said.

Everbody jumped down off the wagon, and we each stopped and dipped us a drink out of the graniteware pot on the front porch. Then the girls, they lit out to have a look around. I told them to watch out for snakes if they was going up to the barn.

I had the chicken and noodles already cooked—my best company meal—and I'd set the table with what was left of Mama's white plates and cups, along with the silverware with the shell design. I also had out her big serving bowl with the hand-painted pink roses. Before we left I'd give Dora the matching platter, and though it was chipped she'd gotten misty-eyed.

"Let's go ahead and eat," I said to Alta Bea and Harold. "No telling when the girls'll get back."

"Pretty table," Alta Bea said. She got out her flask and poured some whiskey in her and Harold's teacups.

All Harold wanted to talk about was the oil business. "The Whitesides, they've got themself a well," I told him. "Got a wildcatter already spudded it."

His eyes lit up. "It prove out?"

"He has this oil book," Alta Bea said. "All he did on the train was read, read, read."

"Big pool north of the ridge, evidently," I said.

"Oil, oil, oil," Alta Bea said.

"And a Mr. Fox, he already put up a couple dozen wells near where the Whitesides' is, and there's a big outfit from back east has put some in."

"Let's go see it, want to?" Harold said.

"Please," Alta Bea said, rolling her eyes. She gestured with her forkful of noodles.

The girls come back after while. Opal, after she eat, begged off going to the oil field, saying she needed a nap. Dacia said she would go, she needed fresh air. The house stunk, in her opinion.

It wasn't but half a mile to the Whitesides' north pasture. Walking through alfalfa gets tangly, but it does give off a sweet, grassy smell. Harold and Dacia, they run ahead up and over the ridge, and me and Alta Bea lagged behind. I asked her how her and Harold got along with the girls during the long trip from Obsidian.

"Dacia's a headstrong girl," she said.

"She'll be fine once she gets used to the place, I reckon."

"*Getting used to* isn't in her way of thinking."

"She's mouthy, don't I know it, but she's a good girl in her heart," I said. "She don't scare me none." I was saying what I hoped was true. But soon as I'd seen Dacia at the depot, and how grown-up she was getting, my old dread had came back to me. Didn't seem like I had no way of keeping her under control—and what might she take it into her head to do, once she realized that? She'd been on a bad road for as far back as I could remember. And now even Alta Bea seen it.

"William told me she talked about running away," Alta Bea said. "More than once."

"Dora wrote me. I said, where-at's she going

to go? Said, she's got no place to go, and that's where she's going—no place." Whistling past the graveyard, is what we used to call it when you was pretending you wasn't scared.

Alta Bea stopped. "Times are changing, Bertie. Girls just take off by themselves, heading west to California and Oregon. They think they'll be in the pictures or strike gold."

This shook me, though I shrugged. "Likes to hear herself talk, is all."

She put her hand on my arm. "Terrible things happen to them. Read the newspapers."

I pulled away and looked to the top of the ridge, where Dacia and Harold had disappeared. "I tell you what, she sure has growed since I last seen her. Don't seem like it's been long enough for her to have growed so much."

"Maybe it's been a long time since you took a good look at her," Alta Bea said. "Maybe you aren't seeing what's there in front of you."

"I see good enough." I heard the sand in my voice.

Neither one of us said nothing for a little bit. The air felt thick.

Finally, Alta Bea said, "Come on, let's go look at that oil well. Harold's liable to buy it before we get there."

The Fox-Whiteside field was little compared to the El Dorado field, which we was told covered more than thirty square mile. But for all that, Whiteside was plenty big. When me and Alta Bea made it to the top of the ridge, we stopped and looked. Besides the derricks, there was machines and outbuildings of all kinds, wagons, trucks, stacks of pipe and parts, men running around carrying things, hammering, climbing up and down, talking and hollering. And everwhere clouds of soot, smoke, and steam.

"Men," she said. "Seems like they can build anything as long as it's big and noisy."

"These is modern times, sure enough," I said.

Alta Bea blinked and nodded.

I seen Harold and Dacia down there standing by the Whiteside derrick, and me and Alta Bea walked down the slope.

"What is that smell?" she said.

"Dead things from deep in the ground don't smell good."

When we got there, Harold was standing just inside a little shack next to the derrick. There was a man with him, black-faced with dirt. He started up a piece of the machinery, which made a terrific racket. I couldn't hardly bear it.

Dust rose in billows all around us.

Harold pointed to a big wooden part of the derrick that looked like a ladder. "Walking beam!" he hollered. "Pull the cable up, boom! Drop the bit! Boom! Big hole!"

"I can't abide the noise!" I hollered.

Harold nodded to the man, and the three of us headed back to the alfalfa pasture. Only when we got there did I notice I'd been holding tight on to my belly.

I looked around. "You seen Dacia?"

Alta Bea and Harold looked at each other.

I said, "She'll be along directly, I expect."

Dacia showed up at the house about an hour after we got home. When I asked her where she went, she said nowheres.

That evening Harold went into town to the hotel, but Alta Bea wanted to stay up and talk, so I asked her to spend the night at our house. After the girls was in bed, me and Alta Bea set out on the porch. The evening was cooling down, not a lot but a little.

"I hate the thought of Harold coming home and dripping oily dirt all over my house," was the first thing she said after she took a big drag off of her cigarette. She wasn't smoking just for the look of it, like some women done. She sucked it hard into her lungs.

"He ain't getting a boss's job?" I said. "Suit and collar?"

She rolled her eyes. "He wants to learn the business from the ground up, he says, so he's starting by working in the field." She shuddered. "I can just picture his clothes, stiff with oil."

I never said nothing.

She smoked for a while, and then she said, "You know, on the train, when the girls were sleeping and Harold was reading his oil book, I had some time to myself. I enjoyed that."

I nodded.

"I love how you can look out the window and watch the world go by." She had a dreamy look on her face. "I was so conscious of how *far* we were traveling."

"It's a long trip."

"Children would wave, and I wondered what they thought about us. I wanted to jump off the train and go look inside their houses."

"You did?" I felt my mouth twitch. She was a strange one, sure enough.

"I wondered, what do they eat, what's in their closets, what do they read, what do they talk about at meals."

I cleared my throat. "You must be wore out."

"It was like the train window was a picture frame," she went on, "and suddenly I could see—I only have one lifetime, and I'll never know what's just outside the frame." She give a big sigh and pulled her flask out of her pocket.

It give me a sick feeling. I hadn't said nothing at dinner since Harold was there, but now I felt like I had to. "I thought maybe you wasn't drinking no more. In your letter—"

"Helps me sleep." She took a sip.

Neither one of us said nothing for a while.

"I hope the girls didn't give you no trouble," I said.

She laughed through her nose. "That Dacia, she pitched a fit when we left. 'My daddy! My brothers! My mama's grave!'" She said this sarcastic, like she thought Dacia'd been faking.

I wondered. I myself had felt those same feelings. Maybe in this new place, me and Dacia would get along better, maybe she wouldn't be so hardhearted, maybe . . . I hardly dared to think what it might be like if me and her got along—for all of us. Life would be different for me, for sure. Dacia hung over me like a cloud about to bust open.

"And when we got here today and I went after her?" Alta Bea went on. "I found her stuck barefoot in the middle of a sand burr patch. By the time we got them all out, her feet were specked with blood. But she didn't say a word."

"She is contrary." I wilted a little bit.

"But Opal, she was so sweet. She never complained about her motion sickness, and she helped us pass the time. 'Let's play poor pussy, let's play poor pussy,' which I'd never heard of."

I smiled. "Opal always liked that game." You try to make people laugh by acting like a cat.

"It took two seconds for Dacia to make Opal laugh, and me too. Dacia does have a gift for mimicry." She took another drink. "She does you, did you know that? 'Now, you childern, you

316

remember how Mama was all the time a-callin' us a buncha heathens? Well, you know she never meant nothin' by it, now quit actin' like a buncha heathens.' "

I felt my face go red.

Alta Bea chattered on. "And Harold, he kept repeating things from his oil book—the driller this, the roughnecks that, the tooldresser, the pumper, and so on and so forth. But what he's aiming for is brokering leases. That's where the big money is, he says."

"I imagine so."

"Funny thing is, they're called lease-grafters, did you know that? But it doesn't mean they're crooked, supposedly. They have to be 'good talkers' and 'have nerve,' the book says. So Harold says, 'That's me! That's me all over!' " Now she rolled her eyes and laughed.

I yawned. "It's awful late."

"You go on. I want to smoke another cigarette. I'll be in soon."

"Good night, then."

I peeked in on the girls in the little bedroom, and they was sleeping real hard. Wore out. I thought about the two of them, how different they was. Opal sick as a dog and never complaining, and Dacia acting like she hated the world, me especially, for no good reason.

I leaned on the doorway and watched as they slept. How come my raising of them didn't take with Dacia—and Opal sweet as could be? How come Dacia, my own blood, to hate me after all I done for her, all I suffered? I recalled when I slapped her on the day of Mama's funeral. Did my jealousy infect her somehow? Is that how come she was so hateful? I wanted to banish that notion. I couldn't hardly bear it.

I leaned my head back against the doorjamb and reached under my blouse and run my fingertips over my belly like I'd done a thousand times, in circles, and circles within circles, as lightly and gently as I could and still touch the skin.

Before too long Harold got on with Cities Service, and him and Alta Bea moved into one of the company houses in Oil Hill. These houses stood all in a line not far from the oil field, ever one of them painted gray. People called them shotgun shacks because they was long and narrow, with the rooms in a row and a door at each end. Four rooms, and free gas piped in. The neighbor ladies brought food the first day, but Alta Bea wasn't much for making friends. She'd ruther travel the eight miles to our house as neighbor with them. I don't know if she thought she was above them—stuck-up, our mothers called it—or if she had turned back to being shy like she used to be. With Alta Bea, it was hard to tell.

One morning, with the men working and the girls off to school, here come Alta Bea in their car they'd bought. She never opened the gate, just set out on the road and beeped her horn till I went outside. She hollered for me to come for a ride, so I grabbed my sweater and off we went. Pretty soon I folded up my sweater and set on it, but, little like I was, I still had to stretch my neck to see out the windows. Cow pasture, creek, alfalfa field, wheat field, cow pasture, a tractor pulling a disc. A field of oil derricks and pumpjacks.

"That smell," Alta Bea said, and it was like I woken up from a dream. "I don't see how a person can ever get used to it."

I just shrugged.

We must have gone six or seven miles when she jerked the steering wheel, sending the car into a skid. I braced my hands, and we come to a stop by the side of the road. Dust rose up all around us.

"What in the Sam Hill." I put my hand on my belly. It hit me—one thing I hated about riding in cars was, you was at the driver's mercy.

She laughed and scooted back against her window frame. She pulled out a cigarette and blowed out smoke, and then she started pulling out pins till her hair fell in loose waves. She was growing it out again, I seen.

"Don't you just *love* cars?" she said, her eyes closed. Now she squinted against the smoke. "You've gained weight around the middle."

"Oh." I felt myself blush.

"You aren't, are you?"

This wasn't the way I planned on telling her. She'd caught me by surprise. I just nodded.

"Damn." She looked at me sideways. "I told you before, there are ways."

"Too late for *that*." I used a smart-alecky tone that made it sound like me and Sam never meant to have a baby so soon, that we wasn't careful, and now I had to go through with it—though none of that was true. Alta Bea brought out the worst in me, seemed like. Made me say things I didn't feel, act like somebody I wasn't, which wasn't something I done except when I was with her. Now I felt so bad about what I said, I never noticed she wasn't happy for me like I thought she would be.

"When are you due?" She reached under her seat and pulled out a glass candy dish and stubbed out her cigarette.

"Soon after the first of the year, looks like."

She never said nothing, just looked past me out the window.

I felt bad. I felt like I had tempted bad luck, just to go along with her. I wanted her to know how I really felt. "Me and Sam, we're excited. It's what we want, tell the truth."

She turned to the front and pushed the button to start the car. She gunned the engine. "I'd have thought you'd had enough of babies."

"We're excited," I said again.

"If you say so." She cranked the steering wheel and turned around, headed toward home.

"I do," I said. "I'm the happiest I ever been."

She sighed. "I'm glad for you, then. Good for you."

Pretty soon I turned a little away from her and petted my belly. I told my baby, *I can't hardly wait to meet you. You got the happiest mama and daddy there ever was.*

Chapter 17

That fall Sam got more hauling business than he knowed what to do with, only this time he was contracting with oil companies, and they paid good money. Not enough to get rich, but enough to pay the bills and put food on the table with a little bit left over. That little bit made all the difference. From the Sears catalog we got Dacia and Opal each their own pair of school shoes. Dacia put hers on the moment they come and wouldn't take them off to save them for school. Then come the rocking chair and the iron crib on legs.

Opal, she never stopped talking about the baby that was coming—the baby this, the baby that— and she sewed up half a dozen gowns and made flannel burp rags. Dacia never said nothing about it. She complained about having to sleep in the bed with Opal—said Opal kicked her—and here she was sleeping in a bed regular for the first time in her life. Wasn't nothing she liked about this new place, seemed like.

Come late one night near the end of November, I started in with my pains early, and I labored with the baby from one in the morning till five the next afternoon. I remember laying in the bed all night till the pale daylight come, and the sun's shadow crept over the quilt hour by hour. Opal come in ever little bit and asked me did I need anything. She was big enough, I counted on her to help if I needed it. Dacia, I don't know where she got to. At the time I reckoned she was afraid I might die like Mama done, and she didn't want nothing to do with it.

When the light was almost gone I knowed I needed help, and I sent Sam for the doctor. When he got there he reached in and pulled on the baby's head. The baby come out finally, but the top half of his left ear got tore off, evidently. We never noticed it for a while, and by the time we did, why, we couldn't find the tip of his little ear. I said, it was probably in the cuffs of the doctor's pants—you'd be surprised what-all gets in pants cuffs, I should know, and the baby's ear was tiny—but when the doctor went to sew it back on, nobody could find it nowhere. So the baby was left with a ragged edge on his ear. I whispered to him, *Never mind, we'll just comb your hair over it, nobody'll notice.*

The baby's head and eyes was too big for the rest of him, seemed like. To me he looked like a baby bird that fell out of the nest, with papery skin pocked where the feathers never come in. Laying there in bed, I rejoiced when he started up squalling and the doctor laid him on my chest and he dug his face into me. Sam leaned over and asked me how did I like our boy, and then he out-and-out bawled, Sam did. He petted the baby on the back and smiled and wiped off tears for a good long while.

We named the baby William Winslow Frownfelter and we called him Will. Early like he was, he didn't weigh but five, five and a half pounds.

Dacia and Opal, they come in the bedroom and looked at him. Dacia said, "Is that what he looks like?" And Opal, she touched her finger to his hair and said she never felt of anything so soft and to be sure to save a lock of it.

But Will, he never sucked very good, and seemed like he spit up most everthing he swallered. Ever little bit he'd open his eyes and look around, but he never curled his hand around your finger. He kept waving his arms trying to dig at his hurt ear. His breaths was raspy.

In the middle of the fourth night I woken up, and when I touched him in his crib he was already cold. I wrapped him in a blanket and carried him outside. He hadn't been outside before, and I wanted him to feel what it was like. It was pitch-black out, with a sliver of a moon, cold. There was a whistling wind in the trees.

I walked over to the little stone wall the Whiteside boys had built, and I set down with him. I put my hand on his face to make sure. I never had sang to him yet, and all I could think of was "Jimmy Crack Corn," so I sung that. *Jimmy crack corn and I don't care, Jimmy crack corn and I don't care, Jimmy crack corn and I don't care, my William's gone away.* Babies, they don't care how silly the words is—could be about pickling watermelon rind, for all they care—only what it sounds like. I heard my voice get real low. It broke into cackling, my throat was so wore out. I set on the wall and rocked him and sung to him. I felt a little warm blood oozing out between my legs, and I clamped them shut.

Directly the sky begun to lighten and the crows started in cawing. Not long after, Sam come running outside in his underdrawers. Soon's I seen him, I jumped up and took off running. I knowed he would take my baby, and wasn't nobody going to take my baby away.

Now I have to tell the part I always left out of the story.

When I got out of bed to check on the baby, I couldn't see good in the half-light, but things was so quiet I had a real bad feeling. I never reached down and touched him and found him cold—that's just the way I always told it. Truth is, I picked him up and pulled him close, and when his little cold face touched the flesh of my neck—well, I can't hardly stand to think about what happened next. Lord help me, I throwed Will down on the floor. I done that. It was like *my very skin* couldn't abide the feeling of him cold on my neck. I throwed my baby on the floor, I did. Then I stood there still and silent, seeing would Sam wake up. Seemed like the whole world would have heard that sickening thump. Standing there in the darkness, it felt like my spirit was cut open like raw meat, and something touched the rawness, and pain went through me, and if I could have took back what I done, I would. I surely would. I wanted to go back five minutes in time, just five minutes. I felt like I could live with him dead, maybe, but not with what I done, and then I thought, *No, go back five hours or whatever it needs, make him alive again and warm against me.* Now according to what Mama told me, wishing unnatural things contrary to the Lord's will, that's blasphemy, it's defiance, it's disobedience. And I said to myself, *The hell with the Lord, where was the Lord when this innocent child breathed his last, ain't nobody taking my baby. Will, he ain't been outdoors yet, I'm taking him outdoors so's he can feel what it's like,* and that's what I done. I said, *The hell with the Lord. The Lord can go to hell, and, Mama, I'm sorry, but ain't nobody going to take my baby away from me.*

I never told nobody what I done, not even Alta Bea. Not even Sam.

Mrs. Whiteside, she talked to Sam and had us to bury Will in their family graveyard up on the hill

327

east of the big house. There wasn't no arguing with her, that's how she was raised, to help people in trouble, we didn't owe her nothing. She told Sam they'd planted lilac bushes on the north for a windbreak, and there was always flowers for Decoration Day. She paid for the funeral home, the coffin, everthing.

A storm come up the night before the burial, coating the branches with ice. I remember they clicked ever little bit as we stood there by the grave. Afterward I walked by the graves of two girls and a boy Mrs. Whiteside had lost herself. That's all I remember from that day.

That, and Dacia asking me, over and over, how come the baby died, what did I do to him, what did I feed him, did it hurt when he died, how come he died. No matter what I said, she looked at me with her eyes narrowed, like I was the liar of the world. It made me hot and cold at the same time. I don't know what would've happened if Sam hadn't pulled her away from me and took her somewheres, I don't know where.

In the months after Will died, I started in having bad dreams. A cat would be talking to me, smiling, and then I would look away, and when I looked back, the cat's face would be a baby's— not Will, some baby I never seen before—and then its eyes would go glassy, and then I knowed it was dead. Or I would feel myself getting pulled into a room, and then I would see a tall iron crib in there, and I'd grab aholt of the doorjamb, trying to keep myself from getting sucked into thc room, but my hands would lose their strength and I'd get sucked in there, and just when I was about to get in sight of the crib—I couldn't look, I couldn't not look—I would wake up sweating and crying. Or I walked up to a winda and just throwed Will out of it, just throwed him out, and then I wouldn't know for sure was he dead first— what if he wasn't dead first?—and a feeling like a razor would come up in my throat. I had a lot of dreams like that. And in the daytime, when the memory of what I done come over me, I withered, and it took all I had to just raise my head up.

In the mornings Sam looked wore out. Over them months his voice got softer and breathy. Seems like he never got shet of that rasp after that. Sometimes when I woke up in the night he would be crying next to me in the bed. When that happened I just laid there. I didn't figure he'd want me to know he'd broke down like that. And wasn't a thing I could do for him.

Day by day I didn't feel like doing nothing. My arms was heavy. I did the chores that had to be done, but I didn't take no pleasure in it. Half the time I couldn't remember, did I just wash this plate or not? Off and on I wondered, would we ever be as happy as we was? I woke up one morning and couldn't remember why I ever liked the house. Now I hated it.

Opal, why, she took to making pies and things to cheer us up. For a while, Dacia couldn't hardly get a rise out of me. I just set and looked out the kitchen window. I felt like I was waiting to wake up.

Alta Bea drove over from Oil Hill most ever day. She was pregnant herself, but she never hardly mentioned it, only casual-like, and we never made no fuss about it, which I reckon she understood. At first she wasn't happy about it. She complained to me her diaphragm didn't work. Now me, I didn't have no use for such a thing, and it half scared me to even think about sticking something like that inside me, but Alta Bea'd said to me many times, she was determined to "space out" her children. But as time went by, seemed like she got used to the idea of the baby. At least she stopped complaining about it.

I ain't never forgot how I felt that winter. It's like you're a bug crawling around in a circle that don't get no bigger nor smaller, and you don't feel like you have no reason to keep crawling, but you do. The memory of throwing my baby on the floor kept floating into my mind, lit onto me like a moth, brushed against me, drug down my spirit while I was doing some everday thing. There it was, there it was, and there it was again—when his face touched me, I throwed the baby down on the floor. I did.

Sometimes life scrapes your insides raw.

Alta Bea had her baby in April, and Harold come and got me in the car. When I seen the baby's face I about fell over, she was so pretty. I told Alta Bea, said, "She's the prettiest baby I ever seen, look at that hair!" Alta Bea had that angelic look new mamas get, kind of dazed, and she said, "Can I go to sleep now? Bring me a cigarette. Is she normal?" They called the baby Alice. Being around the baby, even just smelling her, it made me feel like there was hope in the world again.

I stayed and helped for a week and then come ever little bit for a month. Alta Bea, she was a big healthy gal, and she recovered well. On Decoration Day her and the baby and Harold come over and walked up to Will's grave with me and Sam and the girls. Mrs. Whiteside, she was right—the lilacs was blooming, and there was plenty of them to decorate the grave with. To my mind, there's no flower smells as good as lilacs, no perfume as sweet. Mrs. Whiteside, she'd also had a headstone put in, which later that day me and Sam went back up to the house and thanked her for. She stood at the doorway and never asked us in, and she acted like she was embarrassed we was even thanking her. I was just as glad we didn't go in. It had been a hard day already.

Alta Bea, she started calling like she done before, only now she'd bring Alice with her. Alice was an easy baby—a rag doll, soft-jointed and roly-poly, not stiff and unhappy like some babies is. She was a balm to my misery, sure enough.

I remember one time, Alice must've been about two months old, me and Alta Bea was setting at the table visiting and drinking coffee. I was holding the baby stretched out on my forearms and facing me, and she blinked her little eyes whenever I laughed.

Alta Bea asked me, had I heard the latest rumor about the war in Europe.

"Don't hardly pay attention no more, heard so many." I stuck my lips out and burbled, and the baby pulled her head back and smiled.

"My neighbor said it was in the Kansas City paper. They might call up Harold and Sam's unit."

"Not the National Guard." I shook my head. "I don't believe that. They ain't the army." Sam and Harold, right out of high school they'd both joined up with the 35th Division of the Kansas and Missouri National Guard. Wasn't no war going on then, and they needed the pay. Dora, she'd wrote me that William and Buck had registered for the draft but wasn't called up. William was deferred because he run the co-op, and Buck had a low draft number.

"I hope you're right," Alta Bea said. "I don't know what I'd do if I had to take care of Alice day *and* night." She made a face. "It feels like I'm walking knee-deep in calf's-foot jelly. Like I'm always about to fall asleep, but I never quite get there." She fidgeted with something in her pocket, her silver cigarette case I reckoned.

I didn't know what to say. Harold wanted her to get a girl to come in, but Alta Bea wouldn't have no stranger in the house.

"It's a struggle to even *think,*" she said.

I nodded. "Seems like they fill up all the time there is, sure enough." I pulled the baby up to my nose and smelled of her hair.

"I've never watched the clock so much in my life," Alta Bea said. "You know, counting down to the next thing—lunch, her nap, her next bottle, Harold coming home. The next thing. It seems to take forever."

I swung Alice up and back, and she took to giggling. When I looked up at Alta Bea, a big smile on my face, I seen she had tears in her eyes. If I didn't know better, I would've swore she was jealous.

"Here, Mother, you take her for a while." I held her out.

But Alta Bea stood up and carried her coffee cup to the stove. "Do you think it's possible to be too wrapped up in your children?"

I thought about that. "Well, you can spoil them,

if that's what you mean, but I don't think you can love them too much."

"No, I mean—can you make your own happiness depend too much on theirs?"

This was one of them things Alta Bea said to me that didn't make no sense. I said, "You can't make nobody happy if they're bound and determined not to be." I was thinking about Dacia. But then when I tried to remember something I'd done especially just to make her happy, the only one was that time in the smokehouse when me and her and Opal played house and Dacia mimicked people and I laughed, and we sung songs. It stung I couldn't remember any other times. I told myself there must be some, I just couldn't remember.

Alta Bea's face crumpled. "There's so much to think about—and nothing to think about." She got out a cigarette and held it unlit between her fingers. "You've known me forever. You knew me as a girl." She leaned over toward me. "Don't you remember how I used to be?"

I smiled. "Remember that time we played with paper dolls? And your mama, she—"

"For Christ's sake!" She smacked her hand on the table, and the baby startled. I stretched her out on my legs and rocked her.

"Now I can't think about anything beyond, you know . . ." She looked around. *"Supper."* Her mouth wrinkled.

"Oh! That reminds me," I said. "What time is it? I ain't even shelled the beans yet." I started to get up.

She put out her hand. "Will you watch her for a minute?" She put the cigarette in her mouth and slumped out the door to the porch.

I felt like I should go after her and keep her company while she smoked, but I didn't. I just set there and petted Alice and smelled her. Alta Bea, when she got to talking this way, she made me jumpy. I was glad we'd finally made the last payment on the note we owed her, though she still had a way of making me feel obligated to her.

Summer come, and then fall, and then it was Will's birthday. Me and Sam talked about it that morning and decided we'd just go visit the grave by ourselves. I said, maybe the girls wouldn't notice the date. But at breakfast Dacia said, "Isn't *nobody* going to say *nothing* about the baby's birthday?" so the four of us went up there. It turned out Opal had made him a little stuffed duck with big, floppy lips that was supposed to be its beak, which she left at the grave. Dacia wanted to stay home from school, but I made them both go.

Ever day, bit by bit, it felt like us four was getting used to things as they was. Dora wrote at least two times a week, and ever little bit she sent drawings or things the twins had made, and she said she always had them kiss the envelope where she sealed it. I did the same—wrote and sent things, I mean—but the girls was too big to be kissing no envelope, both of them.

I lived for Dora's letters. Wasn't hardly a day went by I didn't think about the twins, wondering what they was up to at a given minute.

I still carried an ache inside, and once in a while a terrible feeling come over me, but now it seemed like the kind of pain you get when you're healing. The pain meant that the wound had blood feeding into it, so you knowed it would eventually seal up and scar over.

Then when spring come, in April 1918, why, Sam and Harold's unit did get called up for the Great War. We got a letter, and they only had a week to get ready. I know me and Alta Bea took them to the train, and I know Sam kissed me so hard it hurt my mouth, but that's all I remember. It never seemed real at the time, no part of it. It was like I was walking through fog in a dream. Things went on like usual all around us—me and the girls and Alta Bea—but Sam and Harold was gone.

Partly just to keep ourselves busy, me and Alta Bea started putting up a lot of food on her stove. With the free gas, you just lit the stove and it would stay how hot you put it. It stunk, and you had to light it ever time with a match and that scared me a little, but it was the first modern machine I ever used that I liked better than the old way.

One day when we was canning bects, two-three months after the men left, Alta Bea sliced into her finger with the knife. She swore and started crying, and then she said, "*And* I'm pregnant again!"

What was funny was, I was late, and just that morning I'd reckoned I was expecting, too. But I never said so now, not wanting to steal her thunder.

I jumped up and grabbed a rag to bind up her finger. We was standing side by side over the sink, and she put her arms around me and pulled me close and took to sobbing. "It must have happened the night before they left," she said. "I was up late seeing to the baby, and Harold wouldn't wait for me to put in the diaphragm, and I was out of the jelly." She swore again and cried into my shoulder while I stood there and held on to her. After while she pulled away and set down at the table and blowed her nose.

"He did it on purpose," she said. "He knew I—"

I couldn't stand it no more. "I am, too."

"What?"

"Expecting."

Now her tears stopped and her face lit up. "Bertie," was all she said, and in such a kindly way. I felt at peace. I loved my house again. I loved my life. I felt like I was woken up.

Wasn't but a couple days later, when the girls was at school, I was on my knees scrubbing the floor when I felt a hot stream flowing out of me. For a moment I just stayed like I was. I told myself I had wet my pants. But when I looked down, it was blood all right. I laid on my side and pulled my legs up. I heard a noise and then realized it was me, wailing, when a cramp hit me. After while I half turned on my back and set up. I didn't have a lot of clothes to spare, but I knowed, in that instant, I would throw out that skirt.

Then I felt glad I hadn't told the girls or wrote to Sam yet. I wouldn't have to tell them nothing.

When I felt well enough to get up, I pulled myself out of my skirt and set on the chair. I started wadding up the skirt, and in the folds I seen the gray tissue, and inside it, the kidney bean with the two black dots. I don't know what I thought it would look like—like a whole baby, only smaller, I reckon—but not this odd small thing. I leaned over and touched it with my fingertip—soft, sticky, hardening a bit as it cooled. Didn't give off no smell different from the usual coppery stink of blood.

And then I felt myself break to pieces inside. Thoughts come through that'd been hidden in me for a long while. It seemed like the very flesh of my children bore God's rebuke. There was plenty of reasons. I stabbed my own daddy, I wished him dead, and I was short with Dacia, impatient with her ways, and most of all, jealous of how Mama'd ruther spend time with her, even as a baby, than me. And Mama, how come I left her and went to the backhouse, and her all alone when she died? Worse yet, I never kept the family together. On her deathbed she'd give me a sacred task, to look after the children, and I failed it—I let things get worse and worse till there wasn't nothing to do but everbody go different ways. And Will, when his cold face touched me I throwed him on the floor. And Timmy, I hadn't thought about him for a long time, Timmy who I let wander off and drown in the Tenmile, wedged in the rocks. And then in spite of all I done wrong, God had give me Sam, who loved me more than anybody ever had, and now I'd lost two of Sam's children, and who knowed when he would come back from the war so we could try again? Or if? I wondered, would I ever have children of my own, and the very thought made me lose all my breath.

When I come to, I had to hurry to get everthing cleaned up and throwed out before the girls got home.

The next time I seen Alta Bea I told her I was mistaken, it was just my cycle being late, and I real quick asked her, what about them Lister's towels, did they work better than rags when you had your flow? And how much did they cost? And had Alice got a new tooth? Felt like a new tooth coming in, there, could she feel it? And had she got a letter from Harold lately?

As time went by I felt my black misery calling to me, only this time I pushed it away. I seen clear, as clear as anything I ever seen, that this time it would kill me if I let it. I felt like I couldn't dip a toe in it, I had to harden myself against it, and day by day I stared straight ahead and swallowed back my feelings and got stronger. I found out, I could wake up ever day and do what had to be done, and I let it be enough.

Chapter 18

As the months went by and the war went on, there was letters to be wrote ever day, and chickens to dress and ironing to do. Mrs. Whiteside, she give me work, and other people did, too. We needed it. In the war Sam was only making half of what he done when he was home. We got by, is all.

Me and Alta Bea, living outside of Wiley and not being churchgoers, we didn't get to town much. Alta Bea wasn't one to neighbor with the folks in Oil Hill, neither. When me or her did leave the house, it was to go to each other's house. She got the paper, and we kept up with the war news that way. We'd read about battles at the Marne, the Meuse-Argonne Forest, the Belleau Wood—places I had no idea where they was or how to say them—and then months later we'd get a letter and find out if Sam and Harold had been in them. Hardly nobody in Wiley went to the war, being farmers or oil workers. It seemed far away.

I did take pleasure in Opal, couldn't help it. She had a bright and happy spirit, and though she was quiet, there wasn't no dimming her light. No matter how much gloom hung over the house, she went around acting happy, always curious. When she wasn't sewing or in school, why, she'd run all over creation. She'd leave the house in the morning and not come home till dark set in. She loved playing in the oil field. Liked the racket, I reckon. Liked to watch the men, liked to listen to them holler. Probably heard some coarse language, and that probably sent a thrill up her spine, something a child like Opal craves ever little bit.

But Dacia, seemed like she couldn't hardly stand to be in the same room with me. She'd bring up Will. She'd ask me questions she knowed the answers to, like she was a young child, just to be mean. Was he still in the ground, and wasn't he cold? Had coyotes dug him up? Didn't they dig up dead people? Did somebody shoot him, she asked me one time, and I told her of course not, now go do your chores and leave me be. She knowed where my sore places was, seemed like, and she delighted in poking them. Or not so much delighted as wondered what would happen and had to find out.

Just to torment me, she taught Opal a chant they done at school during recess—*Kaiser Bill went up the hill to get a peek at France, Kaiser Bill come down the hill with bullets in his pants.* Dacia thought it was dirty because it said "pants," and she thought she was getting away with something, getting Opal to sing a dirty song. Of course the joke was on her, because it wasn't about underpants. But Dacia relished it anyhow.

Ever time she poked me like this, I felt like the cords in my neck would bust, but I muffled my wrath and left the room ruther than give her the satisfaction.

I had bad dreams ever little bit. When I couldn't sleep at night, I talked to Sam—pretending like he could hear me—and told him my troubles. I tried to picture him in a muddy hole in the Argonne Forest, listening to the big guns booming a few miles off, like he talked about in his letters, but I couldn't. I woke up tired and mean. I jerked the skillet around and broke the eggs, slammed the plate on the table.

Alta Bea had the baby in October, another girl. Named her Ruby. I helped with this one, too, though I never took as much pleasure in it as I done with Alice. Even with a new baby it felt like life was mean and small, there was a filthy, bloody war on, and things might go on this way forever.

To our great relief the war ended in November. But a lot of the soldiers didn't come home right away, Sam and Harold included. Sam wrote me from France that they never knowed, from day to day, was they coming home. Christmas come and went, and no Sam. I felt a cold fury inside. How come he couldn't come home? He wrote me, be patient, which was just like him. Wasn't nothing to do but wait.

That was the winter of the big flu. A couple dozen people we had connections to in Wiley and Oil Hill come down with it. Mrs. Whiteside, she laid in bed for six weeks with a fever and couldn't hardly get her wind, but she got over it. I was worried Alta Bea might catch it, and her with two babies at home, but she never did.

I got the girls to school most days. In January, Dacia broke her arm playing Crack the Whip on the ice. She cried and asked for Sam, wanting him to play her a song on his teeth like he done. I told her to quit acting like a baby, didn't she know we all missed him.

The day come, March 15, 1919, when I got a telegram from Sam saying him and Harold had arrived in New York City. Soon's they could get a seat on a train, they'd be home. I bawled that night till my throat was raw.

Wasn't but two weeks later, why, Sam and Harold did get home. Me, Opal, Dacia, and Alta Bea and her two girls went and met them at the train. Harold, he stood there for a minute blinking and looking around like he didn't recognize nothing. But then Sam clapped him on the back, and Alta Bea and me and the girls, why, we pretty near run them over. At first Alta Bea's babies screamed like they'd been shot, but we wasn't surprised. Takes a while for little children to get used to growed men.

Sam, he like to busted his face smiling, and after while Harold put his arm around Alta Bea's neck and wouldn't hardly let go. I thought she might lose her balance.

We had Alta Bea's car, and it's hard to picture how we all got into it. I think Dacia, and maybe Opal, too, stood on the running boards.

Alta Bea drove. "Hard to believe it's been three years since we moved to Kansas," she said.

"Hard to believe it's been a year since you left," I said to Sam.

"Ain't hard for me," he said. "I believe ever damn minute of it."

"War's over!" Harold hollered. "Time to get rich, fat, and happy!" He stuck his head out the window and let the wind blow his hair. "No more oil field work for me! War's over! You're looking at a lease-grafter!" He brought his head back in and grabbed aholt of Alta Bea. "Time to get cracking! Gonna be a boy next time!"

I couldn't see Alta Bea's face from where I set in the backseat, but I seen her stiffen and the back of her neck get red.

That night after supper Sam got out his fiddle case and headed out to the porch, and me and the girls looked at each other and grinned and followed him. Sam set in one chair and me in the other'n, and the girls on the floorboards with their legs dangling off the edge.

He played for a long time just making chords, tuning the bow, trying it out, back and forth, his eyes closed. For a long time he picked and plucked scales and pulled the bow with his ear up close to it. After while Dacia said, " 'Careless Love'!" and Opal called out " 'Frog Went a-Courtin'!" and Dacia said, "That train song about the oranges!" And so none of us noticed at first when Sam dropped his arms. He give me a bewildered look and shrugged.

"Sam's wore out," I said to the girls. "Had a big day. He'll—"

Dacia stood up and turned to me. "No, he ain't," she said. "He's never too bushed to play *music*."

Sam hung his head. I seen his hands was shaking.

My instinct was to hustle the girls off to bed, but they had gotten too independent in the last year for that. I didn't want to holler at nobody on Sam's first day home.

Opal, she got to her feet and set her hand on Sam's knee. "He's tired in his spirit, ain't you?" she said, solemn as a forty-year-old.

We all froze, even Dacia. I felt spit gather in my mouth, I was so like to cry.

But Sam just smiled his big smile and leaned over and kissed Opal on the forehead, and then he packed the fiddle away in the case and nobody said nothing else. The girls went to their room without being told, and me and Sam went to bed shortly after.

Sam woke me in the middle of the night, must've been three, four o'clock. "My time's mixed up," he whispered. "Can't sleep."

I scooted over and laid on my side with my stomach against him. "I'm so glad you're back." There was a rumble. "That me or you?"

"Thunder, off a ways," he said. "Fixing to rain."

"We could use it." I rubbed my face against his chest.

He sucked in air and sighed real deep. "Can we go to Will's grave tomorrow?"

"Sure enough."

There was a long silence, and I thought he'd went back to sleep. But he said, "Seen a lot of graveyards."

I petted his arm.

"Little white crosses, by the *acre*."

I groaned.

"Didn't want to get buried over there," he said.

"Thank God you never."

"You should've saw them farms. Hedges, they had hedges for fence? So thick a sheep can't get through. You never seen the like."

I started to say, "You told me all this in your letters," but I never did.

Sheet lightning crackled in the window.

"And the houses was made of rock mostly, a lot of them thatch roofs," he went on. "We'd come across a burned-out house, dead horses, dogs." He was talking fast now, like he hardly ever done. "This one time, there was these two old people and a little girl. You could see what happened. Machine gun. They was running through the grass to the house. Got the old man first, fell on his face, old lady, landed on her side with her arms flung out, little girl, throwed her up in the air like a rag doll, landed all twisted." He sniffled. I thought maybe he was crying, but I put my hand on his chest and he wasn't.

"I figured, grandparents, granddaughter. Maybe an orphan. Seen a lot of children wandering around, beg for food."

"That must've—"

"Me and Harold, we was on our way back to camp one night, we eat supper at a family's house in town. This was before the battle of the Argonne. I told you about that, the people in Beauchamp? They'd have some of the fellas over to eat, bottle of wine, flowers on the table? A mother, little boy, daughter, grandmother—nice folks. So Harold, he gets drunk, and I haul him out of there, and we was walking back, and we come up on this little family graveyard. It was dark out. We seen this lady, I thought she was a growed woman, but closer I reckoned she was fifteen, sixteen, she was laying facedown on this grave, new grave, bawling, and Harold, he goes over to her and gets on his knees and touches her, you know, and she screams, and I tell you what, Bertie, I had to punch him a time or two to get him off of her. I thought I might have to shoot him, the son of a bitch."

"Oh," I said.

"Next day, he says, 'I done what? Me? I don't remember.'"

"Hard to trust him after that," I said.

"Things in a war, they ain't . . ." I felt him shrug. We was both quiet for a long time.

"It light enough out yet?" he said.

"For what?"

"Go see Will."

That would have been the time to tell him about the other baby if I was going to, but I never did. I just said, "Let me get my shoes on."

It was cold out, and the air was wet, but the rain hadn't came. There was a thick fog along the ground. We tromped up there, him and me. The little duck Opal had made, we found it stuck in the lilac hedge and put it back on Will's grave. We didn't stay but ten minutes. Sam didn't say much. I had the feeling he'd said all he was going to.

A couple months later Sam come home with a truck that somebody'd made by putting a truck bed onto a Model T Ford. It was already three or four years old, seems like, but Sam had learned a lot about motors during the war, and he knowed how to make it go no matter how old it was.

Opal and Dacia heard him coming and went running out to the road. I watched them from the front porch. He drove that truck right up until the tires almost touched the house. They all three was laughing fit to die.

Sam pumped the foot-feed. "Come take a ride!"

"I got supper to get!"

"That can wait! Come take a ride!"

Well, of course I pulled the pan off the fire, got me a sweater, and went out there and climbed into the truck. It made an awful racket. I had to put my hands over my ears. Off we went, heading toward Wiley.

The road was mostly ruts, and we rocked back and forth and up and down, and after while my breakfast wasn't setting on my stomach too good. I had Sam to stop, and I got out of the truck and throwed up by the side of the road. I felt awful, shaking. Opal climbed down after me and petted me on the shoulder, but then she got a whiff of it and throwed up, too. She was always sympathetic like that.

Inside the truck Dacia got to laughing, and she couldn't hardly stop.

Now Sam got out and come around to where me and Opal was. "You sick, little bird?"

"I bet she's expecting!" Dacia hollered through the window.

"Are you?" His voice had hope in it.

I heaved twice and throwed up again.

Opal groaned and walked to the back of the truck. I heard her choking back her bile.

"They're both expecting! Opal too!" Dacia yelled.

Now Opal was ten or eleven years old and of course hadn't never done nothing, so what Dacia said was preposterous. But still it made me mad. "You take that back," I said to her.

"Bertie and Opal's in the family waaa-ay," Dacia said in a singsong voice.

"That ain't funny," Sam said.

I was so riled, I swallered hard and climbed into the truck and snatched her by the hair and pulled her down onto the ground, her screaming the whole time. "Say you're sorry!" I hollered. "Say you're sorry!" I had her by the arm, and I was shaking her, making her head snap once.

Then I heard Sam say, "That's enough, that's enough, let her go now, that's enough."

I let loose of her hair, and she took off running back toward the house. I was panting like a dog, and my throat gurgled. I heaved again but nothing come.

Sam petted me on the back. "You got to be careful. You got to take care of yourself."

Opal walked toward me. "Are you?"

351

I hadn't told nobody yet, and I was loath to, afraid I would miscarry again and shame myself. But Opal had caught me by surprise, and I nodded, and, to my shock, her and Sam throwed their arms around me and rocked me.

I lost that one a while later, couple weeks maybe. It wasn't as hard as the other one. One night I felt that ache like before, and I went out to the backhouse and that was it. To comfort me, I told myself a story. I told myself this baby come too soon after the war, while the bad feelings from Sam's war stories was still hovering in the bedroom where he told them. So the baby's spirit refused to come into this awful world. It was the kind of a story they used to tell back home in Kentucky, like the Rumpelstiltskin story I made up for Dacia—a story to explain how come something happened—and I thought it through sundry times. It meant that when things settled back down, when the leftover ugly war feelings went away, me and Sam would have our baby and live happily ever after.

Next morning I told Sam and the girls it was just a false alarm, like I'd said to Alta Bea the first time. Dacia, she give me her stink-eye look she had, but she never said nothing.

Chapter 19

They opened a picture show in El Dorado," Sam said. "Let's go Saturday, want to?" He folded the newspaper on his lap and drawed on his cigarette. He and Harold, they'd been back home for a year.

"Ain't you playing at the dance?" I waved smoke out of my face. Only thing I didn't like about setting out on the porch. But I had a mess of peas to shell, and it was a nice summer evening.

"They ain't finished painting the hall yet, so no dance this week."

"Well, if you want to."

"I wouldn't mind it." That was Sam, talking sideways.

Come Saturday, me and Sam and Opal took baths and put on clean clothes. Dacia, she folded her arms and said she wouldn't go. Said we didn't really want her along—meaning me, I didn't want her to go—and I said well of course we wanted her to go, wouldn't have asked her otherwise, and she could just climb down off of her high horse, and she said she didn't want to be seen with us nohow, we was clodhoppers, and I said well, whatever we are, you're one, too. But I told myself she was fourteen now and thought she knowed everthing, so I said she could just stay home by her lonesome then.

It riled me how she was like to spoil our good times over nothing. She looked like a growed woman, a pretty one at that, awful pretty, but you couldn't trust her like a growed woman. She acted like a child, like she didn't care what nobody thought or needed. I often asked myself, what if I'd acted like her at that age? When I was taking care of Mama and Dacia and Opal and the twins? But it wasn't no use. She acted like what she wanted to.

It was an evening like I like, not too hot and not too cold. There was mackerel clouds high in the sky and a little breeze. Sam drove us in the truck. Without Dacia fussing over who got to set where, the trip went quick.

I never seen nothing fancier than the Belmont. The lobby walls was decorated with curlicues made out of plaster and painted gold, and there must've been a dozen giant chandeliers with sparkling crystals swaying with the movement of the air. The ladies' bathroom, which they called the "ladies lounge," had a carpeted room with couches and chairs before you went into the toilets, and that part was white marble, floor to ceiling. Real modern.

I don't remember what was playing—something about Indians and two white sisters. I think Wallace Beery was in it. Opal bawled her eyes out, I know that. Plus there was two silly comedies and a newsreel. It cost a dime apiece to get in.

Opal fell asleep on the way home, and Sam carried her to bed. When I got in the house, I like to died—there was Dacia setting at the table with the scissors and Opal's doll, and all its pretty human hair strung on the floor. Its head was nothing but frizzy clumps.

"What the Sam Hill?" I felt froze to the spot, like I was looking at something impossible. What girl her age would do such a thing?

"She don't play with it nohow." Dacia had already ruined her own human hair doll by leaving it outdoors in the rain. But Opal had kept hers nice all this time and made dresses and coats and hats for it. She treasured that doll. She herself was eleven, just about old enough to give them up, but this one was special because Sam'd give it to her.

"I don't care if she plays with it or not! Ain't yours to ruin!" I grabbed the scissors out of Dacia's hand and throwed them across the room. I felt a fury in me. My wrath felt like it was a long time coming—fierce and righteous.

She jumped up from the table. "She's your pet! You always take her side! I hate you!"

"What in the world? How come you're so hateful? What did Opal ever do to you?"

"Me hateful? *Me* hateful?"

"Ain't nobody in this house acts mean like you do."

"Christ Almighty," she said. "You ain't got no idea. You're blind, deaf, and dumb!"

"You don't even know what 'dumb' means."

"I know ten times as much as you. I know things you never even thought about!"

This brought me up short. It was true, Dacia'd been to school a whole lot more than me. And seemed like she knowed things, things you never learned in school, things I couldn't hardly imagine what they was. She was all the time giving me that narrow-eyed look she had, like there was a secret she knowed.

I was sick of it. "You don't know half the things you think you know!"

She throwed back her head and laughed. A woman's laugh, low-pitched, a laugh that sent a charge up my spine.

"I know things about *Mama*," she said. "You think you loved her and she loved you—well, you don't know nothing. You don't know the first thing about her."

I took in air through my nose. I heard it whistling. "If you think you're too big for a whippin'—"

"Mama, she killed herself, and don't nobody know it but me." She looked me in the eye.

I reached out to slap her face, but she dodged my hand, and I brought both hands up and covered my own face. I stood for a moment not knowing which it was—a lie straight from hell, or a lie but she believed it. Sorrow poured over me, damping down my wrath for the moment. "Don't go saying nothing like that," I said. "Don't conjure." Even I didn't want Dacia to burn in hellfire for all eternity, which might be a real thing for all I knowed.

"You never believe me," she said. "You don't never believe nothing I say."

"Dacia." I was having trouble getting my wind. I wanted to wail like a heathen.

"I swear to God, she did, she killed herself, and I knowed it all along. I knowed it, but I never—I never understood it, what it meant."

I took aholt of myself best I could. "Look, I was with Mama when she died," I said. "I seen her take her last breath. She just drifted away." This wasn't strictly true. I'd went to the backhouse, and Mama was dead when I got back. But I wasn't about to give Dacia something to hold over me.

It was like she wasn't paying no attention. "She was standing in the kitchen," she said. "She was holding that box, you know the one—Rough-on-Rats."

This was too much. I almost laughed. "Oh," I said, sarcastic. "And when was this?"

"The middle of the night, the night before she died." Her voice was calm.

"What time?"

This got a rise out of her, seemed like. She looked at me and squinted. "How do I know what time? It was dark. I got up to pee. There she was. I asked her, 'Mama, can I have a drink of water?' And the box flew up out of her hands, and she hollered."

I sighed. "I never heard her holler. Nobody heard her holler. How comes you to make up this lie? Can't you let her rest in peace?" I knowed I should just let her foolishness roll off of my back, but seemed like I couldn't. I was always asking myself, *Why why why?* Never asked myself that about Opal. Never had to.

Now Dacia frowned. "Maybe it just sounded like hollering to me," she said. "It was the middle of the night, real quiet."

"Listen to me," I said. "She couldn't hardly get out of *bed.* I was *with* her. She was practically dead already the night before, when I fell asleep." Now I pictured the whole thing, me and Mama laying in bed in the blue moonlight. I felt her, hot with fever, against me. I remembered *don't you do this to me* coming from inside the walls. *Don't you do this to me* coming from somewhere.

I pulled out a chair and set across from Dacia at the table, only half aware I done it till I felt myself setting there.

"Rough-on-Rats," she said. "And I said, 'Can I have a drink of water?' And the poison, it flew all up in the air, like sawdust." She cleared her throat. "And she grabs aholt of the broom and starts sweeping it up. Says, 'Go back to bed, I'm gonna blister you.' "

"Quit it," I said. "You're making this up."

"Said, 'Go back to bed, Dacia, I'm gonna blister you.' Couldn't hardly talk. Like whispering."

I dipped my chin and stared at her. "Not one word of this is true."

"Rough-on-Rats," she said. "You remember— had a picture of a dead rat on it. Laying on its back with its legs waving in the air. Flew up in the air like sawdust."

"Of course I remember. She kept it on top of the cupboard."

"She *eat* that rat poison, Bertie, she did. They say if you take a little bit ever day for some while, why then, by and by you just close your eyes and stop breathing. Nobody knows no better."

"She never done that," I said. "She died from the childbed fever."

"She told me, she never wanted no more children. She was too tired. She told me, said—"

"She never told you that!" Now I was so mad, everthing in the room took on a purple tinge.

"The twins, they was little," she said. "One day they got to squalling, and I went over there, and she whirled around and seen me, and

359

she screamed like she seen a bear, and I said, 'Mama, what's wrong, Mama?' And her mouth opened and closed, and she never said nothing for a long time. Her eyes, they had such a look, it scared me. The skin all around them was red, and you could see the whites. Then she started bawling, and I bawled, too, and pretty soon we all four was bawling—me, her, the babies. We was scared. Nothing scares a child more than its mama crying. You know that."

"Dacia!" I hollered. "You couldn't have been more than four or five! Nobody remembers that far back!" I stopped and looked around my own front room to be sure I was in the real world.

"She said, 'I'm tired—I'm going to Heaven,' and I said, 'Can I go?' and she said no, I was to stay and help you look after Opal and the twins. Told me, said, 'Don't you fret,' she was gonna be wearing a snow-white robe and singing with the angels. Said, 'Ain't no tears in Heaven, ain't no dirty diapers neither,' and she *screamed* laughing. Said she couldn't stand to have no more babies, she was too tired."

I set there with my mouth open. *Ain't no tears in Heaven.* Mama was like to say that.

"Her and me, after that, we talked about it ever little bit, though I never knowed she meant she was gonna kill herself, I swear I never," Dacia said in a flat tone. "We just talked about it like it was a trip she was going on. It was like it made

360

her happy to talk to me about it. She said, 'Dacia, you got eyes in your head. You see things how they *is*. Not like Bertie, I don't know where her eyes is, she's always looking somewhere off a ways. But you,' she told me, said, '*you* I can talk to. You see things how they *is*.' "

Dacia looked down at her hands. "Said, 'You and Bertie put together, you're me. She's me on the outside, and you're me on the inside.' " Now Dacia looked up at me. "That's what she said. God's truth."

I set there with my mouth open.

"Said, 'Don't tell Bertie. She'll want to go, and you know what a fuss she'd make. It's our secret.' Oh, I liked that—*loved* it. Our secret, just me and her, not you. I used to look at you and think, 'Mama's going on a trip with the angels, and I know it, and you don't, ha ha ha.' Only thing I had all to myself, see?"

All the while she was saying this, I was picturing times I seen Mama and Dacia together, giggling, Mama so wore out she couldn't hardly hold her head up, but still tickled by Dacia and her ways. And Dacia glancing toward me and then turning her head, something secret in the corner of her eye. Me feeling fretful, feeling left out, tucking the covers around Mama, bawling Dacia out, smacking her, shooing her off. Jealous.

The shame I felt filled me up with pain, but it didn't excuse these lies Dacia was telling. I said to her, "How comes you to blacken our mother's memory this way?"

"It's the truth," she said. "I swear to God. I swear on a stack of Bibles."

"How comes you to tell this lie? You got nothing to gain. Is it just to hurt me? You just evil?"

Now her voice dropped, and it was like she was pleading with me. "It *haunts* me, Bertie— why else?" she said. "Haunts me like a ghost. Gonna haunt me till the day I die. I can still see her standing there, pale white, her nightdress hanging from her shoulders like her body wasn't even there. That snow-white robe she talked about. Singing with the angels."

I pictured that nightdress. I remembered how fragile it was. I remembered ripping it in half when me and Alta Bea was washing Mama's corpse.

Now I lowered my voice. "The kindest thing I can say is, you was dreaming."

Dacia give a long sigh. "I was always so jealous of you."

What? went through me. I almost choked. Her jealous of me?

"You done everthing together, you and Mama," she went on. " 'You're too little, Dacia, you're too little, leave us alone, shoo, shoo, we're getting supper, can't you see? Go play. We're workin', leave us alone.' "

362

Dacia, she was always good at imitating people. In her mouth, my voice was hateful, prideful, mean. Took the air out of me.

She went on. "Me and Mama talking about her trip, it was the only thing I had that was mine, all by myself. Can't you understand that? All I had."

I got out, "I can't help it I was born first." I felt how small that sounded.

"Try to understand," she said. "Me and Mama's secret turned out to be the *awfulest* thing, the horrible, awfulest thing. Mama's trip to Heaven. All that time, what she was really talking about. I only just realized it, not too long ago, what she meant, she was going to kill herself. Maybe just in the past year I put it together in my mind."

It felt like we was rolling downhill like a rock, getting faster, and I tried to slow it down. "You was dreaming, hear me? That night? You was *dreaming* you seen her in the kitchen."

"I never knowed she was going to do it, don't you see? I never knowed she was going to eat that poison, I *swear* I never. I thought she was just going on a trip, all that time, even when I got to be, I don't know, seven, eight, that's all I thought she meant, I swear. Going on a trip."

"Don't matter," I said. "It's all a lie."

"How old was I when she died?"

I heard myself growl.

"Six? Seven?" she said.

"You know how Goddamn old you was." I hated she made me swear.

"No, I don't! I never knowed what year nothing was. How would I?"

"You know what year you was born, and you know what year Mama died."

"How would I?" she said again.

It shocked me, now that I thought about it. None of us at home never said what year nothing was, and Daddy, he never put up no stone on Mama's grave. I knowed what years things happened, but I was older than Dacia, and I cared about them kind of things. "You was almost nine," I said finally.

"So, eight." She nodded. "When she died, I never put it together in my mind. I just thought she died, like people does. Afterward I'd think about it ever so often, but I would get to some certain place in my mind, and then I couldn't get no futher." She cleared her throat. "One night a while back—Sam was still in the war—I dreamed about her, and when I woke up, I all the sudden got it. I just knowed. Mama, all that time she was really telling me she was gonna kill herself if she got pregnant again. Not go on a trip—kill herself. And then, by God, she done it. And the baby, too. Not in so many words, but she was *telling* me."

She fell silent then. I took this all in. The cords in my neck was twanging.

After a little bit she went on. "That night she

died—she couldn't hardly stand up straight. She had one hand on the table, and her other hand around her belly, bent over. Her nightdress, it was draped on her like it was hanging on a hanger."

I heard the tears pooling in her mouth, and then she started crying full out, sobbing.

I was stunned. "Oh my God, you really believe it, don't you?" I said. "You really believe this story you made up out of whole cloth." It was all a lie, of course, but I got a picture in my mind's eye of something like that, true or not, hounding you as a child—something sneaking up behind you ever little bit, something you can't quite see or hear or touch or smell, but you can just barely taste it in the air. You would get close to it, and it would slip away, just out of reach. Something like that would warp you, sure enough. For an instant I seen Timmy, smiling, heard his voice piping *leapfrog, leapfrog,* and I didn't know where I was at or what year it was or if he was really dead or not.

Then I reminded myself, what Dacia was saying wasn't *true.* It wasn't possible in this world. I felt like I had to make her own up to that. "She died of the childbed fever," I said. "You didn't have nothing to do with it." I said it sarcastic, but then it hit me, *Maybe she feels like it was her fault Mama died.* Like she could have stopped it somehow. But she was just a child. What could she have done? Nothing. Just a child.

But anyhow, it was a cock-and-bull story.

Dacia sniffed and took up a napkin and blowed her nose. "Don't matter what I say. You believe what you want to. Don't matter what nobody says. She just *drifted off,* that's what you want to believe, so *by God* that's what happened. Don't matter what nobody says, me nor nobody else."

"Not when it's a lie straight from hell," I said.

Now I heard a throat being cleared behind me, and I like to jumped out of my skin. I whirled in the chair, and there was Sam standing there. He was holding a dishtowel twisted in his hands.

"How long you been there?" Soon's I asked, I realized I'd heard him come in a while back, but it hadn't registered at the time.

Before he could answer, Dacia jumped up and flew at the mess on the table—the doll, the clothes, the bits of doll hair. She flung her arms left and right, scattering the scraps. "She don't believe me!" she hollered at Sam. "She don't believe nothing I say!"

"Dacia—" Sam said.

"You're evil!" she screamed at me. "You're the liar!"

Sam took a step toward her.

"You're a slattern! You was throwing yourself at all kinds of men, trying to get a husband! Don't say you wasn't!"

I let out a howl, and I jumped up from the table so fast I slammed hard into its edge. But

I never paid it no mind. I run to the stove and grabbed my stoutest wooden spoon, my pickle spoon. Now this wasn't no spindly, thin-handle pine spoon like you buy in the store. This one had been Mama's—a big old handmade hickory spoon with a burl in it, a good fifteen or twenty year old, hard as a rock—and I took it and started hitting Dacia with it as hard as ever I could. She screamed and run, but I caught her and swung at her—her back, her behind, her shoulders, wherever the spoon landed, I didn't care. I heard Sam hollering at me to stop, but it was like something had aholt of me. I'd never beat nobody like that before. I kept beating on her, and her running around the room and screaming, till all the sudden I hit something—the wall or the table, something—and the spoon split in two along the line of where the burl was, and one piece of it went flying.

It was like a spell had broke. Sam caught aholt of Dacia and pinned her arms at her sides. "Hold still," he said to her. "Calm yourself. You're gonna make yourself sick."

"She busted the pickle spoon on me!" she hollered. "The Goddamn pickle spoon!"

"I never!" I hollered, but my hands was trembling like I had.

Now Opal come out from their room, sleepy, and stood next to the door. "Please don't whip nobody, Bertie, please."

Dacia hollered to Sam, "Even Mama never whipped us with the pickle spoon!" Her hand went to the back of her neck, where I seen a red welt starting to swell up.

I just stood there by the stove, panting like a dog, holding the pointy end of the spoon. I heard Dacia yelling and Sam trying to talk sense into her, but my mind went someplace else. Of all things, I had a picture of Mama showing me how to kill a hen, years and years ago. If you hold her by the feet and don't joggle her around too much, she'll keep her head upright and level, like an Arabian dancing lady, and she won't get fretful. You just tenderly lay her down on her side in the grass, put the broomstick across her neck, set your feet on the broomstick astraddle her head, and give her feet a good firm yank. "Her head slips right off, see?" Mama'd said. I remembered some kind of a pink tube unspooled from the carcass where the head used to be. "She don't feel a thing, see?"

Now Opal started up wailing, and I come back to the present. My heart was beating so fast it hurt, and my muscles felt electric. I felt like I was about to fly right off of the earth.

"I ain't *never* having no children," Dacia said to me. Her voice was vibrating, but she wasn't hollering no more. "And if you're smart, you'll wish your next baby dead, too." She pointed to my belly.

I started after her, but she wriggled out of Sam's arms and run past Opal into their room and slammed the door.

I groaned and lowered myself into the chair. I felt a bruise on my hip where I'd bumped into the table before. I was still panting.

Sam, he walked over to Opal and petted her arm. "You want to sleep in the bed with us tonight?"

She nodded and walked into our room. She was in a daze, seemed like. I cringed when I seen she was sucking her thumb, and her eleven.

Sam pulled up a chair and scooted close to me. "You hear all that?" I said.

"Enough."

I wiped my nose with my sleeve. "You know I never throwed myself at no men."

"I know." He put his hand on mine.

"Them lies about Mama . . ."

Now he didn't say nothing.

"It was lies, Sam."

He sighed. "I never knowed her."

Anger rose in me. "Well, I'm telling you, it's lies, all of it."

"I know." He petted my arm. "But could—I mean, could some of it be true?"

Now I stood up. "I'm gonna go for a walk."

"Must be coming on ten, eleven." He rose up from his chair.

"I won't be long." I got my shawl and walked

out of the house and onto the road and turned south, away from the big house. I walked along the road for I don't know how long. It was pitch-black out, and there was a warm wind, like breath. I felt sand on my ankles. Thoughts flew at me, one after another. Dacia knowed exactly what she was doing and knowed exactly how I would feel about it, and where on Earth did she come up with that story about Mama? How come her to say such evil things? I felt bad—it was true I favored Opal, who wouldn't?—but that didn't explain how come Dacia was so angry so much of the time. I thought about her playing with cards on Mama's bed when she was little, making up stories about the kings and queens. I felt my shoulders slump. She was doing the same thing now, only she wasn't a little girl no more, and her stories was made up to hurt people. Before, it was horses sprouting wings and flying off, and now, it was rat poison flying up like sawdust, the picture of the dead rat waving its legs, Mama saying *ain't no tears in Heaven*. Rough-on-Rats. I pictured that box up high on the shelf.

And then, just then, I recollected the day, back when Mama was still living, when I was hunting for the blue colander and I dumped out the junk drawer and found that thing—the two pieces of corrugated cardboard with white feathers stuck in the folds, them two cardboard ovals tied together with string. I'd thought it was Dacia's childish attempt to make an Indian headdress. I recollected the blood spots in the feathers, the silverfish chew holes. That thing Dacia made with feathers, that thing she said was something she'd made to play with, I'd threatened to beat her with a switch over it, and she'd gone out and cut a switch and stripped the leaves off, preparing herself for a beating, rather than tell me the truth. Which was, I now understood like I'd been hit over the head with a rock, the truth was, that feathered get-up was angel wings. Dacia'd made angel wings for Mama to take on her trip to Heaven. Mama's big secret trip, the one she talked about with Dacia all that time they was living in her bed.

Walking down the road in the dark, picking my way so's not to step in a hole, I knowed it for the truth. They was angel wings. Mama'd told Dacia if she got pregnant again she was going on a trip to Heaven, and Dacia'd made her wings to fly with, and she'd hid them in that dresser drawer you couldn't hardly open. And when Dacia was telling her stories, them angel wings turned into horse's wings and the horses took off and flew to Heaven.

The truth was right there in front of me, just like it was for Dacia. Mama, my own mama, she'd put this burden on that child, a burden nobody could bear, or should have to. How bad do you need company, to make your child an unknowing partner in something so awful? Bad, I reckon. My mama done that, the very mama who I washed her body after she died and petted the bulge in her belly. Everthing Dacia'd said about Mama was true, and, like as not, Dacia herself didn't understand to this day how bad of a thing it truly was, how much it had warped her.

I felt skinned. I felt like the very meat and blood of me was open to the air. As far as Mama killing herself and leaving everthing up to me— four little children and a drunken father and a failed farm and all the rest—that thought skipped across my mind like a flat rock on a creek. I wouldn't let myself hate Mama that much or, worse yet, let myself picture what she must've been like inside, the part of her that she said Dacia was like. I didn't want to look at that. I put it away someplace deep. I told myself, Mama's over and done with, don't make no difference now. Dacia's the one I got to contend with.

And Lord help me, I'd just beat Dacia till I raised a welt on her neck. And I knowed she had more bruises and welts to come in other places— I'd felt them in my hands by the reverberations in that hard old pickle spoon. Dacia'd took it too far, she had, like she always did. She'd lied in the end, lied to spite me in front of Sam, told a stupid, obvious lie that cast doubt on the whole fantastical story about Mama. That was Dacia, sure enough. But that didn't make the rest of it untrue. I knowed if I thought about it some more

I would remember other things that happened when Mama was sick, little things, things that would point to the truth.

I spread my shawl wide and let the wind swell it like a kite. Then I pulled it in and wrapped it around my face to hide my terrible shame, and I turned for home.

I tried to plan out what I would say to Dacia. I wouldn't say I was sorry for beating her. What she'd said about me, them names she called me in front of my husband, she'd asked for it, she deserved a beating. No—I would say I was sorry for that, it was too harsh, I'd lost my temper. I would ask her to forgive me. No—I would say it was awful hard being the oldest, trying to keep the family together, she never understood . . . No—I would start with Mama. I would ask her about the poison. Did she see Mama eat it? When? Where? And as soon as I thought that, I remembered Mama's mottled rash she got off and on. Was that from the poison? Did she eat it for a while and then quit, and then take it up again? What else did Dacia know about it?

And then I would tell her I remembered the cardboard thing with the feathers, and I would ask her, did she remember that thing? What was it? And listen for what she said. Maybe I was wrong about that. Maybe it *was* all made-up, all lies, maybe . . .

All the way home I planned and planned. One

time my mind wandered, and I even planned a way to tell Sam about the baby I lost during the war. But I drove that thought away when it come to me that Dacia wished the next baby would die, and my stomach turned over, and I vomited there on the road. I told myself, *Stop, just tell her what's in your heart, and, for God's sake, tell her you're sorry, since you are, and tell her you wish to God you could take it all back.*

And even then, I didn't know, could I do that, would I have the fortitude to bear her wrath, her throwing it up to me for the rest of our lives. Maybe it was best just to let it lay there.

In the morning Sam woken me up, breathless, saying he couldn't find Dacia. Her things was gone, the eight dollars he kept hid in the toe of his good boots was gone, he'd looked everwhere, she wasn't nowhere on the place.

Chapter 20

When a fourteen-year-old girl runs off without no note or nothing and you don't know what happened to her, you spend your days in a fearsome place where you dangle between wrath and dread and regret. Your throat gets swole up and stays that way, and your stomach grinds itself into meat. If you get distracted and forget it for a minute, why, soon's you remember again, ever hair rises up. That's where me and Sam was at after Dacia left. It's a hard place. I done my best to act hopeful around Opal, but she wouldn't hardly say two words in a row, only set and embroider like her life depended on it.

That first day, me and Sam acted like maybe Dacia wasn't gone for good. Sam rode into town and asked around for her, and he talked to the sheriff. Nobody seen her, nobody knowed nothing.

Soon's he come into the house he said to me, "She home?"

I was setting at the table, mending the elbow of his good shirt. I shook my head.

"Where's Opal at?" he said.

"Took her up to the Whitesides' to oil their mopboards. Should keep her busy all day."

"I don't suppose any of them seen Dacia?"

I shook my head again.

"Could she be playing a joke?" he said. "Trying to scare us?"

I never answered. We'd already had the same conversation before he'd went to town.

"Wouldn't hurt to go look down at the creek," he said, casual-like. "I'll round up some men."

"Sam?" I said. "Set for a minute." Then, choking and swallowing, I told him what I'd puzzled out the night before—the angel wings, the rash, Dacia's stories. I told him it must've been true, what she'd said—Mama had killed herself, and she'd brought Dacia in on it—and I'd beat her for nothing. When I was done my throat was dry.

It was a while before he spoke. He opened his mouth several times, and finally he said, "She couldn't have been right in her mind, your mama." His voice was quiet.

I nodded. I knowed he was walking on eggshells. Much as I craved that, I hated that he felt he had to.

He got out his cigarette lighter and fiddled with it. "I reckon Dacia can't stand what your mama done, and she takes it out on you."

We was silent for a long while, the both of us. Finally, I said, "I just wish—"

"We'll find her," Sam said. "She couldn't have got very far."

They never found no trace of her down at the creek, nor anyplace else we could think of. We talked to everbody we knowed, and Sam, he called on ever sheriff and pastor he met up with in his hauling work. We wrote William and Buck in case she went back to Obsidian, but they never seen her. We put ads in the papers in Kansas City, Wichita, Omaha, Denver. Nary a word.

There come a time—I don't know when, after a month maybe—when me and him stopped acting like she was coming back, and we settled into that place where dangling people live at. Ever time Sam come into the house, he give me the look that asked had I heard anything, and I give him the look said I hadn't. There ain't no mercy in living that way. You don't feel like you get any rest.

Opal, she slept in the bed with us for a week or two before she give up and went back to sleeping in her and Dacia's bed. I heard her crying in there ever little bit.

Over time, Dacia faded into the back of our minds, like she was bound to. Humans has got to be able to see far enough to put one foot after the other, or else they lose their mind. Me and Sam still had a child to care for, after all.

And things change all around you, all the time. Wiley got electricity in 1922, and Alta Bea and Harold built themselves a big house by the river, and they paid a fortune to have electric wires strung out there. The new house had four bedrooms and three water closets and a telephone. I'd thought Alta Bea's folks' house was fancy, but this one outshone it. I never seen nothing so modern.

One Sunday me and Alta Bea made pickles while Sam and Harold went fishing. Her new kitchen give water with a turn of the faucet handle. Canning takes a lot of water. Seems like there was spoons, rags, jars, jar lifters, lids, pans, pots, teakettles, and cucumbers everwhere you looked. By late afternoon the house smelled like sugar and vinegar and pickling spices. Smelled so strong, her little girls Alice and Ruby run outside to play, like we'd been telling them to all day.

Alta Bea, she was pregnant again. Little Alice'd told me, "We're going to get a baby boy, and his name's Harry." When I asked her how she knowed it was going to be a boy, she said, "Because Daddy said so."

Me and Alta Bea got to a stopping place in the canning, so we set down and put up our feet. Alta Bea made us some ice tea. She poured whiskey in hers.

Pretty soon the side door banged open, and

Harold come in carrying a mess of catfish on a stringer and plopped them down, all slimy, in the middle of a cookie sheet full of lids we'd just scalded.

Alta Bea said something like, "Don't put those filthy things there—can't you see we're canning?"

Harold stood there looking riled, didn't say nothing. Directly Sam come in.

The air in the kitchen was crackling with bad feelings between Alta Bea and Harold. It hit me I seen this before between them, plenty of times, and never hardly noticed how hateful it had gotten. When Mama was alive it was like that ever little bit between her and Daddy, too—there was something there that wasn't getting talked about but everbody felt it. Funny how you can watch something happening like that for a long time without hardly paying it no mind, like you feel something tickle your hair and you reach up and grab it, and when you look down in your hand, there it is, a bug, and you ask yourself, how long has that been there.

"Did you hear me?" Alta Bea said. "Get those fish off my *table.*"

Harold leaned over, picked up the fish in his two hands, and carried them over to the sink, paying no mind to them dripping on the floor, like men will. Plopped them in the sink. Got out his knife. Reached in a drawer, grabbed the sharpening stone, started scraping the knife. It was peculiar to see him in work pants and boots and a dirty, tore-up shirt. You usually seen him in a suit and collar, either leaving for work or coming home from work, all shined up. He was doing real good. Seems like they wasn't finding new pools like they once was, so he'd gotten out of lease grafting. Now he had him a job with a big company from back east, bossing all their drilling and pumping operations in south and southeast Kansas. Getting a little paunch, I noticed.

Sam set down next to me and put his arm around the back of my chair.

Now Harold picked out a fish and thumped it on the head with the knife handle. Grabbed it behind the whiskers with his first and second fingers and under the chin with his thumb, started stripping off the skin with a needle-nose pliers. Of course blue cat don't have no scales, they have skin, and it's slicker than snot. It took some tries before he got all the skin peeled off. Me and Sam and Alta Bea all just set there, watching, not saying nothing.

Then he sliced through the belly and wrenched out the guts, and then there was the gristle noise, ragged, as he sawed off the head. You leave the head for last so you have something to hold on to while you're skinning it. You don't want to touch them whiskers. They're stiff and pointed as a knitting needle, and they can give you a nasty

380

jab. That's how come you keep your fingers flat on the head and curl them around the base of the whiskers.

There was a moaning-like sound as the gills let go of their air. The smell, mixed with the pickling smells, was disagreeable.

I looked over at Alta Bea and seen her staring at the back of Harold's head. She tipped up her glass, but there was only a couple drops left. She licked at them.

I expect it took fifteen or twenty minutes for him to clean the mess of fish. Thump it, strip off the skin, gut it, cut off the head. Nobody moved, nobody said one word that whole time. I got to thinking about the story Sam told me, when Harold pounced on that French girl in the graveyard and Sam like to never got him off of her. I hated to think what kind of a man Harold was, underneath. And Alta Bea, I thought about her as a child, wanting to slide behind the paint on a wall whenever she was around people, and how things in that house seemed off to me. Her and Harold's new house was big and modern and had electric and indoor plumbing, but things was off there, too. I wondered, was Alta Bea sorry she'd married Harold? And her with a third child on the way. And her drinking like she done. I couldn't see no way out of where they was at.

Now Harold rattled the cupboard as he jerked

out a pie tin. He plunked the pink flesh on it and set it down on the table. He glanced at Sam and tromped out the kitchen door. The guts and heads was still laying in the sink where he let them drop.

Alta Bea stood up and got out the fry pan, the lard, the flour, the cornmeal, the salt, the pepper, and proceeded to fry the fish.

Me and Sam set there waiting for somebody to say something, but things was silent till we heard the girls squealing outside, "Daddy! Daddy!" You know, that delirious way children holler when they see their father.

After we eat, we played cards until late. Alta Bea got drunk. Before we left, Sam offered to help Harold get her up the stairs, but he said no thanks, he could handle her.

Me and Sam, we never said much on the way home.

Over time, seemed like we had less and less to talk about, beyond the weather, the bills, Opal's schooling, things like that. For one thing, there was Dacia. But then there was the other thing we never talked about—I was having miscarriages ever four or five months, seemed like. I kept wondering, what if I never was able to carry another baby? What if we went on and on, month after month, never knowing would I or wouldn't I, till I got so old we just give up? After my war year when I lost the first one, I'd felt like I was strong enough to get through anything. But this I didn't think I could bear. Ever time I felt the stickiness between my legs or discovered the stain in my underwear, the shame of my failure fell upon me. I come to dread the sight of blood, which had never bothered me before, and even just seeing the color red give me a feeling of bereavement. I remembered Mama saying, "The Lord tempers the wind to the shorn lamb," but to me it never felt like the wind let up.

The Wiley doctor never knowed how come I kept losing them. "It's just something that happens," he told me. "If you could see the women coming in here with seven, eight, nine of those brats, you wouldn't be complaining." After that I started going to the doctor in El Dorado, but seemed like he didn't know how come neither. Told me to stop several times a day and put my feet up, which I done, but didn't make no difference. Sometimes Sam knowed when I lost one, but if he didn't, I didn't tell him.

I prayed to God, let me carry a baby. I ain't asking for riches or nothing, just a baby. A little head of hair to smell, lips making a little O, arms and legs flailing. Can't I have one, like everbody else? Just one?

But truth is, I never actually believed the Lord heard me. Or if He did, He kept saying no. No, no, no, no, no, and again no, month by month, year after year. No.

Me and Sam, we growed rough edges, prickly, to where we irritated each other when we rubbed together. The months melted away, and then the years.

Chapter 21

In 1925 Daddy died, and Alta Bea, she went with me to Kentucky for the funeral. Sam was busy working, and Opal, she wouldn't go. Said she didn't hardly remember Daddy anyways, she was only a child when we broke up the family and moved to Kansas, and she was only a baby when we left Kentucky, and she didn't know none of them people, and how come was we burying him in Kentucky anyhow, with Mama in Missouri. It was a shock for me to hear all this. The older ones and younger ones in a family, it's like they have whole different lives.

I told her, Daddy bought that plot back home years ago, and maybe *he* was too cheap to take Mama home, but we was too stubborn to do like Daddy done. And I told her, you only got one daddy and he's only going to die once, and you can't go back and do it over again when you get older and understand why you have to go to your daddy's funeral. And I said, what about the twins, and William and Dora and Buck? Didn't she want to see them again?

She told me, *I ain't a child, stop preaching,* and

there wasn't no more time to argue with her. The train come when it come, and you had to catch it or wait another three days.

Only when me and Alta Bea was on the train did I recollect Opal had been sick on the ride to Kansas as a child. I wondered how hard it must have stuck in her mind, that even now she wouldn't complain about it but let me go on and on like I done, and her making up excuses. With Opal, if you wasn't careful you could just forget she even existed.

Buck and William and Dora, they'd already rode with Daddy's remains to Galena, and they met me and Alta Bea at the train when we got there. At first we all stood in the spitting snow and looked at each other, not being huggers. Then Dora broke away and come and throwed her arms around me and started dancing me around. The two of us started crying, and then she let go of me and everbody took a turn. Alta Bea, she stood off to the side. After William embraced me, he offered his hand to her, and she shook it and smiled. "You remember me," she said, like she was surprised.

Then everbody was talking at once, smiling and crying. Something happens when you see your beloveds you last seen years ago, and you see the age on their face, but at the same time you also see them like you remember them. It's like the years come and go on their face even as you're standing there.

Buck, he took Daddy's death hard. He never did get married, and him and Daddy'd lived together over the barbershop for nine years. It's a mystery to me how Buck got along with Daddy like he done, and me and William never did. I will say, Buck was always sweet and patient like that. Opal takes after him, sure enough.

William and Dora had the twins with them, who of course I hadn't saw since we moved to Kansas. They was fifteen now, and both just alike. William had them to look me in the eye, and I babbled on about taking care of them when they was little, but of course they just stood there red-faced and dropped their eyes to the ground like boys does. It was more like they was nephews or cousins than brothers, which I knowed would happen, which is how come I cried bitter tears when we moved. But they was good-looking boys, healthy and sound, and they done William and Dora proud. Them two also had four of their own, two boys and two girls. You could see the Winslows and the Sweets in them.

I'll never forget that trip, and not just because we was burying Daddy. Seems like it was the first time in my life I had the feeling people was looking at me and saying to each other, "That's her." It turned out, I never knowed how notorious I was back home, nor what for.

Seeing Daddy in his coffin made me remember washing Mama. I recollected what she looked like, gray like he was now, and I thought about the sound of the water trickling into the bowl as I wrung out the cloth. The memory of it pierced me. But Daddy's death never hit me like Mama's. I thought, *Well, like everbody else, he won't suffer nor cause suffering no more.*

It was a relief when they closed the lid and my brothers and a couple of cousins carried the coffin out of the church. We had the funeral in Mama's church because most of Daddy's people had scattered hither and yon, and the few that was left wouldn't set foot in our church. Besides, they never had no church, they met in people's houses.

"You ready?" I said to Alta Bea, and we headed to the basement for the funeral dinner. Halfway down I smelled pork and game and corn and greens and meringue. I was back home, sure enough. A girl again, six year old.

They had four long tables for people to set at, and two tables set end to end filled with food. Lines of people was moving along either side. People was talking, laughing, crying. They was putting their hands on either side of people's faces, staring at them like they was looking at a picture.

A heavyset woman, about sixty, trotted up to

us, her hands fluttering. "Albertina, Albertina!" she hollered. "Come set with me!"

I cocked my head to one side.

"I'm Ina, I'm a cousin of your mama, I'd know you anywhere, you look just like your folks, I remember you like it was yesterday, you won't remember me, you was too little, but I remember you like it was yesterday, who's this?" She didn't talk fast like people in Kansas, but she did talk continuous.

"This here's my friend Alta Bea," I said.

Ina grabbed me like a prize and set me down in a folding chair. Then she started in naming our relations and enumerating where each one fit on Mama's side. Behind Ina's remarks I overheard a man's voice. "I walk in the door, and she says, 'If that's a box of candy, you can just throw it in the trash.' So I walked outside and throwed it in the trash."

"Good thing the ground ain't froze yet," a second man said.

"Third funeral we been to this month. Hope Flora don't catch a cold like last time."

I turned back to Ina, who was talking about Daddy and us moving to Missouri, and I said, "Daddy decided to take his hand to farming, but—"

"Horsefeathers!" Ina said. "Albert Winslow never had no desire to be no farmer, nor wanted to leave here neither. It was your mama made

389

him. Said, it's a shame when relations only see each other at funerals." She looked around. "Now, your mama, why, she thought the sun rose and set on you, and that's the truth. Spoilt you rotten."

"She did?" I wondered, did she have me confused with Dacia. I remembered Mama saying when I was a baby I was stiff, saying I was colicky and sour and looked plain like a Winslow.

"We've always thought Bertie was spoiled," Alta Bea said, sarcastic. She must've snuck a drink already.

Ina pursed her lips. "Well, if you want to know, it had to do with the serpents. Your daddy's kin was serpent handlers, but you know that."

"They was?"

"That's something our side don't believe in, of course, never did. Now your mama said she didn't care if he went to them meetings, but she nor any of her children would never go to no serpent preacher or poison drinker. They drink poison, too." She squinted at Alta Bea like Alta Bea might be one of them heathens. "She made him promise on a solemn *oath* he wouldn't expose none of the children to that," Ina went on. "A child don't know no better."

"Amen," Alta Bea said. I poked her in the side.

"Like I said," Ina went on, "your mama give you any little thing your heart desired." She laughed. "She used to tie your hair up in rags and made the prettiest ringlets." Now I knowed she thought I was Dacia, but I never said nothing.

"Your daddy, I reckon he wanted to show you off, you was so pretty." Ina looked around and leaned close. "Sure enough, one day he took you to a serpent meeting."

She may have confused me with Dacia before, but now I knowed it was me she meant. "I was on his shoulders, I remember," I said. "My hair rose up."

"Static electricity," Alta Bea said. When Ina's eyes got big, she added, "She told me, when we were girls."

Ina turned back to me. "Well, do you remember what *happened?* Do you recollect, one of them *struck* you?"

"What?" said me and Alta Bea together.

"I didn't think so." Ina's chin trembled. "Well, your daddy, now he was drunk in the Lord, and he walked up there, and he grabbed your little knee and stuck your little foot out and waved it in front of them snakes." She stuck out her hand, wiggling it, to show how Daddy done my leg.

"Drunk in the Lord?" Alta Bea said.

"But you ain't heard the best part!" Ina cried. "When that snake struck you, Albertina, its fangs—I don't know what kind it was, rattler, copperhead, cottonmouth, Clyde Oberle would know, he knows all the serpents—"

"It bit me?" I said.

"Well, that's just it! The fangs went *in between* your toes! It sprayed its poison but never broke the skin!" She pulled up to her full sitting height. "And you never spoke a word, not one word. Never cried or nothing. Just set there in your daddy's arms, a-lookin' around at everbody like nothing happened, happy as a pig in slop."

For a moment the hair on my arms stood up, and I felt like I couldn't breathe.

"Your daddy and them, they saw it as a *sign,*" Ina said. "There was rejoicing in the Lord, and they say a lot of people got saved from it."

A shiver went up my spine. Me, anointed? Could that be? As a baby? And the Lord, him just waiting all this time for me to answer the call?

"I don't know if their salvation took," Ina said. "Like I said, our side don't believe in the serpents."

The dinner noises went on—people talking, shoes clomping on the floor, somebody laughing.

"That snake, it never kilt you like it should have," Ina said. "By the grace of the Lord, them fangs fell in between your toes. He spared you on your daddy's faith, if not your mama's, though of course we always thought it was your mama's."

"In between your toes, Albertina," Alta Bea said. Her tone was sarcastic, and the look she give me had in it all the things her and me ever said to each other, all the books she ever read and lent to me, all her schooling. The time she told me how a watch worked.

Then I knowed, just knowed like I knowed there was dirt in the ground, that this snake story, or anyway the part about my toes, was malarkey. Maybe there was a scrap of truth to it, maybe people around there thought they seen something, but Daddy, he'd done it up into a whole song and dance for his kin and Mama's. Just like all of his stories—embroideryed on or slanted, if not made up out of whole cloth. Fairy tales.

I felt let down and sad. "If that don't beat all," I said, to be polite.

Ina perked back up. "Well, by the time your daddy come home with you that night, your mama, she'd heard all about it, and she met him at the door with the long rifle. Told him to put you down and leave the premises, or she was going to shoot him like a dog." She arched an eyebrow. "And she wouldn't let him back, neither, till he promised to take you-uns away and never have nothing to do with his kin no more. And bless his heart, that's what he done."

Now, I knowed I was only a baby when this happened, maybe three year old—little enough I was perched on Daddy's shoulders. And little enough that, if somebody hadn't mentioned it at the hog killing, and if I hadn't told Alta Bea the story to fix it in my mind, why, I might have forgot what few things I remembered about it.

And little enough I never noticed nothing about no toes.

And I knowed I was nine when we moved away from Kentucky, after Daddy took me horse-trading and done some foolish wicked thing and got beat up in an alley next to the trash cans, just like he didn't have a young girl with him to take account of. I reckon Daddy never told nobody *that* story. That story never made him look good, like the snake story done, in his eyes. And the two stories had got mixed up in Ina's mind, and only me still alive that knowed better. But I still didn't see no need to say nothing. The less said about Daddy, the better.

Now Ina sighed. "Oh, you're well known around here. Everbody knows about Albertina Winslow and the serpents."

"If that don't beat all," I said again. "Beats anything I ever heard tell of."

Me and Alta Bea stayed in Galena for four days. We spent most of the last day just saying goodbye—who knowed when us Sweets and Winslows would ever see each other again? And me getting my picture took. My favorite is the one with me, Buck, William, Dora, and the twins standing in front of our old house. It was a shame Opal and Dacia wasn't there to complete the family circle. Mama would have liked that. The house, it seemed awful small, like they does.

There's a picture with me, Buck, and William at Daddy's grave, too. As we was standing there I couldn't help but think about Mama's service, with just us children and Daddy lined up there and a few neighbors, and nary a one of Mama's people. Me and William and Buck look old in Daddy's graveyard picture, more like we was in our forties than our twenties. Buck, his eyes is burning right off the paper, seems like.

Later on that day, me and Alta Bea got on the train for home. "I bet your girls is missing their mama," I said to her when we settled in. She had four by then. Harold kept wanting to try for a boy.

She got a cigarette out of her bag. "How are you feeling, Bertie? All right?"

"Wore out, tell the truth."

"I've noticed you putting your hand on your belly, if you don't mind my saying so." She lit the cigarette, leaning her head back to blow the smoke high in the air.

"Eat too much, I expect. Seems like when we get together, all we do is eat."

"You certainly have interesting relatives," she said.

We never said nothing for a while. I looked out the window at the scenery passing by. It's awful pretty in the Kentucky hills. Not like the Flint Hills, where the beauty is in the huge

Kansas sky, and the sun washes everthing else out, and the land don't seem like much. Oh, the land's pretty, in a brownish way, with miles of knee-high brownish prairie grass dotted by brownish rocks and bushes. And the longer you live there, the more you see the million tiny differences in the dun shades. But the sun—seems like you're exposed to the sun's very eyeball, it glares down at you. Makes you feel little, like you might disappear and never be missed. But them Kentucky hills, why, the sky there's a lot smaller, peeking at you through the trees, the sunbeams broke up among the leaves, and in that paler light, the colors is real strong, deep, rich—blues and greens and purples and reds and oranges. After you're in Kansas for a while, seems like the colors of Kentucky look like an oil painting up close—too loud to be real. Kansas, everthing's real, no matter how close you look at it.

Alta Bea jolted me out of my thoughts. "You know who I think about every so often? Little Will."

It took me a second to register what she meant, and then everthing flew from my mind except the memory of me throwing Will on the floor. Felt like I had lightning running from the top of my head to my gut, and then back up into my teeth. I tasted acid.

Alta Bea frowned and put her hand on my arm

and said, "I'm sorry, Bertie. I always say the wrong thing."

A boy come down the aisle selling things from a box. Alta Bea asked me did I want anything, but I said no. She boughten some crackers and a package of cigarettes.

Me and her never said nothing for a while. Finally, I said, "Did I ever tell you, when Daddy was a boy, he heard somewhere that riding on a train would kill you? He thought if you moved thirty mile an hour, like a train does, why it would make your insides explode."

Alta Bea smiled.

"I said to him once, said, 'People's been riding on trains since before you was born, Daddy,' and he says, 'You just wait. Ever one of 'em's gonna die from it sooner or later. You mark my words.'"

"Mark my words." She laughed. "What I remember is him sitting up on your roof, singing. We could hear him at our place."

I always wondered, could they hear him. Now I knowed. "Drunk," I said.

She give me a doubtful look.

"You was in town the day he hung John in the tree for a joke, and I stabbed him with the hay fork."

She nodded, her eyes big.

"Everbody . . ." I looked out the window but didn't see nothing I was looking at. "All them things they said about what a good husband

and father he was? At the funeral? Hogwash. Drink, sleep it off, drink some more, that was Daddy." Now that I got started, seemed like I couldn't stop. "After we moved to Obsidian? Never worked hardly. Me and my brothers, we growed ever onion and radish that was growed on that place, we took care of the animals, we hired ourself out, we brought in all the money was brought in to that house. We seen to it the rent was paid, we kept up the bill at the store, as best as we could." I wiped my nose. "And Mama, she'd say, 'Your daddy's asleep on the floor, mind you don't step on him as you go by.' It was like, he's your daddy, he can do any fool thing he wants to. He wasn't asleep—he was passed out."

"We never knew," she said, which was a lie she was offering as a friend, and I just took it. I knowed she meant well.

We each had our thoughts for a while. She got out her silver flask and sipped from it.

"My father's going to die one of these days," she said.

"He sick?"

She shrugged.

"Oh. You mean someday," I said.

"Now my father never drank." She give a bitter laugh. "Maybe it would have been better if he had."

I sighed. Seemed like she couldn't see herself through nobody else's eyes, but that was Alta

Bea. "I never seen him very much," I said. "Whenever I did, he was dressed up. For the bank."

She lifted the flask and, with it pressed on her mouth, said, "I don't think he ever wanted children."

I felt a chill, and I batted away a thought of Mama.

You could hear the metallic echo of her swallow. "Or anyway, not a girl," she said. "He's never expressed any feeling for me except disapproval. Disappointment. He was always *disappointed* in me."

"He was?" I remembered when she told me, the first day I met her, *I was a surprise.* At the time I didn't know what she meant. Then I pictured her daddy walking into the room where we was at, carrying a newspaper, wroth because Alta Bea'd swore. Even wroth, he'd seemed cold. My daddy, you wouldn't ever say he was cold.

"I tried so hard," she said. "I tried. I tried."

I pictured her as a girl, smacking her face on her knees.

"My father doesn't love me," she said. "There. I said it." There was a kind of awe in her voice.

I reached over and petted her arm. "I don't reckon it's in their nature—not like us." I was thinking of my daddy and hers and most of the men I'd ever knowed. Then it dawned on me, the thing about all the men I knowed—they was afraid. Of what, I didn't know. Not of us, not of women, of course not—but what, then? They was running from something all their lives, seemed like, running as fast as they could. What was they afraid of?

Then I pictured Sam—and his kind, sweet, gentle ways—and I realized he wasn't afraid like other men was. I wondered, how come? I pictured him the first time I seen him at the dance years ago, and I felt heat in the skin of my arms.

I looked over at Alta Bea and seen tears on her cheeks, and I knowed how lucky I was, even with all I had lost in life, to have Sam. He had loved me for years now, and I just now understood—you have to have somebody to love just as much as you have to have somebody to love you. Maybe more.

I was glad we was on our way home, and I couldn't hardly wait to get there.

Wasn't long after Daddy died that Opal saw an advertisement in the Wichita paper for a used sewing machine, one of them heavy factory kind. She bought it out of her own money she had been saving for two years, and she give Kirby Hess six dollars and a half rent for the first month in the corner of his hardware store. Me and Sam was worried would she make out. I asked her, "How're you going to pay the second month?" and she told me she already had a customer—

400

Mrs. Whiteside. She wanted Opal to make her a dress to wear to Kenneth's wedding. Opal never said so, but I think Mrs. Whiteside give her extra money to get started. Her husband had died a few months before, and seemed like Mrs. Whiteside wanted to spend money while she could.

Opal never had no doubt she would make out. Seems like it never come into her head she wouldn't.

She got one of them dress dummies, the kind you can adjust their parts to match the person you're sewing for. Then she'd cut out muslin pieces and pin them to the dummy. When she finished the muslin pattern for Mrs. Whiteside's dress, she had me to come in to the shop and look at it.

"I don't see nothing but pieces," I told her. "I can't picture what it's going to look like done up."

"You don't think it'll be pretty?"

"I bet it will," I said. "What did Mrs. Whiteside say?"

"I ain't showed it to her. I wanted you to see it first."

It touched me she asked me first, though I wasn't no help.

Well, of course when the dress was all done Mrs. Whiteside liked it fine, and then the bride asked Opal to make the wedding dress, too. Opal, she told me she figured the mother's dress was a test, and that just goes to show you how smart she is. Something like that never dawned on me, and that's why I never owned no business but dressing chickens and ironing, which is just chores.

When the wedding picture come out in the paper, Opal never had an idle minute after that. Next thing we knowed, she moved her shop to the whole top floor over the Arbogost store. Soon she had two girls working for her.

Sometimes I helped out when they got too busy. I loved going in there. It smelled like sizing, a pasty smell that always makes me happy.

One winter day in early 1926 I was setting there in the shop doing some handwork when Opal's helper Corinne said, "My gracious, what's that?"

I looked up, and she was pointing at the little chair I was setting on. There was a big red splotch underneath of me. Then I felt the cramping start. "I'm sorry, Opal," I said. "Corinne, get a pan of cold water, would you? Rags? Towels? I'm sorry, I never thought—"

"We need to fetch the doctor," Opal said.

"Don't need no doctor. Don't take but ten or twenty minutes, then it'll—"

"You need to lay down! Don't get up! Lay down!" Her voice rose up high, and I could tell by looking at her face that she was scared half to death.

402

"It's my own fault," I said. "I was feeling puny this morning. Should've stayed home. I always think, *this time*—"

Corinne come running in with towels. "Should I get the doctor?" she said to Opal.

"Help me lift my skirt up, will you? Opal, put them towels there—right there. Oh. Oh."

"Christ!" Opal said. Corinne run out of the room.

"Don't fret yourself," I said to Opal. "Looks bad, I know, but—"

"Jesus *Christ,*" Opal said.

That's the last thing I remember. When I woken up, why, I was in a hospital bed. I seen stripes of yellow light on the ceiling from the blinds. I was scared. I'd knowed people that went to the hospital, and not a one of them'd come home alive.

"She (something) (something)." That was Alta Bea's voice.

Sam leaned over me. His face was pale.

"I feel heavy," I said. "Like I can't lift my head up."

"Don't move. Just (something)." Now Alta Bea leaned over. I smelled cigarettes on her.

"(Something) operation," Sam said.

"What?" My throat hurt, and my mouth was dry. My lips felt cracked. I closed my eyes and went back to sleep.

Next time I woken up, the doctor was standing

there talking to Sam. Their voices sounded like horseflies buzzing.

I heard the doctor say, "(Something) she (something)?"

"Well, she (something) the boy (something). She (something)."

"She (something)?"

Seems like all I kept hearing was "she," "she," "she."

"She (something)," Sam said.

"I mean she (something). How many?"

There was a silence.

"Sometimes they (something), like a cat," the doctor said. "Just (something) and act like (something). She."

"She," Sam said.

"Well, she won't (something) (something)," the doctor said.

I kept hearing "she" over and over again all the time I slept. Seemed like I slept a long time. In my sleep Mama come to my bed and kept saying, "Shhhh, shhhh, shhhh."

Some days later the doctor come in with Sam. "How you feeling?" the doctor said.

"Tolerable."

"You hurting anywhere?"

"In the belly down low."

"Let's have a look." I flinched when he pulled back the blanket—it's surprising how just sliding a piece of material across stitches makes your belly scream—and lifted off the bandages. He looked at the wound and then retaped it and covered me back up.

I caught my breath. "When can I go home?"

"Don't you like the service here?" he said, like it was a joke.

"I got things to do. You know."

"We'll see how things look in a week or two." He wrote something down. Then he nodded to Sam and walked away.

"How you feeling? Really?" Sam said. He set down on the bed, and I felt an itchy pain. He jumped up and the bed bounced, and it felt like I'd got kicked by a mule.

I motioned with my hands for him to ease himself onto the bed. "How's things at home?"

"Don't worry about that. You just get well."

"I'll thank you not to tell me what to worry about," I said.

He sighed. "Opal, I don't hardly see her no more. When she ain't here, she's at the shop all day and half the night."

I nodded. "You getting enough to eat?"

"Mrs. Whiteside sends food down ever little bit." He looked at me. "You in pain?"

I shook my head.

"You look like it."

I closed my eyes and laid my head back, acting like I was falling asleep. I had something to say to him, but I hadn't figured out how. I felt him touch my hair, smoothing it with the back of his fingers.

Pretty soon he said, "Had to call Hollis Laird over to the house. Bluebell, she throwed a shoe."

"Is that right."

"Got a letter—"

"I'm barren, Sam," I blurted out. Waves of shame rolled over me.

I felt him startle. The bed was thrumming. "I know," he whispered.

My face felt so tight it hurt. "You can divorce me," I said. "You got ever right."

"Open your eyes," he said.

I shook my head. "Marry somebody that can give you children."

"Goddamn it, open your eyes."

I gritted my teeth, tasting salt. I opened my eyes and looked at him.

"Don't you never say that again long's we live," he said.

"Sam."

"Don't you know we almost lost you?" Now he covered his face with his hands and broke down.

"Go on home," I said. "I'm wore out."

He drawed his arm over his face to wipe the tears off. "You just get well." He petted my shoulder.

I pressed my hand against my stitches and

heaved myself over on my side, facing away from him.

"You just get well," he said again.

"I'm wore out."

He sighed. Pretty soon I felt the bed rock a little and then settle. He laid a hand on my hip for a second, and then I heard his boots on the slick linoleum floor.

There's punishment, and then there's punishment. I felt like I could endure God's wrath for the things I done, but for one thing—I couldn't bear the look I seen on Sam's face. Pity. Pity like I used to feel for Mama, even as she turned her bed into her coffin.

Now I felt afraid. I wanted to believe Sam still loved me like he done before, but I never had the courage to. Besides, there was things he didn't know I done—to Timmy, to Will—things I never told him, coward that I was. I felt like there would be a lot to go through coming up, and I couldn't see how things could ever be the same between us again.

Chapter 22

After three weeks in the hospital, I come home. Then a couple days later, when Sam and Opal was both at work, I went through all my underwear and rags and gathered up the ones that had bloodstains on them, half a bushel basket's worth. I carried the bundle out in the yard and throwed it on the ground and set a newspaper on fire and throwed it on the pile. I stood there and watched the flames and smoke rise and curl. *Goodbye, you blood, you pain, you Goddamn misery,* I said to myself. I was half scared, acting like such a heathen, but I stood there and let the fire mesmerize me. As it sputtered down, the word that come to my mind was never. I was never going to have another miscarriage, and I was never going to have no children. I was twenty-six. Never seemed to stretch out over a long time.

As the next few months went by, what I felt was just empty. Sam, he was gone, working, in the daytime and sometimes overnight, and the same thing with Opal in her shop. When she was home, it was *the shop* this, *the shop* that, her fabric order was late, Mrs. So-and-So had gotten fat, her best seamstress had the pleurisy. It didn't feel like I had nothing to say to neither one of them, nothing that amounted to very much. Sam, seemed like he didn't hardly play the fiddle at home no more. Seemed like he couldn't keep the look of pity off his face.

I'd set in the daytime and ask myself, what did I used to do? How come I used to be so busy from morning till night, and now I can't hardly fill up the days? There was chickens to dress and ironing to get done, but seemed like they didn't hardly take no time no more. My own chores didn't seem to take much time neither. I hated feeling useless, which was what I felt like.

Alta Bea would come over with her girls, and they'd play outside while me and her talked. One time she told me she'd started sleeping in the baby's room. Harold still wanted a boy, but she was determined she wasn't having no more babies. I wondered how long Harold would put up with that. Me and Sam, when I healed up we started having relations again, but for a long time I never took no pleasure in it. Seemed unnatural—wasn't nothing going to come of it.

Nobody hardly ever mentioned Dacia, but seems like I thought about her more often than before. Seems like most ever night I dreamed I was searching for lost things, with a bear or coyote or flying horse chasing me. I had forgotten the last thing she said to me, and I got to where

I would spend hours thinking about nothing but that last awful night. I felt like I couldn't stand not knowing what happened to her. It gnawed at me.

But like a lot of other things, wasn't a thing I could do about it.

One June day the next summer, I was dressing a chicken when a redheaded boy rode on a bicycle up to the front porch. "You Mrs. Bertie . . . ?" He looked down at a piece of paper and tried to sound out "Frownfelter."

I wiped my hands on my apron and told him to help himself to a dipperful of water while I read the note. A Mr. Newt Stiggins of the train depot said there was three children there by themself, asking for me. Said they was my niece and a nephew and another boy. Said Mr. John Naab at the sorghum mill had told him where we lived at.

Didn't make no sense.

"You got the wrong house," I said to the boy. "I don't have no niece and a nephew—well, but for my brother William's children, but they—"

"Mrs. Frownfelter, south corner, Whiteside farm," the boy said. "That's what it says, look for yourself."

"I'm telling you, child, I don't—" And then something went through me.

The boy said, "You all right, Missus?"

I said, "Lord Amighty. What has she done." I

411

backed up and set down hard on the edge of the porch—collapsed, more like.

"Any answer?" the boy said.

"Surely not," I said. "Surely not."

He swung his leg over his bicycle.

"Wait." I stood up. "If you wait till I get the horse hitched up, you can ride to town with me."

When I got there, there they was. The littlest, the girl, looked like Dacia through and through, but with Mama's eyes. She had long, wavy chestnut-colored hair like Dacia's, filthy though it was. She couldn't have been much more than two or three year old, I reckoned. The middle boy, maybe five, he looked a bit like Opal, with deep-set eyes, bags underneath. He stared down at the ground and never looked up at me. The biggest one was white as a ghost, with the whitest hair I ever seen on a child, white eyebrows, white eyelashes, white hairs on his arms. You would've thought he was an albino, but his eyes wasn't pink. He looked too old to be Dacia's natural child, maybe eight.

They all three was deep-down grimy.

I stood there and stared at them for a good minute. They stared back, except for the middle boy, who kept looking at the ground and fingering his shirt buttons.

It felt like I was spinning.

The pale boy unpinned a note from inside his trouser pocket and handed it to me.

Dear sister. Am sending three mouths to feed but have took ill and cant manage. I pray you still live in the same place, if not they will find you. The older boy is one we tooken in, he was lost. I am certain you will be mercival, you always was. I hope the day will come when I can reclame them. Mama always said, I was her on the inside, and you was her on the outside. My best to Sam.

There wasn't no name, but of course I knowed who it was. She was alive. She wasn't dead on the railroad tracks, or murdered, or raped, or drowned, nothing like that. Then I thought, *well, raped maybe,* and I felt my skin quiver.

For some minutes I stood there just breathing. It was like I hadn't took a natural breath for the six years she'd been gone.

Dacia was alive.

I read the note through three times, studying the scribbly writing like it would answer me all the hundred questions that was in my mind. She knowed I would be merciful? Where was *that* feeling when I was looking after her? "Mouths to feed"? Like I would see her children as livestock? Even in her extremity, whatever it was—"took ill" was like to be a lie—she'd managed to get her digs in.

But I took aholt of myself, swallered hard,

413

and put the note in my pocket. I looked up at the oldest boy. "Where'd you come from?"

He fidgeted.

"I mean, what town? Where did you-uns start out from on the train?"

He sighed. "She took us from camp into town, and then into a bigger town to where the train was at."

The little girl sniffled. You could see she was about to cry.

"You don't know the names of the towns?"

He looked at me and squinted. "There's a long creek, maybe a river, by where the tent was at."

"Tent?"

"Where we lived at."

"You know the name of the river?"

He shook his head.

I nodded. "What's your names?"

"I'm Hiram," the boy said. "This here's Trouble, and her name is Sorrow."

The boy he called Trouble gasped and let out a big breath, and I realized he'd been doing that all along ever little bit without me paying it no mind.

"Can't you get your breath?" I said to him. I tried to look him in the eye, but now his eyes was fixed on my mouth. I dipped my head, but I couldn't catch his gaze.

"He does that," Hiram said. "Don't mean nothing."

I looked from one child to the other. I felt my heart slowing down. They was just children, after all. "You hungry?"

"A man with a round red hat give us bread-and-butter sandwiches yesterday," Hiram said. "On the train."

"Yesterday." I reached out my hand to Sorrow, but she ducked behind Hiram. "Let's go get something to eat, want to?" I said to him, and when he followed me, the other two followed him. I took them to the alley pump to wash them up—they seemed to drink as much water as got on them, they must have been thirsty as fish—and then we took the back door into Arbogost's. Tillie looked close at the children but didn't say nothing. She give me a questioning look, but I didn't feel like talking just then. I got a pound of sausages and a loaf of bread, and me and the children set down in a grassy spot by the tracks and eat sausage sandwiches. They eat like they was starving, which I guess they was. We visited the privy. Then I asked myself, *What now? What happens now? You ever think about that, Dacia?* Then I felt bad. It wasn't like I myself didn't have nothing to be ashamed of.

I got out the note and read it again. *Mouths to feed.*

Seemed like there was only one thing to do, which was get in the buggy and ride on home. Which we done. We didn't hardly say a word to each other. They just looked around, curious, except for the middle boy, who kept his eyes cast down.

Sorrow, she fell asleep on Opal's bed as soon's we got home, but she said her first words to me as she laid there with her eyes blinking. "My mama give me some red mittens."

"She did?"

"Uh-huh. Red ones."

"I bet they was warm."

She held up her hands and waggled them back and forth.

"Mittens is a nice present," I said.

"My daddy let me put a plate in the river."

"He did? What for?" I wondered did this have anything to do with mittens, but children is like that, moving from subject to subject, especially when they're sleepy.

"Trouble, my brother?" she said. "He caught a crawdad."

"In the river?"

She said, "Can I go home now?" Then she closed her eyes and slept like she was dead.

At suppertime Opal come walking up the road as usual, and there we was, me and the children. She took off her hat and give everbody a friendly smile. "Well now, who are you folks?"

"Opal—" I started to say.

"Who're *you?*" Sorrow said.

"Opal Winslow. Who're you?"

Sorrow scooted behind Hiram, and her thumb went to her mouth. Her hair looked like a rat's nest after her nap.

Me, I was trying to find words to explain things to Opal without coloring them for the children. While I stood there with my mouth open, why, Opal smiled at Hiram and stuck out her hand. "Hello there, pleased to meet you."

He nodded. After a moment he shook her hand. "Him, that's Trouble," he said, pointing. "He don't say much." Trouble was standing in the futherest part of the room, with his back in the corner, where he'd been all afternoon. His hands was planted against the two walls like he was about to push the walls back. It was hard to know what he might be thinking. His face didn't have the look of a simple person, but the expression he wore was like he wasn't quite there with you.

Opal looked at Trouble but talked to Hiram. "Trouble? You say his name is Trouble?"

"Yes'm."

Opal bowed her head toward Trouble. "You shake hands?" I seen he was looking at her mouth, like he done me.

"He don't like to be touched," Hiram said.

Opal smiled. "Me neither."

Trouble started rocking on one foot. He still hadn't uttered a word.

I started to tell her who she was dealing with,

but she just kept going. She was having a good time. "How about you?" she said to Sorrow. "Your name Trouble, too?"

Around her thumb Sorrow said, "A course not."

"A course not," Opal said. "Well, let me see. Is it Mary?"

The girl shook her head.

"How about Jane? No? Well then, Adelia? Emily?"

Sorrow stared at her with big eyes.

"I know—Obadiah. That's it, I bet. Obadiah."

"Man name," Trouble screeched. "Man-name, man-name, man-name." His voice was like an animal's, a coyote's maybe. Even as he howled, he stared at the ceiling.

We all looked at each other. "We heard you," I said.

"Man-name," he hollered.

I took a step toward him, but Hiram stuck out his arm to warn me back.

"Man-name, man-name." He was panting.

"What on earth?" Opal said. She looked from me to him and back again.

Hiram took Sorrow's hand, and the two of them walked to the corner. Slowly and softly, Hiram said to Trouble, "It *is* a man's name. It *is* a man's name. We know."

"Man-name," Trouble yipped. He let go one hand from the wall and run his fingers up and down his three shirt buttons, up and down.

Hiram dropped Sorrow's hand and squatted down. "Let's go outside. How about it?" He stretched out his hand, and Trouble took it. As Hiram led him outside, Trouble turned around and walked backward, his eyes on the floor.

"What the Sam Hill?" Opal said.

"You must be thirsty," I said to her. "I made some lemonade, want some? And cornbread?" One thing I knowed, you can always feed people.

"What's wrong with that boy?" Opal said. "Who are these children?"

Sorrow, she walked over to where Trouble'd stood and run her fingers along the wall.

"Wore out," I said. "Rode the train for days. Didn't hardly have nothing to eat."

"Train?"

I got out plates and glasses and set them on the table.

Hiram come back into the house and stood there looking from me to Opal. "It bothers him when things don't make sense."

"There's something wrong with that boy," Opal said. "A blind man could see that."

"Well, at least we know he can hear." I pulled the towel off the top of the pitcher. "And he don't abide teasing, evidently."

"He don't get jokes," Hiram said. "He don't mean nothing by it, he just don't get it." He blinked like he had a tic. "He likes to be in a little place by himself, so I fixed him a nest out

419

by the woodpile, temporary. We stay, I'll build it up."

"Lord Amighty," said Opal.

"Dacia gives him a strong cup of coffee when he gets like that," Hiram said. "Seems to help."

"Dacia!" Opal hollered. "My Lord in Heaven! Dacia! Where's she at?" She looked around. "Where's Dacia?"

"Where's Dacia?" Sorrow said. "Where's my mama?" She begun crying.

"Best not mention D-a-c-i-a," I said to Opal.

"My mama!" Sorrow cried. "Where's my mama!" It near broke my heart, how pitiful that child's cries was.

Then we heard Trouble start up hollering out in his hidey-hole.

Hiram didn't make a sound, but tears started running down his face.

"What the Sam Hill?" Opal said.

About that time we heard Sam come driving up.

I never knowed what to do. I felt like the world had turned upside down, and me with it, which I reckon it had. I'd heard tell of people with a fever, how they might turn delirious, and I always wondered what it felt like. Now I felt like I knowed.

That evening, Trouble took to standing in the corner like he done before. Ever three or four breaths his chest caved in like a hiccup. Now Sam, without so much as a by-your-leave, he brought out his fiddle, and Trouble snuck a peek over there ever little bit. Seemed like he got curious in spite of whatever else was going on in his head. Sam set on the edge of his chair like he always done, and slowly he drew the bow across the strings half a dozen times, and then zing, zing, zing, three short notes, and then he run up and down the scale, and then some more zings. All this real soft without paying no attention to Trouble. Now Trouble, why, he started up fingering the buttons on his shirt again. If he saw you noticing that he was looking at Sam and the fiddle, he looked away and put his hand back on the wall. I wondered, had he ever heard music before?

Sorrow, now, she sidled over to Sam and stood next to the chair and bent over and stuck her fingers on the strings and made a sour sound. Sam laughed and pulled the fiddle up to where she couldn't reach it, and she laughed and jumped up and tried again, and he laughed some more, and they went back and forth like that for a while. Sam, he was being careful not to go too far with his teasing and hurt her feelings, like some people does. There's an art to it.

Trouble, he never said nothing. Hiram looked over at him ever little bit, like a cat keeps her eye on a sleeping baby.

Pretty soon Sam lowered the fiddle and let the girl pluck the strings. Right away she broke one, but Sam never got mad. He just took it and pressed it between his thumb and forefinger and stretched it out a little bit and gently sawed it with the bow and made it squeak. Well, Sorrow screamed laughing. Even Hiram smiled.

This went on for maybe an hour, Sam letting her play with his fiddle and make funny noises. For a player that always took his fiddling serious, it was a wonder how patient Sam was. Then after Sorrow got tired of that game, he played "Three Blind Mice," and then he sung it with his eyes closed and his face transported. Sorrow's eyes followed ever motion he made, and her little mouth moved like she was singing, too. I peeked over at Trouble, and his left hand was fingering his buttons just like Sam done the fiddle. He was looking afar off.

Me and Hiram happened to look at each other in that moment, and I seen his chest rise and fall. I got the chills. The look on his face—a hunger to hope, but a fear to—was one I never seen before in nobody under forty. I didn't know a child that age could even playact what I seen on that face. Them two boys, it was hard to see how they would turn out all right, all they had going against them.

After while Trouble and Sorrow fell asleep where they set, and me and Sam and Hiram went out on the porch. It was gathering twilight, and there was a breeze sprung up. You could see the moon rising and hear the trees rustling. Sam said, "Nice night."

We all three set there for a while thinking our own thoughts.

I looked at Hiram. "Looks like you're the one been looking after them two."

"Yes'm."

"For some while."

He nodded.

Sam pulled out a cigarette.

"You mind telling us how you come to be with them?" I said.

Hiram give a big sigh. "Dacia, she . . ." He sighed again, a ragged sound with tears in it.

Sam said, "Take your time, son. We got all night, or however long it takes."

Chapter 23

Hiram told us it all started when he was living with his own mother and father in a house in some woods. He didn't know where this was at nor how long they lived there. About two-three years ago, he reckoned, when he was about five, his mama woken him up in the middle of the night and hollered, "Run! Run! Get up! The woods! Run! Run!" She raised up the window and pushed him out, and he done like she said to. He run as fast as he could up into the woods.

He run till he couldn't run no more, and when he was wore out, he burrowed in a place between a tree and a bush and fell asleep. When he woken up it was daylight, and he was in his nightshirt, he was barefooted, and his feet was raw and cut up. It took him a minute to recollect what happened.

He wondered how come did his mother push him out the window. Did a bear or a mountain lion get into the house? Did the house catch on fire? He remembered his father coming home one day a while before this, talking about a bad man that killed some people for their gold. Had that bad man come to the house? Should Hiram wait in the woods, or go back home?

He turned it all over in his mind but didn't get no closer to knowing what to do. Directly he decided to walk back home, but soon he realized he was lost. Maybe he'd got turned around when he stopped to sleep. Maybe he'd been walking futher away from home instead of closer. He was scared. But he felt like there wasn't nothing to do but keep on walking, so that's what he done.

He slept two or three nights in the woods. He got hungrier than he ever was before, and so thirsty he couldn't make no spit. He felt like he might die of thirst. Sometimes he thought he seen things.

Then he found himself a little stream. He put his mouth in the water and drunk like a horse till he throwed up, and then he drunk some more. He laid down and slept, and when he woken up he decided to walk downstream. If he stayed close to the creek, he at least would have water. He stopped seeing things.

Inside half a day, he come to the camp. A woman, or maybe a girl, was setting cross-legged on a blanket in front of the tent. He hadn't saw very many womenfolk in his life, and he never had no idea they could be so beautiful.

I wasn't surprised by that. Dacia always had been a pretty girl.

"Are you an angel?" she said to him. "I never seen an angel so white and shiny. Trouble, come out and see this angel." A little boy crawled out of the tent. Hiram heard hiccupping from inside, and he guessed it was a puppy or a baby.

"No'm, I'm lost," Hiram said.

She laughed and raised a brown bottle to her lips and drunk from it. " 'No'm, I'm lost,' " she said. A drop trailed down her neck. The little boy scooted close to her and sucked on his thumb.

Hiram said, "I wonder, could you give me something to eat?"

"Your bellies, that's all you men ever think about," the woman said. "Your bellies and your pricks."

Hiram swallowed. He hadn't heard that word before, but from the way she said it, he reckoned it meant something bad. "I been lost for a long time."

She sighed and jerked her head toward the tent. "Might be some biscuits."

In the tent a baby was laying on a blanket in a wooden box, and next to her there was a cloth bag. He tore into it and eat the three biscuits and a moldy piece of salt-meat. He dug his finger-nails into the seams to get the crumbs. A baby bottle was laying on the blanket. He turned his back to the baby and sucked out half of what was left in it.

After while, a man come, carrying a bucket of little trout. While Dacia and the children slept in the tent, the man, Tom, cleaned the fish and showed Hiram how to pack them in mud. Then he built a fire and put the mud balls on rocks near the edge and left them to bake.

Hiram, he never knowed nothing about living in the woods. He didn't recollect ever seeing a campfire before, nor eating outdoors. His parents must have been city people. He remembered horses walking along mud streets and buildings with windows that went up high and the sounds of many footsteps on wooden boards. They must not have lived in the cabin very long. He wondered, had his mother and father give up searching for him and gone back home by now?

While the fish was cooking, Tom set on a blanket near the fire. He was a short man, thin, with a long beard and long hair. He reminded Hiram of the boogeyman from a fairy tale his mama had told him—the troll under the bridge.

"Come on, boy, I won't bite you." As long as Hiram knowed him, Tom only called him "boy." Hiram had to keep thinking his own name to himself so he wouldn't forget it, but after while—months or years—he did forget his last name.

He set down next to Tom on the blanket. "Where'd you come from?" Tom said.

Hiram told him the story.

"Well, don't fret yourself," he said. "We'll find your folks. Can't be far."

Hiram was relieved. "Yes, sir," he said. "Can't be far."

Tom smiled. "I like a boy that ma'ams and sirs. Your folks done right by you." He got to talking about gold then, his eyes bright. He claimed he'd found lots of gold dust and two nice nuggets, and any day now he was sure to find a big vein. Meanwhile, he was living a man's life, the only life a true man, beholden to nobody, would be content with. That word *beholden* stuck in Hiram's memory.

Some days later Tom walked Hiram into town, set the boy on the bar in one of the taverns, and hollered for quiet, saying the boy was lost and looking for his folks. Hiram looked around, among all them strange faces—mostly men, a few women—for somebody he knowed. By and by the noise took up again, people laughed and drunk, and Tom, he got to talking to a woman over a bottle of whiskey. He whispered to Hiram, "Be right back, boy, keep an eye on things," and left the room with her. When he come back, Hiram jumped off the bar and most knocked him down. Tom vomited on the floor. Somebody carried him outside and throwed him in the street, with Hiram following. Tom laid there all night. Hiram waited next to him like a dog.

After that, Tom nor Dacia made no more effort to find Hiram's folks that he knowed of.

Over the months, Tom showed Hiram how to catch and clean fish, how to clean the pistol and shoot squirrels and rabbits, gut them, skin them, cook them. How to build and stoke a fire, how to make biscuits and coffee.

Tom was careful to do his panning far from camp. Hiram asked him to show him how, but Tom said the boy had no business panning. He never showed Hiram none of the gold he found. He took it to the assay office in town and sold it, and Hiram thought he hid most of the money somewheres away from camp.

Dacia, she showed Hiram how to change and wash diapers, and she learned him, as well as she could, his letters and numbers. Sometimes she wrote down little poems for him to read. She walked him to town once and showed him where to buy canned milk, flour, coffee, and whiskey. After that he went by himself. He went to ever building and asked after his folks, but he had no luck. Once in a while he found a newspaper on the ground. He would take it back to camp and read it, working it out word by word. He didn't know what a newspaper was. The stories seemed like fairy tales.

Tom, he started going futher and futher out to pan, staying for three-four days. Dacia drunk her whiskey, cried sometimes, laughed sometimes, and slept. Mostly slept.

Sorrow, why, she growed and discovered things like a baby does—how to hold her head up, turn over, set up, crawl. Whenever Hiram fetched firewood or fished or hunted, he tied her to a tree so she wouldn't end up in the water.

The children never had enough food to fill them up. They eat meat ever four or five days, and the rest of the time it was biscuits. Hiram learned how to make gravy, and then he started saving grease, and that give them something to eat on the biscuits.

Hiram found out he liked to build things. He started simple: a stick buried in the ground, stacks of rock. Later he fenced in a place for Sorrow to play in so he could stop tying her up. He built a seesaw and a target to throw rocks at.

After two winters and a spring, the day come when Hiram found a gold nugget the size of his thumb. He seen a glint in the water, and he worked the nugget back and forth with his knife till it let go. It was heavier than he expected for as little as it was. He kept it hid for a few days, till Tom left to go panning. Then he give the nugget to Dacia.

"God in heaven," she said. Her eyes got big. "Let's go to town! All of us! Everbody gets a toy! And shoes! And cake!"

"Cake cake cake cake cake *cake,*" said Trouble.

Dacia screamed laughing. She took Trouble by both hands and danced with him around in a circle. "Cake cake cake cake cake *cake!*" Sorrow laughed and burbled.

But as they walked toward town—all of them, even Hiram, chanting "cake cake cake cake

cake!"—Dacia got quiet. She didn't hardly speak at all. When she come out of the assay office, she said, "We're going on a trip. We're going to a fairy land far away."

"Cake cake cake cake cake *cake,*" said Trouble.

"No! No cake!" Dacia said. "And don't you cry or I'll slap you silly! You're going to a fairy land! I been waiting for a miracle, and I got one!"

"Fairy land," said Sorrow.

Dacia lifted the girl to her hip and grabbed aholt of Trouble's hand, and Hiram followed as she walked with them to the livery. The two little ones was excited to see the horses, and Hiram watched them while Dacia rented a buggy. Even Trouble forgot about cake when she piled them in the buggy and it started jerking along. The children never seen the like, nor had they felt what it feels like to be pulled along by a four-legged animal in a buggy. Once you've felt that, you don't never forget it.

They rode for several hours till they got to a bigger town, and then they waited at the train station. Dacia brought them bread and a hunk of dried meat to take with them, and she wrote the note and pinned it inside Hiram's pocket. She forbade him to read it, and he obeyed.

When the time come, she put them on the train and pretended she would be right back and left them there.

• • •

The story finished, Hiram set there on the porch, staring at the floorboards, his forearms on his knees.

"Jesus Christ," Sam muttered.

"Dacia, she ever talk about me?" I said. I ain't proud of it, but that's what was on my mind.

Sam put his hand on my arm, and I shrugged it off. Nobody said nothing for a while.

"I made you a pallet," I said to Hiram.

"Yes'm."

But none of us moved. It was like we was too stunned to.

Hiram said to me, "So you're Dacia's sister, right?"

"What'd she say about me?"

"Her? I don't know. I just thought—I don't know."

Sam cleared his throat. "Don't matter."

Hell it don't, I thought.

After Hiram went to bed, me and Sam set side by side on the porch in the dark. The stars was out, and the cottonwoods was swaying and clacking like they does.

"Well, Bertie," Sam said. "Some fun."

It felt like I was teetering on the edge of a tall cliff. Me and him both. "Get serious."

"What for?" He laughed through his nose.

Some time passed.

"That Dacia," I said.

"No telling what-all happened." Now his voice had an edge to it.

"Well, it happened," I said, sarcastic. "At least twice."

He stiffened and never said nothing.

I felt stung. "You on her side?"

He reached into his shirt pocket and pulled out a cigarette, but he made no move to light it. "None of that don't matter no more, can't you see?"

I felt my wrath rising. He never understood the simplest things, seemed like.

"What do you want to do?" he said. "Tie 'em in a gunny sack and throw 'em in the Walnut River?"

I blowed air out between my lips. "I never said nothing like that."

"What're you so afraid of?" he said, point-blank.

"I ain't afraid." Which of course was a lie. What *wasn't* I afraid of, more like. What if I went through all it would take—looked like it would take plenty, a blind man could see that, like Opal said—and then Dacia come sashaying home one day and wanted them children back, like she said in her note? Be just like her. And what if she didn't, and it turned out Sam couldn't make himself love these children? How could he, rough like they was, and not even his? Children couldn't live just on pity, I should know. And three at once, who'd been through what they'd been through. What if I turned out like Mama, one eye on the rat poison—but I couldn't bear to think about that, never could.

"I know this ain't what you figured on," Sam said.

"They ain't even your kin."

He crushed the unlit cigarette in his fist, drew back his arm, and throwed it out in the yard. I heard him grunt with the effort. It's harder to throw something light than something heavy.

"Well, they ain't," I said.

Now he wrestled his boots off, swearing under his breath, and stood up in his stocking feet. "We ain't going to fix this all tonight," he said. "Better get some sleep."

"You go on," I said. "I'll be in after while."

"Suit yourself." He never touched me, just walked inside the house.

Oh, I was afraid all right, and broody and mean. I knowed I was taking my wrath toward Dacia and trying to wrap it around my shame like a thin, scraggly shawl, just like I always had. Didn't seem like I could help it.

Chapter 24

I woke up before dawn the next day. The bedroom was dark, and Sam was still sleeping. I heard birds scratching around outside, or maybe a possum. My first thought was, *Dacia's alive, she's got children, they come on the train yesterday.* I pictured Opal's room, on the other side of the wall, and little Sorrow sleeping next to her. I pictured the boys' pallet in the front room. It was true all right.

Before I knowed it, my mind was making a list. A couple cots and bed linens for the boys, and clothes and shoes. Plant more squash and potatoes—it was past spring and the garden was already in, but it was worth a try. Maybe set one of the hens to brood. Get the children to a doctor, they was like to have worms. Later on, school, books, pencils, boots, coats—but for now, first things first.

Now I slipped out of bed and tiptoed into the front room. It felt cool in there for early summer, cooler than you would have thought, and then I seen the front door was open. I looked over in the corner where the boys was, and it was just Hiram laying there sleeping with his mouth open.

I went outside. There was a thin line of orange and gray along the horizon. The birds was peeping, but otherwise things was hushed. I walked a ways from the house and softly called, "Trouble? You out here? Trouble?" I remembered Hiram saying he'd made Trouble's hidey-hole out by the woodpile, so I walked around back. The dew soaked my bare feet and drug down the hem of my nightdress.

We kept the wood stacked in a line that jutted out from the back of the house and down a little slope over to a handful of trees. I walked to the woodpile and peeked over it. In the corner where it met the house, Hiram had stacked a couple dozen logs to make a three-sided hideout about three or four foot tall. He'd made a roof over half of it with crisscrossed branches. I wondered, when had he done all this? Must've been after me and Sam went to bed.

There was Trouble setting there, panting. He had a fork in his hand, and it looked like he'd been digging a hole. He must have saw me—he scooted underneath of the branches to where I couldn't see him.

I realized it was him I'd heard scratching when I was laying in bed. I wondered, had he been there all night? He had to be cold, and his pants must be wet from the dew. I fretted he'd catch his death, but I didn't say nothing for fear of spooking him.

I took aholt of a fat log and put it on end and set on it, just to think what to do. I pictured myself luring him out of there with a fried egg and jelly on a plate, the way you'd do an animal.

It took a while for me to notice he was saying something. Not saying exactly—half-singing, half-chanting. At first I couldn't make out the words. The firewood was soaking up his voice, which was wavering like he was rocking. Then I realized he was keeping waltz time—oom pah-pah, oom pah-pah. After while the words come through. *What is a, pickle spoon. What is a, pickle spoon. What is a, pickle spoon.*

It all come crashing down on me at once. I recalled the night before Dacia run off, the picture show in El Dorado, the doll with its ruined hair, Dacia saying Mama'd eat rat poison, me beating Dacia with the pickle spoon. Of course she'd told the children all about it—she would. She'd told them what their cruel aunt Bertie done to her, how I'd drove her away from home. And of course this one, the odd one, the mystery child, he would be the one remembered it, told himself a fantastical story about it. Wasn't no telling what he pictured in his mind. The truth was awful enough.

I wondered, how could Dacia possibly have sent them to me, hating me like she done? How could I possibly mother them? And how could I not?

Then somebody walked up behind me and said, "Oh"—Hiram—and I jumped up.

Fearful he'd hear Trouble, I said, "You hungry? I'm about to fix breakfast, come help me."

"He all right?" Hiram said.

I took his arm. "He's fine, let's go eat."

Wasn't long before the house filled up with the smell of eggs and biscuits and gravy, and pretty soon everbody was at the table except Trouble.

I stood at the stove. Opal swallowed a bite and said to me, "The kids at school's gonna tease 'em over them names."

"What names?" Hiram said.

"Slow down there," I said to him. "Them eggs ain't going nowhere. You want some more breakfast meat?"

He nodded, his mouth full, and I forked some bacon out of the pan for him.

"*Trouble* and *Sorrow*." Opal rolled her eyes.

"What?" Sorrow said. She was setting on Sam's lap, and he was putting egg in her mouth with his fingers.

"Don't you know nothing?" Opal said to her. "Don't you even know what 'Sorrow' means?"

"Opal!" me and Sam said at the same time.

"How'd you like it if somebody made fun of your name?" I said.

"I wouldn't! That's why we got to change it!"

Sorrow had a worried look on her face, but she kept eating. "Don't pay her no mind," I said to her. "Me and you's going to go feed the chickens after breakfast." I clucked like a chicken and flapped my arms, and a smile, a very little smile, stole over Sorrow's face.

"Can I help?" Hiram said.

"Sure you can," Sam said. "You like horses?"

"Only ever seen the one that I remember." Seemed like Hiram was a thinking person and not likely to say nothing he wasn't for sure about.

"You'll like them, if I know boys," Sam said.

Later that day me and Sam decided on "Sarah" for Sorrow and "Travis" for Trouble. Sarah's new name took, but Trouble always stayed Trouble. I called him Travis for a while, but nobody else ever did. Didn't seem to fit him.

The next day I took the three of them to the doctor, and he told me to expect them to grow aplenty in the next year and give them aspirin powder if they complained of pains in their legs. He calculated Sarah was three year old, and Trouble probably about five. He reckoned Trouble would outgrow his affliction, but then he might not. He might be simple, but we ought to wait a while and see how the boy done. He might have rickets, too, so I should give him a spoonful of castor oil ever day. It was the latest thing for rickets, he told me.

Hiram was eight, he figured. Not an albino, just a Swede most likely.

Now I'd took castor oil as a child, and I knowed it was nasty. When I tried it with Trouble, he raised holy hell and started frothing at the mouth. Scared me half to death, and I throwed out the whole rest of the bottle.

A lot happened in the next couple weeks. Trouble slept in his fortress a couple of nights, and the rest of the time he slept in his cot. We'd set two of them up in the front room, him and Hiram meeting head-to-head in the corner. It never seemed to bother Trouble, sleeping outdoors. I guess they was all used to it, though Hiram preferred his cot and Sarah liked sleeping with Opal in her bed.

Sam, most mornings he left the house before the children was up and didn't get home till six o'clock or later. He was taking all the draying work he could get, so he usually worked six days. Me and him, when the children was finally asleep at night, we was wore out. For weeks we didn't talk again about the children's future. Wasn't no point, seemed like. I felt sure Dacia would show up any day, and meanwhile me and Sam would see they was looked after. Wasn't nothing else to do.

Me and the children worked out a routine—get up, eat breakfast, do chores. Hiram, he was crazy about the horses, so he'd curry them down just for fun and then lead them out of the barn and turn them loose on the slope to pasture. We had Bluebell and Clarence then, both geldings, which we mostly used to pull the buggy, so we didn't give them no grain except to call them in. We'd slap the bucket, and here they'd come running. That tickled Hiram. When he wasn't doing chores, he liked to spend time in the tack room, mending and oiling harness, and he'd do whatever I asked him to. Didn't bother him to scrub floors or wash windows.

Sarah, she tagged after me, wanting to do everthing I done. When I done dishes I made up a bowl of soapy water for her, and she splashed around and talked and laughed. Besides dishes, she copied me sweeping the floor, dusting, ironing, things like that. She loved feeding the chickens.

Trouble, now, he tagged along with one or the other of us, ten foot back. He favored the chickens, too, and he never got tired of watching them. After me and Sarah let them out of the chicken house in the mornings, he'd perch somewhere and watch them wander around the yard. I got the feeling, watching him, that he was pretending to be one of them, talking and gossiping, pecking around for bugs and gravel— that he knowed each one like you know a person. I don't know that for a fact, but it sure looked like it. He never said nothing more about the pickle spoon, which I was grateful for, though ever little bit I wondered if he was thinking about it and, if so, what he was thinking. Wasn't no way to tell.

This being summertime, there was time to play, too. Sam showed Hiram how to ride, and Hiram, he'd put Sarah on Bluebell, bareback, and then climb up behind her and ride her all around the place. She loved that. Trouble was deathly afraid of the horses, but he'd set on the fence and watch them. Or him and Sarah would play tag, hide-and-go-seek, things like that.

The three of them run from morning till night, sure enough, each in their own way. They ate good and slept good, which I was glad for.

On Tuesday after they come, we all went to meet Mrs. Whiteside. She already knowed they was there—you can't keep a thing like that secret in a town the size of Wiley—and, to my surprise, she opened the door and let us all in the entry hall. I told her each of their names, and Sarah and Hiram nodded. Mrs. Whiteside give me a look when it come to Trouble, but she never said nothing even though he was staring at her crippled hands and twisting his own to match. I told her my sister had sent them to stay with us, and she just nodded. She give each one a cookie, and they looked at me for permission. They knowed I had a rule against piecing. I told them it was all right, and they stood there and wolfed down the cookies, and then we said our goodbyes. Soon's we was outside, they all three took off running down the slope to home.

I'd been inside the Whiteside house a couple times, but I never noticed before how deathly quiet it was and how it smelled of old people and medicine.

I sent Alta Bea a little note, and in a couple days I got one back. It started out, *My God, Bertie! Can this be true?* She said she couldn't hardly wait to meet Dacia's children, her and her girls. They'd be there Thursday after lunch, which was what she called dinner.

Alice was nine, I reckon. Ruby was seven, Pauline was six or so, and Gladys was three, same as Sarah.

When Thursday come and I heard the car pull up, I walked out of the house carrying Sarah on my hip. Three of Alta Bea's girls jumped out of the car. Alice and Alta Bea, them two stood by the car, watching.

When Sarah saw the three girls, the thumb flew out of her mouth, she got loose of me, and she run right up to them. When she got there she hardly knowed what to do, seemed like, and she come to a stop and stared at them. They stopped, too, the three of them lined up hand in hand. Maybe Sarah never seen other little girls before. Maybe she thought she was the only one in the world.

Gladys said to her, "I got a scab on my ankle."

445

She reached down and pulled up her skirt past her waist. Sarah stepped back a ways, but then dropped down and put her finger on the scab.

"Ow!" Gladys hollered, but then she just stood there and stared at Sarah over the hem of her skirt. "It doesn't hurt," she said, her eyes big.

Then they all started jabbering at once, talking about how Gladys scraped her ankle sliding down the stairs, how their car got dented, what their daddy said, what their mommy said, and all about their dolls, their clothes, their books, their rooms, their kitten. Pretty soon Alice walked over there and started bossing everbody around.

Me and Alta Bea looked at each other and laughed. It was like they'd knowed each other all their lives.

After a little bit Sarah took them to see Trouble's hideout—he was in there but never said nothing—and then she led them over to the barn. Hiram called the horses in, and the girls took turns being led around.

Me and Alta Bea, we set on the porch and visited. She asked me, how did I feel finding out Dacia was alive, how did I feel about the children, how did I feel about Dacia sending the children, how did I feel about this and that and the other? I told her I always liked being busy, and then I changed the subject. She kept poking at me, like she done, and I kept bringing up Harold and the girls and their house and her

446

permanent wave and the new sack dress she had on, things like that. I didn't want to talk to her about Dacia. I felt different ways about her, and that always unsettled me.

After while the girls come over to the porch, and one by one they drunk water out of the dipper, their back turned to their mother like they was getting away with something. They stood there and listened to us talk for a while, and then they run back out in the yard, where Alta Bea's girls taught Sarah how to play ring-around-the-rosy. After while they just set in a circle and talked, like girls will.

This was how I'd pictured it—me and Alta Bea's children playing together. It tugged at my heart to watch it actually happening. Then I reminded myself, we was only looking after them till their mama come for them.

I rose up and said, "All right, girls, time to go home, Sarah needs her rest."

"What are you angry about?" Alta Bea said.

This surprised me. "I ain't."

She got up and gathered her things. "Have it your way." She touched my arm. "We'll have to plan an outing, just us and the girls. Wouldn't that be fun?"

Sarah pitched a fit when they got ready to leave. I tried to pick her up, but she pushed me away and run bawling out to the barn, calling Hiram's name.

I set down on the chair and thought about what Alta Bea'd said. How come she thought I was wroth? Was there something on my face I didn't even know there was? In my voice? After while I noticed I'd twisted the hem of my dress almost into a knot. I set there and finger-pressed it, waiting for Sarah to get over her fit.

Around the house I started finding food scraps in odd places, and seemed like there was more mouse tracks than usual. I put two and two together, and one day I lined the children up in front of the cupboard. "See them glass jars? Them tin boxes? See that food inside there?"

Hiram and Sarah nodded. Trouble was looking at my mouth, like he usually done. I had to stop myself from feeling my teeth with my tongue to see if there was food in between.

"You know why that food's in jars and tin boxes?" I asked.

They shook their heads.

" 'Cause I don't want to feed all the field mice in Creation, that's how come." I looked from one to another. "When people takes food and hides it in their clothes or underneath of their pillow or underneath of their covers, we get mouse tracks all over the house. You know what mouse tracks is?"

Again they shook their heads.

"It's like what people drop in the backhouse,

only it's from a mouse. Little black pellets that stink. You seen them on the floor?"

Hiram and Sarah made a face.

"Well, then, don't go squirreling away food. You want something, tell me. You can have it."

"But you said no piecing," Sarah said.

"I know. But for now, if you're hungry you can piece, just ask me first."

"Yes'm," Hiram said.

Sarah, why, she got out of the habit, being so little. But as long as them two boys lived in the house, they hid food, even Hiram. You don't never forget being as hungry as they used to be, I reckon.

That night before I fell asleep I got to thinking about the life them children had been living, and I went over Hiram's story in my mind. I wondered what might've happened to his folks.

Next morning I left Hiram in charge, went to the library in El Dorado, and found a map of the way west, and I copied down the names of the towns along the route. Then I took to writing letters to the sheriffs, one or two ever day. I told them we had this boy name of Hiram and what he looked like and when he got lost, and did they know anybody looking for such a boy. One by one I marked them off my list. Sarah and Trouble, I figured, their mama knowed where they was at. But Hiram—his folks, if they was alive, I reckoned they must have been out of their minds with grief. Nothing never come of it, though.

A month went by, and one July night after the children was in bed, why, Sam told me he'd been talking to Dick Murphy about a job. I'd just put away the last supper dish, and we was setting at the table drinking coffee.

"Murphy Oil?" I said. "Since when?"

"Pays good. And you get a company house, and free gas. And a telephone." He stretched out his neck till it popped. "I can haul in my spare time."

"Tarpaper shack, you mean."

He poured his coffee into the saucer like he done. "I need something I can still do when I get old, something where you can work your way up to pumper. Something with a pension and disability."

I didn't know what a pension and disability was, tell the truth. We never had nothing like that when I come up. I got up from the table and fetched the cream pitcher.

"Something happens to me, insurance gives you and the children money to live on," he said. "Opal, looks like she can make out on her own, need be."

I set back down and poured cream in my cup. "We don't know if they'll be here next *week.*"

He put a mild look on his face. "Free rent, free insurance—that's worth a lot."

"I can't think of nothing we need that we don't have." I had a feeling he was talking sideways, like he done, wanting to act like this was my idea.

"Well, for one thing, I want to get you a car."

I busted out laughing.

"I mean it," Sam said. "You shouldn't be so far from town without no car. What if one of them needs a doctor?"

"I got a picture of me driving a car."

"You just wait," he said. "Once you start driving, you won't know how you got along without one."

"Ha! Me and Alta Bea, just alike, gallivanting all over the county."

Sam waited till I stopped laughing. "We can't just think of ourself no more."

"But changing jobs? Living in the oil field? After all that, what if Dacia comes back?"

He shrugged. "They're here now, the three of them, ever day." He stared down at the table. "For them, a day's a long time."

"Meaning what?"

"Their mama—that might happen, or might not. Meanwhile, they need to be fed and looked after ever day, rain or shine."

We each thought our own thoughts for a while. Pretty soon I said, "What do you think Mama meant—Dacia was her on the inside, and I was her on the outside?"

He shook his head. "Nobody ain't nobody else,

451

seems to me like." He lifted the saucer to his mouth and drunk.

"I'm serious." I heard the irritation in my voice.

"Fact is, we may never know what Dacia was thinking. We got to live with that."

I shivered. "I don't see how, when you don't know, day by day, is she going to come back after them. I don't see how."

"Them kids need you to, Bertie. You and me both."

"I don't see *how*," I said.

"I don't expect it'll get any easier, time goes by."

We both set for a while. Then he said, "You know me and Murphy's been friends for years. He'll do right by us."

"You been independent all your life pretty much. You think you can work for somebody else?"

"Shit." He got up, smacked his chair against the edge of the table, and dumped out the rest of his coffee in the slop bucket.

I felt the sting of his reproach, but I couldn't understand what we was arguing about.

"You coming to bed?" he said.

"How come you're mad?"

"I ain't mad." He stomped off to the bedroom.

I set there asking myself, what was he wroth about? What was we fighting about? And that same old question—what did Mama mean? What in the Sam Hill did she know about me inside? Far as I could tell, she only ever paid attention to my outside. It seemed like this was a deep-down mystery I could never get to the bottom of.

I pictured Dacia living in that tent, cold in the cold and hot in the heat. Wasn't no doubt she had suffered, and all alone except for a man I wouldn't cross the street to say hello to, and, time was, neither would she. But me and Sam had suffered, too, with her leaving home like she done, no note or nothing. All the years we dangled, not knowing. I wouldn't wish that on a dog.

I hated feeling like so much in my life come down to Dacia. She was like a hair stuck in my mouth, always had been. I couldn't swallow her down, couldn't spit her out.

The next day was a Sunday, so we all had breakfast together after chores. Trouble would only eat if you put one bite on his plate at a time, which Hiram done.

As we was finishing up, Sam said why didn't we all get in the truck and take a ride. Sarah like to had a fit. She loved riding in the truck almost as much as she loved riding a horse.

Soon's Sam turned west, I said, "We going to the Murphy field?" To the best of my recollection, it was eight miles west and two south.

"Just giving the children a joyride," he said.

"Joyride!" Sarah hollered. She was setting in between the two of us. The boys, they was in the bed of the truck.

Sam started singing "Comin' Round the Mountain," and me and Sarah picked it up. I knowed good and well what he was up to, and sure enough, when we got to the Murphy field, he turned in there. It had derricks and pumpjacks scattered around like Whiteside's, but Murphy's also had a dozen tarpaper houses in a row along the dirt access road. Sam pulled up by the first one, closest to the main road.

We all set there and looked at it. First thing I noticed, it was set permanent on cement blocks, and not just laying on skids. Plus, somebody had built a porch on the front. I didn't think I could live without a porch.

But the house itself, it looked forlorn. Not like the Whiteside house had when we first got there, with things broken and falling off and the siding getting eat up by bushes, but like a house in a fairy tale—dark and droopy, a place where elves or goblins might live. Wasn't hardly no trees to protect it from the wind. Tin roof, now that would be noisy. And not much more than a stone's throw from the closest oil rig. Bound to smell.

"Oh my," I said.

"Oh my," Sarah said. Sounded so much like Dacia I like to swallowed my tongue.

"Water pump's right in the kitchen!" Sam said. "Come on, you've got to see the inside."

The house was hot as an oven inside, and dark. Five rooms, but it seemed smaller because it was so dark, and it never had no lean-to you could use as a summer kitchen. It was decent, but it wasn't near as nice as our house at Whiteside's.

One thing, though. The floors in the front room and the kitchen had linoleum tacked on. It looked brand-new, and it had pink cabbage roses on it. I loved that linoleum, tell the truth, not just for the roses but because I love a floor you can scrub clean. Wood can soak up grease till you can't hardly get it out. I suspicioned Sam had something to do with that linoleum.

The children run through each room, looked for a second, and then run out the door to look around out there. Me and Sam ended up in the front room by ourself.

"What do you think?" he said.

"Pretty roses."

He smiled.

"Seems like we'd be going backward, though," I said.

The smile faded. "You don't like it? Gas heat? Gas stove? Pump in the kitchen?" He looked bewildered.

"I don't want to leave the Whiteside house. I love that house. Remember—"

"It's Will's grave, ain't it?"

I took a big breath.

"We can visit it anytime you want to," he said. "Anytime."

"I know."

"What, then?"

I looked around. "I want to stay where we're at."

Now he took aholt of my arms. "You know we can't."

I swallowed hard.

"You know we've got to do this," he said. "The house, the job, all of it." He never said "for the children's sake," but I knowed that was what he meant.

I twisted out of his arms and walked over to the kitchen window. Outside, it looked bleak. We was only just off the road. Trucks went by regular, and dust hung everwhere. There was bound to be rocks and sand burrs, and, with hardly no trees, seemed like the wind would scour everthing down to the nub. Smell of oil outside, and tarpaper inside. I wasn't used to luxury, for sure, but this was a step down, couldn't he see that? And for what? What if Dacia come waltzing into town next week?

I said to him, "But what if she comes back for them?"

"Which are you more afraid of—that she will, or she won't?"

I stiffened. There was a silence, and then I just

456

said it. "If she don't come back, I can't never tell her how wrong I was about Mama. How sorry I am. No way to ask her for forgiveness. But if she does come back . . ."

Now he walked up behind me and tried to embrace me, but I pushed him away. Still looking out the window, I said, "Can you imagine how much she must hate me? I wouldn't blame her."

He took aholt of my wrist and put his mouth close to my ear. "She ain't never coming back."

I cried out, and this time when I tried to pull away, he held on tight. He said, "The way I look at it, she's another one we lost."

I started bawling and kept at it for a while. I couldn't stand the idea of Dacia being lost like me and Sam's own children, lost to us and lost to her children, and her soul lost in the wilderness. I wanted her and me to set down together, to talk it all out—patient and kind and merciful, the both of us—just gaze at each other in compassion and say all the things, answer all the questions, admit all the lies and jealousy and pride and fear that had built up between us back when we hardly knowed each other. I wanted to be able to believe her, believe everthing she said, about Mama or anything else, get to know her truly. I felt like I had a deep and abiding love for her which I never had give voice to, and I needed to hear it maybe more than she did. I had always had a secret picture in my mind, of me and her setting calmly together, and just now this picture played in front of my mind's eye, and I craved it, I craved speaking and hearing the plain truth of her life and mine. I didn't see how I could surrender them children to her without it. And yet it felt like it was a dream, a fairy tale that would never come true.

Finally, I asked Sam, "How come she done it? How come her to send them here, do you think?"

"Turn around. I said, turn around."

I sighed and turned to face him.

"Same reason your Mama give you *her* children." Now he took my face in his hands and looked at me and said, slowly, "To save their lives."

I begun trembling. I so wanted to believe him. If he was right, if Dacia felt like I would be a good mother to the children, maybe me and Dacia—maybe it could come true.

I was full of feelings I wasn't brave enough to share with him, so I turned back around. I felt hot, more than I could bear, and I reached over and tried to raise up the window. I had to lean way over on my tiptoes, but even when I pushed my hardest, it wouldn't budge. I felt my fear turning to wrath, like it often done.

Sam spooned me and worked on lifting the window.

"Stop it," I said. "You're hurting my neck."

"Move then."

I slipped out from under him and watched him wrestle with the window. "I don't like this place," I said.

He made an angry noise and throwed his hands up. Then he turned to me. "How come you to be so hard? Just when things is going so good for us?"

I seen it wasn't no use—we could go back and forth like this forever—and I just didn't have the heart for it, on top of everthing else.

I give a big sigh. "Where we going to put the chickens? I ain't moving here till you get me a chicken house built." I felt how twisted my lips was.

He glared at me for a second and then give me a small smile. "Hiram, I expect he'll build you one, you ask him to."

Opal took time off of work to help me pack, and she walked up to the big house with me to tell Mrs. Whiteside we was moving. I about died when Mrs. Whiteside busted into tears right there at the door, which was about the last thing I expected. She had always seemed like a tough old bird to me, bearing the pain from her crippled bones without hardly a word. I looked at Opal, who stood there like me, her eyes wide.

In a minute Mrs. Whiteside turned inside and limped over and set down heavy in her cushion chair. Opal went into the kitchen and got her a glass of water and set it on the table next to her.

She took out a hankie and wiped her eyes, though she ignored the water. "How come don't you want to live here anymore?" she said to me. She acted like Opal wasn't even there. It occurred to me she seen Opal, the one that made her daughter-in-law's wedding dress, as hired help.

I explained about Sam's new job, the free house, the free gas, the pension.

"Don't be that way," she said.

"What way?"

She glared at me. "I don't need the rent. I could let it go as long as need be."

This surprised me. It never would have occurred to me to ask for such a thing.

She set up straight as she could. "I grew up in that house. I can't *have* strangers living there."

"We was strangers when we moved in."

"And what about your baby?" she said. "Who's going to decorate his grave?" Now she frowned at Opal, but Opal just gazed back without no expression.

"We'll come over regular," I said.

"With *strangers* living in the house?" she hollered.

I felt myself start to crumple. I never imagined she would act like this. I looked over at Opal, who give a little shrug.

"People are so ungrateful," she said. "They don't appreciate what you do for them."

Now that made me mad. "I'm a lot of things, but ungrateful ain't one of them." I felt my knees shaking.

"Me too," Opal said, sweet as a child.

Mrs. Whiteside leaned back and took in a noisy breath. "Well, I never."

"Well, I never neither," Opal said, smiling.

Mrs. Whiteside stared at her for a second and then me. "I can't *have* strangers living there."

Opal said, "Well, that ain't none of our affair, of course."

Ain't none of our affair, of course—now that wasn't nothing I could imagine myself saying, but I felt how perfect it was. I almost laughed, I was so proud of her. But I didn't, out of fear of offending Mrs. Whiteside.

Then the two of us nodded to her and hustled out of that dim, sorrowful house. As we made our way down the hill toward home, I said to Opal, "I still feel sorry for her."

She shook her head. "Don't waste your pity. She don't want it."

"What does she want, then?"

She laughed. "For you to do everthing she says, is all."

This startled me, raw as it was, but I felt like she was right. Mrs. Whiteside helped us, but she wouldn't let us help her, or thank her, and that way she kept us on her string. She reminded me of Mama in this way. She didn't look like her or talk like her, sure enough—Mrs. Whiteside was short with people, and Mama, if she was unhappy with you, she was long. It was the difference between Kansas people and people back home, I reckoned. But Mama and Mrs. Whiteside was alike in one respect—the both of them would have their way or know the reason why.

As for Opal, she had growed up and learned how to deal with the world, all right. I didn't know where she got it from—Lord knowed I didn't have none of it—but I felt like there wasn't no limit to what she might do in this life.

Chapter 25

It was August when we settled into the Murphy house. Sam, he nailed scrap boards up on the inside walls, and I pasted newspapers over them to cut the wind. Then me and Hiram painted over the newspapers, but I didn't like how it looked—mealy—so I pasted up more newspapers to cover it up. We stuffed rags around the window frames to plug up the cracks where they never fit tight. In me and Sam's bedroom we hung up the picture of me and my brothers at Daddy's grave.

Hiram, sure enough, he built me a chicken house, and out back of it he built a fortress for Trouble. Seemed like Hiram could build anything he set his mind to. Don't seem like a hidey-box made out of crates and scraps would amount to much, but Hiram set down a little rock foundation first, and he used a bowl of water to see that things was level as he went along. He figured that out by himself, which like to amazed Sam no end.

Opal never moved with us to the new place. She decided it was a good time to go out on her own. It wasn't no surprise—she'd been sleeping over at the shop more and more and saving up her money, and she had all the work she wanted. She found her a second-floor room downtown, and Sam took her few things to town in the truck. She made curtains and linens and got herself a secondhand couch she fitted with slipcovers. I give her some of Mama's embroideryed dishtowels I'd put away for her. I always reckoned I would give them to her when she got married, but seemed like she was going to end up an old maid. Whenever any bachelors come sniffing around, she shooed them off. Said she was too busy. I recollected how I'd spurned the man teacher because he couldn't give me no children, but Opal, she seemed content not to have any, or anyhow to wait till she was older. I never said boo about it. She knowed her own mind, and I felt like she had ever right to live like she wanted to.

After she moved into town, we put all three children in the second bedroom. It seemed strange there wasn't nobody sleeping in the front room.

And true to his word, why, Sam had me to go outside one day not long after we moved, and there was a car parked next to the house. He told me it was a 1920 Hudson, though that didn't make me no never mind, since I didn't know one kind from another. It was a closed car, I seen that, and it had electric start—I'd told him not to bring home no crank-start car if he wanted me to drive it. And it had four doors and a backseat for the children. I must say, it was handsome.

I asked him how much it cost.

"Wouldn't have bought it if I didn't have the cash money," he said. "Of all people, you should know that."

He had me to get in the driver's side, and he stood leaning against the open door. I seen right away the car was too big for me. "My feet can't reach the pedals."

"How about the gear shift?"

"What's that?"

He threwed back his head and laughed, which made me furious. I swung my legs around and waited till he got out of my way. Then I climbed down out of the car and slammed the door and walked toward the house.

"Come on, Bertie," he called after me. "Don't be like that."

I stopped and turned back to him. "I hope you don't think you're the one gonna teach me to drive."

"Who else?"

"I know somebody."

"Not Alta Bea?" he said, but I never answered.

When I called Alta Bea, it was the first time I used our telephone. She kept laughing and telling me I didn't have to holler, she could hear me. I never have liked to talk on that machine. You can't see the person you're talking to—don't seem natural. I got used to it eventually, but I don't like it.

Now Alta Bea was tickled I asked her to show me how to drive. Soon's her and the girls got to the house, she brought out a bundle wrapped in a heavy wool blanket and put it in the back, and the girls and Sarah crawled into the backseat. Hiram said there was too many girls in the car, so he'd stay home and play with Trouble while we was gone.

I'd made me a cushion, which I set in place in the driver's seat, and then I climbed in. Alta Bea told me what the foot pedals was for and had me to push on them. It took more push than I expected, but I done it. Then she had me to shift the gears, which wasn't too hard on the forward ones, but I like to never got it into reverse. You had to push it in and then yank it clear to the right, past fourth, all the while holding in the clutch with your foot. They didn't make cars to be drove by nobody my size, for sure. But I got it in reverse finally, and off we went. I killed it a few times, like a person will, and I about put us in the ditch the first time I turned a corner, not realizing you had to slow down first and how hard it was to turn the steering wheel. And that spark doodad on the steering wheel you had to play with when the motor started knocking—I like to never got the hang of that.

Alice, the oldest, she gasped ever little bit and said, "Mother?" like I was about to kill us all.

"Quiet down, Worrywart," Alta Bea said finally. To me she said, "Harold just had the driveway graveled, and the tires made this growling sound, and Alice—you know Alice—she said, 'But, Mother, what if they *pop?*'" She laughed, and I smelled the liquor on her breath. Then I leaned forward so I could look in the rearview mirror— it was on the outside of the door—and I seen Alice stick out her lower lip and slide back in the seat with her arms folded.

"Oh, there's a nice grove of elms," Alta Bea said, pointing out the window. "Pull over!"

Now Alice jumped up in the seat. "Why are we stopping? What's wrong?"

"That's for me to know and you to find out. Wait here. Don't move. You too, Bertie." She had her door halfway open before I got the car stopped. She jumped out and went searching among the trees. I seen her take a sip out of her flask. Pretty soon she was out of sight.

Meanwhile the girls reached their arms out the windows and pounded on the car. "Mother!" they hollered. Ruby started to open the door, but Alice said, "Mother said not to move! Mother said not to move!"

Sarah, she climbed into the front seat and slipped onto my lap.

Now Alta Bea come back to the car. "I found

us a place! For Christ's sake, stop screaming, you girls! Come on, we're having a *picnic!*" She threw open the back door, and the girls jumped out of the car, laughing and chattering. Alta Bea took off running. Me and Sarah got out, and I went to the back of the car to get the picnic bundle.

Alice was waiting. "*I* want to carry it."

"It's too big for you," I said.

"I *want* to," she said, and she pulled it away, stretching her little arms around it.

"Mind you don't drop it." Sarah took my hand, and we started walking to where Alta Bea had run off to.

In a moment Alice trotted by us, holding the bundle to one side so she could see her way. "I'm coming, Mother, I have the—" Then *pop!* she barreled into little Gladys, knocking them both to the ground.

Gladys screamed, clutching a bleeding knee. "Mommmm-ee-hee-hee-hee-*hee-!*" Pauline, standing next to her, started hollering, too, sympathetic.

Ruby stood for a moment blinking and then started laughing. Meanwhile, Alice laid there clutching the blanket. A dark spot was spreading from something wet inside.

"Hold still," I said to her, hurrying over. "Might be broken glass in there."

"She's bleeding! There's *blood* on her dress!"

Pauline hollered, meaning Gladys and her skinned knee. "Where's Mother? There's blood on her dress!"

I separated Alice from the blanket and opened it up. Sure enough, there was pieces of glass scattered on the soaked wool, along with soggy sandwiches wrapped in wax paper. Must've been lemonade in a fruit jar. "You all right?" I reached out and took aholt of her arms and turned them over to search for cuts. I didn't see none.

Now Sarah busted into tears. "It's broke! It's broke!"

"Where's Mother?" Alice wailed.

"Stop! Just stop, *everyone* stop!" come Alta Bea's voice a few steps away. There was a screech to it I hadn't noticed before. Everbody froze. There was a stunned silence except for Gladys hiccupping and sniffling.

Alta Bea walked over to her. In a quiet voice she said, "It's just a scratch, for Christ's sake, Gladys—stop blubbering."

"I have a scra-haa-haa-haa-hatch," Gladys said.

"Mother," Alice said, rising to her feet. "It's wet! It's all wet! The picnic's ruined!" She motioned toward the blanket. Me, I was picking out the pieces of glass and wrapping them in my hankie. Sarah was setting next to me, sucking her thumb and blinking and taking it all in.

"There's blood on *my* dress, too," Pauline said. "I have Gladys's blood on my dress!"

Now Ruby busted out laughing. "It's not blood, it's booger-snot!"

"No, it's *not!*"

"Snot! Snot! Booger-snot!"

Now Alta Bea started laughing. She laughed so hard she drooled, and tears come down her face, and she wiped her eyes with her hands. After a minute she lowered herself to the ground and pulled out a cigarette and lit it, still laughing.

"Mother," Alice said. "Daddy says you shouldn't smoke."

"Well, darling, should I *kill my children?*" Alta Bea said. "Because, after all, *those* are my two choices!"

She laid back, laughing and smoking. Then she started to gag, and in a moment it got away from her, and she laid there gurgling and trying to get her breath. I hurried over and throwed away her cigarette and turned her on her side and pounded on her back, and pretty soon she was just regular coughing. You could tell from the high-pitched sound how much her chest must hurt.

"You all right?" I said, pounding on her back. "You all right?"

She nodded and coughed some more. She tried to take in a deep breath, but it set her to coughing again. It took a while for her to get to breathing normal.

The girls never said nothing, just watched her. In a little bit they wandered off, dragging the soggy blanket with them. Alice took Sarah and Gladys each by the hand. The five girls settled in underneath of a tree and started pulling up dandelions and whatnot and playing make-believe like girls does. I kept an eye on them.

Alta Bea laid on the ground for a while, and then she set up and got out another cigarette and pulled the smoke into her lungs. She coughed and cleared her throat and smoked some more.

I was wroth with her—I knowed that words from a mother could haunt their children. But I didn't know how to say nothing like that to Alta Bea, never had. So I just said, "I reckon this is the kind of a day your girls will remember all their lives."

She shrugged. "Alice will, and maybe Ruby. The younger ones, it's just impressions—blood on a knee, crying, spilled lemonade."

"I hope—"

"They'll argue about it when they're older. '*You* broke the jar. No, *you* did. I did *not*.'" She laughed.

"I hope . . ." I said again, but I didn't finish. I wanted to say I hoped none of them would remember what their mother said about killing them, but I was too worried how Alta Bea might react.

She stubbed out her cigarette and pulled out her flask and drunk. Then she put her face to the sky and breathed deep, coughing a little bit. She was about thirty now, and more handsome than ever, relaxed, smiling, like somebody posing for a picture in a magazine. Watching her, I seen something: She was at the peak of her strength as a woman, as a person. Unhappy as she was, this, right now—setting in the sun and smelling the sweet summer breeze—this, slight as it was, was the happiest she would ever be. Clear as anything, I seen the road she was going down, and I seen where it would end up. I wondered—where had it started, this road? When she started drinking? Or was it a long time before that, before I even met her? I remembered thinking, as a girl, that Alta Bea was poor in spirit. So it wasn't the drink made her that way, not exactly. I wondered what had.

"Bertie?" she said. "Why so serious?"

I blinked and looked at her.

"Aren't you the sourpuss," she said. She lifted the flask to her mouth.

I shifted my weight. All the sudden the ground felt awful hard on my hip.

Now she glared at me. "It helps me *relax*."

"I never said nothing."

She rolled her eyes.

I got up my nerve. "Drink kills people."

"Oh, for Christ's sake," she said. "Who do you think you're talking to."

There it was, after all. Her and me, we wasn't on the same road, and finally I faced up to it. I was drawed to her the same way you're drawed to a three-legged orphan lamb—wanting to tend to it, but also wanting to get a close look at the place in its shoulder where the leg's missing. I felt ashamed and downhearted, confused and sad.

I rose and brushed my skirt off. "I reckon we better get on home."

"But the night is young," she said in a mocking tone, raising her flask.

I walked over to the tree and took aholt of Sarah, and Alta Bea's girls followed me back. What was we going to eat, Alice said, the sandwiches was ruint.

I loaded the girls up in the car and got in the driver's seat, and pretty soon Alta Bea got herself to her feet and stumbled over and climbed in. The girls chattered like magpies, but me and Alta Bea didn't say one word the whole way home. I reckon we both knowed—at least I did—that things between us wouldn't be like they was before, and they couldn't be put right.

With everthing that happened, that summer went by before I knowed it. I felt like a horse getting broke to the saddle without no saddle blanket—pretty soon I was too busy paying attention to my new sores to fret very much about the old ones. Looking back, I see it was a blessing.

Chapter 26

Sam's new job was hard on him, harder than driving the truck. Roustabouts, they done the dirty work that other men was too important to do—straightening up the site, lugging tools and materials, scraping and painting, cleaning the drill threads. He come home filthy and wore out. And ever day, the minute he walked in the door, Trouble'd jump up and down and make motions with his hands like playing a fiddle. Sam'd smile and say, "After supper," and Trouble might holler or scream, but Sam'd get himself a bucket of water and take it outside to clean up with, and Trouble'd head to the corner and spread his arms out on the walls, or he'd take off for his fort out behind the chicken house. Then after supper, Sam'd play for a while, with Trouble setting in the corner and rocking and playing with his shirt buttons. Me and Sarah would sing, even Hiram ever little bit. Seemed like Sam was never too tired to play of an evening. Seemed like it revived him. I hoped he would get promoted to pumper soon.

In late August it come time for school to start. On the papers, we give Hiram June 12 for his birthday, the day they'd got to town. On the first day of school he wore new pants and a shirt Opal'd made, and Sam greased up his hair, and we all rode to town with him and walked him to his class. Me and Sam both had tears on the way home.

The teacher set Hiram with the first graders to start out with, but wasn't long before she moved him to the third graders. He was always good at reading, but arithmetic was what he was real good at. I myself was always good with numbers, but I never seen no eight-year-old do number problems like he done. To Hiram, they wasn't hard. Not only that, but Sam showed him how to tinker with my car, and wasn't long before he figured out how it worked. That Hiram, he was one smart boy, and so grown-up acting.

With Hiram gone most all day and Sam at work and the weather cooling down—seemed like fall come early that year—me and Sarah and Trouble started spending more time in the house. When you're in close quarters with young children, why, time slows down. You notice things.

Sarah, now, she poked around in ever cranny of the house, looked inside ever drawer, looked underneath of the beds, just everwhere, like a cat. She looked at ever quilt we had, asking me about the patterns and colors. Sam brought her home a doll one day, and you'd have thought it was a five-dollar bill the way she got excited. Opal brought us bags of scraps and odd notions from the shop—velvet, wool, gabardine, jacquard, fancy buttons, beads, I don't know what-all—and her and me and Sarah made everthing for that doll. Why, that doll had more clothes than I had in my whole life put together, and Sarah played and played and played with her. Done my heart good.

Me and Trouble, though, in the daytime when Sam and Hiram wasn't around, it seemed like we was at each other's throat. Little things set him off, or nothing. When he got in a mood, I would creep around the house and mind I didn't bump into the furniture. It didn't set good with me, spoiling him like that.

More than anything else, he got frustrated when me and Sarah couldn't understand something he was trying to get across to us. He would make his animal sounds and wave his hands, and me and her would guess wrong, and he would get madder and madder. Didn't do no good to say something to him, even something sweet and soothing. Only made him scream the more. Then I'd get frustrated, and him and me would holler at each other, and Sarah would start up bawling. One day I got so desperate I give him a cup of coffee—like Hiram told us Dacia done—which Trouble drunk right down. I give him another one, and he drunk half of it. Then he wadded himself into the corner of the front room and just set there, still as a bird, his face a blank.

Then one day I was hanging out wash when I heard voices coming from Trouble's fort. I wondered who that could be—Sarah was taking a nap. I snuck close to listen. "I tell you what he done?" Trouble was talking. "He had him two sticks, and he was playing them just like a fiddle—just like he seen *you* do. Not sawing, but real fingering and bowing—fast, slow, short, long—you know. Dipping his head and shoulders, then raising up smiling, just like you."

I thought, what's this? It's Trouble's voice, but how?

Trouble said, "His mama, she was good at imitations."

Whose mama? It was Dacia was the one that was good at imitations.

"I wonder, does he hear the music in his head?" "Could be. Him and music, something there. Maybe."

Now the hair on my arms stood up. I recognized this conversation. It was me and Sam, talking in bed, from a couple weeks before. I couldn't hardly breathe. Trouble'd heard us? He remembered ever word? And now he was repeating what we said?

Trouble made a yawning noise. "Gonna go in early tomorrow," he said. "Got to plait cable for Sweeney and them." "Want me to get your

478

breakfast in the morning?" "If you feel like it, but I can."

Then nothing. Things got quiet.

I was flabbergasted. It was a wonder, sure enough. My heart just about wouldn't stop pounding.

I wanted to go over there, but I reckoned he would have a screeching fit if he knowed I was there, so I just walked back to the clothesline and leaned against the post. I thought, as bad as things was when I couldn't understand him, and him able to talk, how come he didn't? Nobody was so bullheaded they'd suffer when they didn't need to.

I stooped over the basket and pulled out a pair of overhauls. As I pinned them up, I took it into my head that we was trying too hard to understand his wants, so he didn't have no *reason* to talk. We had to change our ways.

That night after supper, Trouble made his usual motions and Sam got out the fiddle case and set it on his lap. I said to Trouble, "Don't make motions. Say it in words. You know how."

Sam looked at me. "It's just noises to him. Like the wind in the trees."

"If we let him have what he wants"—here I made motions with my hands—"he won't never talk."

"He don't know what it means," Hiram said.

I said to Trouble, "Say, 'Please play the fiddle.'

479

That's all. 'Please play the fiddle.' I know you can."

Trouble let loose a screech. Sarah put her fingers in her ears.

"Go on," I said, gritting my teeth. "Go on— 'Please play the fiddle.' "

Now Sam set the case on the table and stood up. He took aholt of my arm. "This ain't the way."

"He can talk. I heard him."

Out of the corner of my eye I seen Hiram get up and go over to Trouble and start murmuring.

Sam tightened his grip on my arms. "Let's me and you talk later."

My nose filled with angry tears. "I heard him. Out in his hideout."

"I'm telling you, it's just noises," Sam said.

"You ain't with him all day. You don't know what it's like."

"This ain't the way, Bertie."

I felt myself get hot inside, like I might explode. I put my hand out to Sarah. "Come on, you can sleep in my bed tonight." But she never moved, just set there sniffling.

I felt dizzy with anger and shame both, and I put my chin in the air like a child and walked into our room and shut the door behind me. In a little bit I heard the fiddle start. I took up my book off the nightstand and tried to read, but I didn't have the patience for it.

Pretty soon I heard Sam help the children wash

their teeth. Then he herded them into their room and talked to them a while. Telling them a story, I reckoned.

He come into our room and dropped his boots next to the bed. "He tries a person's patience, sure enough." He set on the bed and pulled off his socks and rubbed his feet.

"He gets in these moods." I put the book on the nightstand. "Seems like I have to creep around the house, and mind I don't look at him wrong."

We both laid down and pulled the covers up.

"You know I'm not the kind of person likes to conform my ways to somebody else's, let alone a child's," I said. "Goes against my grain." I thought, Mama'd know what to do—she'd take a switch to him. But I didn't picture me doing that, and I didn't know why.

I don't know if I said that last part out loud. If I did, I doubt Sam heard me. He was asleep in seconds.

I wondered, was Sam right—talk was just sounds to Trouble? Was his whole life just imitating what he seen or heard other people do? I couldn't help but think, that must be a hard way to live, going through the motions without no feeling behind them. You would have to be guessing how to act all the time. I felt tenderness toward the boy. I wanted to get up and go pet him, and it hurt me that it wouldn't do no good. It'd just set him to screeching.

• • •

When it come up the first cold day, Sam built a brush fire down by the slough in the back of the property. I'd got fat frankfurters at Arbogost's, the juicy kind with the thick skin that squeaks when you break it with your teeth. I threaded the franks on sticks, and me and Sam and Hiram stood there roasting them. We was cold in the back and hot in the front, next to the fire.

Sam asked Hiram, "It get very cold where you was at?"

He shrugged. "Sometimes."

"Ever get any snow?"

"A couple of times. We could see mountaintops with snow on them. Mostly it rained."

Sam nodded.

"How you doing, Trouble?" I said. He was setting there all wrapped up, looking miserable, staring at the fire. Sarah, she was playing among the embers at the edge. She liked to pick up burning sticks and walk around carrying them like they was candles.

"Sure smells good, don't it?" Sam said.

"Makes my mouth water," Hiram said.

"Always tastes better outdoors," Sam said.

"When it first got cold, back in Kentucky where I come up, why, we'd build a fire like this," I said. "Mama, she'd butter up some corn on the cob and wrap them back up in their shucks and set them on the very edge of the fire. That was some good eating."

"What's cob?" said Sarah.

"We didn't have no sweet corn this year, but maybe we'll plant some next year," I said. "Then you'll see what corn on the cob looks like." All the sudden I realized I ought not to have said that—who knowed where they'd be at next year?

"These is done, I believe," Sam said.

I wrapped a slice of light bread around each frankfurter and handed one to Sam. "You children ever see a jack-o'-lantern?" I said.

Hiram and Sarah shook their heads.

"Wait'll you taste turkey and pumpkin pie." I give Hiram a sandwich.

"I heard of that," he said. "Dacia used to talk about it."

"Thanksgiving?" Sam said, chewing.

"Yeah, that's it," Hiram said. "I thought it was made up. She told us made-up stories sometimes."

I smiled. "Well, Thanksgiving's real. It's not no fairy tale." I give Sarah her sandwich and walked over to where Trouble was setting on a tree stump.

"This here's fairy land," Sarah said. "Like Mama said."

I winced and muttered, "She knowed better than to say something like that."

Trouble reached out for the food, and I said, "Can you ask for it?"

"Bertie," Sam said.

"Am I ever going to see my mother again in my *whole life?*" Sarah said through tears.

I held Trouble's sandwich out to him. "Just say the words. I know you can."

Trouble's eyes went almost all white, and then he jumped up and started running around in the half-froze mud, blindly, screaming like an animal.

I stood still for a moment, transfixed. For the first time I was truly afraid of what he might do, afraid of him himself.

Then in a split second, Trouble flew into the fire, his arms and legs whirling, and, just as fast, Sam was in there after him, grabbing him and pulling him out onto the ground, rolling him, and then Sam and Hiram together grabbed him up and carried him into the house. I was steps behind them, Sarah in my arms, without no memory of moving.

When me and Sarah got to the house, Sam'd already ran a bowl of cold water and was holding Trouble's hand in there. Trouble was thrashing, wailing, but Hiram had him pinned like a calf.

Panting, Sam said to me, "Just a blister on his thumb and scorched off his eyebrows."

"Thank God," I said.

"Take her out of here," Sam said.

"What?"

"Go on, get out," he said through his teeth. "She don't need to see this."

I cupped my hand on the back of Sarah's head and carried her into me and Sam's bedroom. She was bawling, and I set on the bed and rocked her. Wasn't long before I was bawling, too.

For a while after that, I never hardly asked Trouble to talk. I got to where, if Sam was present, I looked over at him before I said anything at all to Trouble. Sam, for a long while he never said nothing to me about it. Never had to.

Then the day come when I said I'd help at the thrift shop next to the First Christian Church of Wiley. The church ladies had the thrift shop to raise money for poor people. Me and Sam, why, we was keeping up with the bills, but there was many that wasn't, farming being depressed and oil drilling slowing down. You didn't have to go to the church—which we didn't—to help out at the shop. I'd made a half a dozen baby quilts, along with my dishtowel sets with the appliqued rooster and hen. On the rooster one, I embroideryed, *I rule the roost,* and the hen said, *I rule the rooster.* People liked them for wedding showers.

Sam dropped me and Sarah off at the shop. Sarah, the ladies fussed over her and give her trinkets. She hardly ever stopped talking, seemed like.

Now Sam, he took Trouble to the Community Building, where Sam and his buddies was going to practice for a dance that night. It would only take an hour, he'd told me, and Trouble would be all right for that amount of time. And there would be music.

This is how Sam always tells what happened. His friend Merle Ediger played the piano, Duane Karst played the accordion, and Fred Epling played clarinet and saxophone. Sometimes they had a man who played washboard and Jew's harp, but he wasn't there that day. Alta Bea's husband, Harold, now, he played banjo, but he hadn't played with them for years, since he started working as a lease broker shortly after the war.

Sam come in with Trouble, introduced him around—Trouble never looked at nobody, of course—and found him a place in the corner to set. Then the men visited for a while, tuned up, played some scales, and picked the first tune, "Maple Leaf Rag." Then they played "Missouri Waltz," "Swallowtail Jig," and "Buffalo Gals." On the last one they stopped and started several times since they couldn't decide on who should come in at what place. Then they played three or four more songs and took a break. Merle, the piano player, he got up and left to get beer. It had to do with a bet, I forget the details.

They was standing around talking when Trouble got up and set down at the piano. He put his fingers on the keys, moved his hands around a little, and started up playing "Maple Leaf Rag." He played it all the way through, just like Merle had, without no mistakes and using all the right fingers.

Duane said, "Hey, you didn't tell us—"

Sure enough, before he even finished his remark Trouble started up playing "Missouri Waltz." Now this song was in a different key and different time than the rag, but it didn't make no never mind to Trouble. He played it on through. Then he played "Swallowtail Jig."

By this time Merle was back with the beers, and a bottle of pop for Trouble. "You get a new piano player while I was gone?" he said, joking like.

Trouble never slowed down. He went right into "Buffalo Gals." What was funny was, he played it three different ways, just like they done, at the part where they had made the changes, and then he played it the way they'd decided to, and then he went ahead and finished it. And then, why, he played the other three or four songs they'd done.

Now pretty much everbody in town knowed that Trouble was afflicted. But nobody knowed he could play the piano, including us, of course.

They all started to talk at once, figured he was

done. But then he proceeded to play the songs Sam had played at home on the fiddle! When he was playing before, he was imitating Merle, they all reckoned, which was big enough of a surprise. But when he started playing the songs he only heard Sam play on the fiddle, now that took them aback, because the piano ain't the fiddle.

There wasn't no stopping him, and after while the men just shook Sam's hand, gathered up their things, and left. Sam stayed there and listened to Trouble play for a long while without repeating a song. When he was finished, Trouble got up from the piano and went and set down.

But I didn't know all that when Sam come to the church to get me and Sarah. All I knowed, they was later than I expected. I asked him, "Where you been all this time?"

"We got to get us a piano," he said.

"Where-at are we gonna put a piano?" I helped Sarah climb in the truck.

"What's a yanno?" Sarah said.

Trouble started pretending he was playing a piano on his lap.

"Don't know," Sam said to me. "Don't know how we're gonna pay for it, neither."

I slammed the door shut. "You see what he's doing?"

"Wait'll you hear—"

"We're talking about a piano, and he's acting like he's playing one," I said.

"He *can* play. That's what I'm trying to tell you. He set down—"

"Sam, listen to me," I said.

"I'm hungry," Sarah said.

"He played the *piano,*" Sam said. "Over at the hall. You should have heard him, Bertie."

"What? Look at the road."

"Set down and played a bunch of songs, one after the other," he said.

Trouble was still pretending to play on his lap.

"How?" I said.

"Damn if I know."

"I'm hungry," Sarah said. "When we gonna eat?"

"Beat anything I ever heard," Sam said. "Never missed a note. You never seen the like."

"Wonders never cease." I couldn't hardly take it in.

"Played ever song we played, and—"

"But what I'm saying is—look," I said. "We're setting here talking about a piano, and look at him, what he's doing. It's like he *knows.*"

"I'm *hungry,*" Sarah said.

I petted her. "We'll have supper soon's we get home."

"Trouble?" Sam said. "You hear me? You want a piano to play at home or not?"

Trouble never looked up.

"But I'm hungry *now,*" Sarah said.

"He ain't listening," Sam said to me.

I dug around in my purse. "Ain't nothing to eat in this truck, so there's no use—oh wait, here." I found a mint, and I popped it into Sarah's mouth.

"Don't go and get your hopes up," Sam said.

"I'm not."

"Well, don't."

"I'm not, I said."

After while he said, "Next Saturday, I'm taking the whole day off. We're getting a piano."

Trouble never stopped playacting all the way home. About getting a piano, he never said nothing one way or the other. That was all Sam's idea.

It had been ten years since me and Sam'd been in the Rosewater and Sons funeral home, since Will died. Mrs. Whiteside, she'd made all the arrangements, including picking out the coffin, and me and Sam just come by for the visitation the night before the burial. So I'd about forgot what it looked like inside, though when we walked in, the smell of flowers was real familiar. The front room had couches and tables and lamps and an Oriental rug, plus the two pianos— an upright and a grand, both Steinways. They was there to look at before you ordered one from a catalog, Sam had told me. I never knowed that. I never even knowed the funeral home sold pianos.

Sam walked over to the upright, pulled up the bench, set down, and started playing.

I whispered to him to stop, there might be grieving people in the next room, but he kept on playing. Right away a man come in, about forty, all dressed in black, with a white carnation in his lapel. He didn't make no sound. He seemed to float across the floor like he didn't have no feet. Up close, he smelled waxy.

He laid his hand on Sam's arm. "How may I be of assistance?" he whispered.

"Just looking." Sam pressed the pedal to dampen the sound and started playing scales, his head tilted in the direction of the sound board.

"You have any secondhand pianos?" I said.

The salesman made an O with his lips.

"Don't want no secondhand piano," Sam said.

"Millard Rosewater," the man said, sticking out his hand. Sam lifted his hands from the keys like they was glued on, and he turned and give Millard a quick handshake.

"You're interested in the K-52, I see," Millard said, smiling.

"Just looking," Sam said.

Millard nodded. He reached over and gently closed the fallboard, and then he run his fingers over it. "Satin ebony," he said, kind of breathless. "It also comes in Chippendale mahogany, Chippendale walnut, Louis the Fifteenth—"

"How long's it take?" Sam said.

491

"Pardon?"

"To get here. From the catalog."

Millard glanced at me and back at Sam. "And will you be the main operator, sir?"

"A week, a month, what?"

They went on this way, like men does.

It was a cool fall day outside, but it was awful close in that room. They kept the windows and drapes closed, and the flowers was giving off a smell of brown water. I excused myself and walked outside, standing for a moment under the awning. I pulled in a deep breath and took off my hat to let the breeze cool my scalp.

It was hard to think about anything except Trouble acting like he was playing the piano as me and Sam was talking about it, like he was making a connection with the words. I knowed I wasn't supposed to get my hopes up, but I didn't know how not to. Hope was what I was living off of.

I stepped into the dried leaves scattered on the walkway. I had on the new ankle-high shoes that come in during the twenties. I looked around and didn't see nobody, so I pulled them off and plunged my stocking feet into the crunchy leaves. It felt so good I laughed out loud.

I turned around to get a good look at the building. It looked big and heavy—three stories tall and made of white limestone, with high, arched windows and a bell tower in the back. I wondered if it was originally a church. It looked awful old. I didn't have nothing better to do, so I put my shoes back on and wandered out back to see what was there. Evidently that was where they brought in the corpses—there was a pair of big wide doors, a couple of cars, and a long black hearse. The hearse had AMBULANCE painted on it.

I heard footsteps. Sam was walking toward me, and I seen he had papers rolled up in one hand. He was smiling big, like he done. Five foot away he said, almost hollering, "I talked him into the floor model! They're bringing it Monday after work!"

He took aholt of me and started dancing me around in the sandy gravel. Let me tell you, it'd been a long time since he done that. I felt stiff-legged and stiff-necked both. I let him whirl me for a minute, and then I wriggled out of his arms. "You bought that piano?"

He waved the papers. "Talked him down a hundred dollars!"

That alarmed me. "You talked him *down*—how much did it cost?"

"It's a 1925 model, see, two years old, and I—"

I grabbed at the papers in his hand. One of them tore, and I snatched up the scrap from off the ground. The two pieces together said: *One Steinway, K-52, satin ebony, floor model. Eight hundred and ninety-five dollars.*

A swear word come to me, but I swallowed it back. I stood there with my mouth open.

"It's a bargain," he said. "I know pianos."

I stared at the paper. "This could almost buy a whole Sears *house.*"

He shrugged. "We've got a house."

"Where's this money coming from?" I was looking at numbers I'd never imagined I would have nothing to do with.

"Fifteen down, fifteen a month." He smacked the other paper with his finger.

"We're *borrowing* it? You?"

He took a step back. "We can make the payments. Don't worry."

"We're borrowing? This much money? *Borrowing?*"

"He needs it."

"It's so *much.*" I pictured that satin ebony piano, polished and gleaming, not a nick on it, standing on the linoleum in the corner of the front room, pushed against a wall plastered with newspapers. It seemed comical. Our actual piano—the one I pictured us buying—it would be an old one somebody'd painted pink, scratched up, one leg replaced, a couple key covers missing.

Sam folded his arms. "I told you, we can make the payments."

"I know. But this."

A breeze sprung up, stirring the dust and smelling of ripe leaves and coming rain. Nearby, somebody was burning brush, and the wind had smoke in it, too. I blinked and wiped my eyes on my sleeve.

"You act like I'm not them kids' father," Sam said.

I was startled. I didn't know what to say.

"You tell me," he said. "Back when it was just Dacia and Opal, who's the one said let's move to Kansas so we'd have two nickels to rub together? And now, who's the one took a new job and moved to the oil field for these kids' sakes? And who's the one fought against it?"

I got my back up, and I opened my mouth to speak, but he took a step toward me. "We're doing all right, ain't we?" he said. "Anybody hounding us? Food on the table? Shoes to wear?"

I stared at him. I never seen him so riled.

"It's the both of us, not just you," he said. "The both of us."

"I know that."

"So in the hospital, what did you *do* but offer me a divorce? How do you think that made me feel?" He choked when he said *divorce*.

"You had ever right—"

He let go of me, and his arms flew up. "It ain't about *ever right*, never has been. It's what we mean to each other—or I thought so, anyhow. Where you think I been these ten years? I know you been through a lot. I tried to go through it with you, much as I could. When you let me."

I thought about the babies I lost and never told him about. The one I lost during the war. I felt a cloud of shame settle over me, and I looked at the ground.

"I been here," he said.

"I know. It's just . . ." Now I looked him in the eye. Mama always said, *Might as well be hung for a sheep as a lamb.* "Do you really love these children? Not just tolerate them for my sake?"

He stepped back. He swung his arms apart, taking in the parking lot, the funeral home, the whole street.

"They ain't yours," I said. "Ain't your kin."

He started to speak, licked his lips, and started again. "You think I'm the kind of a man, I can't love them if they're not my blood? You ain't my blood—you think I don't love you?" His face was all creases. "I was in that fire before I give a thought to it, Bertie. I'd do it again."

"I know," I said. "But—"

"Fuck," he muttered.

Shock run up and down me. "You think I done wrong by Trouble."

He sighed and rubbed his eyes with the heels of his hands. "You never meant nothing bad to happen."

"You don't want me no more, how could you?" I said, my voice rising. I was shaking. My throat and my eyes was burning. I couldn't stop the words. "You just feel sorry for me. You'd just as soon . . ."

Now he dropped his hands and looked me square in the eye and didn't say one word.

I lost all the breath that was in me, but I managed to turn away and start running to the front of the building. I jumped in the car and started it up. I waited for a minute, but he never followed me. I ground the car into reverse and drove off. I never knowed where I was going. I never had no tears, only an ache that run along my jaw and down in my throat.

Just west of Browntown I passed the old Sutherland place. In the next section there was a filling station all by itself. Wasn't nothing to see in the field but bushes scattered around, and burnt wheat stubble. Looked like the farmer was late getting it disced if he was going to put in winter wheat. Pretty soon I come upon a raggedy line of trees. Looked like a tree row that had been let go.

These things passed by me, and I seen them and took notice, but I was in a whole other world. It wasn't that I was *thinking* about this other world, or remembering it from the past—I was *in* it, and old happenings was happening all over again. I was back there on the morning Mama died, and *don't you do this to me* come out of the walls, and I was back there singing "Jimmy Crack Corn" with Will cold in my arms as I set on the

497

stone wall at the Whiteside place, singing and cackling, and I was laying on the kitchen floor with my war baby flooding out of me before its time, two black dots among the bloody tissue, and then the other babies, each one of them, and the last one, in the chair in Opal's shop, and the strips of yellow sunlight on the wall through the blinds in the hospital. And then I was sleepy, so sleepy, my head snapping, setting on the quilt next to Mama at the hog killing, and I was in Mama's room the next morning, hearing her wail outside, knowing Timmy was dead and it was my fault, and then I was lying to Mama and Daddy, blaming Timmy himself. And then I throwed Will on the floor, that horrible thump, and Mama and Dacia was playing cards and Mama was eating rat poison little by little, as if she had ever right to, and then I was swinging the pickle spoon, hitting Dacia on the neck, seeing the red welt I'd raised there, and Sam was waking me up, saying *get up, get up, I can't find Dacia nowhere on the place.*

And then I blinked, and I was back in the actual world, driving along a sand road, I never knowed where, just a road like ever other road in the county. I didn't recognize nothing. The car was drifting to the right, and then the passenger side wheels slid off the road and onto the edge of an alfalfa field. I put on the brake, skidded a bit, eased off the brake, brought the car to a stop, and killed the engine. I must've scared up a covey of quail—the birds exploded upward, whistling and chittering and crying, starting low and then climbing and dissolving in the pale-gold autumn afternoon sunlight.

And in a rush the words come to me that I'd been running away from, seemed like, all of my life: *It's no wonder the Lord never seen fit to give you no children.*

There it was, like it was wrote on my forehead. *You know you ain't no fit mother, you got no right to love them children no matter how much you need to.*

The raw green smell of alfalfa rose up and come through the open window next to me. I felt wild. I licked my lips to stop drool from coming out. I had a bright, strange taste in my mouth.

I recollected how I used to picture cocking Daddy's pistol, shooting myself in my forehead, my ears, my eyes. I looked around. I wondered, what would happen if I got the car going fast and drove smack into a tree? How fast would I have to go for it to kill me on the first try? Or would I have to back it up and slam that tree over and over, and what if my arm was broke and I couldn't get it in reverse? It was absurd, what I was thinking, but I had to be sure it would kill me, and how could I be certain sure? I wondered, did Mama go through this, not knowing from day to day which dose would finally kill her?

Then it come to me—if I done this, I'd be doing the same thing to them children that Mama done to me, and Jesus Christ, I was the only mother they had. For another day, year, or their whole life, for better or worse, I was their mama.

Then I heard a sigh or a moan inside the car, and then, strangest thing, I felt breath on my neck, warm and then cool. For an instant it felt like I was dreaming, and at the same time, I was in the dream. Then it vanished, that dream, like they does, and I couldn't snatch it back. I put my hand on the back of my neck, and sweat gathered on my fingers.

I looked outside again, and I seen it was coming up a bad cloud, like it will sometimes in the fall, like winter wants to come early and fall don't want to let go yet. You feel a breeze through your sweater, mild, but there's a chill inside it as it passes between your shoulder blades. You know it might snow the next day—one time, I remember, we got snow on Halloween. The Flint Hills is like to have them kind of storms ever little bit, blowing in huge black clouds you can see coming miles away.

This seemed like it was going to be one of them storms. The air itself looked green, which portended hail, and the bushes was shaking and swirling, and the tree branches was swaying. I scooted up in the seat and clung tight to the steering wheel. I leaned my forehead against it and closed my eyes. For a moment I felt so empty, I felt like if I let go, I would whirl away like chaff.

Then I heard that sigh again, and I looked up, and everthing in the car, ever single thing, was sparkling. The knobs, the rims on the gauges, the levers, the edge of the window glass, all of it sparkling. The wood trim on the dashboard was sparkling, the steering wheel, the gear shift. The tips of my own trembling fingers. Sparkling.

Ever hair on me stood on end.

Now I knowed there wasn't nothing in that car—no sighing and no sparkling—that couldn't be explained by the gathering wind and by sheet lightning in the distance, flickering at the windows and silvering the edges of things.

But what I couldn't explain was the feeling I had, like I'd just took the first deep breath of my life. Like it was the first time I ever filled my lungs clear up to the shoulders. Like I was breathing in air through my skin, my hair, my fingernails, my eyelids. Like I myself was made out of breath, like I was breath itself. But now, instead of feeling empty, I felt light. Light was shining on me and in me, it was filling me and lifting me. I felt like I didn't deserve nothing, but, somehow, I had everthing.

Out loud I said, "Is this what grace is?"

Nobody answered me. I never expected them to. And anyhow I knowed the answer. By the grace of God, I knowed what it was. Grace wasn't hard, like Mama taught me, though it was strong.

And I knowed I had what it took, whatever it was, to do whatever needed doing, and whatever I done would be blessed, and I had everthing I ever needed or hoped for, beyond my desire, beyond my ken.

I started up the car and turned around and headed back to town. Before long it started hailing, the stones banging and clattering on the car roof inches over my head, and after a bit it changed into tinny raindrops. I found my way to the funeral home, and I was soaked head to toe before I reached the front door.

I smelled my wet hair in the stifling room, and I run my hands through it to loosen it off my scalp. I seen Sam was setting and playing the piano. I didn't know the name of the song, but it was slow and sorrowful, tired. I flicked my hands to rid them of the cold water, and I walked up behind him and put them on his shoulders. He jumped a little bit and pulled his hands back from the keys, straightening his back.

"Sam," I said. "I've been so wrong, about so many things. I hope—"

His shoulders buckled then, he blowed out air, and he reached up and took aholt of my cold hands and kissed each one. Then he rose and turned and held me, and the two of us stood there swaying together for a long time, waiting for the storm to let up so we could go home.

They brought the piano Monday evening, two men in a tall truck. The driver, he looked doubtful he was at the right place. Sam walked out and said something to him, and he pulled up to the porch. Then him and a taller man and Sam, the three of them carried in the piano and set it against the wall.

Now Trouble, soon's he'd seen the strange truck, he'd ran out to his fort and hid. We hadn't told him the piano was coming, though it's hard to know if it would've made any difference.

After they got everthing set up, the taller man started playing the new piano. Sam got out his fiddle, and him and the piano man went back and forth, playing notes any which way, seemed like, trying to get the piano and the fiddle to agree, and then *pop!* in through the door come Trouble. The look on his face—he never smiled, but his eyes lit up. He stood in the doorway staring.

"Look what we got!" Sarah hollered at him. "What should we name it?"

Directly Sam started in playing "Bill Bailey, Won't You Please Come Home." The man picked up on it, and Sarah squealed with delight. "I heard that song! I know that song!"

"I heard that song!" Trouble yelled. "I know that song!"

I took in a breath so sharp it seemed to cut me. I reminded myself that just because he made sense, it didn't mean he knowed what he was saying— but I rejoiced just the same.

As the men was leaving, why, Hiram come in the back door from chores. He was washing up when Trouble set down and started playing. I expect Hiram hadn't never heard a piano before. When he turned around, wiping his hands on a dishtowel, and seen Trouble playing, you should have saw his face. He'd heard tell that Trouble could play, but hearing him play, that was a whole nother thing.

"He making that music, or the machine?" he asked me.

"Him."

I don't remember what song Trouble was playing, but it come to an end, and then he started playing "Whispering Hope." I swallowed hard. Where had he even heard it? Then I reckoned Sam'd played it on the fiddle sometime.

"How's he doing that?" Hiram said.

I shook my head. "Don't know."

"Beats anything." He wiped his nose on his sleeve. "Beats anything."

I wiped my nose, too, and I reached over and took Hiram's hand. Pretty soon Sam come over. He put his arm around me and poked Hiram in the ribs with his elbow, like a man will. Hiram smiled.

That piano did look comical in our front room, sure enough. But when I looked at it, I didn't see the piano exactly—I seen the music inside it waiting to come out. No telling what kind or how beautiful it might be, or if it would make you laugh, cry, sing, or get up and dance. I reckoned that was the beauty of it.

Chapter 27

The place where they had the court was in an office next to the jail, plain but for a picture of President Coolidge and the American and Kansas flags in the corners. The floors creaked as we walked in. We settled into the front row of folding chairs. The lawyer was already there, and Sam set down next to him. Then come me, Sarah—she crawled onto my lap, and her four year old—and then Trouble and then Hiram. Opal set in the second row. The lawyer, Jim Nevins, he was trading with Sam for pulling tree stumps. He was a farmer and done law on the side. I'd thought about inviting Alta Bea, but I didn't.

The judge set at a table reading papers. The ceiling fan rotated, making shadows that traveled along the walls, around and around. Even with the fan, it was hot in there. I'd already sweat through my Sunday dress.

Directly the judge lifted his face and took off his eyeglasses. You could see that the bridge of his nose was red where the glasses pinched him.

Our lawyer stood up and said, "Your honor, this

here's Sam Frownfelter and his wife, and these three are the children in question."

The judge nodded. "Sam Frownfelter," he said, "is it your intention and desire to support these children here present until they reach their majority?"

"Here present," Trouble said. "Here present." Evidently he thought he was going to get a present. I slipped him a piece of penny candy, and thank the Lord he started sucking on it and quieted down.

Sam said, "It is." His voice trailed off. He told me later he started to say, "Your Majesty." He knowed that wasn't the proper thing to call the judge, but he couldn't remember what was.

"So ordered," the judge said. He picked up an ink pen and signed his name.

The lawyer leaned over and whispered to Sam, "That's it."

I swallowed. That was it? That was it? We picked up and scurried out of there like we was breaking out of jail, at least it felt like it. Before we headed home we stopped and got our picture took, all five of us together, plus Opal. That's my favorite picture I have.

That night, as me and Sam was getting ready for bed, he turned to me. "If you're gonna be running around town with a bunch of children, we can't have folks thinking you're a trollop." He took my hand and put a gold ring in it.

I was flabbergasted. "Good Lord."

He smiled and run a finger up and down my arm. "Like it?"

"Wc can't afford this." I put it on my finger. It glowed in the lamp light.

"Got it anyhow." He leaned over and kissed me a good one.

I couldn't stop looking at that ring. I never had any earthly treasure so beautiful.

We went to bed and settled in back-to-back.

"Big day," he said.

It was quiet for a moment, and then I said, "You reckon we'll ever see Dacia again?" I'm human, I picked at my scabs to see would they bleed.

"You still afraid she'll come back for them?"

"Might," I said. "I keep dreaming about it." Then I asked him, "Do you think I was too hard on her when she was coming up? Me and her didn't hardly get along."

"She wasn't easy to get along with."

"First thing she said after Mama died, I remember, 'You ain't my mama, you ain't gonna *be* my mama, I ain't gonna do what you say.' And she never did."

"Losing your mama's hard on anybody," he said then. "You and her both."

"But she—"

"You and her both." He sighed. "I sure hate to think of what she had to go through, to get to wherever she's at now." His voice was so soft I

509

could barely hear him. Unless I was mistaken, there was tears in it.

It wasn't like we hadn't talked about all this before. We had. But things wasn't the same since that day at the funeral home.

He spoke again. "It's the ones like Dacia—the ones that are hard to love—" I heard him swallow. "They're the ones need it the most. Mom used to say that."

"Mine too." I reached back far into my memory, and for the first time in years, I was able to picture Mama young, back home, in all her glory, her back bent over the table, her hands dipping into the flour sack like a natural-born woman.

I lost my breath, and I had to suck in air.

"Seems like there's one like Dacia in ever family," Sam said.

Now I seen Dacia in my mind's eye. "Lord knows, she never got no love from me. From nobody really, except Mama, but then Mama . . ." I felt pity for Dacia then, deep-down pity, not strained no more with my own pain and grief and shame.

Now he turned over to face me, and he run his finger along my cheek. "Don't you reckon she sent them here because she knowed you would, though? Love them? Look after them?"

I nodded, and tears sprung to my eyes. I laid my hand against his. "And because she figured you would be here to daddy them."

We laid there like that for a long time. Finally he kissed me and turned back over, and I rubbed his back till I heard him snore.

My muscles felt like jelly. I was so grateful for him, I felt like I could float up to the ceiling. If it hadn't been for the children, I felt like I would gladly have gone to be with the Lord at that very moment.

Then I got to thinking, what name did we put on the court papers—Trouble or Travis? And where did I put the scissors after I used them yesterday? And what did we have in the house for breakfast in the morning, was we out of bread? Did me and Sarah remember to close up the chickens for the night? Did Sam have a clean shirt for work? I was thinking so hard I almost forgot to say my prayer. It was a prayer of joy, sure enough, a prayer of thanksgiving for the good things the day had brought, and all the blessings the Lord seen fit to bestow on me, a sinner saved by grace.

Then I thought, tomorrow I should start writing it all down. The time's going to come when Sarah's going to want to know about her mama.

Acknowledgments

A former working title for this novel was *I Done My Best*, a nod to the young girls of the misty past whose early needlework often bore this humble apologia. Perhaps a better title would have been *We Done Our Best*, in recognition of the contributions of the many people who helped me during the writing.

All the Forgivenesses was inspired by the stories of life in the early twentieth-century oil fields told me by my mother, Sybol Frans Hudson, and her sisters: Eva Mae Barnes, Dorothy Hatfield, and Roxie Olmstead. The voice of this novel is my recollection of the speech of my maternal grandmother, Elizabeth (Lizzie) Murphy Frans, and grandfather, John Madison Frans, without whom so much would not have been possible, although the story itself is fiction. Special thanks go to my aunt Roxie, who generously shared her own written recollections and images of that time and place.

I had many writing teachers. Bob Green of McPherson (Kansas) College provided early encouragement and advice, as did the late Philip Schneider, as well as James Lee Burke, of Wichita State. Years later in Oregon, when I took up serious writing for the second time, a crucial catalyst was a class taught by Carol Watt at Lane Community College. I also learned from the members of the Brookside Writers Workshop, including Jeanne Bishop, John Groves, Wayne Harrison, Judith Mikesh McKenzie, Diane McWhorter, Rebeca Chaison Morales, Connie Newman, Rosalind Trotter, and the late Erica Atkisson.

Connie and Diane, along with Kelly Terwilliger, formed the Waywords writing group. These three women have met with me weekly for some fifteen years and have patiently read and critiqued numerous drafts of large chunks of this work, some of which ended up on the cutting-room floor. Their patient help and encouragement have been vital. My dear friend Erin Bride has read and supported my work for many years, and my alley neighbor Ritta Dreier kindly provided her sewing room as a weeklong private retreat for me at a critical time during the writing.

Sandra Scofield—wonderful novelist, editor, and teacher—edited an earlier draft of this book and provided invaluable help to me in developing the story and characters. More recently, a seminar on fiction fluency by Eric Witchey, sponsored by Wordcrafters in Eugene, has been of great value, as was Eric's early encouragement. I also benefited from twice attending the Willamette Writers Conference in Portland.

My sincere gratitude goes to my agents, Emma Sweeney and Margaret Sutherland Brown, of Emma Sweeney Agency, who guided me through clarifying revisions that strengthened this work, and to John Scognamiglio, my editor at Kensington Publishing, for his help in both focusing and expanding Bertie's emotional life. I'm also grateful to Robin Cook, who handled production, and Kristine Noble, who created the beautiful cover.

To my sisters, Sue Wagerle and Lee Ann Moore—you were my first friends and dearest rivals. To my sons, Curtis and Jeff, and my grandchildren, I hope this book will give you a glimpse of the life and times of people who are gone now and who loved you perhaps more than you know.

And to my husband, Charles Hardinger—whom I met on the school bus and whose patience with my writerly struggles is epic—all my everything.

Elizabeth Hardinger
Eugene, Oregon
September 2019

Discussion

The suggested questions are included to enhance your group's reading of Elizabeth Hardinger's *All the Forgivenesses*.

1. How does Bertie's "voice" affect the way you saw her as a person? How would the story change if it were told by, say, Bertie's mother? Dacia? Alta Bea? Sam?

2. What would you say are the main themes of the novel?

3. The book portrays key relationships between Bertie and her parents, her two sisters, her friend Alta Bea, and her husband, Sam. Other relationships—such as the triad of Bertie, her mother, and Dacia—are also important. Do any of these relationships embody the themes you identified? In what ways? How do these relationships change over the course of the novel?

4. After her father's aborted attempt at farming in Missouri, Bertie says that his "spirit

got broke" by the older boys' embrace of mechanization. She adds, "Daddy wasn't nothing special no more in his own mind." Is she right? What role does drinking play in his psyche? How is it like or unlike Polly's use of "dope" given her by the doctor?

5. Did you find Bertie's plight—social, economic, familial, physical, psychological—relatable? What did you think about the decisions Bertie made to cope with them? Consider also the situations of the other main characters.

6. Bertie says that her finding Sam was "great good luck." What do you think Sam sees in Bertie (and vice versa)? What keeps them together when things go wrong for them? Looking back on the big turning points in your own life, do you think it was luck (good or bad) that determined the outcome? If not, what was it?

7. Bertie says she failed the "sacred task" of parenting her siblings. Why, then, does she still want children?

8. They say every novel has a "monster." Who or what is the monster in this novel? Why?

9. Why does Dacia send her own children to Bertie? Were you surprised by that? Did you sympathize with Dacia? How do you think Dacia's story continues?

10. Bertie struggles to understand how to deal with Trouble. How does Bertie's struggle with her nephew mirror the overall change she undergoes in the novel?

11. Did you learn anything new about the time and place(s) in which the novel is set? How might the outcomes differ if the story took place today, or in a different region?

Center Point Large Print
600 Brooks Road / PO Box 1
Thorndike, ME 04986-0001 USA

(207) 568-3717

US & Canada:
1 800 929-9108
www.centerpointlargeprint.com